This Large Print Book carries the
Seal of Approval of N.A.V.H.

PRETTY BABY

PRETTY BABY

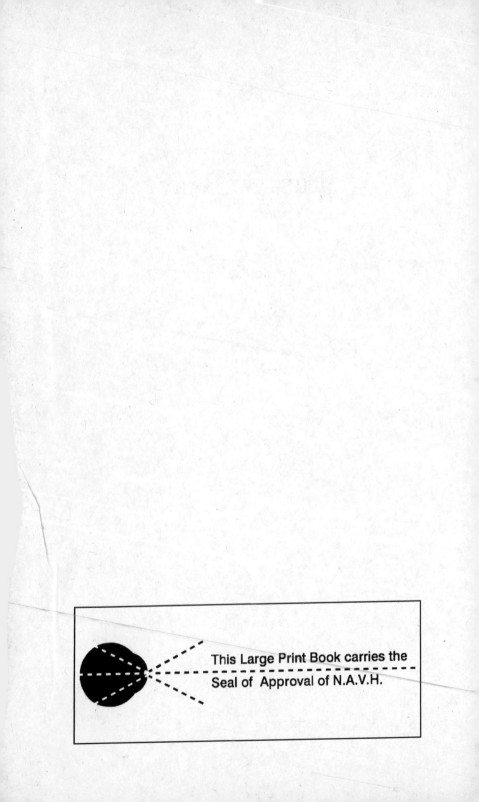

This Large Print Book carries the
Seal of Approval of N.A.V.H.

PRETTY BABY

MARY KUBICA

THORNDIKE PRESS
A part of Gale, Cengage Learning

Farmington Hills, Mich • San Francisco • New York • Waterville, Maine
Meriden, Conn • Mason, Ohio • Chicago

GALE
CENGAGE Learning®

LIBRARY OF CONGRESS CATALOGING-IN-PUBLICATION DATA

Kubica, Mary.
    Pretty baby / Mary Kubica. — Large print edition.
        pages cm. — (Thorndike Press large print peer picks)
    ISBN 978-1-4104-8271-6 (hardback) — ISBN 1-4104-8271-5 (hardcover)
    1. Large type books. 2. Psychological fiction. I. Title.
PS3611.U23P74 2015
813'.6—dc23   2015025033

Published in 2015 by arrangement with Harlequin Books S.A.

Printed in the United States of America
1 2 3 4 5 6 7 19 18 17 16 15

For the ones I've lost

HEIDI

The first time I see her, she is standing at the Fullerton Station, on the train platform, clutching an infant in her arms. She braces herself and the baby as the purple line express soars past and out to Linden. It's the 8th of April, forty-eight degrees and raining. The rain lurches down from the sky, here, there and everywhere, the wind untamed and angry. A bad day for hair.

The girl is dressed in a pair of jeans, torn at the knee. Her coat is thin and nylon, an army green. She has no hood, no umbrella. She tucks her chin into the coat and stares straight ahead while the rain saturates her. Those around her cower beneath umbrellas, no one offering to share. The baby is quiet, stuffed inside the mother's coat like a joey in a kangaroo pouch. Tufts of slimy pink fleece sneak out from the coat and I convince myself that the baby, sound asleep in what feels to me like utter bedlam —

chilled to the bone, the thunderous sound of the "L" soaring past — is a girl.

There's a suitcase beside her feet, vintage leather, brown and worn, beside a pair of lace-up boots, soaked thoroughly through.

She can't be older than sixteen.

She's thin. Malnourished, I tell myself, but maybe she's just thin. Her clothes droop. Her jeans are baggy, her coat too big.

A CTA announcement signals a train approaching, and the brown line pulls into the station. A cluster of morning rush hour commuters crowd into the warmer, drier train, but the girl does not move. I hesitate for a moment — feeling the need to do *something* — but then board the train like the other do-nothings and, slinking into a seat, watch out the window as the doors close and we slide away, leaving the girl and her baby in the rain.

But she stays with me all day.

I ride the train into the Loop, to the Adams/Wabash Station, and inch my way out, down the steps and onto the water-logged street below, into the acrid sewage smell that hovers at the corners of the city streets, where the pigeons amble along in staggering circles, beside garbage bins and homeless men and millions of city dwellers rushing from point A to point B in the rain.

I spend whole chunks of time — between meetings on adult literacy and GED preparation and tutoring a man from Mumbai in ESL — imagining the girl and child wasting the better part of the day on the train's platform, watching the "L" come and go. I invent stories in my mind. The baby is colicky and only sleeps in flux. The vibration of approaching trains is the key to keeping the baby asleep. The woman's umbrella — I picture it, bright red with flamboyant golden daisies — was manhandled by a great gust of wind, turned inside out, as they tend to do on days like this. It broke. The umbrella, the baby, the suitcase: it was more than her two arms could carry. Of course she couldn't leave the baby behind. And the suitcase? What was inside that suitcase that was of more importance than an umbrella on a day like this? Maybe she stood there all day, waiting. Maybe she was waiting for an arrival rather than a departure. Or maybe she hopped on the red line seconds after the brown line disappeared from view.

When I come home that night, she's gone. I don't tell Chris about this because I know what he would say: who cares?

I help Zoe with her math homework at the kitchen table. Zoe says that she hates math. This comes as no surprise to me.

These days Zoe hates most everything. She's twelve. I can't be certain, but I remember my "I hate everything" days coming much later than that: sixteen or seventeen. But these days everything comes sooner. I went to kindergarten to play, to learn my ABCs; Zoe went to kindergarten to learn to read, to become more technologically savvy than me. Boys and girls are entering puberty sooner, up to two years sooner in some cases, than my own generation. Ten-year-olds have cell phones; seven- and eight-year-old girls have breasts.

Chris eats dinner and then disappears to the office, as he always does, to pour over sleepy, coma-inducing spreadsheets until after Zoe and I have gone to bed.

The next day she's there again. The girl. And again it's raining. Only the second week of April, and already the meteorologists are predicting record rainfall for the month. The wettest April on record, they say. The day before, O'Hare reported 0.6 inches of rain for a single day. It's begun to creep into basements, collect in the pleats of low-lying city streets. Airport flights have been cancelled and delayed. I remind myself, *April showers bring May flowers,* tuck myself into a creamy waterproof parka and sink my feet into a pair of rubber boots for the trek to work.

She wears the same torn jeans, the same army-green jacket, the same lace-up boots. The vintage suitcase rests beside her feet. She shivers in the raw air, the baby writhing and upset. She bounces the baby up and down, up and down, and I read her lips — *shh.* I hear women beside me, drinking their piping-hot coffee beneath oversize golf umbrellas: *she shouldn't have that baby outside. On a day like today?* they sneer. *What's wrong with that girl? Where is the baby's hat?*

The purple line express soars past; the brown line rolls in and stops and the do-nothings file their way in like the moving products of an assembly line.

I linger, again, wanting to *do something,* but not wanting to seem intrusive or offensive. There's a fine line between helpful and disrespectful, one which I don't want to cross. There could be a million reasons why she's standing with the suitcase, holding the baby in the rain, a million reasons other than the one nagging thought that dawdles at the back of my brain: she's homeless.

I work with people who are often poverty stricken, mostly immigrants. Literacy statistics in Chicago are bleak. About a third of adults have a low level of literacy, which

11

means they can't fill out job applications. They can't read directions or know which stop along the "L" track is theirs. They can't help their children with their homework.

The faces of poverty are grim: elderly women curled into balls on benches in the city's parks, their life's worth pushed around in a shopping cart as they scavenge the garbage for food; men pressed against high-rise buildings on the coldest of January days, sound asleep, a cardboard sign leaned against their inert body: Please Help. Hungry. God Bless. The victims of poverty live in substandard housing, in dangerous neighborhoods; their food supply is inadequate at best; they often go hungry. They have little or no access to health care, to proper immunization; their children go to underfunded schools, develop behavioral problems, witness violence. They have a greater risk of engaging in sexual activity, among other things, at a young age and thus, the cycle repeats itself. Teenage girls give birth to infants with low birth weights, they have little access to health care, they cannot be properly immunized, the children get sick. They go hungry.

Poverty, in Chicago, is highest among blacks and Hispanics, but that doesn't negate the fact that a white girl can be poor.

All this scuttles through my mind in the split second I wonder what to do. Help the girl. Get on the train. Help the girl. Get on the train. Help the girl.

But then, to my surprise, the girl boards the train. She slips through the doors seconds before the automated announcement — *bing, bong, doors closing* — and I follow along, wondering where it is that we're going, the girl, her baby and me.

The car is crowded. A man rises from his seat, which he graciously offers to the girl; without a word, she accepts, scooting into the metal pew beside a wheeler-dealer in a long black coat, a man who looks at the baby as if it might just be from Mars. Passengers lose themselves in the morning commute — they're on their cell phones, on their laptops and other technological gadgets, they're reading novels, the newspaper, the morning's briefing; they sip their coffee and stare out the window at the city skyline, lost in the gloomy day. The girl carefully removes the baby from her kangaroo pouch. She unfolds the pink fleece blanket, and miraculously, beneath that blanket, the baby appears dry. The train lurches toward the Armitage Station, soaring behind brick buildings and three and four flats, so close to people's homes I imagine the way they shake as the "L" passes by, glasses rattling in cabinets, TVs silenced by the reverberation of the train, every few minutes of the livelong day and long into the night. We leave Lincoln Park, and head into Old Town, and somewhere along the way the baby settles down, her wailing reduced to a quiet whimper to the obvious relief of those on the train.

I'm forced to stand farther away from the girl than I'd like to be. Bracing myself for the unpredictability of the train's movements, I peer past bodies and briefcases for the occasional glimpse — flawless ivory skin, patchy red from crying — the mother's hollow cheeks — a white Onesies jumpsuit — the desperate, hungry suction on a pacifier — vacant eyes. A woman walks by and says, "Cute baby." The girl forces a smile.

Smiling does not come naturally to the girl. I imagine her beside Zoe and know that she is older: the hopelessness in her eyes, for one, the lack of Zoe's raw vulnerability, another. And of course, there is the baby (I have myself convinced that Zoe still believes babies are delivered by storks), though beside the businessman the girl is diminutive, like a child. Her hair is disproportional: cut blunt on one side, shoulder length the other.

14

It's drab, like an old sepia photograph, yellowing with time. There are streaks of red, not her natural hue. She wears dark, heavy eye makeup, smeared from the rain, hidden behind a screen of long, protective bangs.

The train slows its way into the Loop, careening around twists and turns. I watch as the baby is swaddled once again in the pink fleece and stuffed into the nylon coat and prepare myself for their departure. She gets off before I do, at State/Van Buren, and I watch through the window, trying not to lose her in the heavy congestion that fills the city streets at this time of day.

But I do anyway, and just like that, she's gone.

CHRIS

"How was your day?" Heidi asks when I walk in the front door. I'm greeted by the funky scent of cumin, the sound of cable news from the living room TV, Zoe's stereo blasting down the hall. On the news: record rainfall clobbering the Midwest. An accumulated collection of *wet things* resides by the front door: coats and umbrellas and shoes. I add to the collection and shake my head dry, like a wet dog. Moving into the kitchen I plant a kiss on Heidi's cheek, more a force of habit than something sweet.

Heidi has changed into her pajamas already: red, flannel and plaid, her hair with its natural auburn waves deflated from the rain. Contacts out, glasses on. "Zoe!" she yells. "Dinner's ready," though down the hall, between the closed door of our daughter's bedroom and the deafening sound of boy band music, there's no chance she heard.

16

"What's for dinner?" I ask.

"Chili. *Zoe!*"

I love chili, but these days Heidi's chili is a vegetarian chili, loaded with not only black beans and kidney beans and garbanzo beans (and, apparently, cumin), but also what she calls *vegetarian meat crumbles,* to give the impression of meat without the cow. She snatches bowls from the cabinet, and begins ladling the chili. Heidi is not a vegetarian. But since Zoe began ranting about the fat in meat two weeks ago, Heidi made the family decision to go meat-free for a while. In that time we've had vegetarian meat loaf and spaghetti with vegetarian meatballs and vegetarian sloppy joes. But no meat.

"I'll get her," I say and head down the narrow hall of our condo. I knock on the pulsating door and, with Zoe's blessing, poke my head inside to tell her about dinner and she says okay. She's lying on her canopy bed, a yellow notebook — the one with all the teenybopper celebs she's torn from magazines taped to the front — on her lap. She slams it shut the minute I enter, gropes for social studies flash cards, which lie beside her, ignored.

I don't mention the crumbles. I trip over the cat on the way to Heidi's and my bedroom, loosening my tie as I do.

Moments later, we sit at the kitchen table, and again Heidi asks me about my day.

"Good," I say. "You?"

"I hate beans," Zoe declares as she scoops up a spoonful of chili, and then lets it dribble back into the bowl. The living room TV is muted, yet our eyes drift toward it, trying our best to lip-read our way through the evening news. Zoe slumps in her chair, refusing to eat, a cloned version of Heidi, from the roundness of their faces to the wavy hair and brown eyes, everything alike down to their cupid's-bow lips and a handful of freckles splattered across their snub noses.

"What did you do?" Heidi asks and internally I grimace, not wanting to relive the day, and her stories — Sudanese refugees seeking asylum and illiterate grown men — are depressing. I just want to lip-read my way through the evening news in silence.

But I tell her anyway about a customer due-diligence call and drafting a purchase agreement and a ridiculously early conference call with a client in Hong Kong. At 3:00 a.m. I sneaked from the bedroom that Heidi and I share and crept into the office for the call, and when it was finished, I showered and left for work, long before

Heidi or Zoe began to stir.

"I'm leaving in the morning for San Francisco," I remind her.

She nods her head. "I know. How long?"

"One night."

And then I ask about her day and Heidi tells me about a young man who emigrated from India to the United States six months ago. He was living in the slums of Mumbai — *Dharavi, to be exact; one of the largest slums in the world,* as Heidi tells me, *where he was earning less than two American dollars a day in his home country.* She tells me about their toilets, how they're few and far between. The residents use the river instead. She's helping this man, she calls him Aakar, with his grammar. Which isn't easy. She reminds me: "English is a very difficult language to learn."

I say that I know.

My wife is a bleeding heart. Which was absolutely adorable when I asked her to marry me, but somehow, after fourteen years of marriage, the words *immigrant* and *refugee* hit a nerve for me, generally because I'm sure she's more concerned with their well-being than my own.

"And your day, Zoe?" Heidi asks.

"It sucked," Zoe grumbles, slumped in the chair, staring at that chili as though it might just be dog shit, and I laugh to myself. At least one of us is being honest. I want a do-over. My day sucked, too.

"Sucked how?" Heidi asks. I love when Heidi uses the word *sucked.* Its unnatural-ness is comical; the only time Heidi talks about things *sucking* it's in reference to a lollipop or straw. And then, "What's wrong with your chili? Too hot?"

"I told you. I hate beans."

Five years ago, Heidi would have re-minded her of the starving children in India or Sierra Leone or Burundi. But these days just getting Zoe to eat *anything* is an ac-complishment. She either hates everything or it's loaded with fat, like meat. And so in-stead we eat crumbles.

From the recesses of my briefcase — sit-ting on the floor beside the front door — my cell phone rings and Heidi and Zoe turn to me, wondering whether or not I'll ab-scond with the phone in the middle of din-ner to my office, the third bedroom we con-verted when it was clear there would be no more children for me and Heidi. I still catch her sometimes, when she's in the office with me, her eyes roving along espresso office furniture — a desk and bookshelves, my fa-vorite leather chair — imagining something else entirely, a crib and changing table, playful safari animals prancing on the walls.

Heidi always wanted a big family. Things just didn't work out that way.

It's rare that we get through a quick dinner without the obnoxious sound of my cell. Depending on the night, my mood — or, more important Heidi's mood — or whatever emergency cropped up at work that day, I may or may not answer it. Tonight I stuff a bite of chili into my mouth as a rebuttal, and Heidi smiles sweetly, which I take to mean: *thank you.* Heidi has the sweetest smile, sugar-coated and delicious. Her smile comes from somewhere inside, not just planted on those cupid's-bow lips. When she smiles I imagine the first time we met, at a charity ball in the city, her body cloaked in a strapless vintage tulle dress — red, like her lipstick. She was a work of art. A masterpiece. She was still in college, an intern at the nonprofit she now all but runs. Back in the days when pulling an all-nighter was a piece of cake, and four hours of sleep was a good night for me. Back in the days when thirty seemed *old,* so old in fact that I didn't even consider what thirty-nine would be like.

Heidi thinks that I work too much. For me, seventy-hour workweeks are the norm. There are nights I don't get home until two o'clock; there are nights I'm home, but locked in my office until the sun begins to rise. My phone rings at all hours of the day and night, as if I'm an on-call physician and not someone who deals with mergers and acquisitions. But Heidi works at a nonprofit agency; only one of us is making enough money to pay for a condo in Lincoln Park, to cover Zoe's expensive private school tuition and save for college.

The phone stops ringing, and Heidi turns to Zoe. She wants to hear more about her day.

It turns out that Mrs. Peters, the seventh grade earth science teacher, wasn't there and the sub was a total . . . Zoe stops herself, thinks of a better adjective than the one implanted in her brain by misfit preteens . . . a total *nag.*

"Why's that?" Heidi asks.

Zoe avoids eye contact, stares at the chili. "I don't know. She just *was.*"

Heidi takes a sip of her water, plants that big-eyed, inquisitive look on her face. The same one I got when I mentioned the 3:00 a.m. call. "She was mean?"

"Not really."

"Too strict?"

"No."

"Too . . . *ugly*?" I throw in to lighten the

22

mood. Heidi's need to know sometimes puts a strain on things. She's convinced herself that being an involved parent (and by this I mean overinvolved) will assure Zoe that she's loved as she enters into what Heidi calls: *the tumultuous teenage years.* What I remember from my own tumultuous teenage years was the need to escape my parents. When they followed, I ran faster. But Heidi has taken out books from the library: psychology books on child development, parenting with love, secrets of a happy family. She's bound and determined to do this right.

Zoe giggles. When she does — and it doesn't happen often — she becomes six again, consummately pure, twenty-four-karat gold. "No," she answers.

"Just . . . a nag then? A nasty old nag," I suggest. I push aside the black beans and look for something else. A tomato. Corn. A chili scavenger hunt. I avoid the vegetarian meat crumbles.

"Yeah. I guess so."

"What else?" Heidi asks.

"Huh?" Zoe's got on a tie-dye shirt with the words *peace* and *love* written in hot pink. It's covered in glitter. She's got her hair in this side ponytail thing that makes her look too sophisticated for the tangerine braces that line her rambling teeth. She's drawn all over her left arm: peace signs, her own name, a heart. The name Austin.

Austin?

"What else sucked?" Heidi asks.

Who the hell is Austin?

"Taylor spilled her milk at lunch. All over my math book."

"Is the book okay?" Heidi wants to know. Taylor has been Zoe's best friend, her bestie, her BFF, since the girls were about four. They share matching BFF necklaces, skulls of all things. Zoe's is lime green, and draped around her neck at all times, day or night. Her mother, Jennifer, is Heidi's best friend. If I remember correctly, they met at the city park, two little girls playing in the sandbox, their mothers taking a breather on the same park bench. Heidi calls it happenstance. Though I believe, in reality, Zoe threw sand in Taylor's eye and those first few moments weren't so fortunate after all. If it hadn't been for Heidi with her spare water bottle to wash off the sand, and if Jennifer hadn't been in the midst of a divorce and desperate for someone on whom to unload — the story might have had a very different ending.

Zoe replies, "I don't know. I guess so."

"Do we need to replace it?"

24

No comment.

"Anything else happen? Anything *good*?"

She shakes her head.

And that, in a nutshell, is Zoe's sucky day.

Zoe is excused from the table without eating her chili. Heidi convinces her to take a few bites of a corn bread muffin and finish a glass of milk, and then sends her to her room to finish her homework, leaving Heidi and me alone. Again, my cell phone rings. Heidi jumps up to start the dishes and I linger, wondering whether or not I've been excused. But instead I grab some dishes from the table and bring them to Heidi who's dumping Zoe's chili down the garbage disposal.

"The chili was good," I lie. The chili was not good. I stack the dishes on the countertop for Heidi to rinse and hover behind her, my hand pressed to plaid red flannel.

"Who's going to San Francisco?" Heidi asks. She turns off the water and turns to face me, and I lean into her, remembering what it feels like when I'm with her, a familiarity so ingrained in us both; it's natural, habit, second nature. I've been with Heidi for almost half my life. I know what she's going to say before she says it. I know her body language, what it means. I know the inviting look in her eye when Zoe is at a

25

sleepover or long after she's in bed. I know that now, as she slips her arms around me and pulls me into her, locking her hands around the small of my back, it isn't an act of affection; it's one of ownership.

You are mine.

"Just a couple people from the office," I tell her.

Again with the big inquisitive eyes. She wants me to elaborate. "Tom," I say, "and Henry Tomlin." And then I hesitate, and it's probably the hesitation that does me in. "Cassidy Knudsen," I admit, meekly, throwing in the last name as if she doesn't know who Cassidy is. Cassidy Knudsen, with the silent K.

And with that she removes her hands and turns back to the sink.

"It's a business trip," I remind her. "Strictly business," I say as I press my face into her hair. It smells like strawberries, sweet and juicy, combined with a hodge-podge of city smells: the dirtiness of the street, strangers on the train, the musty scent of rain.

"Does *she* know that?" Heidi asks.

"I'll be sure to tell her," I respond. And when the conversation goes quiet, the room silenced except for the indelicate propulsion of dishes into the dishwasher, I seize my

26

opportunity to slip away, wandering into the bedroom to pack.

It isn't my fault I have a coworker who's nice on the eyes.

HEIDI

When I wake in the morning, Chris is gone. Beside me, on the distressed wooden nightstand, is a mug of coffee, tepid and likely filled to the gills with hazelnut creamer, but still: coffee. I sit up in bed and reach for the mug and the remote control and, flipping on the lifeless TV, stumble upon the day's forecast. Rain.

When I finally wobble down the hall to the kitchen, bypassing Zoe's school portraits from kindergarten through seventh grade, I find her standing in the kitchen, pouring milk and cereal into a bowl.

"Good morning," I say, and she jumps. "Did you sleep okay?" I ask, and kiss her gingerly on the forehead. She congeals, uncomfortable with the mushy stuff these days. And yet, as her mother, I feel the need to show my affection; a high-five — or secret handshake as Chris and Zoe share — simply won't do, so I kiss her and feel her

28

pull away, knowing I've planted my love for the day.

Zoe's dressed already in her school uniform: the pleated plaid jumper and navy cardigan, the suede Mary Janes that she hates.

"Yeah," she says and takes her bowl to the kitchen table to eat.

"How 'bout some juice?"

"I'm not thirsty." Though I see her eye the coffeemaker nonetheless, a door that she previously opened and I firmly closed. No twelve-year-old needs a stimulant to get going in the morning. Yet I fill my mug to the brim and douse it with creamer, sit beside Zoe with a heaping bowl of Raisin Bran and attempt to make small talk about the anticipated day. I'm inundated with yeses, noes, and I don't knows, and then she scampers away to brush her teeth, and I'm left with the silence of the kitchen, the steady percussion of raindrops on the bay window.

We head out into the soggy day, bypassing a neighbor in the hall. Graham. He's pressing at buttons on a snazzy watch, the gadget letting out various beeps and bleeps. He smiles to himself, clearly pleased.

"Fancy meeting you here, ladies," he warbles with the most decadent smile I've ever seen. Graham's longish blond hair flops against a glossy forehead, strands that will soon be fully erect thanks to a generous supply of gel. He's wet, though from rain or perspiration, I honestly can't say.

Graham is heading home from a morning run along the lakefront in his head-to-toe Nike attire, an overpriced watch that tracks mileage and splits. His clothing matches entirely too well, a lime-green stripe in his jacket to match the lime-green stripe in his shoe.

He's what one would call metrosexual, though Chris feels certain there's more to it than that.

"Morning, Graham," I say. "How was the run?"

Leaning against the wheat colored walls with their white wainscoting, he squirts a swig of water into his mouth and says, "Incredible." There's a look of euphoria on his face that makes Zoe blush. She glances down at her shoes, kicks invisible dirt from one shoe with the toe of another.

Graham is a thirtysomething orphan, living in this building because the unit next door to theirs was left to him in his mother's will when she died years and years ago, and Graham, consequently, made out like a bandit, acquiring not only his mother's inheritance, but hundreds of thousands of dollars in a hospital settlement, as well, money that he's slowly squandered away on fancy watches, expensive wines and lavish home decor.

Graham planned to put the home on the market after his mother died, but instead he moved in. Moving vans replaced all of her eclectic furniture and belongings with Graham's modern ones, so sleek and stylish it was as if he'd climbed from the pages of a Design Within Reach catalog: the crisp lines and sharp angles, the neutral colors. He was a minimalist, the condo sparse but for sheets and sheets of computer paper that littered the floor.

"Gay," Chris assured me after we'd stepped foot in Graham's new condo for the first time. "He's gay." It wasn't only the home decor that caught Chris's eye, but the closets full of clothes — more clothes than even I owned — that he left purposefully open so we would see. "Mark my words. You'll see."

And yet women came to call quite regularly, stunning women that left even me speechless. Women with bleach-blond hair and unnaturally blue eyes, with bodies like Barbie dolls.

Graham had arrived when Zoe was still a toddler. She took to him like fruit flies to a bowl of browning bananas. As a freelance writer, Graham was often home, staring blankly at a computer screen and overdosing himself on caffeine and self-doubt. He came to our rescue more than once when Zoe was ill and neither Chris nor I could miss work. Graham welcomed her onto his tufted sofa where together they watched cartoons. He is a go-to when in need of a cup of butter, a dryer sheet or someone to hold the door. He's also top-notch at expository writing, helping Zoe with English homework when neither Chris nor I could. He's an expert at dressing a turkey, something I learned that I couldn't do three-quarters of the way through cooking Thanksgiving dinner for in-laws.

In short, Graham is a good friend.

"You two should join me sometime," Graham says about the run. I see the multitude of water bottles harnessed to his waist and think we best not.

"You'd be sorry if I did," I say, watching as Graham tousles Zoe's hair and again she blushes, this time the rosy tint having nothing to do with his sexual innuendos.

"What about you?" he says to Zoe, and she shrugs. Being twelve has its advantages, the fact that a shrug and a shy smile can get her off the spot. "Think about it," he says, flashing that decadent smile, the teeth lined in a row like well-behaved school children, impeccably white. The insinuation of facial hair where he has yet to shave, the down-turned eyes, which Zoe avoids like the plague. Not because she doesn't like him. But because she does.

We say our goodbyes and head out, into the rain.

I walk Zoe to school before continuing on to work. Zoe attends the Catholic school in our neighborhood, nestled beside a cumbersome Byzantine church, with its gray brick exterior, its heavy wooden doors, its heavenly dome that reaches to the sky. The church is entirely ornate, from the golden murals that run wall to wall, to the stained-glass windows and marble altar. The school sits behind the church, tucked away, a regular brick school building with a playground and a mass of children in matching plaid uniforms hidden beneath multicolored raincoats, their backpacks too obese for their tiny bodies. Zoe slips away from me with barely a goodbye and I watch, from the curb, as she unites with other seventh graders and hurries from the waterlogged street into the dry building, staying away from the little ones — those clinging to parents' legs and vowing that they *don't want to go* — as if they have some communicable disease.

I watch, until she is in the building, and then continue on my way to the Fullerton Station. At some point along the way, the rain, with all of its urgency, turns to hail, and I find myself running, gracelessly, down the street, my feet stomping through puddles, splashing dirty rainwater upon my legs.

The girl and her baby come to mind and I wonder if they, too, are somewhere out there, being pelted by rain.

When I arrive at the station, I use my fare card to unlock the turnstile, then dash up the slippery steps, wondering if I will see them: the girl and her baby, but they are not there. Of course I'm grateful that the baby and her mother are not on the platform in this atrocious weather, but my mind begins to wander: where are they and, more important, are they safe? Are they dry? Are they warm? It's the definition of bittersweet. I wait impatiently for the train and, when it arrives, I get on, my eyes anchored to the window, half expecting to see the two appear at any second: the army-green coat and lace-up boots, the vintage leather suitcase and sodden pink fleece blanket, the baby's exposed creamy head, with faint, delicate plumage, the baby's toothless smile.

At work, a third-grade field trip arrives at our literacy center. With a handful of volunteers, we read poetry to the students, and then the students try their hand at writing and illustrating some poetry of their own, which the more adventurous of the bunch share with the group. The students coming to the center are mostly from lower class, urban neighborhoods, mostly African-American or Latino. Many are from low-income homes, and a smattering speak something other than English — Spanish, Polish, Chinese — in the home.

Many of these children come from families where both parents work, if both parents are still around. Many are from single-parent homes. Many are latchkey kids who spend their afternoons and evenings alone. They are overlooked for more pressing matters: food and housing, to be exact. A morning at our facility is about more than literacy and developing a love of sonnets and haiku. It's about the doubt that overtakes the children when they walk in our doors (quietly grumbling about the task at hand), and the fortitude with which they leave after a few hours of hard work and the undivided attention of our staff.

But once they're gone, thoughts of the girl

and her baby return.

The rain has quieted to a needless drizzle when lunchtime comes. I fasten my raincoat and head outside, careening down State Street while feasting on some healthy granola bar in lieu of lunch, heading to the library to pick up a book I have on interlibrary loan. I absolute love the library, with its sunlit atrium (though not sunlit today) and grotesque granite gargoyles and millions and millions of books. I love the quietness of the library, the gateway to knowledge, to the French language and medieval history and hydraulic engineering and fairy tales, learning in a very primitive form: books, something that's quickly giving way to modern technology.

I pause beside a homeless woman leaning against the redbrick building, and set dollar bills in her outstretched hand. When she smiles at me, I see that many of her teeth are missing, her head covered in a thin black hat that's supposed to keep her warm. She mumbles a thanks, inarticulate and hard to understand, what teeth she has blackened from what I take to be methamphetamine use.

I find my book on the holds shelf and then take a series of escalators up to the seventh floor, bypassing security guards and elementary school field trips, wandering vagrant men, and women with other women, talking too loudly for the library. The library is warm and calm, and entirely welcoming as I make my way to the literature aisles in search of something enjoyable to read, the latest *New York Times* bestseller.

And it's there that I see her, the girl with her baby, sitting cross-legged on the ground in the midst of the literature aisles, the baby laid across her lap, its head elevated by a knee. The suitcase sits on the ground beside her. The girl, it appears, is grateful to be free of its weight for the time being. The girl pulls a bottle from the pocket of the army-green coat, sets it into the obliging baby's mouth. She reaches for a book from the bottom shelf and — as I sneak into the nearest aisle, yanking some sci-fi thriller from the shelf and flipping to page forty-seven — I hear her voice softly reading aloud from *Anne of Green Gables* while stroking the underside of the baby's toes.

The baby is utterly calm. I spy through the metal shelves as the baby consumes the bottle, down to the residual bubbles at the bottom, and as she does her eyes become too heavy to keep open, and they slowly, slowly drift closed, her body gravitating to dormancy, perfectly still with the exception of involuntary twitches here and there. Her mother continues to read, continues caressing the tiny toes with a thumb and forefinger and suddenly I'm eavesdropping on a very personal moment between mother and child.

A librarian appears. "Can I help you find something?" she asks, and I jump, clutching the sci-fi thriller in my hand. I feel guilty, flustered, my coat still dripping with rain. The librarian smiles, her features soft and kind.

"No," I say quickly, quietly; I don't want to wake the baby. I whisper, "No. I just found it," and I hurry to the escalators and downstairs to check out my new book.

I stop on the way home from work at the video store and rent a movie, a chick flick for Zoe and me, and a box of microwave popcorn, fat-free. Chris has always been a road warrior. As a young girl, Zoe was adversely affected by her "here one-minute, gone the next" father. When he traveled, we would invent fun things to do when we couldn't be with daddy: movie nights and sleepovers in the big bed, pancakes for dinner, inventing stories in which Chris was a time traveler (much more entertaining) instead of a traveling investment banker (boring).

I take the elevator up to the fifth floor of our vintage building and as I walk inside I find it eerily quiet, strangely dark. Generally it's the blaring sound of Zoe's stereo that greets me. But tonight it's silent. I flip on a lamp in the living room, call out her name. At her bedroom door, I knock. I can see the light leaking out under the door, but there's no response. I let myself inside.

Zoe, still in her plaid uniform — which is a rarity, these days — is sprawled across the creamy shag rug that lines the hardwood floors. Her uniform is usually discarded for something graphic, something with sequins or rhinestone studs the minute she walks in the door. I can tell she is breathing — *asleep* — and so I don't panic. But I watch her, hugging that yellow notebook in her arms, lying aimlessly on the floor as if her body suddenly became too heavy to hold. She's wrapped in a plush blanket, her head propped on a throw pillow that reads Hugs & Kisses. Her space heater, which Chris bought after Zoe's many complaints that her bedroom was too cold, is set to seventy-nine degrees. Her bedroom is a furnace, an oven, and Zoe, lying two feet away, is being cooked. Her cheeks are flushed; it's a wonder the blanket didn't catch fire. I hit the power button and turn the thing off, but it will take hours for the room to cool.

My eyes deviate around the room, something Zoe would bark at if she were not asleep: the exposed brick walls that appear at random throughout the condo, the reason, Chris deduced, that Zoe's room was so cold; the unmade canopy bed with the patchwork quilt; the posters of teen celebs and tropical paradises mounted to the walls with putty. Her backpack is on the floor, spilled open, the granola bar I thrust into her hand before school for an after-school snack lying untouched. Balled up notes from classmates are scattered upon the floor. The cats lie beside Zoe, embezzling the feverish heat for themselves.

I run my hands through her long hair and quietly call her name once, and then twice. When she comes to, she sits up at once, her eyes wide, as if she's been caught doing something wrong. Something bad. She jumps to her feet, the cats falling to theirs, and tosses the blanket to her bed.

"I was tired," she reasons, and her eyes dart around the room wondering what, if any, transgressions I found. None. It's nearly seven o'clock, and outside, somewhere behind the dark, plump clouds, the sun is beginning to set. Chris, in San Francisco, is likely sitting down to an outrageous dinner at some extravagant restaurant, studying Cassidy Knudsen across the table. I push the thought from my mind.

"Then I'm glad you took a nap," I say, eyeing the creases across her cheek, her exhausted brown eyes. "How was your day?"

"Fine," she says, snatching the yellow notebook from the floor. She clings to it like a baby lemur clinging to its mother's fur.

"Was Mrs. Peters there?"

"No."

"She must really be sick," I say. The flu, it appears, is peaking late this year. "Same sub? The *nag*?"

Zoe nods. Yes. The nag.

"I'll start dinner," I tell Zoe but to my surprise she says, "I already ate."

"Oh?"

"I was hungry. After school. I didn't know what time you'd be home."

"That's fine," I tell her. "What'd you have?"

"Grilled cheese," she says and then, for good measure, "and an apple."

"Okay."

I realize I still have on my raincoat, my rubber boots, and my bag is still draped across my body. I thrust my hand excitedly into the bag and produce the movie and popcorn.

"You up for a movie night?" I ask. "Just you and me?"

She's quiet, her face flat, no animated smile like the silly one on my own. I sense the *no* long before it appears.

"It's just . . ." she starts. "I have a test to-morrow. Mean, median and mode."

I drop the movie into my bag. So much for that idea. "Then I can help you study," I suggest.

"That's okay. I made flash cards." And she shows them as proof.

I try not to be overly sensitive because I know there was a time that I was twelve — or sixteen or seventeen — and would have rather had dental work than hang out with my mom.

I nod. "Okay," I say and slip from the room. And, as quiet as a mouse, she closes and locks the door behind me.

CHRIS

We're sitting in a hotel room: Henry, Tom, Cassidy and me. It's my hotel room. There's a half-eaten box of pepperoni pizza (meat!) on top of the TV, open cans of soda lying around the room. Henry's in the bathroom, taking a deuce, I think, because he's been in there so long. Tom is on the phone, in the corner, with a finger pressed in one ear so he can hear. There are pie charts and bar graphs spread across my bed, dirty paper plates everywhere, on the table, on the floor. Cassidy's plate is on the end table, the one with the pepperoni plucked off and left in a neat pile beside her can of diet soda. I snag a piece of pepperoni and pop it in my mouth and when she looks at me, I shrug and ask, "What? Heidi's gone meatless these days. I'm becoming protein deficient."

"The New York Strip steak didn't satisfy that craving?" she asks. She's smiling. A frisky sort of smile. Cassidy Knudsen is

43

somewhere in her twenties, late twenties, right off an MBA. She's been working with us for about ten months. She's a freaking genius, but not the awkward, nerdy type. The kind that can use words like *fiduciary* and *hedging* and actually sound cool. She's built like a lamp post, tall and thin, with a sphere at the top that glows.

"If I wanted my wife here, I would have brought her."

She's sitting on the edge of my bed. She wears one of those pencil skirts with three-inch heels. A woman of Cassidy's stature does not need three-inch heels, which makes it all the more risqué. She runs her hands through champagne hair, a sleek bob cut, and says to me, "Touché."

Outside the window the San Francisco skyline lights up the night. The heavy, hotel curtains are open. From the right angle we can see the Transamerica Pyramid, 555 California Street, and San Francisco Bay. It's after nine o'clock. In the room next to us, the TV is loud, the sound of preseason baseball drifting through the walls. I pluck another piece of pepperoni from Cassidy's plate and listen: Giants are up 3 to 2.

Henry emerges from the bathroom and we try hard to ignore the stench that follows. "Chris," he says, offering his cell phone in an outstretched hand. I wonder if he washed that hand. Wonder if he was on the phone the whole time he was in the bathroom. Henry isn't the classiest guy in the world. In fact, as he walks from the bathroom I see that the fly of his trousers is down and I would tell him, except that he just stunk up my room. "Aaron Swindler wants to talk to you." I take the phone from his hand and watch as he gropes for another slice of pizza and quickly lose my appetite.

It's no coincidence the prospective client's last name is Swindler. I put on my best salesman voice and saunter to my own corner of the cramped hotel room. "Mr. Swinder," I say. "How about them Giants?" though from the catcalls in the adjoining room I bet the Giants are no longer winning this game.

I didn't always want to be an investment banker. When I was six years old I had all sorts of lofty goals: an astronaut, a professional basketball player, a barber (it felt lofty at the time, kind of like a surgeon for hair). As I got older it wasn't so much about the career itself, but how much it paid. I envisioned a penthouse on the Gold Coast, a fancy sports car, people looking up to me. My mind leaped to lawyers and doctors, pilots, but none of those interested me. By the time college rolled around, I had such a penchant for money that I majored in finance because it felt like the right thing to do. Sit in class with a bunch of other overindulged kids and talk about *money.* Money, money, money.

That, in retrospect, is probably what enticed me the most about Heidi when we first met. Heidi didn't obsess with money like everyone else I knew. She obsessed with the lack of money, the have-nots verses the haves, where all I was concerned with was the haves. Who had the most money and how could I get my hands on some?

Aaron Swinder is going on and on about derivatives when I hear my own phone ring from across the room, where it lies on the striped comforter beside Cassidy and now Henry, who, forty and notably single, is staring not so subtly at the sheer pantyhose on her legs. I'm waiting for an important call, one I can't miss, so I motion to her to answer it, and hear her chant, "Hi there, Heidi," into the receiver.

I deflate, like a helium balloon after a party. *Shit.* I hold up a finger to Cassidy — *hold on* — but since Aaron Swinder won't stop talking about damn derivatives I'm forced to listen to a protracted conversation between Cassidy and my wife, about the flight to San Francisco, dinner at an expensive steakhouse and the goddamn weather.

Heidi has met Cassidy exactly three times. I know because after each and every one of these meetings I've been bombarded with the silent treatment, as if I had anything to do with her recruitment to our team or her good looks for that matter. The first time they met was last summer at a work picnic at the botanical gardens. I'd never mentioned Cassidy to Heidi. She had only been working with us about six weeks. It didn't feel like the necessary, or prudent, thing to do. But as Cassidy sauntered near us in a long, strapless summer dress — where we hid in the shade of a maple tree on a ninety degree day, sweating and feeling totally gross — I saw Heidi grope awkwardly at a jean skirt and blouse, which she was clearly sweating through. I saw all shreds of self-confidence dissolve.

"Who's that?" Heidi asked later, after the phony smiles and "So nice to meet yous" were through, after Cassidy had walked away in search of another happy marriage she could muddle. "Your secretary?"

I never knew what Heidi meant by that, if it would have been better or worse if Cassidy Knudsen was my secretary.

Later, at home, I caught Heidi pulling

negligible gray hairs from her head with a pair of tweezers. Soon after, beauty products besieged our vanity, those laden with antiwrinkle agents and age defying vows.

This is what I'm remembering as I thrust Henry's cell phone back at him, making sure to say, "Here you go, Henry," in a powerful tone so that Heidi, back home in Chicago, knows Cassidy and I are not alone, and flee into the hallway with my own phone. Heidi is a beautiful woman, don't get me wrong. Gorgeous. A person would never guess an entire decade sat between Cassidy and my wife.

And yet, Heidi knew.

"Hey," I say.

"What was that all about?" she asks. I envision her at home, in bed, pajamas on, red flannel or maybe the polka-dot nightgown Zoe picked out for her birthday. The bedroom TV is tuned in to the news, her laptop spread across her legs. Heidi's hair is pulled into one of those messy updos — anything to keep it out of her eyes — while she searches online for information on the slums of Dharavi or maybe poverty statistics from around the world. I don't know. Maybe, when I'm not home, she searches for porn. No. I change my mind. Not Heidi. Heidi is much too tasteful for porn. Maybe she's looking up some practical use for vegetarian meat crumbles. Cat food? Cat *litter*?

"What?" I say dumbly. As if I hadn't noticed. The hotel hallway is covered with the most awful wallpaper, some kind of geometric red design that makes my head hurt.

"Cassidy answering your phone."

"Oh," I say. "That." I tell her about my phone call with Aaron Swindler and then change the subject as fast as I can, blurting out the first thing that comes to mind. "Still raining back home?" I ask. There can be nothing more mundane than talking about the weather.

It is. All day long.

"What are you doing up so late?" I ask. It's after eleven o'clock back home.

"I couldn't sleep," she says.

"Because you miss me," I suggest, though of course we know it's not the case. Chances are I'm not there more than I am there, as has been the case since we started dating. Heidi is used to me being gone. As they say: absence makes the heart grow fonder. That's what she says anyway when I ask if she misses me. I think she secretly likes having the bed all to herself. She's a stomach sleeper — and a blanket stealer — with a fondness for sleeping diagonally. For our marriage, me in a hotel room simply works.

"Sure," she says. And then the expected: "Absence makes the heart grow fonder."

"Who said that anyway?" I ask.

"Not sure." I can hear her fingers moving across the laptop. Click, click, click. "How's everything going?"

"Fine," I say and will her to leave it at that.

But she doesn't. Not my Heidi. "Just fine?" she pries, and I'm forced to relay news of the delayed flight due to rain, followed by turbulence and a glass of spilled orange juice, lunch with a client at Fisherman's Wharf, the reasons I don't like Aaron Swindler.

But when I ask about her day, it's Zoe she wants to talk about. "She's being weird," she says.

I chuckle. I slide down the red geometric wallpaper and have a seat on the floor. "She's twelve, Heidi," I say. "She's supposed to be weird."

"She was taking a nap."

"So she was tired," I say.

"She's twelve, Chris. Twelve-year-olds don't nap."

"Maybe she's getting sick. The flu, you know," I say, "it's going around."

"Maybe," she says, but then, "she didn't look sick."

50

"I don't know, Heidi. I haven't been twelve in a long time. And besides, I'm a guy. I don't know. It's probably a growth spurt, maybe some puberty thing. Maybe she just didn't sleep well."

I all but hear Heidi's chin hit the floor. "You think Zoe's going through *puberty*?" she asks. If Heidi had her way, Zoe would have remained in diapers and fleece footie pajamas for the rest of her life. She doesn't wait for an answer. "No," she says, deciding for herself. "Not yet. Zoe hasn't even started menstruating."

I cringe. I hate that word. *Menstruating. Menstruation. Menstrual flow.* The idea of my daughter wearing tampons — or me having to hear about it for that matter — fills me with dread.

"Ask Jennifer," I suggest. "Ask Jennifer if Taylor is —" I grimace and force out the word *"— menstruating."* I know how women are. A little camaraderie can fix anything. If Taylor's going through puberty, too, and Heidi and Jennifer can call and text each other about emergent pubic hair and training bras, then all will be fine.

"I will," she says decisively. "That's a good idea. I'll ask Jennifer." Heidi's voice quiets, the worried thoughts that consume her mind buttoned up for the time. I imagine

51

her shutting down the laptop, setting it on my side of the bed: a snuggle buddy for the night. "Chris," she says.

"What?"

But she reconsiders. "Never mind."

"What is it?" I ask again. A couple walks down the hall, hand in hand. I pull my legs into me to let them pass. The woman, with a very grandiose tone says, "Pardon me, sir," and I nod in reply. They must be sixty-five years old, still holding hands. I watch them, in their matching khaki pants and spring coats, and remember that Heidi and I rarely hold hands. We're like the wheels of a car: in sync but also independent.

"It's nothing."

"You sure?"

"Yeah," she says. "We'll talk about it when you get home," and for the first time she decides that she's tired. Her voice sounds tired. I see her drifting farther and farther under the covers, a stuffy duvet that makes me sweat even in the dead of winter. I envision the bedroom lights off, the TV off, Heidi's glasses on the end table beside our bed, as is always the routine.

An image pops into my head, unsought and unwanted, and I force it out quickly, like a cannonball from a cannon. *What does Cassidy Knudsen wear when she sleeps?*

"Okay," I say. From inside my hotel room, someone knocks on the door. I'm wanted. I rise to my feet and tell Heidi that I have to go and she says okay. We say our good-nights. I tell her I love her. She says "me, too," as she always does, though we both know the verbiage is wrong. It's just our thing.

As I return to the hotel room and spy Cassidy in her pencil skirt and three-inch heels, still perched on the edge of my bed, I can't help but wonder: *A satin slip? A ruffled babydoll?*

HEIDI

I wake up with an image of Cassidy Knudsen in my mind, and wonder if I've been
dreaming about her, or if she arrived, then
and there, in the morning light, a consequence of our awkward exchange the previous night. I hear her voice over and over
again, answering Chris's phone, that lively
"Hey there, Heidi," that to me, sounded like
nails on a chalkboard: sharp and shrill, infu-
riating.

On the commute to work, I try hard not
to think about that girl and her baby. It's
not easy. On the train I try my hardest to
focus on my sci-fi thriller and not stare expectantly out the dirty window, waiting for
the army-green coat to appear. I spend my
lunch with a colleague and not at the public
library, though I long to go. To loiter in the
literature aisles searching for the girl. I'm
worried about the girl, about her baby, wondering where they sleep and what they eat.

I'm contemplating how to help, whether to give her money, as I did the woman with the blackened teeth, hovering beside the library, or to refer this girl to a shelter, to one of the women's shelters in the city. That, I decide, is what I need to do, to find the girl and deliver her to the shelter on Kedzie, where I know she and her baby will be safe. Then I can remove them from my mind.

I'm about to make a break for it — from a mundane lunch meeting with a mundane coworker — when my cell phone rings, a return call from my dear friend Jennifer. I excuse myself and retreat from the lunchroom to my office to take the call, forgetting for a fleeting moment about the girl and child.

"You saved me," I say as I plop into my chair, hard and cold and certainly not ergonomic.

"From . . ." Jennifer prompts.

"Taedium vitae."

"In English?"

"Boredom," I say.

On my desk sits a framed photo of Jennifer and Taylor, myself and Zoe, one of those photo booth strips from about four years ago, when the girls, eight years old, with their sunny, smiling faces and animated eyes, were still tolerant of being seen in public with their mothers. The girls sit on our laps, Taylor with her big, sad eyes and downward sloping smile, beside Zoe; Jennifer and me, heads smashed together so we all fit in the frame.

Jennifer divorced years ago. I've never met her ex, but from the picture she paints, he was inflexible and sour, given to nasty mood swings that resulted in perpetual fights and innumerous nights on the living room sofa (for Jennifer, that is; her ex was too stubborn to give up the bed).

"Taylor isn't going through puberty, is she?" I ask, just like that. Having a best friend is a wonderful thing. There needs be no proofreading, no refinement, of the comments that come from my head.

"What do you mean? Like her period?"

"Yeah."

"Not yet. Thank God," she says, and just like that, I feel some great sense of relief.

But then, because of my tendency to over-analyze, my Achilles' heel if ever there was one, "Do you think they *should* be menstruating?" I ask, having discovered on various internet searches that it can start as soon as eight, as late as thirteen. But the websites I scour suggest that menarche begins about two years after girls start developing breasts. Zoe, at twelve, is as flat as a pancake. "They're not *behind schedule* or anything, are they?"

Jennifer hears the concern in my voice. She works as a clinical dietitian at a local hospital. She's my go-to for all things medical, as if working in a hospital provides her with a free medical degree. "It's not a big deal, Heidi. They all mature at their own pace. There's no *schedule,*" she assures me, and then she tells me that Zoe's adolescence is something I cannot control. "Though I know you'll try," she goads, "because that's just what you do." The kind of blunt statement only a best friend can get away with. And I laugh, knowing it's true.

And then the conversation shifts to the spring soccer season and what the girls think of their hot-pink uniforms, whether or not the Lucky Charms is an appropriate team name for a group of twelve-year-old girls, and the girls' infatuation with their coach, a twentysomething college kid who didn't make Loyola's team. Coach Sam, who all the mothers think is dreamy. And there Jennifer and I are, gushing about his bushy brown hair, his dark, mysterious eyes, his soccer player build — the strength and agility, calf muscles like we've never seen — pushing all thoughts of Zoe's emerging adolescence and that girl and her baby from my mind. The conversation drifts to boys, preteen boys, like Austin Bell, who all the girls adore. Including Zoe. Including Taylor. Jennifer admits to finding the words *Mrs. Taylor Bell* scribbled across her daughter's notebook and I envision the pale skin of Zoe's arm, the name *Austin* tattooed in pink, a heart over the *i*.

"In my day, it was Brian Bachmeier," I admit, remembering the spiky locks that graced the boy's head, the heterochromatic eyes, one blue, the other green. He moved to our junior high from San Diego, California, which was respect worthy in and of itself, but on top of it, the kid could dance, the Carlton and the jiggy, the tootsee roll. He was the envy of the other boys, the one the girls idolized.

I remember asking him to dance at my first boy-girl party. I remember he said no.

I think of Zoe. I think of Taylor. Maybe our girls aren't so different after all.

There's a knock on my door. I look up to see Dana, receptionist extraordinaire, beckoning me for a tutoring session with a twenty-three-year-old woman who was recently granted asylum from the country of Bhutan, a small South Asian country sandwiched between India and China. She'd been living in a refugee camp in nearby Ne-

58

pal for much of her life, living in a bamboo hut with a dirt floor, surviving on food rations, until her father committed suicide and she sought shelter in the United States. She speaks Nepali.

I lay a hand over the receiver and whisper to Dana that I'll be right there. "Work calls," I tell Jennifer and we confirm the sleepover for Zoe and Taylor tonight at Jennifer's home. Zoe is absolutely thrilled about it. So much so that she actually remembered to say goodbye this morning before she ran into school.

The day dawdles by at an excruciatingly slow speed. Outside the rain quiets, though the city skyline remains gray, the tops of skyscrapers lost in the ashen, obese clouds. When five o'clock rolls around, I say my goodbyes and ride the elevator down to the first floor. It's rare that I leave the office at five o'clock, but on a night such as this — Zoe at a sleepover and Chris on a delayed flight that won't arrive until after 10:00 p.m. — I take pleasure in having the condo all to myself, a simple delight that doesn't happen too often. I'm relishing the idea of watching a chick flick all by myself, of lounging on the sofa in my warm, snuggly pajamas and devouring an entire bag of microwave popcorn all alone (and possibly following it up with a scoop of mint chocolate chip ice cream!).

Above me the clouds are beginning to disintegrate, the sun trying hard to don a lovely sunset behind the fissures in the clouds. The air is cold, an unsettling forty degrees and blowing. I slip my hands in a pair of leather gloves and drape a hood over my head, hurrying, with all the other evening commuters to the "L" station. I force my body into the congested train, where we stand like sardines in a can, smashed together, chugging along the winding, choppy track.

When I depart at the Fullerton Station, I make my way carefully down the wet steps. Beside me, a fellow commuter lights a cigarette and the scent of tobacco fills the air. There's a nostalgic redolence to it: it reminds me of home. When I was a girl, living with my family outside of Cleveland in a 1970s Colonial home with the sponge-painted walls my mother adored, my father smoked Marlboro Reds, a half pack a day. He smoked in the garage, never in our home. Never in the car when he was with my brother and me. My mother simply wouldn't allow it. He secreted the scent of tobacco from the pores of his skin. It was on his clothing, in his hair, on his hands.

The garage was suffused with the smell; my mother claimed it oozed through the heavy metal door and into the kitchen, a thoroughly white kitchen — white cabinets, white countertops, a white refrigerator, a chunky farm table. In the morning, my father wouldn't be out of bed five minutes before he was sneaking off to the garage with his coffee and Marlboro Reds. He'd come in, and I'd be at the table eating my Cocoa Puffs and he'd look at me with the most beguiling smile (I knew my mother had snagged a good one when she married my father) and tell me *never* to smoke, just like that, "Don't ever smoke, Heidi. Never," and he'd wash his hands and join me at the farm table for a bowl of Cocoa Puffs.

I'm thinking of my father as I make my way down the steps, my fingers instinctively reaching for the yellow gold wedding band that hangs on a chain around my neck. I trace the grooves and ridges of the ring, the words *the beginning of forever* etched on the inside.

And then, for a split second I'm nearly certain I see him, there, in the crowd, my father in his Carhartt overalls, one hand thrust in a back pocket, the other holding a Marlboro Red, looking straight at me when he smiles. A hammer dangles from its allot-

61

ted loop on the pants, a baseball cap sits on his head — Cleveland Indians it says — atop a mess of brown hair, which my mother always begged him to trim.

"Daddy," I nearly say aloud, but then the image disappears as quickly as it appeared, and I shake my head, remembering. It couldn't be.

Or could it?

Of course it couldn't, I decide. Of course.

And then I'm breathing in that familiar carcinogenic scent — wanting to smell it and yet not wanting to smell it — when I hear it: a baby's wail. My feet have just hit the pavement when the sound grabs me by the throat and I spin instinctively, my eyes searching for the source.

And there I see her, sitting underneath the train tracks, shivering in the nippy air. She's leaning against a brick wall beside newspaper stands and rank garbage cans, beside swollen puddles, sitting on the cold, wet concrete, rocking the baby against her chest. The baby is crying. There's a frenzy to the way she rocks the baby, a mother with an inconsolable baby, moments away from becoming unhinged. Zoe was a colicky baby, prone to endless hours of intense crying. I can relate with the frustration and the overwhelming fatigue in the girl's eyes. But what I can't relate to is her presence on a city street, in the midst of twilight, on a cold spring night. I can't relate to the desperate way she thrusts a waterlogged coffee cup (likely snatched from the neighboring garbage can) at passersby, begging for money, and the way people give her the once-over, dribbling spare change in her cup: a quarter here, a handful of pennies there, as if any amount of spare change has the ability to save this girl from her fate. I feel my breath leave me for a moment. This girl is a child and the baby is a *baby*. No one deserves such a fate, to be penniless and displaced, but certainly not a child. My mind leaps to the outrageous cost of infant formula and diapers, knowing that if this girl is supplying diapers for that baby, there is certainly no spare change left for her own provisions. For food and shelter, for the umbrella with the flamboyant golden daisies.

I'm rear-ended by a throng of commuters departing the "L." I scoot out of the way, unable to join the clique of other wage earners, those retiring to warm, dry homes and home-cooked meals. I simply cannot. My feet are frozen to the pavement, my heart racing. The baby's wail — piercing and miserable and utterly inconsolable — rattles my nerves. I watch the girl, watch the frenzied rocking, hear the tired words fall from her exhausted mouth as she holds out her cup. "Please, help."

She's asking, I tell myself. She's asking for help.

And yet the do-nothings continue on their way home, rationalizing their lack of concern with the change they drop in her cup, change that would have otherwise found its way to the washing machine or some countertop or bookshelf, where it would sit purposelessly in a ceramic pink pig.

I feel myself tremble as I approach the girl. She lifts her chin as I draw near, and for a split second our eyes lock before she thrusts out her cup and looks away. Her eyes are worse for wear, jaded and pessimistic. I nearly balk for a moment because of the eyes. Icy and blue, a cornflower blue, with much too much eyeliner staining the surface of her bloated eyelids. I think about fleeing. I consider pulling a twenty dollar bill from my purse and setting it in her cup and being on my way. Twenty dollars is much more substantial than a handful of change. Twenty dollars can buy dinner for an entire week, if she's thrifty. That's what I tell myself in my moment of hesitation. But then, I realize, she'd likely spend it on Enfamil formula, placing the baby's needs before her own. She's rail thin, skinnier than Zoe, who is a string bean.

"Let me buy you dinner," I declare, my voice much less bold than the spoken words. My voice is quiet, quivering, nearly suffocated by the sounds of the city: taxis passing by and blasting their horns at commuters who jaywalk across Fullerton; the automated message *Attention customers. An outbound train, from the Loop, will be arriving shortly,* followed by the imminent arrival of the brown line on the platform above us; the sound of the baby's cry. People pass by, chatting and laughing loudly into cell phones; a forgotten rumble of thunder rolls through the darkening sky.

"No thanks," she says. There's a bitterness to her words. It would be easier for her if I dropped in my twenty and continued on my way. Easier now, in this moment maybe, but not when the hunger begins to eat away at her insides, when the baby's inconsolable crying makes her snap. She stands and reaches for the leather suitcase, shuffling the baby in her arms.

"It helps," I say, quickly, knowing she's about to make a run for it, "to lay them on their stomachs sometimes. Like this." I motion with my hands. "It helps with the colic." She watches my hands go from upright to horizontal and she nods — to some extent — and I say, "I'm a mother, too," and she sizes me up and down, wondering why I don't just go. Like everyone else, drop in my change and go.

"There's a shelter —" I begin.

"I don't do shelters," she interjects. I envision the interior of a homeless shelter: dozens upon dozens of cots lined in a row.

She's incredibly tough on the exterior. Hardened and rebellious. I wonder if inside she feels the same. She wears the same torn jeans, the same army-green coat, the same lace-up boots. Her clothing is grungy, wet. Her crooked hair carries a slick look, greasy, having not been washed in some time. I wonder about the last time she enjoyed a warm shower, a good night's sleep. The baby, too, from what I can see is far from clean.

I consider Zoe on her own, on the streets. Homeless. The vision, purely hypothetical, makes me want to cry. Zoe, with her saucy exterior and sensitive, defensive interior, begging for spare change beside the "L." Prepubescent Zoe with a baby of her own in three or four inconsequential years.

"Please let me buy you dinner," I say again. But the girl is turning and walking away, the baby slung over her shoulder awkwardly, fussing and thrusting her teensy body about. I'm consumed with desperation, with this need to *do something.* But the girl is moving away from me, swallowed up by rush hour traffic on Fullerton. "Wait," I hear my voice say. "Please stop. Wait." But she does not.

I drop my bag to the moistened sidewalk and do the only thing I can think to do: I shimmy out of my raincoat, fully waterproof and lined, and at the corner of Fullerton and Halstead — where she waits anxiously for a green light to cross the plugged street — I drape the coat over the baby. She delivers me a dirty look.

"What are you —" she starts, accusatorily, but I retreat a step or two so she can't undo the one thing I can think of to do. The cold air rushes my bare arms where I stand in a short-sleeve tunic and useless, lightweight leggings.

"I'll be at Stella's," I say as the light turns green, "in case you change your mind," and I watch as she joins the mass exodus of people crossing Fullerton. Stella's, with its All-American cuisine and pancakes twenty-four hours a day. Completely unimposing and modest. "On Halstead," I call after her, and she pauses, in the middle of the street, and peers over her shoulder at me, her visage hazy in the glow of oncoming traffic. "On Halstead," I say again, in case she didn't hear.

I stand there at the corner, watching until I can no longer see the army-green coat for all the people, until I can no longer hear the baby's cries. A woman bumps into me and at the same time we say, "Excuse me." I cross my arms, feeling naked in the brisk air — more fall-like than spring-like — and, turning onto Halstead, hurry to Stella's. I'm wondering if the girl will show, wondering whether or not she knows where Stella's is, whether or not she even heard me.

I scurry into the familiar diner and the hostess who greets me says, "No coat tonight? You'll freeze to death," as her russet eyes look me up and down — my hair in a frenzy, my clothing insufficient for the weather. I clutch an overpriced quilted handbag, paisley and plum, as confirmation, perhaps, that *I* am not a vagrant. I have a home. As if the burden of being homeless isn't enough — the lack of food and shelter, of clean clothing — there's the horrible stigma attached to homelessness, the disgrace of being thought of as lazy, dirty, a junkie.

"Table for one?" the hostess — a striking woman with snow-white skin and almond-shaped eyes — asks, and I say, "Table for two," forever hopeful, and she escorts me to a round, corner booth that faces out onto Halstead. I order a coffee with cream and sugar and keep watch out the window, as people trek past, city slickers on their commutes home from work, twenty-year-olds en route to a cluster of college bars on Lincoln, their laughter penetrating the drafty windows of the diner. I watch the eclectic city life meander past the window. I love to people watch. Sleek men in charcoal suits and thousand-dollar shoes beside grunge band wannabes in thrift-store clothing beside mothers with posh jogging strollers and old men hailing cabs. But I hardly notice any of them tonight. All I am looking for is the girl. I think that I see her time and again. I'm sure I catch smidgens of her colorless hair, darker when it's soiled and wet; of the nylon of her ineffectual coat; an untied shoelace. I mistake briefcases for her leather suitcase; imagine that the squeal of tires on wet pavement is the baby crying.

I receive a text from Jennifer that she's arrived home from work and the girls are doing just fine. I scan my emails to waste time: most are work related, some junk mail. I check the weather: when will the rain end? No end in sight. The waitress, a fortysomething woman with the most luscious red hair and waxen, winter skin, offers to take my order but I say, "No thanks. I'll wait until my group arrives," and she smiles gently and says, "Of course." And yet, for lack of anything better to do, I skim through the menu and decide on the French toast, but also decide that if my group never shows, I'll settle for coffee. If the girl and her baby don't arrive by — I check my watch — seven o'clock, I will pay for the coffee with an ample tip for the waitress's time and retreat home to my chick flick and popcorn, and my overwhelming concern for the girl and her baby.

I people watch. I watch patrons come and go. I watch them eat, drooling over generous portions of German pancakes and hamburgers with waffle fries. I absolutely hate to dine alone. The waitress returns and refills my coffee and asks if I'd like to continue waiting and I say that I would.

And so I wait. I must check my watch every two and a half minutes. Six thirty-eight. Six-forty. Six forty-three.

And then she appears. The girl and her baby.

WILLOW

"Heidi was the first one in a long time who was nice to me."

That's what I tell her, the lady with the long silver hair, too long for someone her age. Old ladies are supposed to have short hair. Grandma hair. Short, wrapped tightly with hair curlers, the way Momma would do Mrs. Dahl's hair when I was a girl, with the hot-pink curlers she'd plug in to warm, then sit for a half hour or more, painstakingly wrapping the dark gray, brittle hair around the curlers, then plaster it with spray. We'd wait, in that tiny bathroom of ours (my job was to hand Momma the pins), listening to Mrs. Dahl go on and on about how they'd artificially inseminate the cattle on their farm. I was eight years old and so I didn't know what any of it meant, but I sounded out the words they spelled, words like *s-e-m-e-n* and *v-u-l-v-a*.

"Then why'd you do it?" she asks. The

lady with the long silver hair, combed straight. And big teeth. Like a horse's.

"I didn't want to hurt her," I say. "Or her family."

She sighs, leery of me from the moment she walked into the cold room. She hung back, by the door, just watching me with gray eyes from behind a pair of rectangular glasses. She's got thin skin, like tissue paper, *used* tissue paper, crinkles everywhere. Her name, she says, is Louise Flores. And then she spells it for me, *F-l-o-r-e-s,* as if it's something I might need to know.

"We'll start at the beginning," she says, sitting on the other chair. She sets things on the table between us: a recorder, a stopwatch, a pad of paper, a felt tip pen. I don't like her one bit.

"She wanted to buy me dinner," I say. I've been told that being up-front will go a long way with the silver-haired lady. Louise Flores. That's what they said, the others who were here: the man with the chin strap and mustache, the cutthroat lady dressed in head-to-toe black.

"Mrs. Wood wanted to buy you dinner?"

"Yes, ma'am," I say. "Heidi."

"Well, wasn't that nice of her," she says bitterly. Then writes something down in the pad of paper with the felt tip pen. "Ever

72

hear the saying 'Don't bite the hand that feeds you'?"

When I stare off into space, ignoring her, she prods again, "Huh? Have you? Have you ever heard that saying: 'Don't bite the hand that feeds you'?" And she's staring at me with her gray eyes, where there's a reflection of the one fluorescent light off the rectangular glasses.

"No," I lie, letting my hair fall in my face so I can't see her. *What you can't see, can't hurt you.* That's one I know. "Never."

"I see we're off to a great start here," Louise Flores says with an ugly sneer, and presses a red button on the recorder. Then: "I don't want to talk about Mrs. Wood though. Not yet. I want to go back to the beginning. Back to Omaha," she adds, though I know good and well Omaha isn't the beginning.

"What'll happen to her?" I ask instead. I didn't mean to hurt her, I tell myself, honest to God, I didn't.

"To whom?" she asks, though she knows good and well who I mean.

"Mrs. Wood," I say flatly.

She falls backward, sloping into the angles of the chair. "Do you really, truly care? Or is this just an effort to waste time?" She stares at me, hawkeyed, like Joseph used to do. "I'm in no rush here, you see," she adds, crossing her arms across herself, across a crisp white blouse. "I've got all the time in the world," and yet there's a bite to her voice that suggests she does not.

"What'll happen to her?" I ask again. "To Heidi?"

I imagine the warmth of that nice home, the feel of the soft bed, as the baby and I lay together under the brown blanket that felt just like the soft fur of a bunny rabbit. There were pictures on the walls, there in that home, family pictures, the three of them, pressed close together, smiling. Happy. It always felt warm in there, a different kind of warm, one you felt from the inside out, not the outside in. I hadn't felt that way in a long time, not since Momma. Heidi was about the closest I'd gotten to Momma in eight whole years. She was kind.

The lady's smirk is smug, her gray eyes lifeless, though her thin lips compress into a phony smile.

"As the saying goes, 'No good deed goes unpunished,' " she says, and I imagine Mrs. Wood, in an orange jumpsuit like me, that kind smile washed off her face.

HEIDI

The girl stands there, on Halstead, before the door of the diner, peering through the glass. Not sure if she wants to come in. She's come this far and yet she hasn't quite made up her mind. I see through the glass that the baby is crying, still, though not disconsolate. More of a whimper. She has the baby swaddled in my raincoat, lying horizontally on her tummy as best she can manage with the leather suitcase in one hand. Good girl, I think. She was listening. She lays a hand on the door, and for an instant I'm no longer terrified that she won't show, but suddenly terrified that she has. My heart scurries and a whole new quandary comes to mind: what will I say to her now that she's here?

A young man in a hurry sweeps up from behind and nearly plows her over to get inside Stella's. She staggers, retreating from the door, and I think that she's changed her mind. This young man with his persnickety face, with too much pomade slicked in his hair, has made her change her mind. The man steps inside the warmth of the restaurant, holding the door open for the wavering girl. She eyes him, and then her eyes scan Halstead, trying to decide. Stay or go. Stay or go. After a moment of her hesitation, he briskly asks, which I hear vaguely over the clamor of a crowded restaurant, over dishes clinking and a multitude of voices, "You coming or not?" though the look on his face makes clear he might just let the door slam shut on her face and that of the baby.

I swallow hard and wait for her response. Stay or go. Stay or go.

She decides she'll stay.

She steps inside the diner and the hostess with the russet eyes scans her up and down. The army-green coat and torn jeans, the musty smell that schlepps along with those living on the street, the baby, awed suddenly by the lights on the ceiling, the warmth of the diner, the noise that is distracting to me but somehow pacifying to her.

"Table for one?" the hostess asks the girl unenthusiastically, and I quickly stand from my corner booth and wave.

"She's with me," I mouth, and perhaps

then the hostess makes the connection: my bare arms, a second warm, creamy coat swathing the baby. The hostess points in my direction. The girl makes her way through laminate tables, past obese bodies that spill out of banquet chairs, past waiters and waitresses carrying trays full of food.

"You came," I say as she pauses before the corner booth. The baby turns, at the sound of my voice. It's the first time I've seen the baby so close, under the canned lights that line the drop ceiling. The baby offers a toothless smile, lets out a dove-like coo.

"I found this," the girl says, pulling out a familiar green card, which I recognize instantly as my library card, "in the pocket. Of your coat."

"Oh," I say, not bothering to hide my surprise. How silly of me to give away my coat without checking the pockets, and I remember jamming it inside en route from the public library to work the other day, a sci-fi thriller in my hands. She came to return my library card.

"Thank you," I say. I take it from her outstretched hand, feeling the overwhelming need to touch that baby. To stroke her doughy cheek, or sweep the few strands of gentle snowy hair. "You'll join me for dinner," I say. I turn the library card over in my hands, and then stick it inside the quilted purse.

She doesn't respond. She stands before the booth, her eyes — mistrusting, weary — looking down, away from me. "What difference does it make to you?" she asks, without looking at me. Her hands are dirty.

"I just want to help."

She sets the suitcase on the ground, between her feet, and adjusts the floundering baby. The baby, as they tend to do without warning, is becoming agitated, possibly hungry, no longer interested in the recessed ceiling lights.

"It's not what the world holds for you. It's what you bring to it," she nearly whispers, and I find myself staring, dumbly, until she says, *Anne of Green Gables.*

Anne of Green Gables. She's quoting *Anne of Green Gables.* Of course, I think, imagining her and the baby on the floor of the library the other day, reading aloud from the L. M. Montgomery classic. Which makes me wonder what other classic children's books she's read. *The Wind and the Willows*? *The Secret Garden*?

"What's your name?" I ask. She doesn't tell me her name. Not at first anyway. "I'm Heidi," I say, opting to go first. It seems only right. *I,* I remind myself, am the adult. "Heidi Wood. I have a daughter. Zoe. Who's twelve."

The mention of Zoe must help. She sits after a moment, readjusting the baby against her chest. She and the baby slide awkwardly into the corner booth and she pulls a dirty, formula-encrusted bottle from a coat pocket and fills it with ice water from the table. She sets the bottle into the baby's mouth. The water is too cold, lacking in the nutrients of formula or breast milk. The baby quibbles for a moment, and then makes do. This is not the first time the baby has gotten by on water alone. Anything to fill the void in her tiny tummy.

"Willow."

"That's your name?" I ask and she hesitates, then nods. Willow.

Chris and I chose Zoe's name because we liked it. The alternatives — Juliet, Sophia, Alexis — were all, we believed, to be used in time. For boys, we thought of Zach, to complement Zoe, and of course, Chris threw his own name into the hat. We talked, many times, about how we would trade in our vintage condo for a single family home farther north, Lakeview, or west, Roscoe Village, than our current home, where the mortgage would be slightly less, though the commutes to school and work exponentially longer. I found myself shopping for white, slatted bunk beds when we picked out Zoe's crib; I foresaw rows of shabby chic comforters and dollhouse bookcases and an abundance of toys scattered across the floor. I thought of homeschooling as an alternative to the pricey private school that Zoe now attends, a much more practical alternative to the forty thousand dollars a year we would spend on tuition for all of our imaginary children.

The doctor used the word *hysterectomy*. I lay in bed at night when I should be asleep, considering that word, what it means. To the doctor, to Chris, it was a term, a medical procedure. To me it was carnage, plain and simple. The annihilation of Juliet and Zach, Sophia and Alexis. The end of that vision of shabby chic comforters and homeschooling.

But of course, by then Juliet was already gone, a simple D&C procedure that was anything but simple. There was no way to know whether or not she was a girl — that's what the doctor said, what Chris restated time and again, that there was *no way to know* — and yet I knew, I knew with certainty it was Juliet who was discarded as medical waste, right along with my uterus, my cervix, parts of my vagina.

I found myself, still, stockpiling baby clothes that I found in boutiques in the city — lavender petti rompers and organic animal print bodysuits — hidden in bins that I purposely mislabeled *Heidi: Work* and stored in our bedroom closet, knowing full well Chris would never reconnoiter what he thought to be austere literacy statistics and college textbooks on ESL.

"It's a beautiful name," I say. "And your baby?"

"Ruby," the girl says undecidedly.

"Lovely," I say, and it is. "How old?"

There's a pause, and then she says, as if not quite sure, "Four months."

"Have you had a chance to look over the menu?" the redheaded waitress asks, appearing from out of nowhere, it seems. The girl, Willow, starts and looks to me to answer. The menu lies before her, untouched.

"I think we need some time," I say, but suggest a mug of hot chocolate for Willow, who shivers on the other side of the vinyl booth from the cold. I secure my hands around my own mug, cooler now, but still retaining some heat of the coffee which the waitress now refills for a third time.

"Whipped cream?" the woman asks, and Willow looks to me for approval. Funny, I think, how in that split second she becomes a child, just at the very mention of whipped cream. She strikes me as an optical illusion, like the famous Rubin's vase: depending on how one looks it at, one of two scenes appear, two profiles, placed face-to-face, or the vase which lies perched between them. They flip-flop before your eyes. Profiles, vase. Profiles, vase. Strong, independent young woman with a baby; helpless young girl with an affinity for hot chocolate and whipped cream.

"Of course," I declare, perhaps too fervidly. Moments later the waitress returns with the heavenly drink, a warm white mug and saucer, with a plentiful mound of frothy snow on top, speckled with chocolate shavings. Willow reaches for a spoon and dips the tip into the whipped cream, and licks it off, savoring the taste, as if she hasn't tasted hot chocolate in years.

How is it that someone like her comes to be living on the streets? To be living alone, no caregiver, no guardian. Of course asking the question seems entirely inappropriate, a sure way to send her running. I watch as she appraises the whipped cream, and then goes at it, full tilt, ladling spoonfuls into her mouth until it is gone, until it spills from the corners of her mouth and the baby watches her with covetous eyes, no longer enrapt with the ice-cold water, but with this bubbling white substance oozing from her mother's mouth.

She raises the mug to her lips and drinks too fast, wincing at a burned tongue. With my spoon, I scoop an ice cube from a water glass and sink it into the hot chocolate. "There," I say. "That will speed things along." She hesitates, then tries again, and this time, she doesn't burn her tongue.

There's a bruise hidden above her left eye. An ochre color, as if it is healing. Her fingernails, as she grabs for the menu and decides what she'll have to eat, are long and craggy, with an abundance of dirt wedged between the skin and nail. There are four earring holes placed in either ear, including the cartilage at the top of the ear that's pierced with a black stud. Running the length of the earlobe are a set of silver angel's wings, a gothic cross and ruby red lips, in that order. The red lips on the left lobe are missing. I picture them, lying on the filthy city sidewalk beneath the Fullerton Station, being squashed by passersby, or in the middle of the street, getting run over by cabs. Her bangs hang long, over her eyes. When she wants to look at me, she brushes them away, but then lets them enshroud her eyes once again, like a wedding veil. The skin, on her hands, her face, is chapped and red, creating fissures in the dermis, her hands riddled with dry blood. Her lips are cracked. The baby, too, Ruby, has hints of eczema, crusty red patches along her otherwise milky skin. I reach into my purse and produce a travel-size lotion and, sliding it across the table, say, "My hands get dry in the winter. The cold air. This helps." And as she sets her hand on the lotion, I add, "For Ruby, too. Her cheeks," and she shoves the bangs away and nods, and without hesitation, applies the cream to the baby's cheeks. Ruby cringes at the coldness of the lotion, her noncommittal slate-blue eyes watching her mother curiously, with a bit of resentment mixed in.

"How old are you?" I ask, and I know that her immediate, premeditated answer is a lie.

"Eighteen," she says, without looking at me. Every other question I've asked was met with hesitation. It's the immediacy of her answer that makes me certain it's a lie. That and the naïveté of her eyes when the optical illusion does an about-face, and she is again a helpless girl. A helpless girl like Zoe.

Children legally become adults at the age of eighteen. They become independent beings. Parents lose their rights over their children; they also lose financial responsibility. There are many things an eighteen-year-old can do legally that a seventeen-year-old cannot, such as living alone on the city streets. If Willow is only seventeen, or fifteen or sixteen for that matter, then certain questions are called to mind: where are her parents and why is she not living with them? Is she a runaway? The consequence of child abandonment? My eyes revert to the ochre bruise and I wonder if it's a product of child abuse. If she was seventeen, she could be forced to return home, if such a home exists, or forced into the foster care system.

But I let these suspicions fall by the wayside and take the girl's word at face value: she's eighteen.

"There are shelters specifically for women and children."

"I don't do shelters."

"I work with young women. Like yourself. Women from other countries. Refugees. I help them, sometimes, to get settled."

The waitress returns to take our order. I order the French toast and Willow says she'll have the same. I realize then that she would have had whatever I was having. She didn't want to be presumptuous, to order a half-pound burger when I was having a salad, or breakfast when I was having dinner. The waitress removes the menus from our table and disappears behind a swinging aluminum door.

"There are some wonderful holistic shelters out there. They offer a safe haven, medical care, psychological care, education. There are caseworkers to help you get on your feet. Help you put together a resume, find childcare for Ruby. I can make some calls," I offer, but I see that her eyes are cinched on an elderly man sitting at a booth alone, neatly slicing a deli sandwich in half.

"I don't need any help," she says, piqued. Then she's silent.

"Okay," I acquiesce, knowing if I continue down the same path, she'll take the baby and the leather suitcase and leave. "Okay," I repeat, quieter this time. A concession. I stop meddling and she will stay. So she stays and devours her dinner in near silence and I watch as the baby becomes slowly lethargic and drifts to sleep on the girl's lap. I watch as the girl tears apart the French toast with the side of a fork, and drenches each and every piece in a pool of maple syrup before plunging it into her voracious mouth. I eat slowly, watching the syrup drip down her chin, watching as she wipes it away with the sleeve of the army-green coat.

When is the last time she's had a square meal?

This is only one of the infinite questions I have for her. How old is she, *really*? Where is she from? How did she become homeless? How long has she been living alone on the streets? Where is Ruby's father? How did she acquire the ochre bruise? How often does she visit the library? Does she always haunt the literature aisles, or just whatever suits her fancy on the given day? I nearly mention the librarian with the kind smile — a contrived comment for the purpose of small talk — but I stop myself in time. Of course the girl has no idea I saw her at the library, that I tarried in the neighboring aisle, spying as she read aloud from *Anne of Green Gables.*

And so we eat in silence. In place of small talk, there are the sounds that accompany eating: mastication and swallowing, more maple syrup spurting from the plastic bottle, a fork dropping to the floor. She reaches down and picks it up, and plunges it into the French toast like a torture victim who's been denied food for days. Weeks. More.

When the meal is through she sets her hand on the suitcase and rises from the booth. "You're leaving?" I ask. There's a pang in my voice. I hear it. She hears it.

"Yes," she says. Ruby wakes briefly from the movement and then returns to the Land of Nod.

"But wait," I say, and there is that desperation I felt on the street: her, drifting away, and me, unable to stop her. I flounder for my purse and find a single twenty-dollar bill, not enough to cover the cost of dinner. I will need to wait for the waitress to bring the bill, will need to pay for the meal with a credit card. "Let me take you to the drugstore," I beg. "We'll buy you some things. Formula," I say. "Diapers." Hydrocortisone for those inflamed cheeks. Cereal bars for Willow. Diaper rash cream. Toothpaste. Toothbrush. Shampoo. Hair brush. Vitamins. Bottles of purified water. Gloves. An umbrella. And then it sounds harebrained, even in my own mind, for how could she tote all of those so-called necessities up and down the city streets.

She eyes the twenty in my open wallet and I yank it out, without a second thought, and extend it to her. "You'll go to the drugstore," I say. "Buy what you need. For yourself. For the baby." She hesitates for a brief second, and then yanks the bill from my hand. She nods, which I take to mean yes and thank you.

88

"Wait," I say, before she slips away. Without thinking, I place a hand on the nylon coat and stop her before she goes. The nylon feels strange to my touch, foreign. When the frosty blue eyes turn to me, I withdraw the hand in haste, and beg, "Please. Wait. Just one second," as I unearth a business card from my bag. A simple black business card with my name and phone numbers — cell and work — in white, in an easy-to-read Comic Sans font. I force it into her hand. "In case —" I begin, but a waiter rushes past in haste, a tray full of food perched on a palm above his head, and sing-songs, "Excuse me, ladies," and the girl retreats from him, retreats from me and withers slowly away, backward, like buttercup roses in a cylinder vase, shriveling up and fading away.

And there I stand, all alone, in the middle of Stella's, thinking, *Please. Wait.* Though by now the girl has vanished from the diner and the redheaded waitress, apathetic to my distress, passes by and hands me the check.

I take the long way home, anesthetized to the cold, to the fine mist in the air. I go the long way, stopping by the used bookstore on Lincoln to pick up a copy of *Anne of Green Gables.*

I pay two dollars for the book because there are pages falling out, random, forgotten treasures tucked inside the aging pages: a bookmark with tassels, an old photograph of a little girl in white knee highs beside her grandfather in blue plaid pants. There's an inscription in the book, and a date: To Mom 1989.

I find my neighbor Graham in the hallway on my way upstairs, about to drop an empty bottle of wine down the garbage chute. "That's recyclable," I remind him, hearing a pestering quality to my voice that drives Chris mad.

But Graham just laughs. He's left his condo door wide-open, a blonde beauty queen on the sofa with a fresh glass of Chablis. We exchange a look, and I force a smile, one that she doesn't return.

"Caught by the recycle police, again," he says, withdrawing the bottle from the chute. There are recycle bins by the freight entrance of our building, a long walk for someone who doesn't think much of the environment. But I do. I stop myself before reminding Graham that it takes some one million years for a glass bottle to decompose.

There's an overwhelming need to tell *someone* about my night at Stella's, knowing that Chris won't do. Not even Jennifer will do — she is much too logical, too left-brained for this kind of insanity. I need someone who's ruled by the right brain like me, someone driven by feelings and emotions, by their imagination and beliefs, someone inspired by fantasy.

Someone like Graham.

But from the open condo door, I hear the sound of acoustic guitar on his stereo, the beauty queen beckoning him by name. He tucks the empty wine bottle beneath an arm and tells me he has to go. "Of course," I say, and watch as he closes the door behind himself and I find myself staring at a square boxwood wreath, listening to a squeal from his date.

Inside my own home, I forget all about my movie and tuck myself into bed with *Anne of Green Gables.* When Chris finally returns home from his trip, I hide the book quickly underneath the bed, behind a flounced charcoal bed skirt where only cats and dust bunnies dwell, and pretend to be asleep.

He crawls into bed beside me and kisses me long and slow, though his lips are laced with the image of Cassidy Knudsen.

WILLOW

My momma was the most beautiful lady in the world. Long black threads of hair, a thin face with high cheekbones, perfectly arched eyebrows and the bluest eyes I'd ever seen. *I love you like a squirrel loves nuts,* she'd say to me, or *I love you like a mouse loves cheese.* We'd spend half a day trying to think of the silliest ones we could: *I love you like a fat boy loves cake.* And we'd die laughing. It was our thing.

We lived in a rural Nebraska home, in a tiny little unincorporated town just outside of Ogallala. Momma and Daddy, Lily and me. Ogallala came long before Omaha, just like Momma and Daddy came long before Joseph and Miriam. It was another whole world to be exact, another whole *me.*

Momma used to tell me all the time about the day she and Daddy got married. She said that by the time they said "I do," she was already pregnant with me, which didn't matter none to her or Daddy, but her own momma and daddy didn't like it one bit. Turned out they didn't like Daddy much, either, and so one day, when Momma was nineteen years old, she and Daddy drove out to a chapel in Des Moines, and they got hitched. Momma told me about it, about their wedding in a cozy little church on the side of the road, as we sat on the front step of our tiny prefabricated home, painting our toes candy-apple red while Lily slept the afternoon away. I was eight years old. Momma told me about the chapel, about her walking down the aisle in a strapless, tea-length vintage wedding dress the color of snow; she told me about her veil, a birdcage veil she called it, and I imagined canaries perched on the top of her head. She told me about the man who did their wedding, some man named Reverend Love, and even at that age, at eight years old, I had a hard time believing that was his real name. Reverend Love. I remember the way Momma said his name, that very day we sat on the front step of our prefab home, staring down the boring old street at some boys playing kickball on their lawn, the way she elongated the word *love* until we both about died laughing.

But she said that Daddy was handsome as

all get out, dressed up in a shirt and tie, a sport coat he'd borrowed from a friend. I tried hard to imagine that, 'cause I didn't think I'd ever seen my daddy in a shirt and tie before in my whole entire life. There were no photos from their wedding, 'cause Momma and Daddy didn't own a camera back then, but they had a piece of paper that said they were married, and that was even more important to them than some picture. Momma showed it to me, that paper. Certificate of Marriage, it said, and there, at the bottom, the words *Reverend Love.*

And then, some six months later, I was born. Momma told me about that day, the day I arrived. She told me how I took my sweet time coming out of her, how I was in no rush. She told me how Daddy held on tight to me, there at the hospital, as if he thought I was gonna break. I didn't meet my grandparents when I was born, not then, not ever. Momma's momma and daddy didn't want a thing to do with us, and Daddy's, well, Daddy's were dead. We visited them every now and then, over at the cemetery on Fifth Street, leaving browning dandelions beside the headstones that read Ernest and Evelyn Dalloway.

My momma was convinced by her own

momma that she was Audrey Hepburn, the reason she was named *Holly,* as in Holly Go-lightly. She'd pull her long black hair back into a beehive hairdo and prance around our home with a *Breakfast at Tiffany's* style cigarette holder though Momma didn't smoke. She'd walk around our home in old polka-dot shift dresses on any old day of the week and plagiarize Audrey Hepburn quotes, as if they were her own, and I'd sit there, on the couch, and just stare.

It never surprised me one bit that Daddy wanted to marry her. I'd never seen anyone as beautiful as Momma was.

I asked Momma more than once to tell me how she met my daddy. It was a story she never tired of telling. She told me how she met Daddy in town, at some saloon where he was tending bar, about how some oaf of a man was trying to get friendly with her and how Daddy didn't like it one bit, how he didn't like the way that man talked to her, didn't like the way he kept holding her hand after Momma had told him to quit. Her knight in shining armor, she said. Momma always said that marrying Daddy was the best decision of her life, though as it was, her marrying Daddy made her own parents all but disappear. *Poof,* she said, holding her hands up in the air like some kind of magician, *like magic.*

Daddy, being a truck driver, was gone more than he wasn't. Daddy was an OTR driver, which meant "over the road." He spent his days traveling from sea to shining sea, hauling some sort of freight or hazmat across the country. We missed him more than anything when he was gone, Momma especially, but when he came home, he made up for it, as he showered Momma with slobbering kisses and touched her in places that made her blush. She would get all dressed up for his return, curling her hair, and painting her lips berry bliss. He always had something for Lily and me, something he'd picked up from Vermont or Georgia or wherever it was he was traveling — a key chain or a postcard, a mini Statue of Liberty. It was like Christmas morning when Daddy was home, like summer vacation. And he brought stuff for Momma, too, but that stuff he wouldn't show her, not until Lily and I had gone to bed, but I could hear them at night when they thought I was asleep; I could hear them in their bedroom, laughing.

We didn't have a whole lot of money, there in that prefab home just outside Ogallala, but Momma, she sure loved to shop. Of course we didn't have the money for the kind of stuff she wanted to buy, so instead she took Lily and me to the fancy stores just so she could try on dresses and stare at herself in the mirror. This was one of those things we did when Daddy was away, though Momma said, "don't ever tell Daddy," 'cause she didn't want him to feel bad. But Momma talked a lot about *one day. One day* she was gonna have that salon of her own instead of cutting hair in that bathroom that belonged to Lily and me. *One day* we were going to get a bigger house that hadn't been premade. *One day* she was going to take us to some place called the Magnificent Mile in a city known as Chicago. Momma told me about it, about this Magnificent Mile. She talked about it as if it was a fairy tale, and I wasn't really sure if it was real or not. But Momma was sure. She talked about stores with names like Gucci and Prada, and what she would buy in those stores if she could. *One day.* She had a list of those things, what she wanted to see before she died. The Eiffel Tower, Audrey Hepburn's gravesite in some small town in Switzerland, the Magnificent Mile. We didn't have a lot. Even at eight years old, I knew that, though there wasn't ever a time I wished for more. I was happy there in that prefab home near Ogallala, and even though

Momma talked all the time about her *one days,* I didn't ever want a thing to change. Momma used to say, "We don't have much, but at least we have each other."

And then one day, we didn't even have that much.

CHRIS

Heidi has this need to make everything right. She recycles to a fault. Cans and bottles, the newspaper, batteries, remnants of aluminum foil. She returns hangers to the dry cleaner; rips me a new one when I come home with a plastic shopping bag instead of remembering to bring a reusable one from home. I hear her words, haunting me in my dreams, her metallic tone parroting: *That's recyclable,* in the off moments I attempt to slip an envelope or a scrap of paper into the garbage can of all things. Our milk comes in glass bottles which are reusable and insanely expensive.

In our home, trespassing spiders are never killed but rather, relocated to the balcony or, in the case of inclement weather, to the basement storage units where they can reproduce among cardboard boxes and unused bikes. Smashing them with a shoe or flushing them down the toilet would be simply inhumane.

It's the reason we have two cats. Because she found them as kittens under the Dumpster behind the building. What was left of their mother lay nearby in a bloody tangle, the rest of her serving as fodder for a stray dog. One day Heidi carried them into our condo, each one of them only a pound or two, dirty, covered in shit and garbage, their bones showing through sporadic fur, and declared, "We're keeping them." And as is the case with most things in our marriage, she didn't ask. She told me. *We're keeping them.*

I named them One and Two because Odette and Sabine (yes, both girls; I am indeed the only Tom in this household of Queens), as Heidi suggested, sounded plain dumb. Feral cats don't deserve human names, I told her. Especially not fancy French ones. One is a calico, *chatte d'Espagne,* as Heidi says. Two is all black with longish hair and neon eyes. Bad luck. Evil. The thing hates me.

And so it came as no surprise to me on Saturday morning when I rolled out of bed that there she was, standing in the middle of our living room, displaying her saddest "orphaned kitten" eyes. She'd just finished up a phone call and was going on and on about the poor girl at the Fullerton Station. It was nearly ten in the morning, but from the darkness out the window, you might have guessed it was five, maybe six o'clock. What I had in mind for the day, after an exhausting trip to San Francisco, was sitting in the leather recliner, watching endless hours of professional basketball. But there was Heidi, clearly up at the crack of dawn, clearly having digested too much caffeine. She was in her robe and slippers, clutching her cell phone in the palm of a hand, and I *knew* there was more to this story than she was letting on. This wasn't just about a homeless girl she'd seen. There must be a hundred thousand homeless people in Chicago. Heidi notices them, don't get me wrong. She notices each and every one of them. But they don't keep her awake at night.

"That's why God made homeless shelters," I say. Outside, there is rain. Again. The TV stations are flooded with reporters standing on roads and highways that are underwater. Dangerous and impassable, they say. Even the major expressways — portions of the Eisenhower and the Kennedy — are closed down. Apparently we've entered a state of emergency. The news cameras pause on a yellow street sign: Turn

Around, Don't Drown, it says. Words to live by. A dripping reporter in a golden poncho stands in the Loop getting whammed by rain (as if *seeing* the rain on TV rather than listening to the way it pelts the windows and roofs of our homes will drive home the point) warning that even a few inches of rapidly flowing water can carry a car away. "If you don't need to travel this morning," she says, giving a concerned look as if she actually gives a shit about our safety, "then, please, stay home."

"She doesn't *do* homeless shelters," Heidi replies in a knowing way, and it's then that I understand. Heidi didn't just *see* this girl. There was an exchange. A conversation.

What she's told me thus far, or what I've dragged out of her involuntarily, is that she saw a young homeless girl beside the Fullerton Station, begging for change. A young girl with a baby. I arose from bed and came into the living room — my mind on one thing: TV — to find she'd just finished up a call on her cell, and when I asked who she was talking to, she said, "No one."

But I could tell it wasn't no one. It was clear to me that it was *someone,* someone that mattered to Heidi. But she didn't want me to know. This is what happens to men who travel all the time, I thought. Their wives cheat on them. They rise from bed first thing in the morning to carry on clandestine conversations with their lovers while their husbands are catching some much-needed sleep. I spied my wife: guilty, frenzied eyes, suddenly not as chaste as I knew Heidi to be, and asked, "Was it a guy?"

I thought of Heidi, last night, of the way she pulled away from me in bed. Was he here? I wondered. Before me? I didn't get home until after eleven, to find Zoe AWOL, Heidi in bed, and I remembered when Zoe was little, the way she and Heidi would create welcome-home banners and plaster them with stickers, drawings, photos and whatever other frilly little embellishments they could find, for when I came home, and now, five or six years later: nothing. Only the cats were waiting for me beside the front door, their annoying squawks not a warm welcome but rather an ultimatum: Feed us or else . . . The tiny stainless-steel bowls that Heidi never forgets to fill were empty.

"Heidi," I asked again, my voice losing patience. "Was it a *guy*?"

"No, no," she responded immediately, without hesitation. She laughed, nervously, and I couldn't tell if she was lying, or if my suggestion put her dirty little secret into perspective. Some covert affair or . . .

"Then *who* was it?" I demanded to know. "Who was on the phone?" I asked again.

She was quiet, initially. Debating whether or not to tell me. I was about to get really pissed off, but then she grudgingly told me about the girl. The girl with the baby.

"You talked to her?" I ask, feeling my heart decelerate, my blood pressure decline.

"She just called," Heidi replies. Her cheeks are flushed, either a symptom of caffeine overdose or she's embarrassed.

My chin drops. "She knows your *phone number*?"

Heidi is stymied by guilt. Unease. She doesn't answer right away. And then, sheepishly: "I gave her my card. At dinner. Last night."

This, I think, is getting weird. I stare at the woman before me in dismay — at the bedhead of auburn hair, the manic, caffeinated eyes — and wonder what she's done with my wife. Heidi is a dreamer, yes. A visionary, an optimist. But there's always a dose of reality mixed in.

Except that this time, it appears, there's not.

"Dinner?" I start, but then shake my head and start again, getting down to the more pertinent details: "Why did she call?"

I find myself staring into Heidi's demented eyes and wishing it was another guy.

Heidi marches to the coffeemaker as if she has any business drinking more caffeine. She tops up a personalized mug Zoe and I gave her for Mother's Day a few years back, a black ceramic mug garnished with photos of Zoe that the dishwasher has begun to wear away. She dribbles in the hazelnut creamer and I think: *Sugar, too. Perfect. Just what Heidi needs.*

"Ruby was crying all night, she said. All night long. Willow was really in a tizzy. She sounded exhausted. It's colic. I'm sure of it. Remember when Zoe was a baby and had colic? The crying all night long. I'm really worried about her, Chris. About both of them. That persistent crying. That's the kind of thing that leads to postpartum depression. To shaken baby syndrome."

And really, I can think of only one thing to say: "Willow? That's her name? And Ruby?"

Heidi says that it is.

"People are not named Willow, Heidi. Trees are named Willow. And Ruby . . ." I let the rest of that sentence fall by the wayside, for Heidi is looking at me as though I might just be the devil incarnate, standing in the middle of our living room in checkered boxer shorts and nothing more. I bypass Heidi, and head into the kitchen for my own cup of coffee. Maybe then this will make more sense. Maybe after a cup of coffee, I'll come to realize this has all been a misunderstanding, the translation lost somewhere in my tired, sluggish brain. I take my time, fill the mug and hover before the granite countertops, ingesting the coffee, waiting for the stimulant to arouse the neurons in my brain.

But when I return from the kitchen, Heidi is standing before the front door, slipping a long, orange anorak over her robe.

"Where are you going?" I ask, bewildered by the coat, the robe, the messy hair. She kicks the slippers from her feet and submerges her feet into a pair of rubber boots lounging before the door.

"I told her I'd come. Meet her."

"Meet her *where*?"

"By the Fullerton Station."

"Why?"

"To see if she's okay."

"Heidi," I say in my most rational, objective tone. "You're in your pajamas." And she looks down at the lilac fleece robe, the gaudy, cotton floral pants.

"Fine," she says and races into the bedroom and replaces the floral pants with a pair of jeans. She doesn't take the time to remove the robe.

This is absolutely absurd, I think. I could tell her, make a bullet point list or maybe a bar graph for her to see it, visually, how this is absolutely insane. On one axis, I'd list all the anomalies of the situation: Heidi's fetish for homeless people, the lack of discretion when handing out her business card, the hideousness of the lilac robe and the orange anorak, the rain; the other axis would show the values of these anomalies, the outfit far outranking the business card, for example.

But all that would do is land me in hot water.

And so I watch from the leather recliner out of the corner of my eye as she grabs her purse and an umbrella from the front closet and disappears through the door, chanting, "See you later." My lethargic reply: "Bye."

The cats jump to the sill of the bay window, as they always do, to watch her leave through the building's main entrance and down the street.

I make myself scrambled eggs. I forget to recycle the egg carton. I warm slices of limp bacon in the microwave (which feels entirely wrong to do in Heidi's absence: eat meat in our pseudo-vegetarian home), and eat in front of the TV: ESPN pregame shows that will eventually turn into NBA games. During commercial breaks I flip to CNBC because I can never be too far away from Wall Street news. It's the part of my brain that never sleeps. The one consumed with money. Money, money, money.

Lightning flashes; thunder booms. The entire building shudders. I think of Heidi on the street in this weather and hope she does her business and hurries home soon.

And then another pop of thunder, another lightning flare.

I pray to God that the power doesn't go out before the game.

It's about an hour later that Zoe is escorted home by Taylor and her mother. I'm still in my boxers when Zoe lets herself inside, and there, hovering in the doorway, is the throng of them, mouths agape, dripping wet like a bunch of wet dogs, staring at me, in my boxer shorts, at the traces of dark hair on my chest. My hair is waxy, standing every which way, an old man smell stuck to me like glue.

"Zoe," I say, jumping from the recliner, nearly spilling my coffee as I do.

"Dad." Mortification fills Zoe's eyes. Her father, half naked, in the same room with her best friend. I wrap a faux fur blanket around myself and try to laugh it off.

"I didn't know when you'd be home," I say. But of course, that isn't a good enough excuse. Not for Zoe anyway.

This, I'm certain, is only the first of many times I will humiliate my daughter. I watch as Zoe grabs Taylor by the hand and they disappear down the hall. I hear the door to Zoe's bedroom creep shut and imagine Zoe's words: *My dad is such a loser.* "Heidi home, Chris?" Jennifer asks, her eyes looking everywhere but me.

"Nope," I say. I wonder if Jennifer knows about the girl. The girl with the baby. Probably. When it comes to Heidi's life, Jennifer knows most everything. I grip the blanket tighter and wonder what Heidi tells Jennifer about *me.* I'm absolutely certain that when I'm being an asshole, Jennifer's the first to know about it. About my smoking-hot co-worker or the fact that I'm traveling *again.*

"You know when she'll be home?"

"I don't."

I watch as Jennifer fidgets with the strap of her purse. She could be a pretty woman, if she'd get out of her scrubs and put on some real clothes for a change. The woman works in a hospital, and I'm half-certain the only clothes hanging in her closet are scrubs in every color of the gosh darn rainbow and clogs. Medical clogs. They look comfortable, I'll give her that, and yet whatever happened to jeans? A sweatshirt? Yoga pants?

"Anything I can help with?" I ask, a polite but dumb offering. Jennifer, a bitter divorcée, hates me simply because I am a man. A half wit, no less, lounging around the house in my underwear in the middle of the day.

She shakes her head. "Just girl stuff," she says, and then, "Thanks anyway."

And then she retrieves Taylor, and when they leave, Zoe turns to me, glaring disapproval in her preteen eyes and says, "Really, Dad. *Boxer shorts?* It's eleven o'clock," and retreats to her bedroom and slams the door.

Great, I think. *Just perfect.* Heidi's off chasing down homeless girls, but I'm the one who's weird.

HEIDI

I don't know if she drinks coffee or not, but I bring her a café mocha nonetheless, topped with extra whipped cream for good measure, the perfect pick-me-up for anyone who's having a bad day. I get a scone to go with it, cinnamon chip, plus the "very berry" coffee cake, in case she doesn't like cinnamon or scones. And then I scurry down the quiet, Saturday morning streets, elbows out, in a defensive position, ready to tackle anyone who gets in my way.

It's raining, the April sky dark and disgruntled. The streets are saturated with puddles, which passing taxis soar through, sending rainwater flying into the air. Car lights are on, and, though it's after 10:00 a.m., automatic streetlights have yet to register that nighttime has turned to day. My umbrella is up, keeping my hair dry though my lower half becomes soaked by puddles, by the surges of water that splash from the tires of passing cars. The rain cascades from the sky, and I chant to myself: *It's raining cats and dogs. It's raining pitchforks and hammer handles. When it rains it pours.*

She's right where she said she'd be. Pacing up and down Fullerton, jouncing a desolate Ruby who screeches at the top of her lungs. Sopping wet. Onlookers — a handful of zealot joggers in water-repellant running gear — circumvent the scene, stepping onto Fullerton to risk their lives in oncoming traffic rather than assist Willow, the young girl who appears to have aged thirty years in the course of a single night, carrying the facial features of a middle-aged woman: dramatic creases on her face, baggage under the eyes. The whites of her eyes are red, the blood vessels of the sclera swollen. She trips over a crack in the sidewalk, tosses Ruby roughly over a shoulder, patting her back in a manner that verges on unkind. *Shhh . . . shhhh,* she says, but the words are not gentle, not pacific. What she means to say is *shut up. Shut up. Shut up.*

She bounces her angrily, as I remember willing myself *not* to do when Zoe was a baby, when her yowling kept me up all night long and it was all I could do *not* to lose control. I don't know much about postpartum depression, personally, but the media is quick to spin sensationalist stories of unstable, disturbed women driven by the intrusive thoughts that jump unsolicited into their minds: thoughts of hurting their babies, of stabbing them or drowning them or throwing them down a flight of stairs. Thoughts of driving their minivan to the bottom of a retention pond with their children buckled safely in the backseat. I know there are women who, fearing they might hurt their babies, abandon their newborns instead, in an effort to avoid physical harm. I commend Willow for *not* leaving Ruby on the steps of a church or shelter, for *not* telling her to shut up when I know it's exactly what she wants to say. The joggers look and frown — *what is that girl doing with that baby?* — but what I see is a tenacious girl with more gumption than half the grown women I know. Without my mother to complain to on the phone, without Chris to steal a hysterical Zoe from my arms when I'd had enough for one day, I'm not certain what I would have done, how I would have survived that first year of motherhood (though now knowing the perplexities of a twelve-year-old girl, infancy doesn't seem so bad).

"I brought you coffee," I say, sweeping up from behind and startling the girl. As if coffee will truly fix anything, steal her away

113

from a life on the streets, provide any nourishment for her meager body. She is completely exhausted, her body heavy, her legs on the verge of collapse. I know without her having to tell me that she's been pacing up and down Fullerton since the middle of the night, any effort to calm Ruby down. Her body is sleepy, though her eyes are rabid, like a dog in the furious stage of rabies: aggressive and ready to attack. There's a loss of coordination, an irritability in the forceful way she snatches the cup from my hand, in the way she drops to the wet ground and devours both the cinnamon chip scone *and* the "very berry" coffee cake in a matter of moments.

"She's been crying all night," she says between mouthfuls, crumbs escaping the corners of her mouth and falling to the concrete, where she ambushes them and forces them back in. She tucks herself and Ruby into a doorway, under an indigo awning on the steps of an eclectic little shop with wind chimes and ceramic birds in the front window. The store is open, the contour of a woman watching us through the window, from afar.

"When is the last time she ate?" I ask, but Willow shakes her head, delirious.

"I don't know. She won't eat. Kept pushing the bottle out. Screaming."

"She wouldn't take the bottle?" I ask.

She shakes her head. She removes the top of the café mocha and begins lapping up the whipped cream with a tongue. Like a dog, lapping water from a bowl on the floor.

"Willow," I say. She doesn't look at me. There's a rotten smell coming from her: clothing that has been soaked by rain — damp and filthy — days, maybe weeks, of body odor. An atrocious smell wafting from Ruby's diaper. I peer up and down the street and wonder: where does Willow go to use the facilities? The employees at local restaurants and bars would shoo her away like a stray cat, a *feral* cat. I've seen signs plastered in storefront windows: No Public Restrooms. I think of the park, blocks away, and wonder if there's a public toilet, a port-a-potty, anything for her to use? "Willow," I start again, this time dropping to the concrete beside her. She watches me closely, cautiously, and scoots a bit away, regaining her three feet of personal space. But she claws the coffee, the microscopic pastry crumbs that remain in the soppy paper sack, in case I have the gall to steal them from her hand.

"Willow," I say again, and then, "Would you let me hold Ruby?" finally forcing the

115

words from my mouth. Oh, how I want to hold that baby in my arms, to feel the weight of her! I recall that wonderful baby smell from Zoe's youth: a conglomeration of milk and baby powder, sour and unpleasant, and yet entirely delicious, wistful, nostalgic. What I'm expecting from Willow is a firm *no,* and so I'm taken aback by the ease with which she hands me the hysterical child. It's not instantaneous, no. Not by any means. She scrutinizes me up and down: who is this woman and what does she want? But then, perhaps, some literary verse runs through her mind, some proverb about faith and trust and, as J. M. Barrie would say, pixie dust. She slips the child into my hands, grateful to be free of the thirteen or so pounds of body weight that hampered her all night, that must make her feel waterlogged, snowed over. Willow's body relaxes, her bones sink into the cold concrete, her muscles slack against the glass door.

And in my arms, Ruby quiets. It has nothing to do with me, per se, but rather a change in position, new eyes to see, a smile. I collapse the umbrella and stand from the ground, protected, to some extent, from the elements beneath the indigo awning, and in my arms, sway her back and forth in a gentle lilt, humming. My mind time travels to Zoe's baby nursery, pale purple damask sheets, the sleigh glider where I would sit for hours on end, rocking the tiny figure in my arms until long after she'd fallen asleep.

Ruby's diaper alone must weigh ten pounds. She's soaked through and through, urine and diarrhea seeping through a Onesies jumpsuit and onto my coat. Her jumpsuit, which used to be white, with the words *Little Sister* embroidered in a pastel thread, is caked with throw up and spit up, some milky white, others Technicolor yellow. She's warm to the touch, her forehead radiating heat, her cheeks aglow. She's running a fever.

"Ruby has a sister?" I inquire, trying, with the back of my hand to determine the baby's temperature. 101. 102. I don't want to alarm Willow and so I try to be sly, try to make small talk so she doesn't see the way I press my lips to the forehead of the baby. 103?

"Huh?" Willow asks, turning white with confusion and I point out the jumpsuit, the lavender *L,* the salmon *I,* a pair of baby blue *T*s and so forth.

A cyclist passes by on the street — bike wheels spinning wildly through puddles on the road — and Willow's eyes turn to watch him: the red sweatshirt and black biker shorts, a gray helmet, a backpack, calf muscles that put my own to shame. The way the water mushrooms beneath the tires. "I got it at a thrift store," she says, not looking at me, and I reply, "Of course." Of course, I think. Where would the sister be?

I stroke a finger down Ruby's cheek, feeling the soft, cherubic skin, staring into the innocent, ethereal eyes. The baby latches on to my index finger with her chubby little fist, the bones and veins tucked away under layers and layers of baby fat, the only time in one's life when *fat* is adorable and heavenly. She plunges a finger into her mouth and sucks on it with a vengeance.

"I think she might be hungry," I suggest — hopeful — but Willow says, "No. I tried. She wouldn't eat."

"I could try," I offer, adding, "I know you're tired," careful not to usurp her role as the mother. The last thing in the world I want to do is offend Willow. But I know babies can be more confusing than preteen girls, more baffling than foreign politics and algebra. They want a bottle, they don't want a bottle. They cry for absolutely no reason at all. The baby that devours pureed peas one day won't touch them the next. "Whatever you think is best," I say.

"Whatever," she says, shrugging, indifferent. She hands me the one and only bottle she owns, filled with three or four ounces of formula, put together in the wee hours of morning. It's curdled now and though I know Willow intends me to plunge this very bottle, this very formula, into Ruby's cavernous mouth, I cannot. My hesitation makes the baby wail.

"Willow," I say over the sound of Ruby's hysterics.

She takes a drink of the coffee and flinches from the heat. "Huh?"

"Maybe I could wash out the bottle? Start again with fresh formula?"

Formula is horribly expensive. I remember. I used to cringe each and every time Zoe didn't suck her baby bottles dry. When Zoe was born, I was a staunch believer in breastfeeding. The first seven months of her life, I relied on nothing but breast milk. I planned to do so for a year. But then things changed. Initially the doctor and I discounted the pain as an effect of childbirth. We went on as if all was normal.

But all was far from normal.

By then, I was pregnant again, pregnant with Juliet, though of course, there was no way to know at that point if she was a girl.

It had been less than six weeks since Juliet was conceived when the bleeding first be-

119

gan. By this time in her life, her heart was pumping blood and her facial features were taking form; arms and legs were about to emerge as tiny buds from her tiny body. I didn't have a miscarriage; no, that, of course would have been too easy, too simple, for her to just *die.*

Instead, I made the decision to end my Juliet's life.

Willow gives me a look that is hard to read. Wary and dubious, but also too tired to care. A handful of girls — college aged, in sweatshirts and flannel pants — pass by, huddled close together, arm in arm, under golf umbrellas and hoods, giggling, recalling hazy, drunken memories of last night. I overhear words: *jungle, juice, pink, panty, droppers.* I look down at my own attire and recall the purple robe.

"Whatever," she says again, her eyes following the coeds until they round the corner, their laughter still audible in the slumberous city.

And so I hand the quivering child back to Willow and, releasing my umbrella, scurry to the nearest Walgreens where I pick up a bottle of water from the shelf and acetaminophen drops. Something to bring that temperature down.

When I return to our little alcove, I dump

the used formula on the street, watching as it races into the nearest storm drain, then rinse out the bottle and start anew. Willow hands me the coveted formula powder and I mix up a bottle, and she returns Ruby to my arms. I plunge the bottle into the baby's expectant mouth — full of hope that *this* will quiet the hysterical child — but she thrusts it out with a horrified look, as if I'd slipped formula laced with arsenic into her mouth.

And then she begins to scream.

"Shh . . . shh," I beg, bouncing her up and down and I remind myself — already tired, already frustrated — that Willow did this all night. All night long. Alone. Cold. Hungry. And I wonder: Scared? Lightning flashes in the not-so-far distance, and I count in my head: One. Two. Three. Thunder crashes, loud and angry, full of wrath. Willow staggers, searching the heavens for the source of the jarring noise and I see in the way her eyes dilate that she's scared. Scared of thunder, like a child. "It's okay," I hear myself say aloud to Willow, and instantly I'm transported back in time to Zoe's preschool bedroom, cradling her body in my arms while she nuzzled her head into me. "It's okay," I say to her, "it's only thunder. It won't hurt you one bit. Not one bit at all," and I see Willow staring at me, though the look in her blue eyes is impossible to read.

I'm absolutely soaking wet, as are Willow and Ruby, and the woman in the shop has the audacity to knock curtly on the glass door and tell us to go away. *No loitering,* her lips say.

"What now?" I ask myself aloud, and Willow responds in a hushed voice, more to herself than me: "Tomorrow is a new day," she says, "with no mistakes in it yet."

"Anne of Green Gables?" I ask and she says, "Yes."

"Your favorite?" I ask, and she says that it is.

I'm slow to move, to draw Willow and her leather suitcase from the safety of the indigo awning and into the rain. "I bought a copy of *Anne of Green Gables,*" I confess. "On the way home last night. I've never read it before. I always wanted to read it. With my daughter, with Zoe. But she grew up too fast for it," I say. It was as if I merely blinked, and the baby girl I once read board books to was suddenly too old to share a book with me, with her mother, because then, what would her friends at school think? It would be embarrassing if they knew, or so Zoe assumes.

A thought crosses my mind, as it often does in moments like this: if I had to do it all over, what would I do differently? If Zoe could be a baby again, a toddler, how would I be different? How would Zoe be different? Would things have been different with Juliet?

But of course, the question is entirely null and void, seeing as how there would be no more children for Chris and me.

"Did you and your mother read *Anne of Green Gables*?" I ask, wondering if she will humor me with this tidbit of personal information.

Hesitantly, she answers, "Matthew."

"Matthew?" I repeat, worried that her confession will end there, with that one word.

But to my surprise she continues, the dark bangs shrouding her eyes as she watches a robin hunt for worms on the street. The first sign of spring. There are tiny buds on the trees that line the city streets, crocus shoots poking through holes in the sodden ground. "Matthew, my . . ." And she hesitates — there's a distinct hesitation before she says, "my brother," and outwardly I nod, but inwardly my heart leaps. One piece of the puzzle. Willow has a brother named Matthew. Willow has a brother, *at all*. A brother who read *Anne of Green Gables.*

"Your brother read *Anne of Green Gables*?" I ask, trying to ignore the peculiarity of it, of Willow reading a book such as *Anne of Green Gables* with her brother, a book that a mother and daughter should share. I want to ask her about her mother. About why she didn't read the book with her mother. But instead, I say nothing.

"Yes."

I see a wistfulness come over her when she mentions her brother. Matthew. A tinge of sadness, a mournful sigh.

I wonder about this Matthew and where he may be.

And then Ruby's bloodcurdling scream makes me remember the acetaminophen. I tread lightly. "I think Ruby is running a fever," I say. "I bought some Tylenol at the store. It might help." I hand Willow the box so that she can see it is, in fact, Tylenol, that I'm not trying to drug her baby.

Willow looks at me with concern in her eyes and her voice becomes that of a child. "She's sick?" she asks, her own naïveté showing through.

"I don't know."

But I see that the baby is a drooling, boogery mess. Willow concedes to the Tylenol and I read the directions for the dosage.

Willow holds Ruby while I squeeze the berry flavor medicine into her mouth, and we watch as Ruby goes silent, and then smacks her lips together. It's yummy, the Tylenol. And then we wait for the medicine to kick in, for Ruby to stop crying. We wait and think. Think and wait. Wait and think. Think and wait.

What will I do when Ruby does, if ever, stop crying? Say goodbye and return home? Leave Ruby and Willow here, in the rain?

With the diarrhea soaked diaper, a red, swollen, boiled and blistered diaper rash on her genitalia and buttocks (as I imagine there to be, hiding beneath the diaper). That, alone, would make me scream.

"When's the last time she saw a doctor?" I ask.

"I don't know," says Willow.

"You don't know?" I ask, taken by surprise.

"I don't *remember*," she corrects.

"We could take her to the doctor."

"No."

"I could pay. For the bill. Medicine."

"No."

"Then a shelter. Protection from the elements. A good night's sleep."

"I don't do shelters," she says again — a replay of last night in the diner — the tone

125

of her voice hammering the message home. I. Do. Not. Do. Shelters. I can't blame her. I, myself, would think long and hard before checking into a homeless shelter. Shelters themselves can be dangerous places, brimming with desperate men and women, turned by circumstance into violent predators. There are communicable diseases in shelters: tuberculosis, hepatitis and HIV, and, sometimes, the homeless are not allowed to bring their personal possessions inside. Which means, abandoning Willow's vintage suitcase and whatever treasures it may hold. There are drugs in shelters, drug addicts, drug dealers, there are infestations of lice and bed bugs, there are people who will steal the shoes from your feet while you sleep. In the coldest months, people wait in line for hours to be assured a bed in a shelter. And even then, there may or may not be space.

"Willow," I say. There's so much I want to say. The "L" comes soaring in on the tracks above us, drowning out the sound of my voice. I hesitate, wait for it to pass and then say, "You can't stay out here forever. There are things Ruby needs. Things *you* need."

She looks at me with those cornflower eyes, her skin drab, remnants of eye makeup intensifying the baggage beneath her eyes.

126

"You think I want to live on the streets?" she asks. And then says to me, "I've got nowhere else to go."

CHRIS

The front door opens and there they stand like two drowned rats. There's a baby in Heidi's arms, a scent far worse than cumin wafting from the girl. I rub at my eyes, certain I'm hallucinating, certain *my* Heidi would never bring a homeless girl into our home, into the home where her own daughter lives and breathes. The girl is a ragamuffin, a street urchin. She's barely older than Zoe. She won't make eye contact with me, not when Heidi tells me her name is Willow or when I say lackadaisically (I don't want to appear *too* stupid when the cameramen appear to inform me that I'm on the next installment of *Candid Camera*) that mine is Chris.

Heidi announces, "She's going to stay with us tonight," just like that. Like those damn kittens, and I'm too stupefied to say yes or no, not that anyone bothered to ask my opinion. Heidi shepherds the girl into *our* home, and suggests she remove the soused boots from her feet, and as she does so, about a gallon of water pours from their insides and onto the floor. Beneath those boots, her feet are bare. No socks, her feet macerated and covered in blisters. I wince, and Heidi and the girl's eyes follow mine down to the bare feet. I know Heidi's thinking about how to remedy the girl's ailing feet, but I'm just hoping whatever she's got isn't contagious.

Zoe appears from her bedroom, the words "what the . . ." dropping from a gaping mouth. I'm guessing our daughter isn't overly familiar with the *f* word that follows that statement, so I nearly say it aloud for her. *What the fuck are you thinking, Heidi?* But already Heidi is showing the girl into our home, introducing her to our daughter, who stares dumbly at this waif and then looks to me for an explanation. I can only shrug.

The girl's eyes get lost on the TV, on some basketball game: Chicago Bulls versus the Pistons, and I hear myself ask — for lack of anything better to say — "You like basketball?" and she flatly answers, "No," and yet she's staring at that TV as though she's never seen an electrical appliance before in her life. When she talks, I catch a scent of bacteria fermenting in her mouth: halitosis. I wonder when she last brushed her teeth. They've probably got that "fuzzy sweater" thing going on. There's an ungodly smell coming from her and when I move to the window and open it a crack, Heidi shoots me an evil eye, to which I reply, "What? It's stuffy in here," and hope the rain stays at bay long enough to air out the stench.

The girl is nervous, like a trapped tomcat, eyes darting around the room, searching for a bed under which she can hide.

I can't figure out what is the weirdest of all: this strange girl in our home, or the way Heidi cradles that baby as if it is hers, the way she supports its head with the palm of her hand and rocks it back and forth intuitively. Her eyes gaze at that baby in a covetous way, an almost silent hum sneaking from her when the TV breaks for commercial and the room is filled with a split second of silence.

"I'm going to my room," Zoe declares, and walks down the hall and slams the door.

"Don't worry about her," Heidi apologizes to this girl — Willow — and says, "She's just . . . she's twelve."

"She doesn't like me," Willow guesses. *Nope,* I think, *she doesn't.*

But Heidi says, "No. She just . . ." She

fights for an appropriate answer and comes up near empty. "She hates everything," she says instead, as if somehow *everything* does not encompass this strange new addition to our home.

"You can stay in here," Heidi says as she leads the girl down the hall and into *my* office where we keep a classy leather sofa bed for when guests come to stay. Except that this is not a guest. I watch from the doorway as Heidi hands the baby back to the girl, then removes stacks of my work from the sofa and sets them on the desk with a thump.

"Heidi," I say, but she ignores me, too busy removing the cushions from the sofa and tossing them to the floor.

"What you need," she's saying to the girl, who stands, grappling with the infant and a sopping suitcase in her hands, standing as uncomfortably in the room as I feel, "is a good night's sleep. A square meal. Do you like chicken?" she asks, the girl's wavering nod barely visible before Heidi says, "We'll have chicken tetrazzini. Or better yet, chicken potpie. Comfort food. Do you like chicken potpie?"

And there's only one thought running through my mind: *I thought we were vegetarians.* Where has Heidi been hiding the chicken all this time?

In her haste, Heidi knocks a dozen or more Excel spreadsheets and my fancy financial calculator to the floor. I push my way inside, losing patience, and collect the spreadsheets one by one. The girl reaches over and picks the calculator up off the floor, running her fingers over the numbers and buttons before returning it nervously to me. "Thanks," I mutter, and then, "Heidi," I say again, but this time she pushes past me — leaving the girl and me alone in the room for all of twenty seconds — in search of a set of chambray sheets from the linen closet. I snatch my laptop as the girl watches me, unplug the printer from the wall and carry the both of them, with great difficulty, from the room, tripping over the printer's electrical cord as I do. I bypass Heidi in the doorway and snap this time, *"Heidi,"* and when her brown eyes pay me the time of day, I growl, "I need to speak with you. *Now,"* and she sets the sheets on the pull-out bed and follows me — piqued, as if I'm the one being bullheaded and impetuous — from the room.

"What the hell are you thinking?" I seeth at her as we drift down the narrow hall. "Bringing that girl into our home." The printer is heavy; I lose balance and stumble into the wall. Heidi doesn't offer to help.

"She had nowhere to go, Chris," she insists, standing before me in that heinous lilac robe, her hair flattened by the rain. Her eyes are aroused, bizarrely similar to the night I came home from work, some twelve years ago, and there she was in the midst of our dining room, candles everywhere, perched in the nude. A bottle of wine open on the table: Château Saint-Pierre, and her impeccable body sitting cross-legged beside it, sipping from a handcrafted wineglass. The ten-dollar ones that we saved for special occasions.

"How long is she staying?" I ask.

She shrugs. "I don't know."

"A day, a week? What Heidi?" I ask, my voice escalating. "Which is it?"

"The baby has a fever."

"So take it to the doctor," I insist.

But Heidi is shaking her head no. "She doesn't want to," she says.

I trudge through the hall, set my now-traveling office on the kitchen table. I throw my hands up in the air, miffed. "Who the hell cares what she wants, Heidi? She is a little girl. A runaway, probably. We're harboring a runaway. Do you have any idea what kind of trouble we could get into for harboring a runaway?" I ask as I find the phone book in a kitchen drawer and start flipping through the thin pages for the non-emergency police number. Or is this an emergency? Strange girl in my home. Sounds like trespassing to me.

"She's eighteen," Heidi insists.

"How do you know she's eighteen?"

"She told me," she replies foolishly.

"She's not eighteen," I assure my wife. "You need to report her to the *authorities*," I demand.

"We can't do that, Chris," she says, stealing the heavy book from my hands. She snaps it shut, pages getting crimped between the yellow covers. "How do you know she wasn't abused? Molested? Even if she is a runaway, she must have a good reason for leaving home."

"Then call DCFS. Let them sort it out. This is not your concern."

But of course it is. Every neglected, mistreated, overlooked, ignored, abandoned, forgotten, emaciated, abused, derelict creature on God's green earth is Heidi's concern.

This, I know without a shred of doubt, is an argument I cannot win.

"How do you know she's not going to kill us?" I ask instead. Good question, I think. I see us on the morning news: Family Slain in Lincoln Park Condo.

And there she is, *that girl,* standing in the office door, watching us from down the hall. Her eyes, a capricious blue, though blood-shot and tired. Her hair slung across her face, her mouth refusing to smile. A bruise perched on her forehead as if implying what Heidi said is true. "I could ask the same about you," she mutters, her eyes moving up the ecru wall and settling on the pop-corn ceiling above before she says, "When I am afraid, I put my trust in you," and I'm 100 percent sure Peter Funt is about to come barreling through the front door with a cameraman in tow when I ask stupidly, "In *me?*" my mouth having plummeted halfway to the ground below.

"In the *Lord,*" the girl says, and Heidi gives me this look like I'm some godless heathen.

Heidi glowers at me, and then spins on her heels, and, heading down the hall, de-clares, "Why don't I draw you a warm bath, Willow? You can soak awhile and I'll hold Ruby. It will feel so good to get on some clean clothes. Some dry clothes. I bet you wear the same size as Zoe. I'm sure she'd be happy to share."

Bullshit, I think. Zoe doesn't want to share the same oxygen as the girl, much less her clothes. Zoe flips on a stereo from the alcoves of her bedroom and blaring boy band music fills our home.

I watch as Heidi scoops the baby from Willow's hands, and leads them both into the bathroom.

When the door closes, I ransack the cabinets for Lysol spray.

WILLOW

My memories of Momma are slim to none these days. There are no photos left to remember her long black hair, her swarthy skin, her pretty blue eyes. Joseph made sure of that. He said I couldn't keep living in the past as he stood there, in that bedroom that was mine, the one with the patchwork quilt, the drafty windows so that in the winter it was never warm — and in the summer it was always hot — the flowery golden wallpaper that peeled from every seam, from every corner of the room. But there are glimpses of her that rattle in my mind from time to time. Glimpses of Momma. Her profile in the bathroom mirror while she cut Mrs. Dahl's hair. The sound of her giggling at something on TV. Watching her lie on a beaten-up plastic lounge chair in the parched lawn sunbathing, and me, in the grass beside her, digging dirty fingers down in the earth for worms. Baking in the kitchen from the worn Julia Child cookbooks we got at the public library, and Momma, standing there with a half bottle of Dijon mustard spilled down the front of a white shirt. Laughing.

I watched as Joseph tore what pictures I had of Momma right in two before my very eyes. And then into a million tiny slivers so that even if I tried to piece them back together, it would never be just right. He made me pick up the scraps from the floor. Made me march them down the steps and into the overflowing trash while the boys watched on and then he sent me to my room. As if the mess had been my doing. "I don't want to hear a word from you. You hear?" Joseph ordered, all six-foot-six of him, with that full pumpkin colored beard of his, with his serious, hawkish eyes. And he added, "Beg God for His forgiveness."

As if loving Momma was a sin.

After that the memories I had of Momma were scattered, so that I never knew if those visions were true or not, and I'd find myself second-guessing it all — the sound of her laugh, for instance, or the way her fingers felt when they ran through my mucous-colored hair. I'd lie in that bed of mine, covered up with the quilt, and rack my brain to come up with some tiny crumb of Momma to get me through the night. The shape of her nose, whether or not she had freckles, what it sounded like when she said my name.

"How did your parents die?" she asks me. Louise Flores. She slips a navy suit jacket from her haggard body and folds it precisely in two, like a greeting card, then sets it on the table beside the recorder and stopwatch.

"I'm sure you know, ma'am," I say. There's an officer in the corner, a sentry keeping watch, though he tries hard to pretend he's not here. She said I didn't have to answer her questions, not yet anyway. I could wait for Ms. Amber Adler, she said, or my attorney. But I pictured Ms. Adler's disappointed eyes when she came in the room and knew it was best to fess up soon. Before she arrived.

"How about you tell me," the silver-haired lady says, though I know that somewhere in that pad of paper it says. About Momma's old Datsun Bluebird. About the accident, a rollover accident, as someone said, out on I-80, just outside of Ogallala, about how eyewitnesses claimed they saw the car zigzag and swerve. About how Daddy lost control of the car, then likely overcorrected, sending the car in circles on the road. I imagine it, Momma's old Bluebird doing summersaults down the interstate while Momma and Daddy hung on for dear life.

Lily and I were home at the time. Alone. We never had a sitter. Momma trusted me to take care of Lily, even when I was eight years old. I got pretty good at it: changing her diaper, putting her to bed. I cut her apples and carrots into teensy bites so that she wouldn't choke — like Momma said — and always made sure the dead bolt was secure, that I didn't answer the door for no one, not even Mrs. Grass from next door, who was forever trying to embezzle our milk and eggs. Lily and I would lie in front of the TV anytime Momma and Daddy were gone, watching *Sesame Street* because *Sesame Street* was her favorite show of all. She liked Snuffleupagus the best, Snuffy, the big old mammoth who always made her laugh. She'd lie on the living room floor beside me, on the shaggy green carpeting that reminded me a bit of Snuffy's fur, pointing at that mammoth on the TV and laughing.

It wasn't as if Momma left Lily and me home alone that much. But there were times, she said, that *an adult's got to do what an adult's got to do.* That's what she said to me the morning she and Daddy climbed into the Bluebird and she stuck her head out the window as they pulled from the

140

gravel drive, her long black hair getting caught up in the wind so that I couldn't see her face, but I could hear her voice anyway: *Take good care of Lily,* and something or other about *love* and *you.* I love you like a bee loves honey. I love you like peanut butter loves jelly. I love you like a fish loves water.

Momma told me to take good care of Lily. They were the last words she said to me, the last vision I have of her: her with her head stuck out the busted window of the junky old Datsun, the wind blurring her face with a mass of black hair. *Take good care of Lily.* And that's what I intended to do.

But then, just like that, Lily was gone, too.

HEIDI

We bathe Ruby first. I draw the water so that it is tepid: warm enough, but not too warm for the baby's frail skin. I'm about to leave the room, to give Willow privacy, when she turns to me and asks, with those tuckered-out eyes, her body enervated, ready to drop, the tone of her voice fraught with fatigue, "Will you help me? *Please?*" And I say of course, elated to feel the slippery child in my hands as Willow scoops handfuls of water over her body. With the baby in my hands, I find myself thinking of Juliet, knowing that the loss of Juliet wasn't only about the loss of one baby; it was about the loss of all the babies. All the babies I was meant to have. There was a time I found myself thinking of little Juliet for hours on end, dreaming about her and what she may have looked like had I carried her full term. Would her hair be light and sparse like Zoe's when she crawled out of my womb, or would it be dark and plentiful as Chris's own mother said his was, hampering her with months of heartburn as the old wives' tales claimed they do?

It had been quite some time since I allowed myself to think of little Juliet, to let her image creep into my head. But there she was, once again, taking up residence in my mind's eye, reminding me of all the babies I would never have. *Juliet,* I nearly uttered allowed. *Juliet Wood.* She would have been eleven years old now, if life had gone according to plan. Eleven years old, with a parade of little ones following her out, every two years like clockwork. Sophia and Alexis, and baby Zach.

And then Ruby squeals and I return to the present, to the here and now. I watch as the bathwater seeps up the green sleeves of Willow's coat, transforming the army green to black. I offered to take the coat from her before she sunk her arms into the water, but she said no. Her callow hands shake as she lathers the vanilla body wash onto her hands, and caresses the baby's scalp and underarms, her rear end. Ruby's bottom is encrusted with a scarlet diaper rash, as I knew it would be, a rash that is not limited to just the genital area, but under her arms and in the folds of skin elsewhere along her tiny body. Her bottom is besieged by a yeast infection, a white crust at the periphery of the red rash. I devise a grocery list in my mind: diaper rash cream, clotrimazole cream and, as the vanilla body wash seeps into the corners of the baby's eyes and she lets out a shriek: No More Tears baby wash. Willow has no spare diapers and so, when the bath is through, I swathe Ruby in an organic harbor blue towel, and seal it shut with safety pins. Add to the checklist: diapers and wipes.

I am about to take Ruby from the room, to give Willow privacy for her own bath, when she stops me. I can see that she does not want the baby to leave. She doesn't trust me. Not yet. And why should she, I think, when I am a complete stranger. Wasn't I the one to stop the neonatal nurse from removing Zoe from my birthing room, on doctor's orders that I rest?

Though I want nothing less than to make Ruby a fresh bottle, to sit with her in the living room until she falls to sleep, I lay a second towel on the porcelain floor and the baby on top of that, sucking like the dickens on her own adorable toes. I linger for a half a second or more, staring as she unearths the appendages from that harborblue towel, and like an agile gymnast, thrusts them into her mouth.

Willow locks the door behind me. I stand there, in the hall, hand on the wall, all the breath suctioned right out of me with a vacuum's upholstery attachment thrust deep into my lungs.

From the kitchen, I see Chris sitting at the table, typing furiously on his laptop. The printer is plugged into the wall, an ugly black cord that stretches across the room.

A safety hazard.

But I don't dare say this. His eyes meet mine and remind me, once again, of how he disagrees with my decision. He shakes his head, disgruntled, and his eyes revert to the LCD screen, to the microscopic numbers that fill the lines of the incomprehensible spreadsheets. Zoe's pop music suffuses our home, making the walls shake, the framed photographs that line the hallway walls dance. I stare at the images of Zoe: smiling through gaping teeth, and then, years later, her nose ruddy with a cold. Crooked teeth, much bigger than the space that nature allowed for them, followed by braces. Zoe always adored picture day at her Catholic school, the one and only day of the year when uniforms were not required. When she was younger I had a say in what she wore for pictures, and so we relied on sateen dresses and woolen jumpers, with corsage headbands or tulle poufs in her hair. But as the years went by, and adolescence settled upon my once baby girl, a sudden change altered those photos, no longer awash with ruffles and bows, but now animal prints and graphic tops, hoodies and dark vests, each article of clothing as reclusive and moody as the individual inside them.

My knuckles come to rest on Zoe's bedroom door.

"What?" she grunts from inside the room. When I let myself inside, she is sitting on the bed with her adored yellow notebook close at hand. The space heater is on, set to seventy-four degrees after a recent request that she not let her room feel like the fiery furnace of hell. And still, Zoe is wrapped in a blanket, sulking. On her arms: arm warmers, another recent fad that has me nonplussed. Zoe's are black with sequins, given to her by a friend. *Are your arms cold?* I had asked blunderingly the day she arrived home from school with them secured to her hands.

Her eyes confirmed what she already knew to be true: her mother was an idiot.

Even I could hear the cowardice in my voice, fearful of rejection from my twelve-year-old daughter. "Do you have something

Willow could wear? After she's through with her bath?" I ask, hovering in the doorway like a scaredy-cat.

"You've *got* to be kidding me," Zoe replies as she gropes for her phone and begins texting furtively with dexterous thumbs. I can only imagine what mean words she is sending to Taylor via cell phone towers.

"You can't," I say, springing across the canopy bed for the cell phone. I snatch it from my daughter's hand, and see a series of text abbreviations of which I can't make heads or tails. J2LYK.

Zoe cries out, "That's mine," as she lunges for the phone and tries to yank it from me, but I remind her that, "It's not. Your father and I still pay the bill." I stand firmly before the bed, holding the phone behind me. That was our agreement after all. Zoe could have a cell phone so long as Chris and I were allowed to peruse her text messages for any red flags.

But the look on her face is reminiscent of a child being slapped.

"Give it to me," she orders, staring at me with those big brown anime eyes of hers, the disproportional eyes that always look sad. She holds her hand out expectantly, blue ink doodled across a forearm. Oh, how I want to give her the phone, to not have her be mad! I see the piping hot indignation leaching from my child and know her mind is bursting with hatred. Hatred toward me.

Whoever said motherhood was easy . . .

I long for those days when Zoe and I would rock before an open window, on the long forgotten sleigh glider, the one with the deep tufted seat I had to roll myself out of and the antique scrolled arms. I'd rock her until she fell asleep, and then I would cradle her for hours, swaying back and forth until the lullaby music petered out and the white hot sun fell below the horizon.

Out Zoe's bedroom window, I stare at the city's skyline, lost in the fleecy clouds. Being on the fifth floor of our own building, our view skirts right over the top of smaller neighboring buildings and south, to the Loop. It was the reason Chris and I were smitten with the condo some fourteen years ago when we decided to buy it. The view. The Loop out our south-facing windows, a nibble of Lake Michigan to the east. We didn't bother making a low-ball offer; we paid asking price, too terrified someone would snatch it from our hungry hands.

"We can't tell anyone about Willow," I say calmly. "Not yet anyway."

"So I'm just supposed to *lie* to my best friend?" she asks exasperatedly. What I think is: *yes.*

But what I say is a cop-out, a carbon copy of my first response. "We just can't tell anyone, Zoe. Not yet."

"Why not? Is she in witness protection or something?" she asks like only a twelve-year-old can.

But I disregard this query and ask again, "Do you have something she can wear after her shower?" Zoe arises from her bed melodramatically and moves to the closet with resentment. I see from behind that her pants hang too loose on her, her rear end all but lost in the fabric. "She won't be here for long," I hear myself say, and then, "We should take you shopping for some new clothes soon," a poor attempt at entente.

And Zoe, chock-full of sarcasm and chagrin, says of Willow, "I know. She's just one of your *clients.*"

"Not exactly," I say, seeing how Zoe would make a quick connection between Willow and my clients, the stories I tote home from work of the homeless, illiterate people I attend to all day. "She needs our help, Zoe." I am ever hopeful that I can appeal to her civic duty better than I can that of Chris. When Zoe was younger, we trudged through snow to deliver outgrown winter coats to the homeless at a women and children's

149

shelter; collected toys and books for the patients at the children's hospital, those suffering from leukemia and lymphoma and other cancers I couldn't bear to imagine a child having. I reminded Zoe of others who were far less fortunate and how it was our obligation to help.

Zoe yanks a pair of hot-pink drawstring pants from her closet and a striped shirt, plum and light gray. As she tosses them into my waiting hands, she mutters, "I don't like these anyway," and I'm left wondering if she forgot about the less fortunate, or if this — sarcasm and chagrin — is all she has to give. "They're ugly," she says.

"This is only temporary," I murmur as I retreat from the room. In the hall, Chris's eyes rise from the laptop and again he shakes his head.

I lay the clean clothing on the sofa bed and hover in my bedroom until Willow emerges from a steamy bathroom swathed in her own harbor-blue towel, Ruby clutched in her wet hands. She tiptoes into the office, and closes the door.

The lock clicks shut.

I let myself into the bathroom and collect a pile of clothing from the floor, heaping it into an empty hamper with the laundry detergent, dryer sheets and stain remover on top. In the kitchen, I remove a change purse of quarters from a drawer and tell Chris that I'll be back, before descending six flights of stairs for the community laundry room tucked away in the basement. Before I go, Chris eyes me and asks, "And what do you expect me to do with *her*?"

"Five minutes," I say, "that's all," an inadequate response to his question, and then I hurry from the room before he can say no.

I find the laundry room empty. It's a small space with an outdated inlaid parquet floor, five washing machines and an equal number of dryers, each of which eats more quarters than they put to good use. I lay Ruby's "Little Sister" jumpsuit atop the washing machine and saturate the stains with stain remover, followed by the pink fleece blanket that smells of sweat and sewer gas. I reach into the hamper and pull Willow's clothing from the pile: the army-green jacket that I zip shut before snapping the buttons, a pair of jeans that I fear will turn the white jumpsuit blue. I set them aside to wash in their own machine. And then I yank a once-white undershirt from beneath a sweater.

And I freeze.

I check twice, half-certain that it's the poor lighting in the laundry room that makes me think I see blood spatters across the undershirt. Something red, of that I'm certain, but I do my best to convince myself that the flecks are ketchup. Barbecue sauce. The juice of a maraschino cherry. I smell the shirt for whispers of tomato paste, Worcestershire sauce, vinegar, but I come up with nothing but body odor. Body odor and blood. My eyes scan the other articles of clothing for a second time: the frayed jeans, the raveling sweater, Ruby's jumpsuit. They're each caked in their own filth, but none other than the undershirt carry the distinct carmine color of dried blood. I fumble for the stain remover and begin squirting the life out of it, but then stop — suddenly — knowing that little can be done about dried blood. I wad the undershirt into a discreet ball and on the way upstairs to our fifth-floor condo I drop it in the garbage shoot.

I envision that undershirt with whatever secrets it may hold, tumbling down five flights and into the Dumpster perched beside the service entrance.

Of this, Chris can never know.

WILLOW

Momma used to say she had a sister, Annabeth, but if such a sister existed, she never came forward to claim Lily and me.

"How is it that you came to live with Joseph and Miriam?" asks Louise Flores, the ASA — assistant state's attorney, she told me when I asked. The clock on the wall reads 2:37 p.m. I lay my head on the cold steel table of the interrogation room and close my eyes. "Claire," the stark woman prods, laying a hand on my arm to shake me awake. Roughly. She'll have nothing to do with this, nothing to do with my "shenanigans," she says. I yank my arm away and hide them, both of them, under the table where she can't reach.

"I'm hungry," I say. I can't quite remember the last time I ate, but I remember sifting through a garbage Dumpster sometime before the cops caught me, finding a half-eaten hot dog, cold and covered in pickles

153

and relish and mustard, the mustard thick and gluey, lipstick marks on the bun. But of course, that's not where the police found me. They found me smack-dab on Michigan Avenue, staring through the window of the Gucci store.

"We'll eat when we're through," she says. She's got old-lady hands, wrinkled and veiny. A tight gold wedding band that cuts into the skin. Surplus skin that hangs from the bottom of her arms, her chin.

I pull my head from the table and look at her, into those gray eyes behind the rectangular glasses and say again, "I'm hungry." And then I put my head back on the table and close my eyes.

There's a hesitation. Then she tells the man in the corner to get me something to eat. She drops some coins on the steel table. I wait until he's gone and then I say, "I'm thirsty, too."

I won't lift my head until the food arrives, I decide. But already she's asking questions, questions which I readily ignore. "How did you end up with Joseph and Miriam?" and "Tell me about Joseph. He is a professor, is he not?"

Joseph is a professor. Was a professor. It's the reason that when he and Miriam showed up, claiming to be the second cousin twice removed (or something to that effect) on my daddy's side, my caseworker thought it was a lucky break. Joseph and Miriam lived with their two boys, Matthew and Isaac, in a home in Elkhorn, Nebraska, which sat right outside of Omaha, the largest city in all of Nebraska, so that the two were practically holding hands. Their home was nice, much nicer than our prefab home back in Ogallala, with two floors and three bedrooms and big old windows that stared out at the hills that surrounded that home. We lived in a neighborhood with a park and a baseball field, though I didn't ever see any of those things, but I heard about them, heard about them from the neighborhood kids I watched out those big old windows, riding their bikes up and down the street and calling for someone or other to grab their bat 'cause they were going to play ball.

But Joseph said I wasn't allowed to play with those kids. I wasn't allowed to play at all.

I spent my days doing chores, taking care of Miriam, missing Momma and Daddy. The rest of the time I stared out that window, at the kids, coming up with as many "I love you likes" as I possibly could.

I love you like cinnamon loves sugar.

I love you like kids love toys.

But by the time Joseph and Miriam arrived, Lily was already gone.

Lily only lasted about three weeks in the home. After Momma and Daddy died, we were sent to some group home for orphaned kids like us. *Orphans.* That was a word I'd never heard before. There were eight of us living in that house with a whole bunch of grown-ups who'd come and go. There was a couple, a woman and man, who lived there with us all the time, Tom and Anne, but others passed through: everyone's caseworker, who all seemed to be different; a tutor; some man who was always trying to mess with my head. *Tell me why you're upset, Claire. Tell me how you felt when your mother and father died.*

It wasn't a bad place, in hindsight. Later on, after living with Joseph and Miriam, the group home seemed like a palace. But for an eight-year-old girl who'd just become an *orphan,* it was about the worst thing in the world. No one wanted to be there, but especially not me. Some of the kids were mean. Others just cried all the time. Those other kids at the group home were taken away, given away or just flat out rejected by their folks. The fact that Momma and Daddy died was somehow or other a good thing; it showed that someone actually loved us, actually wanted us in their lives.

Lily was adopted, which was the be all and end all of life for an orphan.

Orphan. One day I'm just a little girl from Ogallala, and the next, I'm an *orphan.* There was a whole lot crammed in that small word: the way folks would look at me with pity in their eyes, would stare at my cheap, undersized clothes, which some charity dropped off for us, donations from kids who'd outgrown them though they sure as heck didn't fit me, and say *oh* as if to say *that explains it.*

That explains the sad look in my eye, the quick temper, the tendency to sulk in a corner and cry.

Paul and Lily (yup, that's right, *Lily*) Zeeger were the ones who adopted Lily, *my* Lily, little Lily. Sweet little Lily with her ringlets of black hair, black like Momma's, the pudgy little hand that clasped my finger, the chubby cheeks and unselfish smile. The one I was meant to take good care of before Momma died. I eavesdropped on their conversations with the caseworker, Paul and Lily's conversation with her: the irony of that name, *Lily,* whether or not it was destiny. "But of course," said Big Lily, a beautiful blonde woman with turquoise jewelry, as if she was talking about a dog, "we'll need to change her name. Can't hardly both be called Lily," and the caseworker agreed, "Of course."

I threw a fit. Screaming. About how Momma gave Lily that name and they had no right to change it. I grabbed Lily and ran, through the house and out the back door, desperate for a place to hide. I ran into the woods, but with Lily in my arms, they caught me easily. The woman who ran the house, Anne, stole Lily right from my arms, saying, "This is just the way it's got to be." And Tom scolded me: "You don't want to upset her, now do you?"

I saw that Lily was crying, her chubby arms reaching past Anne for me, but the woman kept walking, away, away, away, and Tom was holding me though I squirmed and kicked and chances are I bit him. I remember him screaming, and that's when he finally let me go.

I tore into the house, searching every nook and cranny for my baby sister. "Lily! Lily!" I was screaming, crying, calling out her name so many times the word no longer sounded right in my head. I pushed my way into the other kids' bedrooms, into bathrooms that were in use.

And then I saw it, out the window: the silver minivan pulling away down the drive.

It was the third to last time I would ever see my sister.

They renamed her Rose.

They weren't bad people. That I'd come to realize later. But when you're eight years old and you've just lost your folks, and now your sister's been taken from you, too, you hate everyone. And that's just what I did. I hated everyone. I hated the world.

"Tell me about Joseph," says Louise Flores.

"I don't want to talk about Joseph," I say. I lay my head on the table sideways, where I can't see her eyes, and ask, "How'd you find us anyway?" picking at the dry skin of my hands, watching the way they bleed.

"How'd we find *you*?" the woman repeats, and I catch sight of a curl of her lip out of the corner of my eye. She doesn't like me. She doesn't like me one bit. "That was dumb luck," she says, the dumb, I'd bet, being me. "But if you're asking how we found the *baby*, well, that was a tip."

"A tip?" I ask, lifting my head to see her, the satisfaction that fills her eyes. *You really are dumb, aren't you?* those eyes say to me.

"Yes, Claire, a tip. Short for tip-off. A phone call from an individual —" she starts, and I interrupt with, "Who?"

"— an *individual,*" she continues, "who

159

wishes to remain anonymous."

"But why?" I wonder out loud, though I don't really have to think too long or hard to come up with an answer. My mind settles on one man. He never did like me anyway, that's for sure. I heard them, right there, in that very next room. Fighting about me when they thought I couldn't hear.

"Tell me about Joseph," she says again.

"I told you already. I don't want to talk about Joseph."

"Then how about Miriam. Tell me about Miriam."

"Miriam is a troll," I say, letting my chip bag dance to the floor.

The woman is straight-faced. "What does that mean?" she asks. "A *troll*?"

"An imp," I say. That's just it. Miriam in a nutshell. I didn't like Miriam, that's for sure. But I did feel kind of sorry for her. She was small, maybe four feet tall, with mousy gray hair, her skin knobby like a streusel topping. She sat in her bedroom all day and night. She hardly said more than two words to me. She only ever talked to Joseph.

But that's not the way she looked when she and Joseph, Matthew and Isaac showed up at the home to fetch me. No, that day Joseph made her up in a pretty gingham dress, short-sleeved with a V-neck and a big bow that wrapped around her like a hug; he made Matthew and Isaac put on nice shirts and pressed pants. Even Joseph was handsome in a striped shirt and a tie, a kindness to his eye that I never saw after that day. He made sure Miriam was taking her pills, that she put her lipstick on and that she smiled every time he so much as nudged her side. At least he must have because I don't remember seeing Miriam smile a day in her life. But something or other impressed the caseworker who was convinced that living with Joseph and Miriam would be a wonderful thing for me. *Blessed* and *fortuitous* were the words she used. Cursed and damned were more like it. My caseworker swore that Joseph and Miriam had gone through a screening process and foster care training; they had children of their own. They were now licensed foster parents and were, for me, or so she claimed, a *perfect fit.*

No one asked if I wanted to live with Joseph and Miriam. By then I was nine years old. No one gave a hoot what I wanted. I was supposed to feel lucky that I was moving onto a foster home, that I didn't have to stay in the group home forever. Joseph and Miriam were an extended sort of family, which was also a good thing. Supposedly.

Though my relationship to Joseph and Miriam was so spotty I had a hard time connecting the dots. But there was *paperwork,* the caseworker said. Proof. And then she sat me down and looked me in the eye and said, "You've got to understand, Claire. You're getting older all the time. This might be your one and only chance at a family."

But I had a family: Momma and Daddy and Lily. I didn't want another one.

Lily got swept up in an instant because she was two years old. Infertile couples, like Paul and Lily Zeeger, were looking for just that. A baby, if possible, but a toddler if a baby was hard to find. Little Lily barely remembered Momma and Daddy. In time, she wouldn't remember them at all. She'd come to believe that Paul and Lily were her parents.

But no one wanted a nine-year-old, and sure as heck, no one would want a ten-year-old or an eleven-year-old, either. Time was ticking away, or so my caseworker, Ms. Amber Adler, said.

I packed what few belongings I'd been allowed to bring with me: some clothes and books, the photos of Momma that Joseph would later tear to shreds.

"And Joseph. Is he a troll, too?"

I pictured Joseph in my mind. The towering man, the sinister eagle eyes and aquiline nose, his short, military-style pumpkin-colored hair and the bristly beard that kept me awake at night, as I lay on my bed, listening in fear for the sound of unwelcome footsteps on the creaky wooden floor outside my door.

The bristly beard scraping across my face when he lay down beside me in bed.

"No," I said, looking the silver-haired lady straight in the eye. "No, ma'am. Joseph's the devil."

HEIDI

I can't stop thinking about it, about the blood.

As I pass my neighbor, Graham, on the way up from the laundry room, I'm unsettled, incognizant of the way he says to me in that always jovial, always dependable tone of his, "You just get more and more beautiful every time I lay eyes on you," and I have to ask him to repeat himself.

"What's that?" I ask and he laughs.

I'm reminded of my robe and messy hair, the fact that I have yet to shower. I can feel the hallway spinning and I wonder when the last time was that I ate. I lay an unsteady hand on the wall and study Graham coming at me, completely unaffected by personal space. He is impeccable as always, in a pullover sweater with a half zip, a pair of dark wash jeans, leather loafers.

But somehow or other, I believe Graham, though I know I look an atrocious mess, I believe him when his eyes come to a stand-still on mine and he tells me that I look beautiful. His eyes look me up and down as if proving it to be true. He grabs me play-fully, by the hand, and begs me to go out with him tonight, to keep him company at some god-awful engagement party at Cafe Spiaggia. I can't imagine Graham without a date in tow, some stunning blonde in a little black dress and four-inch heels.

My hands are shaking out of control, and seeing this, Graham asks if I'm feeling all right. There's this sudden urge to fold into Graham's sweater, to bury my face into the heather gray and tell him about the girl. The baby. The blood.

His eyes show concern, the space between his eyebrows all puckered up so that a crease runs vertically between them. He holds my gaze, trying hard to read what I won't say, until I'm forced to look away.

He can see that something isn't quite right, can sense that Heidi Wood, who al-ways has everything under control, is com-ing undone.

"Fine," I lie. "I feel fine."

Physically, the truth, but emotionally, a lie. I cannot get the blood out of my mind, the sight of the yeast infection devouring the baby's bottom, Chris's eyes suggesting that what I'm doing — helping this poor girl who desperately needs help — is wrong. The image of baby Juliet that has returned to me after all these years in exile.

Graham doesn't cave so easily. He doesn't move on as others would do, taking my words at face value. He continues to stare until I repeat, with an obligatory smile this time, that I am fine. And after some time he concedes.

"Then come with me," he says, as he pulls on my hand and I feel my feet drag down the carpeted hall. I laugh. Graham can always make me laugh.

"I want to," I say. "You know I want to."

"Then come. Please. You know I hate small talk," he claims but nothing could be further from the truth.

"I'm in my robe, Graham."

"We'll stop off at Tribeca. Find you something sumptuous to wear."

"I haven't done *sumptuous* in years."

"Then something pretty and practical," he concedes, but I'm drawn to the suggestion of sumptuous, the idea of masquerading around town as Graham's date. I find myself wondering, often, why it is that Graham's still single, and whether or not he, as Chris insists, is gay. Are all the gorgeous women simply a cover, a security blanket of some sort?

"You know I can't," I say, and his eyes take on a crestfallen look before he bids me adieu and saunters off down the hall alone.

I pause beside my own door, dwelling on it all, letting the fairy tale exist for just a split second longer before reality throws a monkey wrench to it: Graham and sumptuous attire from Tribeca, dinner at Cafe Spiaggia. Me on Graham's arm, posing as his date.

Back inside, Willow is sitting on the edge of the pull-out sofa, holding the baby. She's dressed in Zoe's garb, the wet towel returned to a bathroom hook. "My clothes," she says, in a panic. "What did you do with my clothes? They're not . . ." her voice is shaking. Her eyes unsteady. That rickety way she rocks the baby, more spasmodic than calming.

"I'm washing them," I interrupt, seeing panic rise up inside her swollen blue eyes. "There were some stains," I admit, quietly, quickly, so Chris, down the hall at the kitchen table, will not hear. I stare at her, willing her to explain so that I will not have to ask her outright about the blood. I don't want her and her baby to leave, but if Willow's being here is dangerous for Zoe, for my family, then I cannot allow her to stay.

167

Were it up to Chris, she would already be halfway out the door.

But instead, I stare at her, solicitously, begging her to explain. Explain the blood. Something innocent, I pray for something . . .

"A bloody nose," she interjects then, disrupting my thoughts. "I get bloody noses," and she peers toward the ground, as people do when they are nervous or perhaps, when they are lying. "I had nothing to wipe it on," she says, "just the shirt," and I consider the cold spring air, aggravating the nasal tissues, making them bleed.

"A bloody nose?" I ask, and she nods her head meekly.

"A bloody nose, then," I say, "that explains it," and with that I walk out of the room.

WILLOW

Matthew told me once that what his father intended to do, long before he married Miriam, was go into the seminary and become a Catholic priest. But then he got Miriam knocked up, and all hopes of the priesthood vanished in the air. Just like that.

"Knocked up?" I asked Matthew. I was young, like maybe ten or eleven years old. I knew what sex was; that Joseph taught me though he didn't go as far as to give it a name, what it was he was doing when he came into my room at night. What I didn't know was that what Joseph did when he lay on top of me, crushing me to the bed, a rubbery, wet hand pressed against my mouth so I wouldn't scream, was the same thing that led to babies.

"Yeah," he shrugged. Matthew was six years older than me and knew things that I didn't. Lots of things. "You know. *Pregnant.*"

169

"Oh," I said, still not sure how *knocked up* and *pregnant* had a darn thing to do with Joseph not becoming a priest.

Matthew rolled his eyes. "Duh."

But that all came later, much later.

At first Matthew and Isaac, the both of them, wouldn't have a thing to do with me. Joseph forbade it. Forbade them from talking to me. Forbade them from looking at me. Just like me, Isaac and Matthew weren't allowed to do much of anything. There was no TV, no playing ball or riding bikes with the neighborhood kids, no listening to music, no books — none other than the Bible, of course — and when Matthew and Isaac came home from school with something or other to read, Joseph would hold it up disapprovingly and call it blasphemous.

Momma and Daddy hadn't been religious at all. The only times they talked about God were what I later came to know as *in vain.* We didn't go to church. There was only a drawing of Jesus in the old prefab house, which Momma said used to belong to her own mom and dad, and we kept it in the kitchen, and more than anything else, it covered up a hole in the wall where I accidentally threw a ball when Daddy and I were playing catch in the house. The man in the picture might as well have been the president of the United States for all I knew. He might have been my grandpa. We never spoke of the picture. It was just *there.*

"You're telling me your foster father sexually abused you," Ms. Flores says, though her eyes say I'm full of it. Full of crap. "You ever tell your caseworker about this?"

"No, ma'am."

"Why not? She checked up on you, did she not? Brought letters from Paul and Lily Zeeger."

I shrug. "Yes, ma'am."

"Then why didn't you tell her?" I look out the one barred window placed too high on the wall for me to see what is outside. There's just a hint of blue sky, some white fleecy clouds. I fantasize about what's on the other side: a parking lot, cars, trees.

The caseworker was okay. I didn't hate her. She drove a beat-up junker car and carried about half a million case files in a mangled Nike bag that, at the age of thirty or maybe forty, made her back sag like those old ladies with osteoporosis. She worked out of her car, with all her files stored in the backseat. She moved from group home to foster home, back to group home, meeting with all the kids on her ever growing caseload. Apparently she had an office — somewhere — but I don't think she was ever there. She was nice enough, but she was up to her ears in her caseload (if she told me that once, she told me a thousand times) and half the time when she showed up, she thought my name was Clarissa and once or twice, Clarice. She talked fast and moved faster. She wanted things *done.*

The day I went to live with Joseph and Miriam was just one more checkmark on her to-do list.

"You see, Claire, I've seen your files. I know that your caseworker made visits to the home, to Joseph and Miriam's home, and I know that this so-called sexual abuse was never discussed. What *was* discussed at these visits —" she reaches down into a briefcase at her feet and pulls out a chunky green file, flipping to a page she's marked with yellow sticky notes "— were your mood swings, your quick temper, your refusal to follow rules, complete chores, obey orders, your defying authority, your poor grades in school." She sits, still as a mouse, her eyes bearing down on me across the table, and then adds, "Your flights of fancy."

I'd been in that house just outside Omaha for all of a month before Joseph came into my bed that first time. At first he just wanted to see parts of me I didn't think he had any business seeing, and then he wanted to touch me in places I didn't want to be touched. When I said I didn't want to do these things, he said to me with a kindliness that waned with every split second it took to undress, "Come on now, Claire. I'm your daddy now. It's okay to let your daddy see," and then he'd stare as I pulled a shirt up over my head.

I was scared like I hadn't been in a long time, not since Ivy Doone, in the first grade, dared me to summons Bloody Mary from my bathroom mirror. In that first month I'd rarely seen Miriam leave her room. Miriam wore her nightclothes all day and all night, the same fusty, crusty ones, without bathing, until her stench filled the home. She rarely said more than two words to the boys or me, only to Joseph, when she was begging his forgiveness for something or other she'd done. She'd drop to her knees before him, sobbing, and kiss his feet, begging *Please, Joseph, forgive me* and he'd kick her away and move on, saying she was pathetic, worthless, a tramp. He said once, in a fit of rage, that Miriam should be tossed out the window, her corpse left to feed vagrant dogs.

"Have you got anything to say to that?" Louise Flores asks. Any comment about my delinquency.

Joseph said no one would believe me. It was his word against mine. No one would believe me if I told them what he did.

And besides, he was only doing what a good daddy was supposed to do.

"No," I mutter.

The woman rolls her eyes, closes the file before her and says to me, "This *alleged* sexual abuse. Tell me about that."

I learned later, when copying from the Bible, word for word until my hand cramped and the muscles burned and I could barely hold the pencil without shaking, which was Joseph's punishment for me when I misbehaved, of the Phoenician princess Jezebel, who was thrown through a window for killing the Lord's prophet, her blood splattered on the walls. She was trampled and left to be eaten by dogs, so that when the people returned, all that was left was her skull, and feet, and the palms of her hands.

Matthew and Isaac were sent to school while Miriam and I were left at home alone. If anyone ever came to the door, we weren't to answer it. We were to stay real quiet so no one knew we were inside. Joseph told me if ever I did dare answer that door it might be bad people on the other side, bad people who wanted to hurt me. So I didn't dare open that door. The house was dark, the curtains always closed. Except in my bedroom, where I'd peek out my window as Matthew and Isaac walked through the neighborhood where we lived, past the kids on the bikes with their baseballs and footballs, past little girls with pigtails who drew murals on the sidewalks with chalk. They'd wait, at the end of the block, for the big yellow school bus to come and sweep them up and drive them to school. I watched as some of the kids called Matthew and Isaac mean names because, in that neighborhood, Matthew and Isaac were deemed weird 'cause they didn't ride their bikes and they couldn't catch a ball if their life depended on it. They didn't have friends, and if ever some of the neighborhood boys came to the door to see if they could play, Matthew and Isaac, like me, had to be real quiet, pretend no one was home, and in time, none of those kids came to call anymore. Instead they called them names at the bus stop, they pushed and shoved them, they threw snowballs smack dab at Matthew and Isaac's heads.

I believed Joseph when he said, coming into my bedroom night after night, hearing me sob for Momma and Daddy, and feeling so lonely and alone and scared, that he would take care of me like a good daddy should. He told me that this, what he was doing when he lay his sweaty body beside me under the patchwork quilt, was what a real daddy was supposed to do.

He told me that my living with him and Miriam was my momma and daddy's last request. That this was what they wanted.

And he told me that if I didn't do what he said, he'd take it out on my Lily. *Oh, yes,* he'd say if ever I hesitated to undress. *You don't want anything to happen to Lily now, do you?*

I thought about Lily all the time. I thought about Lily, out there, somewhere. I wondered if that was Momma and Daddy's wish, too: that Lily live with the Zeegers when they died.

But I didn't think that was true.

By then, Lily was three years old. She only knew Paul and Big Lily as Mommy and Daddy; she didn't have any memory of those folks buried at the cemetery back in Ogallala off Fifth Street, under a maple tree that was half as dead as they were, their corpses rotting in matching pine boxes in the ground. I dreamed of Momma and Daddy there, in those boxes, the ones I watched with Ms. Amber Adler being lowered into the ground, before she drove Lily and me in her junker car to the group home.

I dreamed of Momma and Daddy's skeleton arms trying hard to reach through the pine boxes and touch hands.

CHRIS

I watch Heidi sauté the chicken, carrots, peas and celery in a skillet in the kitchen. In a saucepan, she adds butter and onion, cans of chicken broth. I bless my lucky stars for real chicken and not chicken crumbles. She pours it all into a pie crust and pops it in the oven. She tries not to look at me. When our eyes do intersect, she says, "She needs our help," just like that: her new catch-phrase, her mantra.

I haul my laptop and printer to the floor so we can eat at the kitchen table. I try hard to be theatrical about it so Heidi can see what an inconvenience this has become. She ignores the moan, the heavy thwack of the printer on the hardwood floor, the "oh, shit" when my legs get tangled up in the cord and I all but trip. Heidi is still unshowered for the day, still sporting the lilac robe, her hair now thrust into an unruly bun. She's wearing her glasses.

Her hands tremble as she yanks dinner plates from the kitchen cabinets. Zoe is in her bedroom, still listening to boy band music and, no doubt, inventing all sorts of scenarios in her mind in which her parents disappear. Little does she know her best chance of ridding herself of Heidi and me lies on the other side of the bedroom wall, resting at Heidi's suggestion. From time to time I detect the babble of that baby, doped up on Tylenol to keep a fever in check.

"You're shaking," I say.

She frowns at me and says, "I haven't had anything to eat all day."

But I imagine there's more to it than that.

On the edge of the counter, her cell phone, placed nose to nose with Zoe's confiscated one, rings, and she picks it up, her eyes roving over the display screen before she sets it back down, the call ignored.

"Who was that?" I ask, arching my back after the weight of the printer.

"No one," she says, "telemarketer," but when she goes to retrieve Zoe and that girl for dinner, I sneak a peek and see that Jennifer called for the second time today. Two missed calls, the phone reminds her, from Jennifer Marcue. Two waiting voice mails.

We sit at the table, like one big happy family. Heidi holds the baby. The girl, Willow,

Heidi reminds me with a firm kick to the shin when I mistakenly call her Wilma, scarfs down the meal as if she hasn't eaten in a week. She won't make eye contact with me, though every now and then her eyes stray to Heidi's, but for me, there's no such luck. She stays away from me, three feet or more, as if I might just carry the plague. I tell myself it has something to do with men, but maybe it's just me. She jumps when I move too quickly, skidding my chair out from the table and standing to fetch a glass of milk.

Heidi is watching the baby, the way her eyes oscillate under translucent eyelids in her sleep. A smile toys with her lips, and I wonder what life would have been like if Heidi had been given the big family she always talked about. Heidi hungered for a huge family, a half dozen kids, maybe more. I was never really sure how I felt about it. Kids, sure. I wanted kids. But five or six, like Heidi talked about, I didn't know. Of course it didn't matter how I felt because it never came down to that. Before I could be too concerned with a houseful of kids, we got the diagnosis from the doctor that would forever change our lives.

Suddenly kids weren't the issue; it was whether or not my wife would live or die.

But still, I wonder what it would have been like had Zoe not been an only child. Would family meals have been like this — strained and unnatural, the only sound the gnashing and grinding of food — or would dinnertime have been rambunctious: hair pulling and knock-knock jokes, name calling and kids taunting each other, rather than withdrawing themselves into silent seclusion as our sole child chooses to do? Those stereotypical only-child myths — that they are lonely, selfish and maladjusted — all seem to apply to Zoe, and I watch as, out of the corner of her eye, Zoe peeks sideways at the girl beside her, and I wonder: what *is* that expression that crosses her face? Hate? Envy? Or something more? Something different?

Zoe, sitting at the table, wrapped up in a gray blanket because she is perpetually cold, scoops the innards of her chicken potpie out with a fork, and then asks, "What even *is* this?" while staring at the broth that oozes across her plate like water from a dam.

"Chicken potpie," Heidi says, setting a forkful in her mouth. "Try it. You'll like it," she says. I watch her manage the baby and eat her meal, a woman skilled in the art of motherhood. It wasn't that long ago that she juggled baby Zoe at the kitchen table.

Zoe says that she hates peas, and we all watch as she draws her fork through the goo, separating piles of carrots and peas, chicken and celery. She picks at the crust, and lays a nibble of pastry on her tongue, letting it dissolve.

"What kind of name is Willow anyway?" I ask as the room drifts into silence. The TV is on: a roundup of the day's basketball games, but as is always the case during dinnertime, it's on mute. I see scores flash by, replays of bank shots and alley-oops.

"Chris," Heidi barks, as if I'd asked some kind of inappropriate question: her bra size or political affiliation. No one ever accused me of being shy. The irony, of course, is Heidi's practice of interrogating me on my day, and yet allowing this stranger to sit at our kitchen table without knowing her vital statistics, a surname, whether or not she's an escaped con.

"It's just a question. I'm curious, that's all. I've never heard the name. Not for a girl anyway."

Maybe a tree.

"It's a beautiful name. Like a Willow tree," Heidi says, "graceful and lithe."

"There's a Willow in my earth science class," Zoe states, her arrival in the conversation astounding us all. Almost as unexpected as if Willow herself opened her mouth and said something. "Willow Toler." And then Zoe adds, "The boys call her Pussy," and an awkward silence takes over the room. Again. All but for the damn black cat who attacks the exposed brick wall as if there are roaches living inside it.

"You have a last name, Willow?" I ask, and again with Heidi's, "Chris!"

"Yes, sir," she says quietly. There's a kind of Arcadian simplicity to her, hidden there under the tough disguise. I can't quite put my finger on it. A twang in her voice, or maybe it's the fact that she said sir. I stare at her, plunging forkfuls of chicken potpie into her mouth, too much food in each bite. She nearly licks the plate clean and, without asking, Heidi dishes up another slice. She eats the insides of the pie first, saving the crust for the very end. Her favorite part. The part Heidi pulled from a box. Store bought.

She's not eighteen. I know that much. But I don't know how old she is. I tell myself she's eighteen because that way, when the authorities show up at our front door, I can claim ignorance. *But, sir, she* told *me she was eighteen.* She smells better than she did hours ago, cleaned up and wearing Zoe's castoff clothing. But she still looks like a vagabond, the messy eyeliner she painted on following her shower, the ersatz color of her hair. An earring hole, or two, that look infected, fingernails bitten to the quick. Eyes that are erratic, trying hard to escape my probe. The bruise that looms from behind the mantle of dyed hair.

"Care to share?"

"Chris. Please."

The girl mutters something cryptic beneath her breath. I imagine words of a religious nature, *trust* and *God.* But when I ask her to repeat herself, she breathes out, "Greer."

"What's that?" I ask. A car alarm starts squawking out the still open window.

She repeats, louder this time, "My name is Willow Greer."

Later, after we're through with dinner and the dishes have been cleared, I write it down on the back of a receipt I pull from my wallet. So I won't forget.

When I awake in the morning, there is sun. After days and days of clouds and rain, there's something perplexing about the sun. It's bright. Too bright.

My entire body is stiff. Like an old man's. I can barely feel my hip. I roll over, onto my back, my right hand smacking the metal edge of the bed frame. All sorts of expletives run through my mind as I try to remember why I'm on the floor to begin with, why my now-aching hand is even close enough to accost the bed frame. I find myself on the not-so-soft boucle rug that lines Heidi's and my bedroom floor, wrapped up in Zoe's magenta sleeping bag.

And then I remember: sleeping on the floor at my own insistence that Zoe not be left alone in her bedroom for the night. Not when we had an outsider in the home. Heidi told me I was being ridiculous and offered to swap places with Zoe. But I said no. I wanted my flock where I could see them. All of them. Even the cats were allowed to stay, sealed in a locked bedroom across the hall from that girl, an extra chair buttressed beneath the door's handle in case she tried to force her way in.

I roll over, onto my side, and get an angle of the bed I've never seen before: the underside. There are all the expected things one finds underneath a bed: a dusty sock divorced from its partner some time ago, a stuffed bunny of Zoe's that went AWOL when she was eleven, the back of a woman's earring.

"What's wrong?" Heidi asks as I slip out of the bedroom and into the kitchen. The house is filled with the aroma of pancakes and eggs, freshly brewed coffee. Heidi's hovering before the stove, baby placed on one hip, flipping pancakes with the opposing hand. It looks shockingly natural, Heidi and that baby. As though we've stepped in a time machine or something, and there she is, holding baby Zoe in her arms. The baby's got her gold chain, the one Heidi won't leave home without, wrapped up in the palm of its fat hand, tugging hard. I see Heidi's father's wedding band dangling from the end, the one and only thing in the world Heidi wanted when he died. She made a bargain with her mother: her mother could have everything else of sentimental value, but the ring went to Heidi. She searched high and low for a chain of the very same yellow gold as the ring, a twenty-four-karat gold chain that cost nearly a thousand dollars. And now, I watch as the baby yanks on it, the loop of the chain dangling from her grip like a uvula at the back of someone's throat.

"Nothing," I lie as I yank a mug from the cabinet and fill it with coffee. "Morning, Willow," I say to the girl who sits alone at the table, dragging pancakes and eggs into her mouth with a trail of syrup that runs its course across the mahogany table and up

186

Zoe's striped shirt.

I make a quick trip out to purchase the *Trib* from the stand on the corner, and then I take my pancakes and eat outside, on the insignificant wooden balcony that sits at a tilt. I can't stand to stay in the same room with Heidi and that girl, the discomfort filling the room like pea-soup fog. Outside it can't be more than fifty degrees. I stare at my bare feet resting on the balcony's rails and think that I've been duped by the sun. Flipping through the paper I find the high for the day: 56 degrees. I can't help but scan for images of missing girls, as well — teenage runaways, articles on kids wanted for questioning in the killing of their parents. I scour for the words: *homicide, butchery, torture,* and find myself wondering what, exactly, Lizzie Borden's folks did to piss her off.

The night before, Heidi sent me out for supplies. After dinner I walked to the drugstore, where I found myself staring stupidly at a variety of baby diapers in the empty aisle. I'm too old, I thought as I groped for a box and stuck it under an arm, to be buying diapers.

At home I watched as Heidi laid that baby out on the hardwood floor and removed the blue towel — covered now in stinky shit —

187

from her body and set it aside. The baby kicked her feet, thrilled to be naked, while Heidi wiped her bottom with one of those powder-scented wipes, setting the dirty ones in the towel that would later be hurled down the garbage shoot.

When she lifted her up, I choked at the sight of the rash, a foul red rash that covered her rear end. As Heidi lathered one cream, and then a second, onto that baby's behind, that girl stared on, as if no one ever told her about changing a baby's diaper before, about how sitting in all that shit and urine couldn't possibly be good for her skin. Her eyes looked sad as Heidi slipped a white jumpsuit and footed pants from their plastic packaging and onto the baby, covering up a birthmark the size of a sand dollar on the baby's leg.

When she was done, Heidi passed the baby back to Willow, who held her awkwardly, without Heidi's obvious expertise, without the natural maternal instinct girls were supposed to be blessed with. I watched her shuffle that baby like a sack of potatoes, wondering whether or not that baby was *really* her child.

But I didn't dare suggest this to Heidi because I knew what she would say. She would remind me that I'm a cynic, a skeptic. *Of course it's her child,* Heidi would say as if she had some sixth sense about it, as if she *knew.*

We'd sat around the TV for what felt like an eternity, an awkward, hellish eternity, where for an hour or more, no one spoke. And then, when I couldn't stand it anymore, I shut the TV off and said it was time for bed. The clock on the wall read 8:46 p.m.

There were no complaints.

Before we went to bed, I pulled Heidi aside and said, "One night. That's all," and watched as Heidi shrugged, and said to me, "We'll see."

I gathered Zoe's magenta sleeping bag from her bedroom closet, and propped that extra chair before the door, listening to Zoe go on and on about how my insistence on a sleepover sucked. About how impossible I was being. About how she hoped her friends would never find out about *this,* our little ménage à trois, she called it.

Since when does my twelve-year-old know about ménages à trois?

189

WILLOW

Joseph was a professor of religion at the community college. He taught about the Bible, but mostly the Old Testament. He taught about a God who wiped out the world with a flood, who rained down fire and brimstone on entire villages, killing everyone there. Women and children, good and bad. Everyone. I didn't know what brimstone was, but he showed me drawings in those college textbooks of his, pictures of fire pouring down and devouring the towns of Sodom and Gomorrah, turning Lot's wife into a pillar of salt.

"This," he told me in that somber voice of his, with the solemn, spongy face that never smiled, the reddish-orange beard, thick and disgusting, "is God's wrath. You know what wrath is, don't you, Claire?" and when I said I didn't, we looked it up in some big, heavy dictionary, together. *Extreme anger,* it said.

"This," Joseph said, showing me again, the pictures of fire and brimstone, "is what God does when he's mad."

Joseph convinced me that thunder was my doing, something or other I had done to upset God. I lived in fear of thunder, lightning and rain. When the sky turned black — as it often did in Omaha in the middle of summer — on one of those hot, humid July days when the threatening black clouds raced in to swallow the calm blue sky, I knew that God was coming for me. When the wind started whirling, the trees stretched down to touch their toes and sometimes snapped clear in two, garbage from the Dumpster on the corner jetting through the air, I would drop to my knees, as Joseph had showed me to do, and pray, over and over and over again, for God's forgiveness.

What I did wrong, I never quite knew. The explosive lightning and ear piercing thunder immobilized me, and once or twice, and probably even more, I peed my pants as I knelt there, in that bedroom of mine, praying to God. I'd keep watch out the window for the fire and brimstone, falling from the sky. I'd stare for as long as it took, for the storm to settle, to move on to Iowa, and then, Illinois, to punish some other sinner like me.

Joseph told me about hell. The place that sinners go. A place of never-ending punishment and torture, with demons and dragons and the devil himself. Eternal punishment. Lakes of fire. Fiery furnace. Unquenchable fire. Fire, fire, fire. I lived in fear of fire.

I tried to be a good girl. I did. I cleaned up the house when Joseph was teaching and Isaac and Matthew were at school; I made dinner for Joseph and the boys, carried Miriam a tray, though it was rare that she would eat on her own, without some arm-twisting from Joseph.

Miriam spent most of her days in either one of two ways, in a sleep-like daze, wide-awake but totally still, like a statue, or she'd be up and in a panic, throwing herself at Joseph's feet and begging for his forgiveness. There were days when she was agitated, snapping at Joseph and the boys about reading her mind. She'd tell them to *stop it, stop reading my mind.* And then *get out, get out, get out,* and she'd smack at her head with the palm of her hand as if she was pushing them, pushing Joseph, Isaac and Matthew right on out of her brain. On those days Joseph would lock her in her room with a lock and key. He kept that key with him at all times, even when he wasn't home, so that when it was just Miriam and me, I could hear her screaming from her bedroom all day long about how Joseph was reading her mind, how he was putting thoughts inside her head.

I thought that Miriam was crazy. She scared me. Not like Joseph did, but in her own way.

I did my chores, the laundry and cleaning and such, made dinner for when Joseph and the boys came home. And I hummed loud enough to drown out the sound of Miriam's screams. But I only hummed when Joseph wasn't around, because Joseph would swear that whatever I was humming, usually Patsy Cline like the records Momma used to play, wasn't right by God. Blasphemy, he'd say. Sacrilege.

But Joseph never did lock me in my room. Not back then, at least. Joseph knew I wouldn't run away 'cause over and over again he told me about Lily. How he'd do things to her if ever I misbehaved. So I didn't ever misbehave.

But when Miriam was being statue-like, I'd go into her room, and it was as if she didn't know I was there. Her eyes, they wouldn't look at me, wouldn't follow me as I helped her move from the bed. They wouldn't blink. From time to time, I pulled

193

the dirty sheets from that bed and washed them. And then I'd go back inside to help Miriam into the tub, to scrub her body with my bare hands because Joseph told me that it was mine to do.

I did what Joseph asked of me, nearly all the time.

Once and only once did I say no to Joseph as he climbed into bed beside me. Only once did I admit that it hurt, what he did to me. I pulled my legs up as high as I could and wrapped my arms around them so that maybe, just *maybe,* he wouldn't find a way in, and he stood before me, before the bed, and said, " 'An eye that mocks a father and scorns to obey a mother will be picked out by the ravens of the valley and eaten by the vultures.' Proverbs 30:17."

And I imagined that. Being picked apart by ravens and vultures. My carcass being torn apart by their beaks and talons because God was angry with me. Because I was refusing my father what was his duty and obligation.

And then I parted my legs and let him climb up on me and I held real still, like Momma used to say when we'd go to the doctor for a shot. "Hold still and it won't hurt so much." And I did, I held real still. But still, it hurt.

It hurt there, in the moment. Hurt long after he'd gone, after he'd told me what a good girl I'd been, how he was pleased with me.

I thought long and hard about that, about me being a good girl. I wondered what it would take, how many times Joseph would have to let himself into my room, before this good girl turned bad.

CHRIS

I finish my breakfast and head in for a shower, making sure to scour the tile first to remove any trace of the vile sores on that girl's feet. Thirty minutes later, Heidi stands before me, hands on hips, and asks, *"Really?"* when I appear before her with briefcase in hand and I reply, "Yes, *really,*" as I say goodbye to Zoe and head for the door.

I drag Heidi by the hand and into the hallway before I go. The scent of Heidi's breakfast fills the space. A neighbor passes by, presumably headed for the newsstand on the corner.

"I want you to call me," I say as the elevator chimes in the distance and our neighbor friend descends to the first floor. "Every hour on the hour. If you're so much as a minute late, I'm calling the police."

"You're being unreasonable, Chris," she says to me.

"Every hour, Heidi," I repeat. "It's that

simple," I say, asking rhetorically, "How much can you really know about another person?"

And then I kiss her cheek and leave.

On the train, I eavesdrop on twentysomethings' conversations about the previous night's drunken adventures, their lingering headaches, whether or not they puked when they got home.

Later, relishing the quiet solitude of my office, I slide the receipt from my wallet and peer at the name on the back: Willow Greer. I stretch in a leather executive chair on the forty-third floor of a skyscraper in the North Loop, and realize then and there that my offering memorandum — the one hanging over my head, the reason for the commute to work this sunny Sunday morning — is the furthest thing from my mind. I consider that booklet I'm to put together, the one that details the inner workings of some company we're to sell — financial statements, business description, the works — and then push it from my mind.

I fire up the computer and type in the words *Willow Greer.*

Enter.

While the computer does its thing, I find myself staring at a blank spot on the wall, thinking that I should've stopped on the way in and picked up some coffee. My office is windowless, though I'm supposed to be grateful I have an office at all, and not a ceilingless gray cubical as many of our analysts do. I forage through the desk drawers for two shiny quarters, planning a trip to the vending machine as soon as I solve the mystery of Willow Greer. The phone rings and I snap it up. Heidi's sarcastic voice is on the other end, announcing, "Eleven o'clock check-in call." I peer at the numbers in the corner of my computer screen: 10:59. In the background, the baby wails.

"Why's she crying?" I ask.

"Fever's back," says Heidi.

"Did you give her medicine?"

"Just waiting for it to kick in."

"Try a cool washcloth," I offer, "or a lukewarm bath," remembering how sometimes, with Zoe, that worked. But what I really want to say is *Serves you right,* or *Told you so.*

"Will do," says Heidi, and we hang up the phone, but not before I remind her, "One hour. I'll talk to you in one hour."

And then I go back to the computer.

The first thing I do is look through the images, expecting to see Willow's face staring right back at me. But instead I find some redheaded celeb of the same name. A brunette blotting various social media pages, appearing far too immodest — boobs spilling out of a scoop-neck shirt, a paunch overhanging a pair of cutoff jeans — to be our Willow. A town called Willow in Greer County, Oklahoma. Various homes for sale in Greer, South Carolina. According to the virtual phone book, there are six people living in the United States with the name Willow Greer. Not to be confused with Stephen Greer who lives on Willow Ridge Drive in Cincinnati. Only four of six Willow Greers are listed. I yank a sheet of scratch paper from the printer and begin jotting the information down. Willow Greer of Old Saybrook, Connecticut, is in the forty- to forty-four-year-old age range. Too old. Willow Greer of Billingsley, Alabama, is even older at 65+. She could be ninety. I write it down anyway; maybe Ms. Greer of Billingsley, Alabama, is our Willow's grandma. Or great-grandma. The others don't list an age range.

I jot down what sparse information I can find, and then it occurs to me: do you have to be eighteen to be listed in the phone book? Or, more importantly, own property?

I quickly type in Zoe Wood in Chicago, Illinois, and come up empty.

Damn.

I twiddle my thumbs for a split second, thinking. Where would I find Zoe online, if not the white pages? I quickly scan the various social media pages I'm familiar with, which are few and far between. Facebook. Myspace. I'd probably get a lot further in my investigation if I let my twelve-year-old help, the same way she navigates my cell phone for me when I'm stuck. I consider calling her, a stealthy call to her cell, but then picture the confiscated phone at home on the counter beside Heidi's. Crap.

I begin searching for variations of the name Willow Greer. I try Willow G., followed by Willow Grier. I try Willow with one *l*. I humor myself and drop the second *w:* Willo. You never know.

And then I come across a Twitter account for a W. Greer, username @LostWithoutU. I know nothing about Twitter, but I find the tweets dark and depressing, made up of all sorts of suicidal innuendos and allegations. Gonna do it. 2nite. But the profile shot of this girl, of *this* W. Greer, is not the one living in my home. This girl is older, a legitimate eighteen or nineteen years old, showing off lacerations on her wrist, a disturbing smile. The last tweet was posted two weeks ago. I wonder if she did it, if she made the decision to end her life.

And how.

"Hi there, stranger."

I minimize the screen lightning fast, relax in the chair as if I haven't just been caught red-handed, doing something wrong. Is stalking a crime? *Never mind stalking,* I think. *This is research.*

And yet, I'm certain a declaration of guilt is plastered to my face.

Cassidy Knudsen stands in the doorway. She's replaced the pencil skirt and three-inch heels with something a little less formal — and a lot more attractive in my opinion: skintight jeans and a roomy ebony sweater that falls from a shoulder, leaving a lacy red bra strap exposed. She tugs on the sweater, as if trying to amend its crookedness, but it falls back out of place. She leaves it alone, crosses one foot over the other — her Converse All Stars are, somehow, hotter than the three-inch heels — and leans against the frame. "Thought you were working from home this weekend."

"So did I," I say as I reach for the receipt — the words *Willow Greer* on the back — and crumple it into a ball. "Offering memorandum," I add, tossing the wad of paper back and forth between my hands, and then, "Things were a little too chaotic at home."

"Zoe?" she asks because, of course, who wouldn't think the twelve-year-old was responsible for the chaos?

"Actually," I admit, "Heidi," and Cassidy apologizes sympathetically as if I've just alluded to marital problems. This über-concerned look crosses her face: the buttery-blond hair and gray-blue eyes, the fair skin.

"So sorry to hear that, Chris," she says, welcoming herself into the office and having a seat on one of the armless teal chairs that sit facing my desk. "Anything you want to talk about?" she asks as she crosses her legs and leans in, like only a woman can do. Men catch a whiff of melancholy and go running in the opposite direction; women lean into it, the need to talk it out feeding their soul.

"Just Heidi being Heidi," I say, instantly sorry for saying anything in the realm of negativity about my marriage. "Which isn't a bad thing," I add shamefacedly, and Cassidy offers, "Heidi is a good woman."

"The best," I agree, willing thoughts of Cassidy Knudsen in satin slips and ruffled babydolls from my mind.

I married Heidi when I was twenty-five years old. Heidi was twenty-three. I stare at a four-by-six photo of us on our wedding day, thumbtacked to a bulletin board on the wall. *Classy,* she said the last time she was in my office, running her fingers over the picture, and I shrugged and said, "The frame broke. I knocked it right off the desk in a last-minute rush," and she nodded knowingly, understanding that the entirety of my career hinged on last-minute rushes.

But there was something telling about that photograph, I thought; our protective glass frame shattered and now here we were, punctured with microscopic holes that might one day tear. Those holes all had names: mortgage, adolescent child, lack of communication, retirement savings, cancer. I watch Cassidy's manicured fingers — the long clear nails with the white tips — fondle a lamp on my desk, one of those antique banker's lamps, vintage green; I watch her stroke the chain, watch her wrap it around a slim finger and pull — and think: infidelity?

No. Never. Not Heidi and me.

A soft yellow light fills the room. A nice contrast to the blinding white flourescent lights that line the ceiling.

We had dated for mere months when I asked Heidi to marry me. Being with Heidi was something I knew I needed: like air. Something I knew I wanted: sitting there at the top of my Christmas list to Santa that year. I was used to getting what I wanted. In my formative preteen years I lived with a mouth full of metal and headgear. I used to groan and gripe about those braces, the way they would puncture the gum and tear up the inside of my cheek. *You'll thank me one day,* my mother used to say, having suffered her entire life with overlapping teeth she hated. And I did. Thank her, that is. After years of orthodontia, I was left with a smile that could sway most everyone in my direction. It worked wonders at fraternity parties, interviews, client dinners and, of course, with the ladies. Heidi used to tell me that that smile was what first caught her eye the night we met at some charity ball. It was December, I remember that much, and she was wearing red. I'd paid about two hundred bucks to go to the darn thing, at the encouragement of my firm. *Giving back* was our motto that year. It was supposed to look good that our firm had snagged two tables, sixteen or twenty seats, at two hundred bucks a pop, even though not a single one of us knew what cause we were supporting.

Not until I found myself on the dance floor with Heidi later that night, learning more about illiteracy in Chicago than I ever cared to know.

I was used to getting what I wanted. Before I married Heidi that is.

"So what seems to be the problem, Mr. Wood?" Cassidy asks. She leans back in her chair, runs those well-manicured nails through her hair. "You want to talk about it?"

But I say, "No. Better not," thinking how the last time Heidi conceded to something I wanted it had to do with slipping on a pair of jeans before tracking that homeless girl down; the time before that, chunky peanut butter versus creamy. Things that were trivial.

When it mattered, I lost. Every time.

"C'est la vie?" Cassidy asks and I repeat, *"C'est la vie."*

Such is life.

And then I watch her blue-gray eyes and call to mind the way I knocked an espresso down the front of my houndstooth shirt the first time she walked into our conference room, wearing a red suit with the tight, ankle-length pants that only Cassidy Knudsen could wear, a pair of black shoes with, of course, three- or four-inch heels, my boss — suddenly seeming short and impotent — introducing her as "the new gal in town" and staring at her ass as she found her way to an empty seat beside me. She reached for a stack of take-out napkins left behind from dinner the previous night and began to pat my shirt dry in a way only Cassidy Knudsen would do.

She's like a femme fatale, isn't she? Heidi had asked that day at the botanical gardens, the first time Heidi and Cassidy met, last summer at the work picnic, as she watched the other woman drift away, hips swaying back and forth like a tetherball, somehow unattached to the rest of her body.

What's a femme fatale? Zoe had asked, and Heidi nodded her head to the woman in the strapless cherry dress and said simply, *Her.*

I reach for the quarters on my desk and announce that I'm making a trip to the vending machine. "Want anything?" I ask, hoping that when I return, I'll find the office empty. She says no thanks and I take off, down the all but deserted hall for the vending machine in our inadequate office kitchen. I press the button for the highly caffeinated drink I need, and crack the can open while making my way back to my desk.

I'm plotting the next steps in my "find Willow Greer" adventure when I step onto the metallic gold carpeting that separates my office from the ceramic tiles of the main hall. I find Cassidy on her hands and knees on the carpeting, collecting a dozen or so pens that fell. That roomy ebony sweater nearly drags on the ground, exposing the rest of the red bra that I previously couldn't see: the low cut, the Chantilly lace, the underwire cups, a delicate front bow.

She's holding my cell phone in her hand. I squint at the clock on the wall, 12:02 p.m., and my heart sinks.

"Heidi," Cassidy says, holding out the phone to me. She's smiling. But it's not a smile that's nice or polite. "For you. Hope you don't mind. I answered it."

HEIDI

"What *is* that woman doing answering your phone?" I growl into the phone, as Chris's reluctant voice says hello, the tone of his voice — cautious and yet strangely chipper — saturated with guilt. I drift from the living room where Willow sits on the edge of the sofa, baby pressed to a dish towel on her shoulder, burping her with a steady pat, pat, pat to the back as I showed her to do. And yet I see that the baby's face is pressed awkwardly to the towel so that I wonder how well she can breathe, her body sloping at an angle that looks anything but secure. Anything but comfortable.

"Hey, Heidi," Chris says, an unnatural attempt at remaining calm, cool and collected. "Everything okay?"

I imagine *that woman* sitting in his bland, box-like office, listening to our conversation. I envision Chris, checking his watch, making some sort of blah-blah-blah hand gesture to Cassidy Knudsen, to indicate that my rant — *why is she answering your phone; and why didn't you tell me you were going to the office to work with* her; *and who else is in today? Tom? Henry?* — has gone on for far too long. I feel the blood creeping up my neck, turning my cheeks to crimson. My ears burn. A headache begins to form. I place two fingers to my sinuses and press. Hard.

I click the end button, not quite as fulfilling as slamming a telephone into its base. I stand in the kitchen for a moment, breathing heavily, reminding myself of all the reasons I don't like Cassidy Knudsen. She's breathtaking. She's smart, shrewd. Very chichi, as if she should be in the pages of a fashion magazine, and not staring at Chris's insipid spreadsheets all the livelong day.

But the biggest reason I don't like her? It's quite plain and simple, really. My husband spends more time with her than he does with me. Flying to bustling metropolises around the country, spending the night in pricey, sophisticated hotels where Chris and I only ever dreamed about going, dinners at expensive restaurants that we saved for special occasions: birthdays, anniversaries and such, rendering them ordinary on days which were far from ordinary.

I hear her strident voice reverberating in my mind, the overly animated, "Hey there, Heidi," as she answered the phone. "Chris just ran down the hall. He'll be back in a bit. Want me to have him call you?" she'd asked, but I said no, I'd wait. And I did just that, staring at the time on the microwave clock for the four plus minutes it took my husband to return to his phone, all the while listening to Cassidy Knudsen tinker with the items on Chris's desk, hearing a crash and envisioning her knocking over his pencil cup — the painted pottery one Zoe made years ago — pencils and his ballpoint pens tumbling to the ground.

"Oops." She giggled, like a scandalous teenager.

I imagine that once Cassidy Knudsen was a cheerleader, one of those girls in the skimpy polyester skirts and the half shirts, dropping her pencil to the floor before the supposedly perverse male science teacher, reaching down from her chair spread eagle to reclaim it and then later claiming foul play.

While I gather myself to return to Willow and Ruby, I hear the squeak of a bedroom door, Zoe drifting from her bedroom hide-out and into the living room. There's silence, and then Zoe's voice, a bit thorny and stiff.

"Were you ever scared?" she asks. I lurk in the kitchen, wondering what she means. *Were you ever scared?*

"What?" asks Willow and I picture the girl, still wearing Zoe's clothing from the previous afternoon, now sticky with syrup and wrinkled with sleep. She's perched on the edge of the sofa and as Ruby lets out the belch of a male drunkard, the girls snicker.

There's nothing like a little gas to break the ice.

"Out there, I mean." And I imagine Zoe's finger pointing out the bay window, to the commotion of the city outside: the taxis that soar up and down the street, sirens, horns, a homeless man playing the saxophone on the corner of the street.

"Yeah. I guess so," Willow replies, admitting sheepishly, "I don't like thunder," and I'm stricken again by the clear truth that this girl, sitting in my living room with an infant in her arms, a tough mollusk shell protecting all that's valuable and vulnerable on the inside, is a mere child. A child who devours whipped cream and pancakes, and is afraid of something as innocuous as thunder.

Profiles, vase. Profiles, vase.

I imagine the vigorous city when it finally

does fall asleep for the night. When the sun sets somewhere over suburbia, and the lights of the Loop are ablaze. It's stunning, really. But here, in our neighborhood, a mile or two north of downtown, nighttime means total darkness. Pitch blackness spotted with the occasional streetlight that may or may not work. The time of day when zombies come out to play, loitering in the city's parks, in the darkened alcoves of closed businesses that line Clark and Fullerton Streets. Living in an upscale neighborhood doesn't exclude us from crime. The morning news talks frequently of crime waves throughout Lakeview and Lincoln Park, of overnight robberies, about how violent crimes are on the rise. You hear all the time about women being attacked as they walk home from the bus, or as they make their way into their apartment building, grocery bags in hand. The neighborhood at night — strangely dark, fraught with an ear-splitting silence, must be a terrifying place to be. Ghastly.

I make my way into the living room and find the girls eyeballing one another awkwardly. Zoe jumps when I enter and says, "What do you want?" as if I have no business being in my home. She's embarrassed that I caught her talking to Willow when it wasn't required, embarrassed that she showed any interest whatsoever in the girl.

"I have something to show you," I say, "both of you," and I disappear down the hall.

It took over an hour for Ruby's Tylenol to kick in, for the fever to subside. During that time she was irritable and moody, inconsolable whether in Willow's or my hands. We tried feeding her, rocking her, thrusting a pacifier into her wide-open mouth, but all of our efforts were in vain. And then, per Chris's suggestion, we sunk the baby into a lukewarm bath, which seemed to appease her a bit, and followed it up with layers of emollients to her bottom, a fresh diaper, a change of clothes. Because Chris had only purchased a single pair of blue pants to partner with the white jumpsuit, I lug the bin of baby clothing from Chris's and my bedroom closet — the one mislabeled *Heidi: Work* — into the living room where the girls and I can sort through rompers with ruffles and animal print bodysuits, Onesies with tutus, organic fleece pajamas and satin ballet slippers made just for pudgy infant feet.

"Shh," I say to Zoe as I set the indigo lid aside, "don't tell your father about this," I say. Out of the corner of my eye, Willow reaches out and touches fabric, but then withdraws her hand quickly, as if afraid she might break something or make it dirty. I have this sudden vision — a clairvoyant image — where some adult slaps Willow's timid hand away from something that she desires. She withdraws, her eyes downcast, feelings hurt. "It's okay," I say, pulling out the most luxuriant thing I can find and placing it in her hand, watching as she runs her fingers across the vertical ribs as if she's never felt corduroy before. She lifts it, cautiously, to her face and rubs a cheek to it, a pair of maroon overalls with flowers on the bib.

"What *is* all this?" Zoe asks, pulling a velvet dress with a taffeta skirt — size 2T — from the bin, her mouth falling open when she spies the obscene number on the price tag. "Ninety-four dollars?" she asks, ogling the thirty-six inches of fabric no one ever wore, the midnight-blue color and elephantine bow and, somewhere in that bin, pricey tights to match.

"And that was ten years ago," I say, adding, "or more," remembering those days I sauntered into boutiques in the Loop during my lunch break and purchased a romper here, a bodysuit there — on the sly — telling Chris, if ever he asked, that the outrageous debit on our credit card bill was for an expectant coworker or an old college friend, ready to burst forth with child.

"Were these . . . *mine*?" she asks, reaching for a pair of floral bloomers that accompany a summer dress. She holds them up before her and I think, *How do I explain?* I could say yes and leave it at that. But then of course there are the price tags, evidence that these garments were never used.

"My hobby," I admit. "Like collecting bottle tops or sports cards," and the girls look at me as though I just climbed out of a spaceship from Mars. "They're hard to resist," I say, "when they're just so cute," holding up a pair of furry booties and offering them as proof.

"But . . ." Zoe begins, having inherited her rationality from Chris, "I never even wore them," she says. "Who were they for?" she demands to know. I eye Zoe and Willow, their eyes staring at me questioningly. Good cop, bad cop, I think. I find it impossible to stare into Zoe's big brown eyes — both cynical and demanding all at the same time — and admit that they were for Juliet, that even after the doctor said I could have no more children, I continued to pine for children, to envision an imaginary world where Zoe and Juliet coexisted, playing with Tinkertoy sets or Little People on the living room floor, my belly fat and round with number three. I refuse to admit that the notion of an only child left me feeling bilious and cold, the home — where I always envisioned an overabundance of kids — lonely, even when Zoe was there. Even with Chris. My family, the three of us, felt suddenly insufficient. Not good enough. There was a hole. A hole I stuffed full with Juliet, with ambitions and expectations and a bin full of clothing she would one day wear.

In my heart of hearts, I convinced myself that she would arrive, one day. That day just hadn't come yet.

But I interrupt Zoe's rationality and say, "How about we see if we can find something for Ruby to wear," and the three of us begin pulling at the bin with a renewed purpose, though the sight — and the smell: an uncanny blend of upscale boutiques and optimism — of the clothing reminds me of the gaping hole inside my womb.

Or of that place where my womb used to be.

We settle on the maroon overalls, a white jumpsuit beneath with a scalloped edge. I watch as Willow undresses the baby, then tries to force the jumpsuit over Ruby's malleable head. Ruby lets out a wail. She protests on the floor, kicking her legs in defiance. Willow moves with hesitation, with apprehensive hands. She stares at the jumpsuit, at the neck hole that appears far too small for Ruby's round head, and then tries to force it on, forgetting altogether to allow clearance for the nose, to get it over her mouth quickly so the baby can breathe.

"Let me do it," I say to Willow, the words coming out more abruptly that I intended them to do. I feel Zoe's eyes on me, though I refuse to make contact. I shift into Willow's position and, stretching the elastic of the jumpsuit, slide it over Ruby's head without hesitation. I snap the buttons of the crotch closed, sit her up and snap the buttons up the back. "There now," I say, as Ruby's fingers settle upon the gold chain that dangles from my neck, her eyes lighting up like a Christmas tree. "You like that?" I ask, taking the bright eyes and the big, drooling, toothless smile as a yes. I set my father's gold wedding ring in the palm of her hand, and watch as her pudgy little fingers begin to squeeze. "That was my daddy's," I say, and then I focus on the task at hand, sliding the maroon overalls over the jumpsuit, a pair of white lacy socks over her rapidly moving feet. Ruby squeals in delight, and I press my face into her and say, "Coochy, coochy, coo," the kind of nonsensical gibberish babies adore. I all but forget that Willow and Zoe are still in the room, watching as I blow raspberries on the exposed parts of Ruby's skin: the insides of her arms, the nape of her neck; I overlook the horrified look on my preteen's face as I speak fluently in baby talk, the type of skill, like riding a bike, that one never forgets how to do.

"Coochy, coochy, coo," I say, and it's then that Zoe rises to her feet, unexpectedly, and says, "God! Enough with the baby talk already," in that high frequency, falsetto voice only an adolescent girl can attain, before waltzing down the hall and slamming the door to her room.

WILLOW

"What *was* Miriam's medical condition? Was she schizophrenic?"

I shake my head. "I don't know."

Outside the single, barred window, the one placed too high on the cinderblock wall, the sky is turning colors: red and orange quickly displacing the blue. The sentry in the corner yawns, a long, drawn out, exaggerated yawn, and Louise Flores looks at him sharply and asks, "Are we boring you?" and he stands suddenly at attention: chin up, chest out, shoulders back, stomach in.

"No, ma'am," he replies and the jagged woman eyes him until even I begin to blush.

What was wrong with Miriam, I didn't know, but whatever it was, I was pretty sure it was Joseph's doing.

"You said that Miriam would take medicine on occasion?" Ms. Flores asks and I nod my head, yes. "What kind of medicine?"

"Little white pills," I say. "Sometimes another one, too." I tell her that the pills made Miriam look better, made her feel better and get out of bed for a while, but if she got to taking them too much, they just put her back in bed again.

But Miriam was always tired. Whether or not she was taking the pills.

"Did Joseph ever have her to a doctor?"

"No, ma'am. Miriam didn't leave."

"She didn't leave the house?"

"No, ma'am. Never."

"Why wasn't Miriam medicated all the time?"

"Joseph said if God wanted her well, he would make her well."

"But sometimes Joseph gave her the medicine?"

"Yes, ma'am. When Ms. Amber Adler came."

"The caseworker?"

"Yes, ma'am."

"Where did Joseph get the pills? If he didn't take her to the doctor?"

"In the medicine cabinet. In the bathroom."

"Yes, Claire, but *how* did the pills get *there,* if there was no doctor? You likely need a prescription for such medication. A pharmacy."

I say that I don't know. Joseph would tell

me to fetch them, the little plastic baggies — she stops me there: *"Plastic baggies?"* she asks, and I say yes, and she scribbles something down on that notebook of hers beside the word *z-e-a-l-o-t* which I've been reading upside down for half an hour now, and still have no idea what it means. He'd pull some pills out and force Miriam to take them. Sometimes he had to pry her mouth open while I popped in the pills and then we'd wait, for as long as it took, for her to swallow. Miriam didn't like the pills.

But once or twice a year, Joseph would get her to take the pills for a while, and she'd come out from the room and bathe herself, and we'd open up all the windows and it would be my job to get that god-awful Miriam smell out of the home before Ms. Amber Adler, in her junker car with the too-big Nike bag, arrived. He'd get out his toolbox and start fixing things around the house, paint over stains that had cropped up here and there around the home. Only when Amber Adler came to call did the dead lightbulbs get replaced, and squeaky hinges get oiled.

Joseph always had a new dress for me as opposed to the small, musty duds he dropped off in my room in a large white garbage bag, like he'd picked it up at the

221

end of someone's drive on garbage day. Once he even brought me a pair of shoes, patent leather which were far too big, but he told me to put them on nonetheless so Ms. Adler could see.

The caseworker brought letters from Paul and Lily Zeeger. She said she could give the Zeegers my new address, but after Joseph tore the photos of Momma into shreds, I said no thanks, that was all right, she could just bring the letters along when she came. Lily Zeeger wrote beautiful letters about my baby sister, Rose (Lily) with the name Lily always in parenthesis just in case I didn't know who it was she was talking about. She said that Rose (Lily) was growing bigger and bigger every day, and that from the photos she's seen, Rose (Lily) was looking more and more like our Momma, who was a stunning, sensational, dazzling woman (as if the many compliments might negate the fact that she's dead). She said that Rose (Lily) was learning her ABCs, and how to count to ten, and that she could sing as well as the Yellow Warbler which, according to Big Lily, surrounded their Colorado home, and there were photos attached, of a charming little A-frame home snuggled right in the middle of the woods, with mountains in the background and a tiny dog, like a cocker spaniel or something, running around the legs of my Lily. And there she is, Little Lily, with the ringlets of black hair, black like Momma's, that had grown longer and were clipped back in ladybug barrettes, and she was wearing a bright yellow sundress with ruffles and a bow as big as her head. And she was smiling. Paul Zeeger stood on a balcony in a shirt and striped tie, looking down at Little Lily, and I imagined Big Lily took the picture 'cause she was nowhere to be seen. Even the dog looked happy. The letter said how Rose (Lily) was taking a ballet class and loved to practice her pirouettes and relevés for Paul and Lily, and how she absolutely adored her cerise leotard and tutu, and that in the fall Rose (Lily) would begin preschool at the Montessori school in town.

"What's a Montessori school?" I asked Ms. Amber Adler and she looked at me and smiled and said, "It's a good thing," while patting my hand.

I asked her why Paul and Lily Zeeger didn't have any kids of their own. Why'd they need *my* Lily? And she said sometimes things just worked out that way. One or the other of them couldn't have kids. It just wasn't meant to be. And I thought of Joseph saying that if God wanted Miriam to be well, he'd make her well, and I thought that if God wanted Paul and Lily to have kids, he would have given them kids. Kids of their own. Not my Lily. Lily was mine.

I thought a lot about that A-frame house where Lily now lived. I thought about the tall, tall trees and the mountains and the dog. I thought how I'd like to go there, to that house in the woods, and see my Lily again. I wondered if I ever could.

Big Lily said that I could write a letter back to Rose (Lily) if I wanted to and she'd read it to her. So I did. I told her about the tulips outside our home (of which there were none) and what I was learning in school (there was no school). The only reading that went on in our home was from the Bible; the only writing was when Joseph made me copy word for word from *Deuteronomy* or *Leviticus*. The school reports that Joseph handed over to the caseworker — those which showed my poor grades in school — were forged, photocopies of Matthew's or Isaac's report cards that had been altered with my name, with failing grades in math and science, with teacher comments that detailed my disregard for authority figures, my misbehavior.

"Don't you like school?" the caseworker would ask.

"I like it just fine," I'd say.

"What's your favorite subject?" she wanted to know. I didn't know much about subjects. So I said math. "But, Claire, it says here that you are failing your math class," and I would shrug and say that it was hard and she'd remind me, as she often did, how lucky I was to have Joseph and Miriam in my life. How other foster families would not be so flexible and understanding. "You need to try harder," she would say to me, and to Joseph and Miriam, she'd suggest a tutor.

In my letters, I told Little Lily about living in the big city — Omaha — and I described the buildings; though I'd never once seen the buildings, I had an inkling they were there. This Omaha place was much different than Ogallala. I could tell that from the smells, the sounds, the kids on the other side of the window. Momma used to talk about Omaha when we were kids. About the people and buildings, museums and zoos. In my letters I told Lily about my brothers (who I barely knew). I told her about the friends I'd made in school (there were no friends) and how my teachers were an absolute delight (there were no teachers).

In Big Lily's responses, she told me of

Rose's (Lily's) fourth birthday present: a new bike, mint green and pink, with training wheels and tassels, a white wicker basket and a banana seat. There were pictures. Little Lily in a helmet on the bike with Paul Zeeger pushing from behind. The little cocker spaniel running after them. She told me of an upcoming vacation to California to see the beach. She said that this would be Rose's (Lily's) first time ever seeing the ocean and wondered: had I seen the ocean before? They'd picked out a new swimsuit and cover-up for the occasion. The next time the caseworker arrived, there were drawings from Lily herself, of the ocean and fish and blobs in the sand that may or may not have been seashells. And a bright yellow sun with rays that swept off the page. On the back Big Lily had written in her perfect penmanship: Rose (Lily), 4 years old.

They weren't bad people.

In time I understood that.

But knowing it in my mind and in my heart were two very different things.

HEIDI

In the morning, Zoe — reluctantly — offers up another outfit for Willow to wear. This time black leggings that are far too short for Zoe's own legs — and much shorter on Willow's — and a sweatshirt with paint splatters on the front, an art smock from the previous school year.

"Zoe, please," I say, "this one is a mess."

"Fine," she gripes, yanking an extra school cardigan from its hanger and thrusting it into Willow's hands, "here."

The girls eat breakfast — heaping bowls of Frosted Flakes — and then Zoe disappears to bathe and dress. Ruby, on my lap, is sound asleep, finally, having been up and agitated since before 5:00 a.m., awoken in the early hours of dawn by a fever. Because unhappy babies need to be rocked when they're upset — and we, of course, had no rocking chair — I pressed her to my chest and moved back and forth, back and forth in a seesaw motion until she finally began to settle, until the muscles in my back began to burn. But I didn't mind. There was something gratifying about it, something so satisfying when Ruby finally began to grow tired and slowly closed her eyes.

It was then that I lowered my body onto the leather armchair, completely immersed in the way Ruby's eyelids fluttered when asleep, the way her tiny fingers folded over my thumb, refusing to let go. Completely immersed in the tiny toes of her left foot where she'd wiggled the lacy sock right off and onto the hardwood floor. Completely immersed in the filaments of hair that emerged from her head, in the softness of her scalp, the blanch skin.

So immersed, in fact, that I lost track of time completely, forgot about the need to walk Zoe to school, the need to go to work.

Before I know it, Zoe stands, hovering before the front door, her backpack thrown over a shoulder. She has her coat on, partway zipped, and an umbrella dangling by its cord from her wrist. "You ready to go?" she asks and I peer down at my own attire: at the robe and a pair of sheepskin slippers still warming my feet.

"Mom," Zoe snaps this time, having just discovered that I'm still in my pajamas. I

make no effort to move, fearful of waking Ruby from her nap. I feel my mouth open, a *shh* emerging so that Zoe's voice will not rouse the baby from sleep.

Zoe, in a huff, frowns, her eyes bouncing between a clock on the wall and me, her body antsy. Her posture sags, her shoulders slump forward, the small of her back arched. Her backpack falls from her shoulder and into the crook of an elbow before she thrusts it back up and sighs.

I whisper, "I'm not going to work," just like that. "You'll have to walk yourself to school," I say, expecting her to leap up and down with joy, for this is the one thing she's been begging for years to do. To walk herself to school, alone, as her best friend Taylor is allowed to do.

But instead of joy, her mouth drops open and she says to me with disdain, "What do you mean you're not going to work? You *always* go to work," a fact altogether true, for the times that I've called in sick for work — even when a young Zoe was home sick with the flu — were few and far between. Often times it was Chris I begged to stay home from work, or when he was unable, his parents beckoned from their west suburban home, or, in moments of desperation, Graham.

But the weight of Ruby, sound asleep on my lap, reminds me that I cannot leave.

My finger, nestled in the flabby clutches of her hand, assures me I cannot go.

"I have plenty of vacation time accrued," I say in a hushed tone, and then remind Zoe about the paper lunch sack awaiting her on the kitchen counter with ants on a log inside, a recent fad now that she's watching her weight. I wonder if I watched my weight when I was twelve, doubtful, imagining that that, too, came later, sixteen or seventeen perhaps. She gropes for the bag, the paper crinkling loudly in the palm of her hand. Ruby stirs on my lap and opens her eyes ever so slightly, before stretching her arms high above her head and falling back to sleep.

"Have a good day," I whisper to Zoe before she leaves, and she responds with a noncommittal, "Whatever," before disappearing into the hall, leaving the door wide-open so that I have to ask Willow to close it please.

I'm hopeful that Zoe will remember to keep Willow a secret, that she will remember that she's not to mention our guest to her classmates at school, to her teachers. Harboring a runaway for more than 48 hours is deemed a crime, a Class A misde-

230

meanor punishable by up to a year in prison, years of probation, a hefty fine.

But knowing this and believing this are two different things. I find it hard to believe that I could ever be caught, or that the police would enforce such a penalty when what I am doing is helping this girl. I wonder where the police were when someone thwacked Willow so hard that the ochre bruise formed on her head, or when some lecherous man laid himself atop her body. Was she alone when Ruby was born, tucked down some dark alley at night, beneath rusting fire escapes and dripping air conditioner units, beside rat infested Dumpsters, leaned up against some brick wall covered with graffiti, the sounds of the city invalidating the sounds of her screams.

There's an image I carry in my mind, that image of Willow, down a darkened alley, giving birth to a baby. As I sit on the leather armchair with Ruby sound asleep in my lap —Willow perched by the window in silence, watching pedestrians come and go — I count back four months in my head: March, February, January, December. Ruby would have been born sometime in December. Add to my image: dirty, slushy snow; the biting cold, freezing the blood as it oozed from the birthing canal.

In my image, Willow is replaced by Zoe: a daughter, someone's daughter.

Where is her mother?

Why wasn't her mother there to protect her from this ghastly fate?

I find myself staring at Willow, at the hair that hangs in her face, covering eyes that are slowly catching up on sleep, skin that is beginning to soften from the cold, spring air. She isn't a tall girl, per se, about six inches shorter than me, so that I can see the top of her head, the place where tawny roots grow in from her scalp, uninterrupted by the imitation red.

I reach out and, without thinking, lay my fingers briefly on her infected earring holes, the skin red and crusty, the lobe beginning to bulge. She withdraws quickly from my touch, blanching as if I'd slapped her with the back of a hand.

"I'm so sorry," I gasp, withdrawing my hand. "I'm sorry. I didn't . . ." My voice wanders off. I gather myself, and try again with, "We should take a look at that. A little Neosporin might do the trick," knowing that between Ruby's ever-present fever and *this*, we may need to see a doctor before long.

After some time Willow asks, apprehensively, to borrow my copy of *Anne of Green Gables,* and I, of course, say yes, watching as she retires to Chris's office to read. I watch as she carries the worn copy pressed close to her heart, and I wonder what significance the novel holds for her, its narrative committed to her memory like biblical text. I could ask her, I could ask Willow about the book, but I imagine her curling into a ball like an armadillo — or a woodlouse — at my interrogation, and hiding inside her armor shell.

I slip from the leather armchair and settle down at the kitchen table with my laptop and a mug of coffee, Ruby swaddled in a blanket and set on my lap. I pull up a search engine and type into the box: *child abuse.*

I come to learn that over a thousand children die each year in our country due to abuse or neglect on the part of their caregivers. Over three million child abuse reports are made each year, by teachers, local authorities, friends of the family, neighbors or the ubiquitous anonymous calls that child services receives. Child abuse can result in physical injuries: bruises and bone fractures, the need for sutures, damage to the spinal cord, the brain, the neck, second- and third-degree burns, and so on and so forth. Emotionally, the abuse is damaging, as well, leading to depression in even the youngest of victims, withdrawal, antisocial behavior, eating disorders, attempts at suicide, illicit sexual activities. And — as my eyes drift over the words, my mind forms an image of Willow, pregnant with a fetal Ruby growing inside her womb — *teenage pregnancy.* Victims of abuse are more likely to use alcohol and drugs, to participate in criminal activity, to fare poorer in school than the comparable child who has not been abused.

Who is the father of that child? I wonder as I get a second cup of coffee, dribbling creamer along the countertop as I do.

A lover? A boyfriend? A sadistic school teacher, one who took advantage of his position of power to seduce a student or maybe tempt her with an easygoing smile and an approachable manner? Or perhaps her own father? A neighbor? A sibling?

And then I remember: Matthew. Her brother Matthew. Who reads *Anne of Green Gables.*

Is Matthew the father of that child?

The sound of Willow's feet pitches me across the room, and I slam the laptop shut so she doesn't see the words scattered at random across the screen: *assault* and *molest* and *sexual abuse.* I stand, breathing hard, with hands on hips in an overdone impression of relaxation, as she asks permission to turn on the TV and I say, yes, of course, so long as she keeps the volume low. I watch as she settles on the leather chair and turns the TV to *Sesame Street,* the kind of kids' show Zoe hasn't watched since she was four or five. I find it odd, odd indeed; I'm not quite sure what to make of it.

But then, somehow or other, my concern for Willow starts to wane and I find my attention focusing on Ruby instead, the on-line child-abuse investigation morphing into a shopping expedition for rocking chairs, thinking less about that ochre bruise atop Willow's head and more about a baby's need to rock, about nestling before the big bay window with Ruby in my arms and watching for hours as raindrops fall from the sky.

CHRIS

One night turns into two.

Then two nights turn into three.

I'm not quite sure how it happens. I come home from work, ready and motivated to tell Heidi it is time for her to leave. I make a plan in my head, how I will give the girl fifty dollars — no *a hundred bucks* — enough for her to make due for a while.

I'll map out the homeless shelters within the city limits, so Heidi can see I'm trying.

I'll get her there myself. In a cab. Make sure she gets inside the shelter. Make sure they accept babies.

I go through the words in my head, what I will say to Heidi. I jot down a numbered list in my notes on the way home from work, the writing like chicken scratches from the motion of the train. As I walk from the Fullerton Station, I polish the words in my head. We'll be *generous,* I'll say. Give her *plenty.* Make sure she has everything she *needs.*

I'll gaze into Heidi's bewitching brown eyes and make her understand that this is the way it has to be. I'll be tactful and delicate, I'll use Zoe as justification.

Zoe might think you care more about Willow's needs than you do her own.

Then she'll see. If I pit Zoe against Willow, Heidi will see.

But as they say, the best laid plans of mice and men often go astray.

I'm not a block from home when thunder explodes in an otherwise quiet night, when the rain — cold, thick rain — begins to drop from the sky. A band of clouds rolls in across the city like a cinderblock wall. I break into a jog, aware that the temperature has begun to plunge, as well, a fifty-degree day morphing into a thirty-degree night.

What kind of monster would I be if I sent this girl off into a monsoon? That's what Heidi would say, I think, as I climb the steps to our home, shaking the rainwater off my coat and hair.

I come in to find the girl on the couch, the evil black cat on her lap. Heidi and Zoe are at the kitchen table, discussing probability. Probability of simple events. Probability of over-lapping events.

What is the probability of another rainy night

during the wettest April on record?

Heidi has not gone to work for two days now in a row. Two days. It was me who, days ago, forbid her from leaving *that girl* alone in our home as my eyes roved from personal files to jewelry boxes to various electronics, pointing out all the things she was liable to steal. Heidi had eyed the forty-inch TV perched on the wall, imagined the girl walking down Fullerton with that in her hands, and asked, "*Really,* Chris?" pointing out what a pessimist I could be.

And I had said, "Don't be so naive."

But she has used this to her advantage, as an excuse to stay home from work rather than kick the girl to the curb as I had hoped she'd do. She said she couldn't leave Willow alone for fear she'd steal something, the forty-inch TV or her father's wedding ring.

The baby is on the floor, sound asleep. There are weathermen on the TV, talking about the string of storms set to pass through the city during the night, the type of storm system, they say, that produces tornadoes, causing widespread damage. *If you live in the towns of Dixon or Eldena, take cover now.* The storms are headed our way from central Illinois, from Iowa, red and orange blips on the Doppler radar that the weathermen flash on the TV screen.

238

Heidi asks, "Raining again?" as I hang my saturated coat on a hook by the door and slip out of my shoes, her voice elevated over the thumping sound of the rain. I say that it is.

"Just started up," I say. "Getting colder, too," as a clap of thunder rattles through the sky, shaking the building and everyone inside.

"Going to be a doozy," says Heidi, about the storm, her eyes set on Willow across the room, stroking the cat with the palm of her hand, staring vacantly out the blackened windows. Lightning brightens the sky and she jumps, withdrawing into the sofa cushions as if she's trying to hide.

I kiss Heidi and Zoe on the cheek, and take my leftover dinner, the plate on the countertop, tucked beneath a paper towel, to the microwave to reheat it. I peek under the paper towel and see pork chops.

Maybe this girl isn't so bad after all.

The cold air disseminates through our home, through the breaches in the drafty windows. Outside, the wind howls and the trees sway. Heidi rises from her chair, crosses the room and flips on the gas fireplace to warm the space.

It's then that I see, out of the corner of my eye, a look of dread that overtakes Willow, as she springs to her feet, the black cat plummeting to the ground. Her eyes are fastened to that fireplace. The fire glowing orange among the artificial embers. The flames, how they dance dramatically behind the mesh screen, coaxing the cats, enticing them, the both of them, to the warmth of the fire. They sprawl out beside it, oblivious to Willow's distress.

"Fire," she says, her voice shaky and subdued. She's pointing. At the black fireplace with its black louvers on the white wall, surrounded by built-in nooks and crannies that house Heidi's knickknacks: her snow globes and vases, a collection of vintage jars. "Fire," she says again, and I'm reminded of cavemen discovering fire for the very first time. Her eyes are glassy, like marbles; her face has gone white.

It's a knee-jerk reflex when Heidi flips the fireplace off.

The flames disappear. The gas logs return to their hand painted, blackened state.

"Willow," she says, her voice as wobbly as Willow's when she said *fire*. But there's a calmness in Heidi's voice that the girl doesn't possess. A hint of reason. The rest of us in the room, we're silent. The cats stare at the fireplace, growing cold.

"It's okay, Willow," Heidi declares, "it's

just a fireplace. It's safe. Perfectly safe," and her eyes stray to mine, begging to know what in the hell just happened. My shoulders rise and fall as Willow settles back down on the sofa, shaking the image of that fire from her mind.

I eat my dinner and excuse myself, into the bedroom to make a call. A work call, I say so that I won't be interrupted.

But it isn't a work call at all.

I've been doing my own research on Willow Greer, hitting one dead end after the next. I've widened my search to more than a Google search. In every spare second of downtime, I'm on my laptop, searching for the girl.

I've moved on to the National Center for Missing & Exploited Children and to searching active AMBER alerts. I even signed up to receive AMBER alerts via email, and am now being notified every time some alienated spouse tries to run off with his or her own kid. But so far, nothing. Nada.

After discovering the Twitter account @LostWithoutU linked to a W. Greer, I spent more time than I'd ever admit reading the girl's bleak tweets, the threats of self-destruction, staring at photos she's posted online, her arms scratched to smithereens, or so she claimed, by the sharp edge of a razor blade. Cutting. There were responses from all sorts of other hooligans, their photos of self-inflicted wounds trying to one up each other, jagged, red words chiseled into the skin: *fat* and *pain* and *whore*. There were challenges made in response to @LostWithoutU's suicidal threats: Do it, and I double dog dare you.

There were more photos, too, of her various tattoos: assorted occult symbols on a shoulder and leg, some sort of butterfly with black-and-yellow wings, spread across the palm of a hand. A close up of her face and there, hidden behind gangly red hair, a pair of cross earrings much like the ones our Willow wore. A pair of angel's wings.

Could it be a coincidence? I stare long and hard at those earrings and think: probably not.

Could our Willow Greer be the same girl, with a profile photo that is not her own? Maybe. I browse others' profile photos: a dog, a cat, Marilyn Monroe. There's no law that says your photo has to be *your* photo. On a whim I set up my own Twitter account. @MoneyMan3. I upload a photo I find online, some male model with blue eyes and bushy blond hair, shirtless, flaunting six-pack abs.

A man can dream.

I send a tweet to @LostWithoutU.

Does it hurt? I ask, about the parallel red lines lacerated into the skin.

And then I make my phone call.

I have an old college friend who does some PI work around town, mostly in the realm of cheating spouses. Martin Miller. He's got the best stories to tell, stories of high-class women winding up in seedy hotels. His website claims to find lost loves, college sweethearts, teenage runaways. Maybe he can help.

When Martin answers I tell him about our little situation. He vows to be utterly discreet.

The last thing I need is Heidi to know I've hired a PI. Or for this information to wind up in the wrong hands. If he turns the information over to authorities . . . *No,* I think. I scan the website again. *Utmost discretion,* it says. And besides, I know this guy.

How is it, then, that I know about the high-class women and the seedy hotels? No, I think, pushing that thought from my mind. I hear him laugh about it at some dive bar out in Logan Square. It was about five years ago, maybe more. We were drunk.

I know this guy.

Later that night, as I lie in the magenta

sleeping bag on the floor, I think of that girl, the look on her face when she saw the fire. How does a teenage girl come to be terrified of lightning? Of fire?

Zoe hasn't been scared of those things since she was eight.

I almost feel sorry for her. Almost.

But then again, being solicitous isn't really my thing. It's Heidi's.

HEIDI

Willow settles into our home slowly, like the natural weathering of rocks over time, breaking into smaller and smaller pieces. Pebbles. She reveals little about herself, nearly nothing, and yet that alone becomes commonplace. I stop asking questions, stop trying to solicit information about her, her family, her past, knowing the responses will be sparse and incomplete.

There is a brother. A brother named Matthew. That much I know.

In what little time she's been with us, each of us takes to her in our own way, Chris in a synthetic way, his empathy manufactured and strained. He tolerates her, though each day I'm barraged with questions about how many more days she will stay.

"One night?" he asks. "Two?" though I tell him I don't know. He shakes his head at me and says, "Heidi. This is really getting out of hand," and I make him see that for

245

all the days she's been with us, she hasn't done a single harmful thing: our lives are still intact, electronics have yet to be swiped from the home while we sleep.

She's harmless, I tell him. But he is not so sure.

And yet, from time to time my mind retreats to the blood on the undershirt, hurled down the garbage shoot and now taking up residence in some landfill in Dolton. I wonder whether or not it truly belonged to Willow as she said it did, an effect of the cold spring air, or if perhaps . . . But I stop myself, refusing to consider other options. I see those blood splatters at the oddest of times: when taking a shower, when making dinner. Quiet moments when my thoughts wander away from me, away from the everyday busyness to blood.

I find myself thinking about the baby, about Ruby, all the time, when I'm not thinking about the blood. Holding Ruby and listening to her wail, it reminds me of all the imaginary children I once longed to have. The ones I was supposed to have. I find myself dreaming night after night about babies: living babies, dead babies, cherubic babies, cherubs, with their angelic wings. I dream of Juliet. I dream of embryos and fetuses, and baby bottles and baby shoes. I dream of giving birth to babies all night long, and I dream of blood, blood on the undershirt, blood oozing from between my legs, red and thick, coagulating inside my panties. Panties that were once a brilliant white, like the undershirt.

I wake in a panic, sweating, while Chris and Zoe never stir.

Zoe takes to Willow as she does most everything in life: with hostility. There are days she eyeballs the girl from across the room with something akin to loathing in her eyes. She grumbles about sharing her clothing with the girl, or not being allowed to watch some kitschy show on the TV. She refuses to hold Ruby for a split second when Willow is in the restroom, and I'm otherwise occupied. She refuses to give the baby a bottle, and when she cries, as she often does, pathetic, persistent crying, Zoe rolls her eyes and walks out of the room.

I take to making three-course meals, grateful that someone is there to lick her plate clean. I make salads and soups, lasagna, and chicken tetrazzini, watching as Willow devours the meals one by one, always grateful for seconds, while Zoe stares desolately at the food, asking questions like, "What even *is* this?" and, "I thought we were vegetarians," in that way only a preteen can, the

247

falsetto of her voice, whiny and shrill. I watch Zoe pick at the lettuce leaves of her salad like a rabbit, thankful that Willow, across the table, is completely ravenous, and will not let good food go to waste.

In the afternoon, when Zoe is at school, and I am home from work, I find myself staring at Willow. At Ruby. At the way Willow handles Ruby, heavy-handed and inept, until I lift the baby from her arms and say, "Here, let me," sure to tack on, "You could use a break," so as not to insult her. I don't know what she makes of it, of the way I remove the baby from her arms. I'm not entirely sure I care. I press my lips to the baby's forehead and whisper, "There now, sweet girl," as I bobble her up and down ever so gently, trying hard to make her smile.

I settle into the new rocking chair, purchased online and delivered this morning via FedEx, a delivery which Chris has yet to see. I paid extra, nearly a hundred dollars, for expedited delivery, though this detail I won't mention to Chris. I press my back into the lumbar support and the baby and I begin to sway. I hum Patsy Cline lullabies under my breath, songs that my mother one day hummed to me, which seems to get Willow's attention, though she tries hard to pretend she doesn't care.

I watch the girl out of the corner of my eye, wondering ominously if or when she will want the baby returned to her custody, when she will tire of staring at Muppets on the TV screen, and wish to retreat to the office with *Anne of Green Gables* and the baby. My arms tighten around the baby automatically, like a seat belt in an auto collision.

Willow has been with me for over forty-eight hours now, and all I know is her first name, if, as Chris points out, that *is* her real name.

And that she has a brother. Matthew.

She doesn't offer a thing about herself, and I don't ask, certain that any interrogation will scare her away, and she will leave, taking with her the baby. My mind makes up for the lack of information, inventing all sorts of narratives that brought her and her baby into our lives, tales of spring tornadoes sweeping through the Midwest and carrying her from her home, tales of her running away to escape the huntsman who's to return to the castle with her heart. From time to time she starts to say something, only ever a single word, or sometimes just a syllable or two that sneak between her lips, but then she stops herself suddenly and

249

claims oblivion.

She's grave. She doesn't smile. She might as well be an elderly lady, what with all the baggage she carries in her eyes and meek demeanor. She's quiet, virtually silent, sitting on that sofa, staring blindly at the TV. She watches cartoons mostly, almost always *Sesame Street,* staring at the TV longingly, until Chris or Zoe or I break her reverie.

She eats quickly, passionately, as if she's been deprived of a home-cooked meal for the greater part of her life, and at night, as I hover in the hallway after we've parted ways and she's drifted into her room, I wait for the door to lock, as it does every night, for that latch to assure her that no one will be slinking into her room, prowling in the shadows while she sleeps.

I hear her, sometimes, in the middle of the night. I hear her subconscious murmur a single phrase while she sleeps: *Come with me.* Over and over again, *Come with me,* her voice escalating at times until the words verge on desolate, a do-or-die attempt at persuasion.

Come with me. Come with me.

But who is she talking to, I wonder, and where does she want them to go?

She cleans up after herself, bringing her dishes to the sink, where she washes and dries them by hand though I beg her not to. "Please," I say. "Leave them. I'm just going to load the dishwasher," but she does anyway as if she feels she has to, double- and triple-checking sometimes for remnants of food encrusted to the plates or left behind in the tines of the forks, as if such a simple oversight would elicit admonishment, and I picture her, picture Willow, bent over a kitchen chair, receiving the prescribed number of lashings for leaving food behind on a plate, and then a knock on the head to deliver the ochre bruise.

The baby and I sway in the rocking chair, Willow sitting on the sofa in silence. Ruby wiggles in my arms, her mouth plugged with a pacifier, unable to cry, though she wants nothing less than to belt out a bloodcurdling scream. I see the agitation in her eyes, eyes that are shellacked thanks to yet another fever.

I moisten a washcloth and press it to her head, and continue to hum lullabies in the hopes of pacification.

It's then that Willow turns to me — her voice, in that moment of near-silence startling me — wanting to know in her generally timid, generally submissive tone, "How come you didn't have any more babies? If you like them so much?" and I feel the air

251

in the room become too thin to breathe.

I could lie. I could evade the question altogether. No one has ever asked me such a question. Not even Zoe. I think back some eleven years. The beginning of the end, or so it felt at the time. Zoe was less than a year old, a cuddlesome creature when she wasn't in the midst of a colicky rage, the kind that brought neighbors to our door to see what they could do to silence the child so they could sleep. She was just five, maybe six months old when I discovered I was carrying another child, that I was carrying Juliet. We weren't trying to conceive, Chris and I, but we weren't taking precautions not to, either. I was absolutely elated when I found out I was pregnant, certain that this was just the beginning of that vast family I longed to have.

How Chris felt about it, I wasn't entirely sure. *It's soon,* he said the day I told him, standing before the bathroom door with a positive pregnancy test in my hand. *We already have a baby.*

But then he smiled. And there was a hug. And there were conversations over those fleeting few weeks: what we would name the baby and whether or not the baby and Zoe could share a room.

What I noticed first was blood, a watery

discharge that turned crimson with time. And then there was the pain. I was certain I was having a miscarriage when I caught sight of the blood there, in my panties, but the doctor assured me the baby was just fine.

A biopsy confirmed stage 1B cervical cancer.

The doctor recommended a radical hysterectomy, which meant first ridding my womb of Juliet. "It's a simple procedure," the doctor assured Chris and me, and I read online how they would dilate my cervix, and then scrape the contents of my uterus clean, and I imagined Juliet as the pulp of a pumpkin, being scooped out with a spoon.

No, I said, and *Absolutely not,* but somehow or other Chris convinced me that an abortion was something we needed to do. *If it was later in the pregnancy,* he'd said, mimicking the doctor's words, and *If the cancer wasn't so advanced.* And then: *I can't raise Zoe alone,* he'd said, *if something happens to you.* And I thought of Chris and Zoe all alone, and myself, dead, in a tomb. Had the cancer not been so advanced we could have delayed treatment until after the delivery. But such was not the case. As it was, it was the baby or me, and I chose me, a decision that would haunt me for the rest of my life.

The doctor and Chris corrected me every time I said *baby.* They called her a *fetus* instead. *There's no way to know,* the doctor had said before they discarded my Juliet as medical waste, *whether or not she's a girl. Reproductive organs don't develop until the third month of pregnancy.*

And yet, I knew.

I stared at the pamphlets the doctor handed me in the office, angry that I had gotten so busy with work and Zoe that I'd fallen behind on regular Pap tests, that I'd missed my own six-week postpartum checkup because I couldn't be bothered. Cervical cancer, the pamphlets said, could be detected early with routine Pap smears, something I'd failed to have. I was angry that I fit none of the risk factors: I didn't smoke, I wasn't immunosuppressed and, as far as I knew, I hadn't come in contact with HPV.

I was the exception. The rarity. The one in a million.

This wasn't supposed to happen to me.

The doctor chopped out my uterus. And while he was down there he thought, what the heck, and cut out my fallopian tubes and ovaries, as well. The cervix, part of the vagina, the lymph nodes, too.

It took nearly six weeks to recover. Physically. Emotionally I never would.

What I hadn't expected were the hot flashes that flared up out of the blue. The sudden, intense heat waves that washed over my body. The rosacea that took over my skin. My heart, beating out of control, the need to drop into a chair and catch my breath as I saw older women — *older women* — often do. The night sweats that kept me up when I wasn't being kept awake by my young child. The insomnia that gave way to moodiness and irritability. The ember flashes that lingered for years after the hot flashes were through.

I was going through menopause. I wasn't yet thirty years old.

I noticed that my metabolism, too, had slowed, inches accumulating on my once-slim waist. Chris claimed not to notice, but I most certainly did. I noticed when pants went from a size four to a size eight, when I began to eye women like Cassidy Knudsen — young, slim and *fertile* — like some green-eyed monster. Green with envy. They were bountiful, fruitful, productive.

And I was barren. Dry and desolate, unable to support growth.

Growing older all the time, much too fast for a woman my age.

"Think of it this way," Chris had said, in an effort to appease me. "You'll never have to worry about getting your period again," uttering that word — *period* — in a squeamish way, and yet I imagined it longingly. What I wouldn't give to go to the drugstore and buy a box of tampons. To experience that monthly flow, a reminder of the life inside me. The anticipation of a life inside me.

But that life was gone.

"Cancer," I whisper, forcing that ugly word out. "Cervical cancer. They had to remove my uterus." I wonder if Willow understands what any of this means.

She sits on the sofa, staring at that TV. Bert and Ernie pass through, with their beloved rubber ducky. Ernie begins to sing.

Her voice is subdued, like a pale shade of pink. Pastel. Subtle. "But you wanted more babies?" she asks.

"Yes," I say, feeling vanquished by that hole in my heart. The one where Juliet used to reside. "Very much so."

Chris said we'd adopt more children. *All the orphans in the world,* he said. *Every last one of them.* But after giving birth to my own flesh and blood, I didn't want those children. I wanted my own. Adoption was no longer a viable option; I couldn't imagine raising a child who was not my own. I felt cheated, swindled. My heart was closed for business.

"You make a good momma," Willow says, and then her eyes drift to the lightning outside, the rumble of thunder that encroaches into the city, like a cancerous growth, and she says, more to herself than to me, "My momma was good."

"Tell me about your momma," I breathe.

And she does. Waveringly.

She tells me about her dark hair.

She tells me about her blue eyes.

She tells me her name. Holly.

She tells me that she did hair. In the bathroom. Cuts and perms and updos. She tells me she liked to cook, but she wasn't too good at it. She'd burn things, or else they'd be undercooked, the inside of her chicken still pink when she bit into it. She liked to listen to music. Country music. Dolly Parton, Loretta Lynn. Patsy Cline.

She isn't looking at me when she speaks, but rather at the Muppets on the TV screen, Big Bird and Elmo, Cookie Monster. She stares at their bright colors, their eccentricities.

"Where is your mother?" I ask, but she ignores this.

I tell her about my father, and as I do so,

a hand instinctively goes to his wedding band dangling from the gold chain around my neck. At the mention of Patsy Cline, her voice returns to me, running like a soundtrack through my mind. Patsy Cline's death left such an impression on my own mother during her teenage years that songs like "Crazy" and "Walkin' After Midnight" became part of my childhood, as did the images of my mother and father twirling around the copper brown living room carpeting, hand in hand, cheek to cheek, dancing.

"That ring," Willow asks, pointing at it. "That's his?" and I say that yes, it is.

And then for whatever reason I tell her about the wild-goose chase Chris and I went on to find a gold chain that matched. It had to be a perfect match. *Close* wasn't good enough for me, wasn't good enough for my father. Chris special ordered the chain, a purchase that cost him over a thousand dollars.

"We could buy a TV for that kind of money. A new computer," he said. "Put it toward a vacation."

But I said no. I had to have the chain.

"This ring," I had said to Chris that day, standing on Wabash in the midst of Jewelers Row, tears dousing my tired, insomniac eyes, eyes which hadn't slept since before my father died, "is all that remains of my father. The rest is gone."

I don't tell Willow how I fell into a state of deep depression after my father died, a quiet, placid death following an altercation with lung cancer, small cell lung cancer, that is, the kind that had metastasized to the brain, the liver and the bone before he ever knew it was there. I don't tell her how he refused treatment. He continued to smoke. Marlboro Reds. Half a pack a day. I don't tell her how my mother buried him with a carton of Marlboro Reds and a neon green lighter, for use in the afterlife.

I do tell Willow about the glorious fall day that we buried my father in the cemetery beside the church, beneath a sugar maple that had turned tangerine overnight. I tell her how the pallbearers carried that casket out of the church, up a spongy hill and to the cemetery. It had rained the night before and the ground was wet. I tell her how my mother and I followed behind. How I held on to my mother so she wouldn't slip, but more so, because I couldn't let go, because I was already burying one parent and I couldn't bear to lose another. I tell her how we watched them lower him in, and then we laid roses on top of the casket. Lavender roses. Because it's what my mother carried when they were wed.

It's then that she looks at me with those tired cornflower eyes and says — in that way one says they hate terrorists or Nazis, as if they are truly an abomination to all mankind, and not just how people say they hate the smell of burnt popcorn or hate the sight of overweight women in midriffs — "I hate roses," and I try hard not to take offense, reminding myself: *to each his own,* and yet it seems a terribly odd response to my confession.

And then she says, after a period of silence so long that I'm all but certain our revelations are through, "My momma is dead."

And that word — *dead* — sneaks out noncommittally, as though she isn't quite sure whether or not she's dead, or what that word really means to her. Like someone told her that her mother was dead, like one says *A drop in the bucket,* or, *a piece of cake.* An idiom. The kind of word or phrase that makes no logical sense.

My momma is dead.

"How?" I ask, but she won't say. Instead, she curls into a ball, hiding inside her armadillo shell. Her eyes remain locked on the TV, though they've grown glassy and inexpressive, as if she's made a hard-line decision not to cry. I ask again, "Willow?" but she ignores this completely, as if unaware of my voice, unaware of the way my eyes are cemented to her, cemented to the wayward hair and the lips caked in ChapStick, desperate for an answer to my question.

An answer that doesn't come.

And then, in time — when she tires of my staring perhaps — she lifts the baby from my arms and leaves the room.

CHRIS

I'm taking the steps, two at a time, down to the "L" platform when the call comes in on my cell. Henry. I stop midstride and retreat to street level, leaning against the fence that encloses the steps leading underground. The street is full of cars and pedestrians heading home from work. It's not quite dark outside, one of those rare workdays I leave the office on time. A bus is holding up traffic on the street; some suburbanite or out-of-towner tries to bypass it, nearly killing a half-dozen pedestrians at the same time. Brakes squeal. A horn blares. Someone yells, "Asshole!" and shoots the driver the finger.

I shield the setting sun from my eyes with the back of a hand, and say, "I don't even want to hear it," into the phone. It's hard to hear Henry over the commotion of the city, but I make out the sound of his laugh, loud and obnoxious, like nails on a chalkboard.

"Hello to you, too, Wood," Henry says, and I have visions of him on the commode making this call. His pants are down around his knees. There's a magazine spread across his lap. *Playboy.* "Kiss that pretty wife of yours goodbye. We head out in the morning."

"What now?" I ask and he says, "Road show. Denver by way of New York."

"Damn," I say. It's not that this comes as a complete surprise. We've been preparing for this dog and pony show for weeks. But still. Heidi is going to be pissed.

The train ride home is quiet. I depart the "L" at the Fullerton Station and walk down the steps onto the street. There is a homeless man leaning against the cast-iron fence beside the newspaper stands, eyes closed as if he's fast asleep. Beside him sits a black garbage bag, stuffed full with all of his earthly possessions. He shivers in his sleep in the biting fifty-degree day.

My first thought: those big legs of his, long and gangly, lost in a pair of light blue hospital scrubs, are in my way. Like the other people moving down the street, I step over him with exaggerated strides. But then something makes me stop and turn, to see the redness of his cheeks and ears, the way he's got one hand on that garbage bag in case someone tries to steal it in his sleep. I pull my wallet from a back pocket and search inside, forcing the sound of Heidi's voice from my mind. I drop a ten-dollar bill beside the man, hoping the wind doesn't carry it away before he opens his eyes.

It'd be just my luck if my good deed went unnoticed.

When I come into the condo, the TV is on. *Sesame Street.* Heidi's got that baby laid out on its stomach in front of the TV, and she's educating Willow about the fine art of tummy time, hoping the big furry monsters distract the baby long enough that she forgets how much she hates being on her stomach, floundering around like a fish out of water.

Zoe stands in the kitchen, eyeing her cell phone on the counter. She jumps when I come bumbling through the door, as if caught red-handed doing something wrong. She ebbs slowly away, one step at a time, before Heidi can see her proximity to the phone.

Heidi greets me with, "I thought you were going to be home sooner." She barely raises her eyes from the baby, who she inundates with all sorts of shrill baby talk and overblown facial expressions, but for me, nothing.

It's nearly seven o'clock.

"Can I speak to you, Heidi?" I ask as I hang a jacket on the hook by the door. Her eyes graze mine as she lifts that baby from the floor and hands her to the girl who handles her so maladroitly that for a split second I think the baby may fall. And then that stupid woolly mammoth is on the TV, Aloysius Snuffleupagus, and the girl stares, dumbstruck, and it occurs to me that Zoe hasn't watched *Sesame Street* since she was about two years old.

Heidi follows me into the bedroom, her feet light as air on the hardwood floors. Mine, in contrast, are heavy, clobbering the floor as if I have something to prove. The cats scamper away, so I won't step on their tails, and hide under the bed. While I change out of my work shirt and into a white and maroon sweatshirt — my old alma mater, of course, *Go, Phoenix, go!* — I tell her about the road show. About how I'll be in New York for a day or two, followed by Denver for a few days. How I'm leaving in the morning.

I'm expecting a lashing — fingers wagging and eyes rolling — some dismissive comment about Cassidy Knudsen, a grilling about whether or not *that floozy* will accompany me on this trip . . . and yet, none of it comes.

She's quiet for a split second, and then Heidi simply shrugs her shoulders and says, "Okay," and goes so far as to heave the laundry basket downstairs to make sure I have plenty of clean undies for my trip.

I should be concerned. I know that. But not being reprimanded like a ten-year-old boy is pure bliss.

I pack. I warm up leftover pizza for dinner while Heidi gathers quarters and excuses herself to throw the laundry in the dryer. Zoe is in her bedroom, working on earth science, or so she claims. But I see her instead, on her bed, with that yellow notebook across her lap. The one where she keeps her intimate thoughts about how her father's a doofus, her mother loony. Or maybe in that notebook she writes about Austin, or maybe Willow. How would I know? Maybe, just maybe, she's a closet poet, filling the pages with limericks and odes.

In the room with Willow and me, there's nothing but dead air.

And baby noises: coos and squeals and grunts and such.

I find myself staring at the palms of her

hands for evidence of a tattoo, the butterfly with its black and yellow wings. I wonder: if she'd had it removed, would there be a scar? Bleached out skin? Leftover remnants of the tattoo?

But on her hands there is nothing, nada. And yet there are those earrings, the very same earrings as in the Twitter profile. How could that be?

I peek to make sure Willow isn't paying attention, and then I check my Twitter account stealthily to see if *@LostWithoutU* ever responded to my Tweet. No such luck. But I have eight new followers, a fact that I let go to my head.

How would Willow ever reply, I wonder, if she doesn't have access to a computer? *Does* she have access to a computer? I think about that nasty old suitcase she lugged into our home, the one perched in the corner of my office, the leather cracked and brittle, losing shape. Is there a laptop inside, some smartphone with Wi-Fi where she could respond to tweets? I've never seen her on it, never heard it ring.

The girl has enough trouble handling a remote control. I find it hard to believe she's got a smartphone or a computer. But I don't know. Mine and Heidi's are both password protected; there's no way she's getting on them at night.

The girl is staring lifelessly at the TV. I've changed the channel to the news. A roundup of the day's baseball games. It's opening day. I'm guessing she doesn't give a hoot about baseball, but she stares at the TV so she doesn't have to talk to me. She sits far away, as far as she can get, hugging the far end of the sofa though I'm at the kitchen table, a good ten feet away or more. She sips from a glass of water and I watch the way her hand, the water, how they shake, ripples forming on the surface of the glass.

"Where are you from anyway?" I ask. I hate the silence. But more than that, I'm reminded that I'm the only one in this house intent on figuring this girl out. And this — two minutes or so alone with Willow, my interrogation uninterrupted by Heidi's watchful eye and regulations — may be my only chance at doing just that.

She stares at me. It's not a nervy kind of stare. In fact, it's the exact opposite. Meek. Timid.

But she says nothing.

"You don't want to tell me?" I ask.

She's slow to respond. But then she shakes her head, a movement so subtle, if I blinked, I would've missed it.

"No, sir," she whispers. I like that she calls me sir.

"And why's that?" I ask. I listen to her response, try to decipher a dialect but come up empty. She sounds like a standard Midwesterner. Like me. Standard American English.

Willow says cautiously, her voice so quiet I have to lean in to hear her over the baby's babble, "You might make me go home."

And I ask, treading lightly, "Is there a reason you don't want to go home?"

The news blares from the TV, opening day games giving way to the day's top stories. A brutal home invasion and stabbing on South Ashland that instantly catches the girl's attention. I grope for the remote control and change the channel just as body bags are ushered out of the home on stretchers. I land on home shopping.

"Willow," I say again, hoping the accuracy of her name will earn me bonus points. "Is there a reason you don't want to go home, Willow?"

"Yes, sir," she admits, picking at the fringe on the edge of a throw pillow. She isn't looking at me.

"Why's that?"

"It's just —" She stutters. "It's just — that . . ."

I think she'll never finish that thought, and then she says, "I don't like it very much, is all."

An inadequate response if there ever was one.

"Why not?" I prod. There's no response and so I ask again, *"Willow?"* this time with a jagged edge to my voice. I'm losing my patience.

Heidi will be back soon.

An invisible wall goes up around the girl. She doesn't do well with impatience. She needs to be prepped first. Like flower seeds needing to be soaked in water overnight for faster germination. She isn't going to open up until we penetrate that outer hull.

I lower my voice, and turn on the charm. I smile and try again. "Was somebody mean to you?" I ask instead, my voice as comforting as it can be. I'm not known for my compassion. But I try.

Her eyes rise to mine. Blue eyes that carry much too much baggage for someone her age, the blood vessels swollen, sagging tissue around the eyes, blood pooling under the skin, causing dark circles to form. I'm on the edge of my seat. Waiting. Desperate to hear what she has to say. She opens her mouth to speak. To tell me. "It's okay," I say. "You can tell me."

But then I hear the sound of Heidi's keys jiggling in the lock and I silently will her back downstairs to the laundry room, in vain. Willow jumps at the sound, scared to death by the harmless tinny sound of keys. I see the fear take over her eyes, as the water glass slips from her hand, tumbling to the ground below. The glass doesn't break against the shag rug, and yet, water spills. Everywhere. She drops frantically to her knees and begins to clean up the mess, to spot the water with the edge of her shirt, her eyes darting between Heidi and me as if she thinks she might be punished for this little blunder.

Beneath her breath she mutters an incomprehensible jumble about forgiveness and sins.

Keys. Keys in a lock. Being locked in?

I make a mental note of this.

I'm not one to feel sympathetic, but for a split second I feel the slightest bit sorry for the girl floundering around on the floor, praying to the gods for mercy.

"Honey, please," Heidi begs as she retrieves a towel from the kitchen drawer and hurries to Willow's side, "please don't worry about it."

I do my part, leaning over to retrieve the glass from the floor.

But I see the terror in the girl's eyes and know that I cannot undo what has been done.

We sleep, Heidi, Zoe, the cats and me locked in the bedroom. In the early morning before I leave — the sun just rubbing at its eyes and preparing to start the day — I wake and remind Heidi that this is as it should be every night that I am gone, her and Zoe in the room together, door locked.

I am out the door by five, lugging my suitcase and briefcase down the hall for a cab ride out to O'Hare.

The girl and her baby are asleep when I go, their own door pulled to and presumably locked, as well, my office chair possibly slid under the door's handle for an extra safeguard in case we try to force our way in while she sleeps.

The sun is beginning to rise, painting the sky gold. As the cabbie, with his talk radio and the overwhelming smell of a pine-scented air freshener filling the cab, careens down I-90, I lay my briefcase on the seat beside me. I reach inside for a notebook and pen, to get some work done on the ride. It's a solid thirty minutes out to O'Hare on a good day, and judging by the buildup of cars already on the interstate, I'm guessing it won't be a good day.

I toss open the briefcase, and there I see it, a note, scribbled on a purple sticky note, the answer to last night's unanswered question.

A note that sucks the oxygen right out of the cab.

Handwriting I've never seen.

The simple inscription: *Yes.*

WILLOW

Louise Flores wants to know more about Matthew and Isaac, my *foster brothers* if that's what you call them. The term *brother* implies some kind of familial tendency, of which there was none. Not with Joseph. Not with Miriam or Isaac.

But Matthew. Matthew was different.

Sitting there in the meager room, across the table from Louise *F-l-o-r-e-s,* I picture Matthew, tall, like his father, but with hair the color of chocolate brownies, Momma's chocolate brownies, and dark brown eyes. I imagined that this was what Miriam must have looked like once, long ago, before she became a mousy gray. Isaac, on the other hand, was Joseph through and through: a carrot top with orange hair on his arms, his legs, his chin.

"What about them?" I ask, and the lady says: "Did you get along with them? Did they participate in this *alleged* sexual abuse as Joseph did? Or were they victims, as well? What was their relationship with their catatonic mother?"

"Catatonic?" I ask.

"Yes. In a daze. Unresponsive." She says that she assumes Miriam suffered from a condition called catatonic schizophrenia, based on my description. *If,* she says, *what you say is true,* as always implying that it is not.

A troll, I think. An imp. I envision Miriam parked in the corner of her room on the wicker armchair, staring into space, while in the room next to hers, her husband did as he pleased.

My bedroom shared a wall with Matthew and Isaac's bedroom, and for the first year or so, that alone was the only association we had. We ate no meals together. Looked away or downward when we passed each other in the halls of the home. Matthew and Isaac were made to share a room when Joseph and Miriam brought me in, and I didn't know if they liked it or not because no one talked much in that house. Matthew and Isaac spent much of their day in school, and when they were home, they were in their room, doing homework and reading from the Bible. Joseph didn't allow any exchange with me, and he would readily remind Matthew and Isaac that: "Bad company ruins good morals," when their eyes so much as wandered in my direction.

To this end, Isaac never changed. If anything, he became more like Joseph as time went on, a lemming ready to plunge off a cliff at his father's request. But Matthew was different.

I remember the night, the first time we really spoke. I was ten. I'd been living in that house for almost a year, and in that time, Joseph had visited me two dozen or more times. I laid in bed, well after midnight, unable to sleep as was almost always the case. I was thinking of Momma and Daddy and rattling off as many "I love you likes" as I possibly could. And then there were footsteps, outside in the hall, moving along the wooden floorboards to my bedroom door. I held my breath, waiting for Joseph to come in, to slide his clammy body into bed beside mine. I began to shudder as I always did when Joseph's footsteps clamored down the hall and that, in itself, set in motion a whole slew of things: my heart beating as though it might jump from my chest, the sweaty hands, sweaty everything, the inability to see straight, the ringing in my ears.

And then the door slid open and standing there, in the darkness, was a much different

276

profile than that which I was used to seeing. And the voice was different, softer somehow, tender, equally as scared as I was. "Did you know that cockroaches can live for a week without their heads?" he asked. And then I knew, by the sound of his hushed voice: Matthew.

"They can?" I whispered, sitting upright in bed, propped on my elbows in the nearly black room, the only light from a nearby streetlight that flickered off and on, off and on. All. Night. Long.

"Yup," he said. "Sometimes a month. They die from lack of water."

"Oh."

And we stood like that in absolute silence, for a minute or more, and then he closed the door and went into his room.

The next day I found a book slid under the mattress of the bed, sandwiched in between the patchwork quilt and a scalloped dust ruffle: *A Children's Guide to Insects and Spiders.* I knew it was from him. When Joseph went to work, and Matthew and Isaac disappeared down the street, joining the other kids at the bus stop, those kids who heckled them and called them names, I sat on that bed of mine and devoured the book.

Momma had sent me to school back in Ogallala, and that school had taught me to read, and Momma used to make me read to her every night before bed, everything from her fashion magazines to the Julia Child cookbooks to the mail. I was a good reader. I wolfed down that book from Matthew on the very first day, and then slipped it back into his room, under his bed before he and Isaac, or Joseph, got home. I learned everything I could about earwigs and mantids, cicadas and damselflies. I learned that horseflies live for thirty to sixty days, that queen bees hibernate in the dirt in winter, that periodical cicadas only appear every thirteen or seventeen years.

A few days later, a new book arrived: *Sea Anemones.* I read how they looked like flowers, but really were not. Instead, they were predators of the sea. They didn't age like others plants and animals. They had the ability to live forever, to be *immortal,* the book said. That book taught me how the sea anemone injected venom into its prey, and how that venom paralyzed the prey so the sea anemone could swoop fish, shrimp and plankton into their carnivorous mouths.

I didn't like those sea anemones one bit: so pretty and celestial, and yet assassins. Would-be murderers in delicate, angelic bodies. It didn't seem fair. It was a trick, a trap, an illusion.

A few days later: *Rocks and Minerals.* And then another book, and another. Nearly every week Matthew was slipping another book from the school's library under my mattress: *Charlotte's Web* and *The Diary of a Young Girl* and *From the Mixed-Up Files of Mrs. Basil E. Frankweiler,* which I read in the moments that I wasn't cleaning house or bathing Miriam, or making tuna salad sandwiches for dinner.

Every now and again, Matthew would pause by my bedroom door in the middle of the night, along the way to the bathroom or to the kitchen for a glass of water. I got to know which footsteps were Matthew's and which belonged to Joseph. Matthew's footsteps were light and airy as they moved down the hall, then hesitant as he closed in on my room, as if not knowing whether or not they should pause by my bedroom door. Joseph's, on the other hand, had their minds made up. They were coming to my room, right through the white door without a second thought or a moment's hesitation.

Matthew pulled the door open carefully, so it wouldn't squeak, while Joseph flung it straight open, never mind if its bellowing woke someone in the house. Matthew stayed a couple seconds, at best, and would offer some tidbit of information that really, I didn't give two shits about and chances are he didn't, either. I came to understand it wasn't about the information itself but the exchange: a pact, a bond.

I was not alone.

One night: "Did you know a crocodile can't stick out its tongue?" And another: "Did you know nothing rhymes with orange?" and I admitted that no, I didn't know that, and spent the rest of the sleepless night trying to come up with *something* to rhyme with orange. Something so that I could tell him about it the next time he passed by. Porange. Yorange. Florange.

Nope. Nothing.

"Did you know Venus is the hottest planet? Its surface can be 450 degrees Celsius. That's over 800 degrees." And I kind of just stared because really, I didn't know much about Celsius or Fahrenheit, and in all honesty, I was starting to forget all about Venus. It had been so long since I'd sat in a classroom back in Ogallala and learned about the planets and weather and all that. The next day there was another book: a book on astronomy.

One night Matthew passed through and said to me, "Did you know my folks get almost twenty bucks a day to foster you?"

"What?" I asked. I'd never heard of such

a thing. "From who?" I wondered if the money was coming from what little money Momma and Daddy used to have, or if my caseworker was paying my fare.

But in the near darkness, Matthew shook his head and said, "From the good ol' state of Nebraska. That's who." He stood in the doorway, in the plaid pants he wore every night to bed, and a white undershirt with yellow stains down the front, two inches too short for his lanky body.

"Lily, too?" I asked, wondering if Paul and Lily Zeeger were making twenty bucks a day to care for Lily.

But Matthew said no. "Not when you're adopted. The Zeegers had to *pay* for Lily. Like ten thousand dollars or something."

"Huh?" I asked, disbelieving. Ten thousand dollars was a lot of money. The Zeegers bought my Lily like you'd buy a shirt at the store. I didn't know how I felt about that, if I was supposed to feel good that they'd fork over that much money to own my Lily, or if I was supposed to feel bad because she was just like any other commodity you might find at the supermarket. Clothing. Peanut butter. Bug spray.

I wondered if one day, if I ever had more than ten thousand dollars, if I could buy my Lily back. Or maybe, one day, the Zeegers would want to return her, like a shirt that didn't quite fit right. Maybe one day Lily would be for sale again, and I'd figure out a way to buy her myself.

But what really rubbed me the wrong way was that Joseph and Miriam were getting *paid* for keeping me. They didn't buy me like the Zeegers bought Lily.

"How do you know?" I asked.

He shrugged, like *duh.* "I just *do.*" And then he closed the door and walked away.

"Why didn't you ever try to run away?" asks Ms. Flores. By now the man in the corner, the guard, has leaned in and I know he's wondering the very same thing. Why didn't I try to run? I glance at him, his brown eyes prodding me on from behind a navy uniform that looks like something his dad should be wearing, not him. He is a boy, not a man.

"Well," they say, those eyes, "why didn't you?"

"I was scared," I say. "Scared to stay and scared to go. God would be mad at me if I disobeyed Joseph. That's what he told me. That's what he made me believe."

I knew that there was no way I could go. Not at first anyway. Not that there was anywhere *to* go, but if I left, Joseph would do something to harm Lily — that he told me nearly a million times — and if by some chance he didn't, then God would send his thunderstorms and vultures after me, and I wouldn't stand a chance. He'd turn me into a salt pillar. Drown me with a flood. "I was a kid," I remind her. Before going to live with Joseph and Miriam, I believed in Santa Claus, the Tooth Fairy, the Easter Bunny. Until I lost a canine tooth, that is, and stuck it under the pillow on my bed and waited all night for one of the shiny gold coins the Tooth Fairy used to leave me back in Ogallala.

But she didn't come.

I made believe she couldn't find me, there in that house in Omaha, that she was flying all over Ogallala looking for me.

And then I started to wonder about things back home, in the prefab house on Canyon Drive. I wondered if another family had moved into that home, into *my* home, and if some other little girl was sleeping in *my* bed. The one with the hot-pink quilt — with orange polka dots all over — and lacy indigo curtains Momma had made with fabric she found on clearance, though they didn't match a thing. I wondered if that little girl was hugging *my* favorite stuffed purple kitten, all wrapped up in *my* hot-pink quilt, reading aloud from *my* favorite picture books with her momma, awakening in the morning to find *my* shiny gold coin tucked neatly under *my* fluffy pillow.

I told Matthew about it, one night when he passed by my room. I told him how the Tooth Fairy couldn't find me. How I was still holding on to that shiny canine tooth. How I didn't know what to do, how to get it to the Tooth Fairy so she could use it to build her gleaming white castle in Fairyland.

"Fairyland?" he whispered. And I told him how the Tooth Fairy used all those millions of teeth she collected to build a shimmering castle and village for her and all of her fairy friends. And they called it Fairyland.

He just stared at me, dumbly, like he didn't know what to say.

And then he kinda stuttered, "There ain't no Tooth Fairy, Claire," he said. It was quiet for a real long time. And then, "Throw it away."

And just like the day Momma and Daddy died, a little part of me died, too.

I was too scared to ask about Santa Claus and the Easter Bunny. But when Christmas came and went again, with no presents, I knew the reason. And it wasn't that I'd been a naughty girl that year.

Days later Matthew left a new book under

my mattress: a book of fairy tales. *Goldilocks* and *The Three Little Pigs, Rumpelstiltskin.*

But the one that interested me the most was the story of *The Pied Piper of Hamlin,* the tale of a funny-looking man who played his magic pipe to lure the children away from town. They were never seen again. I envisioned Joseph, dressed like a medieval jester from the pages of the fairy-tale book, in a motley coat and tights, playing his pipe up and down the streets of Ogallala to lure the children from their homes. Children like me.

I wasn't sure what scared me the most about living with Joseph and Miriam. Joseph with his hawk eyes and aquiline nose or the vengeful God Joseph told me about or the things he said he would do to my Lily if ever I misbehaved, how he would trap her and skin her alive. He told me how he'd do it, too, how he'd hang her by her feet, then cut her jugular and carotid veins with a blade so that she'd bleed to death. Then, with slow, deliberate movements, he sliced his cold fingers against my throat, so I knew exactly what he meant. He used words like *sinews* and *corpuscles,* words that I didn't know, but they scared me nonetheless.

Funny how thinking about that God of Joseph's, and of all the things Joseph would do to Lily if I was bad, somehow made me feel safer inside that home, staring out at the boys on their bikes and the girls with their chalk, kids like me who had no idea what was going on inside Joseph and Miriam's home. To them we were just the odd ducks on the block, what Momma used to call old Mrs. Waters from down the street, the widow, who walked around talking to her dead husband as if she were chatting on the phone. I imagined those kids out that window, the kids with the bikes and the chalk, and their own mommas and daddies telling them never to play with Isaac and Matthew 'cause they were weird. Not to talk to Joseph because he was an *odd duck,* and then later, when all was said and done, it would be those mommas and daddies who told police that they felt something funny was going on inside our home, all along, they felt that something wasn't quite right. Something they couldn't put their finger on.

But they didn't do a thing about it.

HEIDI

I slip from bed once Chris leaves, quiet so as not to wake Zoe from sleep. Beside me, she sleeps like a newborn, on her back, arms up in the air: the starfish position, the rising sun casting a golden hue across her face. I watch her sleep, the sass and defiance at bay for a time, her features relaxed, her lips flirting with a smile. I wonder what it is that she dreams about, as she lets out a sigh, and rolls over onto her side, taking the warm spot on the ivory sheets where my body has just been. I reach for the comforter from the end of the bed, and pull it up over her shoulders, closing the blinds so the impending sunlight stays out of her eyes.

I walk into the hall, pulling the door to, and find my feet traipsing across the hall to the closed office door, my hand coming to rest on the satin nickel knob. I press my ear to the door and listen for signs of movement, of which there are none. My heart beats loudly, quickly in my chest. My palms begin to perspire.

I'm overwhelmed with a sudden need, a very basic human need, like food, shelter, clothing.

A need to hold that baby in my arms.

There's no logic as I set my sweaty palm on that satin nickel knob, only an instinct, a reflex, some innate behavior.

I know that I shouldn't and yet I do; I turn the knob silently, astonished to find it unlocked.

An omen.

They lay side by side on the pull-out couch, Willow and the baby, a green chenille throw covering their bodies. Willow has her back turned to the baby, a pillow set over her head as if trying to tune out the sound of midnight cries or coos, or maybe Chris's early morning shower before he departed for New York. Willow breathes deeply, evidence of a deep sleep. I tiptoe across the room, cursing a cat who follows me in, scampering under the sofa bed for a place to hide. The drapes are drawn, keeping the outside world out, tiny bands of light sneaking in through the opening in the middle, lustrous early morning light tinged with pink and gold.

In her deep sleep, Willow fails to notice

the way my feet tread lightly across the carpeted room, and in my mind I'm envisioning no Willow, no sleeper sofa.

Just a beautiful baby in a bassinet waiting for someone to arrive.

The baby's eyes are wide-awake when I finally adjust to the darkness of the room and can see her clearly. She is staring with wonderment at the white ceiling, and when she sees me, she smiles. Her legs start kicking in excitement, her arms flailing wildly about. I slip my hands under the weight of her body and lift her from the bed. Willow lets out a sleepy sigh, but doesn't open her eyes.

I press that baby to my chest, my lips to her head, and together we walk out of the room.

I settle into the rocking chair with the baby. "There now," I utter aloud, swaying rhythmically with the baby on my lap. I count her fingers, I count her toes. I run my hand across her silken head and breathe in the silence of the room, silent save for the steady ticktock of a wooden wall clock, its distressed white finish and Roman numerals just barely visible in the light of the rising sun. Outside the sun begins its ascent over Lake Michigan, turning the east-facing sides of the buildings a golden hue. There are clouds in the sky, cottony clouds, in shades of silver and pink, a pale pink clutching the edges of the clouds. A flock of birds flies through the sky, sparrows I assume, and a mourning dove perches on the edge of the wooden balcony, staring in through the bay window, watching me. The baby and me. Its beady eyes stare, its small head tilting from side to side, side to side, asking a question only it knows. The street below is quiet, just the occasional early morning pedestrian headed to work or out for a jog. The city bus passes by, quickly, not bothering to stop at the vacant bus stops; taxis soar by without pause.

I press my bare feet to the hardwood floors and force the chair back and forth, back and forth, aware of the way the baby presses her face to my flannel pajamas, rummaging around for food, for a nipple from which to feed, like a hungry, suckling piglet pressing its way into its mother's teat to drink.

I was a firm believer in breastfeeding Zoe when I still could. Chris and I never truly talked about it; it was something I planned to do. And Chris wasn't about to argue; my breastfeeding Zoe meant there would be no midnight feedings for him, no hungry baby awakening him in the middle of the night.

He could sleep the night clear through while Zoe and I sat together on a glider in her nursery for hours on end.

There were many benefits to breastfeeding, everything from financial benefits, to breast milk's ability to fight disease, though Chris eyeballed me squeamishly whenever I nursed. But for me, it was also about convenience. It was far more convenient for those late-night feedings to simply place baby Zoe on my breast and let her eat to her heart's content. There was no need to prepare bottles, to wash bottles and, more than anything, I felt an intimacy to my newborn, an indispensability that I haven't felt from Zoe in many, many years now. She needed me. As she needed me to rock her to sleep, to change her diaper, but unlike those things, this — breastfeeding — was the one thing only I could provide for her. It was something only I could give.

I planned to nurse until she was a year old and then I planned to wean her from the breast.

But once I fell ill and caring for my own health became a priority, my plans changed. Zoe's breastfeeding was quickly discontinued, and she was forced onto a formula-filled bottle, something that she didn't take to well. There was a part of me half-certain that she, my baby, resented me for the sudden change, for the fact that I never asked her opinion before thrusting a silicone nipple in her mouth. She would scream when I did, refusing to latch on to the foreign object, refusing to drink the foreign milk. In time, she learned to adapt, of course, through trial and error, a half dozen types of bottles and nipples, a half dozen brands of formula until we found one she would consume, one which didn't upset her stomach, one she didn't refuse.

But Willow — I think, completely cognizant of the way the baby roots around in the pleats of my shirt — I've never seen Willow breastfeed.

Why, then, is the baby exploring the shirt of my flannel pajamas for a nipple, the agitation brimming in her tiny little body because she can't make her way past the clear plastic buttons to find my breast.

But I don't have the time to think it through, to come up with a list of sensible scenarios, like engorgement or an inadequate milk supply, because there she is, Willow, standing before me in the room. Her long hair sweeps across her face so that all I can see are her eyes — moody and mistrusting eyes, which fall on me like meteors from the sky. Eyes that make me suddenly wonder how virtuous this girl is, how trust-worthy.

And once again my thoughts go to the blood on the undershirt.

She says, "You took the baby. You took Ruby from my room."

And I say calmly, "Yes. I did," and then I think fast for some excuse. "She was cry-ing," I lie. It's instantaneous, spontaneous, far too easy a thing to do. "I didn't want her to wake you," I say. "I was up anyway. Just about to start a pot of coffee. When I heard her crying."

"She's hungry," Willow says to me, her voice soft, watching as I watch the baby paw at my chest.

"Yes," I say, "I was just about to make her a bottle," but Willow says with a sureness I'm certain I've never heard from her be-fore, "I'll do it," and her eyes stray to the coffeemaker, yesterday's remains now syr-upy and cold.

"You haven't had your coffee," she says, and I tell myself she is simply being helpful, doing her share. I tell myself there isn't an edge to her voice as she gropes the baby awkwardly and removes her from my lap. Suddenly, I feel as if something has been taken from me, something that was mine.

Perhaps Willow isn't as wide-eyed and

green as she's led me to believe.

She's taken the baby and stands now in my kitchen, baby thrust to a hip, holding her awkwardly as she tries to prepare a bottle, as the baby wiggles ferociously in her arms, her eyes glistening with tears. The baby stares at me, her arms reaching past Willow for me — I'm just sure of it — as I remain on the rocking chair, unable to rise and make my coffee because I can think of nothing but wanting that baby returned to me. My blood pressure is rising, sweat pooling under my arms, sticking to the flannel. I feel suddenly unable to breathe, unable to find enough oxygen to fill up my lungs.

The baby is staring at me, her eyes still, though everything else is flailing about. Her feet kick at Willow, her hands pull madly on Willow's sepia-toned hair. The baby's skin has turned a beet red, and at Willow's sluggishness, she begins to scream. Willow takes the abuse as if she barely notices, and yet it makes her clumsy, makes her knock the formula-filled bottle to the floor, the white powder creeping its way into the cracks of the floorboards. And I could help. I could, but I find I'm frozen still, like a statue, my body glued to the rocking chair, my eyes locked on the baby's.

A door parts from down the hall, followed

by the sound of Zoe's voice, half-asleep and annoyed, the child who once clung to my breast needing me and only me. Now she didn't want a thing to do with me.

"Doesn't anybody sleep around here?" she asks, piqued, not making eye contact with Willow or me as she emerges into sight.

I manage a, "Good morning," my voice breathless, as Zoe slides drunkenly down the hall, the strands of her auburn hair in a complete state of lawlessness and anarchy.

Zoe says nothing. She drops to the sofa and flips on the TV, MTV, the preteen equivalent to caffeine.

"And good morning to you, too," I mutter to myself, sarcastically, my eyes staring at the baby with longing, craving another chance to do this right.

WILLOW

Ms. Flores asks to know more about Matthew. Just talking about Matthew somehow brings a smile to my face. I don't say anything, but Ms. Flores sees that smile and says to me, "You like Matthew, don't you?" and suddenly that smile goes away. Just like that.

"Matthew is my friend," I say.

I tell her about Matthew passing by my room at night, about how he left the books under my mattress so I didn't turn into a dimwit like Miriam.

But that was before.

Matthew was six years older than me. He was fifteen when I came to live in that home in Omaha. I was nine. It wasn't too long before he was done with school, and by the time I was twelve or thirteen, maybe fourteen, he'd moved out of the house. Just one day, when Joseph was at work, he packed up his things and decided to leave. But he

296

didn't go far.

Instead of going to college like his friends were doing — Matthew couldn't afford college — he worked at the gas station down the road, and for a while, instead of bringing books for me, like he did when he was in school, he brought candy bars and bags of chips when he came to visit, the kinds of foods Joseph swore were the devil's creation.

I didn't know where Matthew slept at night. He didn't talk about it much. Sometimes he'd talk about living in a big, tall brick building with an air conditioner and a big-screen TV but even I knew he was lying. Other days it might be that he was traveling down the Missouri River in a barge. He just didn't want me to feel bad for him, is all. But of course, anything would be better than living there, in that home with Joseph and Miriam, with Isaac, whose own eyes had started to have that same thirst I saw in Joseph's the nights he came into my room.

But still, sometimes, Matthew would come to the home in Omaha on the days when Isaac was at school and Joseph was at work, and Miriam, of course, was in her own room, oblivious to the world around her. He'd tell me how he might just join the army, how he was making more than I might think in that gas station down the street.

But even I could tell how his eyes looked tired, how sometimes he smelled as though he hadn't bathed for days, how his clothes always smelled, how sometimes he'd nap on that bed of mine while I washed a shirt or a pair of his jeans, or scavenged the cabinets for something for him to eat. Every now and then he'd search around that house for some money, a dollar bill here, some forgotten coins there, and he'd stuff them in a pocket, and I came to believe that Matthew was getting by on that money alone, on whatever money he could steal from Joseph. Once he found a twenty-dollar bill in the pocket of an old coat Joseph didn't wear anymore, and I could see in Matthew's eyes: it was as if he'd struck gold.

Matthew wanted to get me out of the house. I knew he did. He just didn't know how, is all. One day, he swore, when he had more money. Like Momma, Matthew was starting to talk a lot about *one day*. One day he'd have enough money. One day he'd get me far, far away from there.

I thought about Joseph and Miriam getting paid to foster me, and I wished that maybe Matthew could foster me instead.

But that was the child in me talking, the

real me knew nothing like that would ever happen.

I could tell that something was changing in Matthew. He talked about bigger things than cockroaches and Venus now. He talked about getting me out of that house, away from Joseph. Homeless people living on the city's streets.

Matthew continued to bring books for me that he picked up at the public library. I fantasized about that library, about the fact that without any money, you could read all the hundreds of thousands of books for free. Matthew told me about it time and again, about the four floors of nothing but books, and I wondered how long it would take me to read them all. Matthew would bring a book or two when he came by to visit, and let me keep them until the next time, and when I finished the cleaning and the laundry, and I had taken out the trash, I would lie down on my bed and read from the pages of whatever it was that Matthew had brought.

Matthew and I would perch together on the edge of my bed, sometimes, him looking too big for my room, like a full size man trying to squeeze into a doll's house, and together we would read. I could tell that Matthew was changing from the boy who

299

used to stop by my room and tell me about Venus and dumb stuff about bugs. He was filling out, no longer a broomstick, but now a man. His voice was lower, his eyes much more complicated than I remembered in the days when he and Isaac would walk home from school, staring down at the concrete, trying hard to ignore the punches they received.

I felt like something was changing in me, too. I felt different around Matthew, somehow. Nervous like I'd only ever been that first time he came into my room, when I wasn't sure what he was there to do. Matthew looked at me like no one in the world ever had. He talked to me like no one had since Momma and Daddy. We'd read together from this book or that — my favorite being *Anne of Green Gables,* one I must've asked Matthew a hundred times to get from that four-story library — and when we got to a hard word I didn't know how to say, Matthew would help me with it, and never did he give me that look like I was dumb.

I learned a lot in those books, about science and nature, about how unstable air caused thunderstorms, about how, in some parts of the world, thunderstorms happened every day. About how lightning was actually *good* for people and plants, not something to fear.

I started wondering if Joseph was wrong, about the fire and brimstone and all that stuff. I started thinking that maybe when the thunderstorms rattled across the land, shaking the living daylights out of our small Omaha home, it wasn't God coming for me because he was mad.

It was just a thunderstorm after all.

But I didn't dare tell Joseph.

One day Matthew arrived with burns on his arms and hands, the skin raw and red and blistery. I could tell that it hurt, the way he cradled one hand in the other, one of his forearms wrapped up in a gauze bandage. He came into the house quiet-like, like maybe he wasn't sure I should see. I gasped when I saw him, hurrying into the kitchen to get him a bag of ice.

What he told me was there was a fire at the shelter where he was staying. When I asked him where he was staying, he said a homeless shelter. I thought of Momma collecting our old clothes for the *homeless,* but otherwise that word didn't have a whole lot of meaning to me. I thought of Matthew wearing someone's old clothes, sleeping on someone's old bedspread, and the thought made me feel sad.

I knew Matthew wasn't lying about the homeless shelter because when he told me about it, he actually looked at me, but when he told me about riding barges on the Missouri River, he looked away, at the peeling wallpaper in my room or the old paint that lay hidden beneath.

He had a bag with him, stuffed near full with everything he owned. He said he wouldn't be going back to that or any other homeless shelter ever again. He was through.

At first he didn't tell me exactly what happened to give him those burns. But he did tell me about the shelter itself. How it was too crowded. How there weren't enough beds for everyone, how some nights he had to sleep on the floor. How he kept his belongings tucked beneath his bed, feeling lucky if they were still there come morning. He told me about the rows of identical bunk beds with the gaunt mattresses and mismatching bedspreads, some stained and torn, others brand-new. *Donated,* Matthew told me, *because they weren't good enough for the rest of the world,* and I could see in his eyes that that's how he felt: not good enough for the rest of the world, and I wanted to tell him that it wasn't true.

He said that the others there, they were drug addicts and drunks, and the people that ran the place, they couldn't care less. He told me that in order to get clean sheets or a square meal, sometimes he had to do things he didn't want to do.

"Like what?" I asked.

"You don't want to know," he said.

And then he told me what happened there, in that homeless shelter, to give him those burns. He didn't tell me because I asked, because I didn't ask. I wasn't sure I wanted to know that, either.

He told me about a fire. Maybe faulty electric wiring, he said, but more likely arson. I asked him what that meant — *arson* — and he said someone was upset when there wasn't enough room in the shelter for them to stay, and so they took a match to the place, and torched it, he said, leaving two dead, a man and his ten-year-old son. The fire escapes were barred with beds and belongings, so that there was only one way in or out.

I looked hard at those burns, the red skin that bulged from his hands. I pictured a building consumed in fire the way Matthew said it was, the walls left black and charred, everything inside burned to a crisp. This picture made me think of that place Joseph told me about, the one where sinners go. Hell. A place of never-ending punishment and torture, with demons and dragons and the devil himself. Eternal punishment. Lakes of fire. Fiery furnace. Unquenchable fire. Fire, fire, fire.

And I decided then and there that I wouldn't ever step foot in a homeless shelter. Didn't even matter that I didn't know what a homeless shelter really was.

"Where did Matthew stay after he left that shelter?" Ms. Flores asks, her voice tearing me away from my thoughts. I'm thinking about Matthew and a complicated look that had developed in his eyes, one which I liked, the brown somehow browner, warmer, like the syrup Momma poured on our hot fudge sundaes.

That's what I thought of Matthew's eyes: warm and sweet like hot fudge, rich and delicious.

"Claire," she says. "Are you listening to me?"

But before I can answer a phone rings and Ms. Flores dives her hands deep into the pocket of a bag and sets it free. She gazes at the screen, her eyebrows wrinkling up like raisins.

She skids her chair back from the table abruptly, making me jump. "Stop there," she says. "We'll talk about Matthew in a minute." And then, to the boy in the corner, "Watch her. I'll be back," and with that, excuses herself from the cold room, the sound of her heels clattering down the concrete floor.

When she's gone, the barred door sealed shut by a second guard who follows her out of view, the boy in the corner whispers to me, "If it was me, I would've killed 'em, too."

HEIDI

In the morning, there's a knock at the door.

Zoe is in her bedroom, preparing for the school day, getting dressed, brushing her hair and such. Willow is in the bathroom. I pass by, en route to the front door, the knock beckoning me from the master bedroom where I've partially dressed in a pair of tweed pants and a cami, a cardigan left abandoned on my bed. My hair is wet, drying more quickly than I'd like.

I tote the baby on a hip, seeing that Willow has left the bathroom door slightly ajar as I pass by. I catch a glimpse of her in the reflection of the bathroom mirror, staring at her own image. Her hair, like mine, is still wet from a shower, dripping idle drops onto a shirt of Zoe's. There is dark eyeliner placed on a single eye. She leans in close to the mirror to plant it on the second eye, but instead, hesitates, and pulls down the front of Zoe's vintage wash shirt, far down, to the tender skin around her breast. I feel myself gasp for breath, willing the baby to remain silent. She runs her fingers over a lesion right there on the milky white skin, so close to the areola that I can see where the pigment changes colors. It's instinctive when I lean in, desperate for a better look, of what appears to be teeth marks, the imprint of incisors and canines, teeth pressed hard enough to leave a mark. Hard enough to deface the skin forever.

And then another knock, and I jump, moving quickly through the hall so that Willow doesn't have a chance to see my mouth, gaping open at the sight of her scar. So that she won't see me.

Graham stands on the opposite side of the door. In his hands are two mugs of coffee, an outline of the Chicago skyline printed on their surface. Upon seeing the baby, he slips past me in the doorway and sets the mugs of coffee on the kitchen table. "So this is who I'm to thank for the ruckus these past few nights," he says. "You didn't tell me you had company coming," and he sits down, kicking a second chair out with the toe of his shoe, inviting me to join him at my own kitchen table.

"Where's Chris?" he asks, his eyes moving about the mess which is my home, the baby's paraphernalia taking up more than its fair share of space: baby bottles litter the kitchen sink, stacks of diapers and containers of wipes on the living room floor, a heaping laundry basket pressed up next to the front door, something that smells shockingly like feces wafting from the garbage can. "Off to work already this morning?" he asks, trying hard not to wrinkle his nose at the atrocious scent. It's approaching seven o'clock.

"New York," I say, sliding into the chair beside him and catching the heavenly fragrance of his cologne, that earthy patchouli smell, blended with the intoxicating scent of coffee. I press the mug to my lips and inhale.

Graham is dapper as always, his blond hair spiked to perfection, his body cloaked in a fitted crew-neck sweater and jeans. He says that he's been up writing, since five, as is the case most mornings. During business hours, Graham works as a freelancer, writing for websites, magazines and sometimes the newspaper. But the early morning hours are reserved for his true passion: fiction writing. He's been working on a novel for umpteen years, his baby, his pride and joy, which he hopes might one day work its way onto a shelf at the local indie store. I've read bits and pieces, here and there, an honor acquired only after three or four glasses of wine, after begging and pleading, after an exuberance of flattery and praise. It was good. What I read of it, that is. I hired Graham to tweak the wording on my nonprofit's website, to help with pamphlets and to more or less write our annual appeal. Graham and I spent many late nights together, pouring over that appeal — over a bottle or two of my now-favorite Riesling — while Chris and Zoe were next door. I came home late, drunk, giddy, sensing no jealousy in Chris as I most certainly would have felt if the situation were reversed.

What's there to be jealous of? Chris asked, when I pressed him on it, something I never would have done in a sober state of mind. And then, the words that hurt the most: *I hardly think you're Graham's type,* and I remember the look of satisfaction on his face. The gratification at saying those words aloud.

I spent days, months, years wondering what those words meant. Not Graham's type, as in not the beautiful bombshell women who frequented his bed, who made the wall that separated our homes rattle from time to time, fragile baubles scooting dangerously close to the edge of a shelf. Is that what Chris was saying? That I was not good enough for Graham? That what I was, was the weathered woman next door, the one with brown hair being invaded by gray, with skin being annexed by wrinkles. I was the friend. The confidante. The chum. But I could never be more.

Or maybe all Chris meant was that *women* were not Graham's type, that Graham preferred men.

I would never know. But now, I sit across the table and wonder if, in some other life, in some parallel universe, Graham could ever see me as something other than the lady next door.

But inside I can think of little beside Willow, in the bathroom, running her fingers across the disfigurement on her chest. Teeth marks. *Human* teeth marks.

And then she appears, as if beckoned by my mind, standing there in the hallway, and Graham turns his eyes and smiles, the most bewitching smile of all, and politely says hello. Willow says nothing. I can see her feet start to flee, but then she must settle upon that smile: warm and welcoming, entirely kind, and she smiles in reply.

It would be next to impossible to see Graham's smile and not beam.

"Willow," I say then, "this is Graham.

310

From next door," and Graham says, "How do you do?"

"Fine," replies Willow. And then: "She's awake?" meaning the baby, and I say yes, that she is.

Willow asks if there's more toothpaste, and I direct her to the linen closet at the end of the hall. She's gone for a split second before Graham turns to me, his eyes wide with curiosity as if I've just given him the plot line of his next novel, and says, "Do tell," his brain making the quick connection between the baby on my lap, and teenage girl fumbling around in the linen closet for a tube of toothpaste.

We sit on the "L", side by side, and as we drive off, north this time, the baby becomes mesmerized with the motion of the train, the bright sunlight, the buildings that shoot past so fast that their colors and shapes begin to blur, redbrick bleeding into reinforced concrete and steel frames. I sit close enough to Willow that our legs touch and as they do, she pulls away instinctively though on the crowded train there's no where else to go. Willow finds proximity with others to be disturbing, painful almost, in the way that she grimaces and recoils, as if my standing or sitting too close is as painful as

311

a slap across the face. She'd prefer people to stay at an arm's length, literally, in that extrapersonal space, that space which she can't touch and, perhaps more importantly, can't be touched.

She doesn't like to be touched. She winces at the slightest touch of a hand. She avoids eye contact as best she can.

Is this the behavior of someone who's been maltreated, I wonder, staring out the corner of my eye at the erratic hair she lets disguise her face, or the one who's mistreated others? Are the dark, shadowy eyes — and the way they leer at Chris and Zoe, at me — an effect of abuse, or an indication of her own dishonorable behavior? I watch as others watch the girl beside me, the one with a baby on her lap, the one whose eyes wander off into space, her mind teleporting her to some distant realm outside this crowded train, while I secretly stroke the toes of the baby, with a single finger so Willow will not see.

Are they seeing something I've failed to see?

Are they plagued with some thought — some reservation — that never crossed my mind? Or perhaps it did cross my mind, that reservation about Willow, and I chose to ignore it, as I chose to ignore the blood on the undershirt, to take her words at face value and not consider that it could be more. *A bloody nose,* she'd said.

And yet, in the time she'd been with us, her nose had yet to bleed.

We take the train to a walk-in clinic in Lakeview. The baby's fever still lingers, lying in wait for the most inopportune times to rear its ugly head. Tylenol soothes her, yes, and yet it's only a temporary fix; we have yet to get at the root cause of the temperature, the discomfort that makes her miserable for hours on end.

Zoe's pediatrician was out of the question; I knew that much. There might be questions. But a walk-in clinic where I could pay cash — that was much better. Much better indeed.

We depart the "L" and walk the block or two to the clinic, a corner unit on a busy intersection that is loud at this time of day: cars screaming past, sawhorses and caution tape blocking parts of the sidewalk that the April rain has turned into lakes. People step into the street to get around it, stepping into oncoming traffic so that some driver lays on their horn and beeps.

Willow has the baby tucked into her coat, the army-green coat with tufts of pink fleece poking out, a reminder of the day I first laid eyes on the duo, hovering at the Fullerton Station in the rain. I offer to carry the baby but Willow glances at me and says no. "No, thank you," is what she says, but all I hear is no. A denial, a rejection. My face flames red, embarrassed.

And so I wait until we're in the vestibule, Willow and me, that quiet space between glass doors, to take the baby abruptly from her hands — so sudden she doesn't have time to react — she is unable to react because the eyes on the other side of the glass may see — and say, "We'll say she's mine. It's more believable this way. Fewer questions," and I push through the second glass door and into the lobby of the clinic without waiting for her to respond.

Willow lags behind, a half step or more, watching me, the flare of her icy blue eyes burning a hole in my shirt.

WILLOW

"I'd never been out of the house," I say. "That was the very first time."

I tell Ms. Flores how Matthew appeared after Joseph and Isaac had gone for the day, how he had an old pair of gym shoes with him, with laces he had to help me tie, how he told me to put them on because where we were going, I couldn't go barefoot.

I didn't know where he got the shoes. I didn't ask. I didn't ask where he got the sweatshirt, a thin hooded sweatshirt the color of tangerines that he helped me put on.

"Where are we going?" I asked him, the first of three times.

"You'll see," he said and we walked right out the front door of that Omaha home.

"You're telling me you hadn't been out of that house in what — six years?" Ms. Flores asks, doubtfully. She sinks a tea bag into a steaming mug of water, moving it up and

315

down, up and down like a yo-yo because she hasn't got the patience to wait for the tea to steep.

Momma used to love tea. Green tea. I catch the scent of Ms. Flores's tea and in an instant, it reminds me of Momma, of the way she swore her green tea fought cancer and heart disease and old age.

Too bad it didn't do anything to stop Bluebirds from tumbling down the road.

"Yes, ma'am," I reply, trying hard to ignore the way Ms. Flores's gray eyes call me a liar. "It was the first time I'd been anywhere, at least," I say, "other than the backyard," and even that was rare.

"Didn't you think it was a bad idea?" asks Ms. Flores.

My minds drifts back to the day that Matthew and I left the Omaha home. I tell Ms. Flores that the air was cold. It was fall. The clouds in the sky were thick and heavy.

I can picture it still, that first day Matthew took me outside.

"Yes, ma'am."

"Did you tell Matthew that? Did you tell him it was a bad idea?"

"No, ma'am."

She yanks that tea bag from the cup and sets it on a paper napkin. "Well, why not, Claire? If you knew it was a bad idea, then why didn't you say that to Matthew?" she asks, and I feel my shoulders rise up and shrug.

I remember that I walked close to Matthew, terrified to be outside. Terrified of the way the trees shook in the wind. Terrified of the cars that zoomed past, cars which I'd only ever seen from my bedroom window. I hadn't been in a car since that day six years ago when Joseph and Miriam drove me to their home. For me, cars were bad. Cars were how Momma and Daddy died. Cars were how I ended up there, at Joseph and Miriam's home.

I remember that Matthew tugged on my sleeve and we crossed the street. I peered back to see the house from outside, a house that was pretty almost, almost quaint. It wasn't the newest house on the block, but it was charming nonetheless, with its crisp white paint, and the black shutters, and the gray stone that wrapped around the home. The front door was red.

I'd never seen the home from that angle before, from outside, from the front yard.

And then, for some reason, I got scared.

And I started running.

"Hold on, hold on," Matthew said, tugging on my shirt to stop me from running. The gym shoes felt big and clunky, like ten pound weighs on the bottom of my feet. I wasn't used to wearing shoes. Around the house, all I did was walk barefoot. "What's the hurry?" Matthew asked, and when I turned to him, he could see the panic in my eyes, the fear. He could see that I was shaking. "What is it, Claire? What's wrong?"

And I told him how I was scared of the cars, the clouds, the naked trees that shivered in the cold November air. Of the kids who peered from behind curtains of their own homes, the kids with the bikes and the chalk, and their mean names: dickhead, retard.

And that's when Matthew clasped me by the hand, something he'd never done before. No one had held my hand for a real long time, not since Momma did when I was a girl. It felt good, Matthew's hand somehow warm though mine was made up of ice cubes.

Matthew and I kept walking, down the block and around a corner, where he dragged me to a funny blue sign. "This is our stop," he said. I didn't know what that meant: *our stop.* But I followed him over to the sign where we stood and waited for a real long time. There were others there, too, other people hovering around the sign. Just waiting.

318

Matthew let go of my hand to feel around in his pants pocket for a handful of coins, and when he did, the cold November air whooshed up and snatched my hair. A car lurched by, with music that was loud and mad. I felt suddenly as if it was hard to breathe, as though I was choking on that raw air, like everyone was looking at me. *What you can't see, can't hurt you,* I reminded myself, and I pressed in close to Matthew, trying to forget the cold air, the loud music, the brassy eyes.

A big bus — white and blue with tinted black windows — came to a stop right before us. Matthew said, "This is our bus," and we climbed up the huge steps with the other people, and feeling me hesitate, Matthew said, "It's okay. No one's gonna hurt you," before dropping a handful of quarters in a machine and leading me down the dirty aisle to a hard blue seat. The bus lurched forward, and I felt as though I was gonna fall from my seat, onto the dirty floor. I stared at that floor, the one with an oozing soda can and an old candy wrapper and the gook from someone else's shoes.

"Where are we going?" I asked Matthew again, and again he said, "You'll see," as the bus seesawed down the busy street, pitching me back and forth on that hard plastic seat, stopping every block or so to let more and more people on, until the bus nearly burst with folks.

I did what I usually did when I was scared. I thought of Momma, with her long black hair and her blue eyes. I thought back to Ogallala. Just whatever random memories I could bring to mind. They were few and far between these days: stuff like riding on the back of the shopping cart at Safeway, staring at an abandoned grocery list the last shopper left behind in the basket of the cart, the blue ink smeared across the page in a billowing cursive I couldn't read — with Lily tucked in the seat. I thought about biting into a ripe ol' peach and laughing with Momma as the juice dripped from my chin, and sitting under that huge oak tree that nearly consumed the backyard of our pre-fab home, reading to Momma from books that were meant for adults only to read.

"If you were so scared, why didn't you tell Matthew you didn't want to go?"

I thought about that for a minute or two. I watched Louise Flores nibble a prepackaged shortbread cookie and I thought about her question. I was scared for a whole bunch of reasons. I was scared about the people outside the home, but even more than that, I was scared about Joseph finding out we'd been gone. I knew in my mind that Joseph was at work, and that Isaac would be at school first, followed up by an after school job as was usually the case, but still, I wasn't so sure. And Miriam? Well, Miriam hardly knew when I was there so she'd hardly know when I wasn't. But still, I was scared.

So why didn't I tell Matthew I didn't want to go then? It was simple really. I *did* want to go. I was terrified, but I was excited, too. I hadn't been out of that house for a long time. I was fourteen or fifteen by then. Getting out of that home was the third biggest wish I'd had for six long years, the first being that Momma and Daddy come back to life, and the second being to get Lily back. My Lily. I trusted Matthew like I hadn't trusted anyone in the past six years, even more than Ms. Amber Adler who'd come to the home in Ogallala with the police officer to tell Lily and me that our folks were dead, as she kneeled down before me on the laminate flooring and with the kindest smile on her simple face, promised to take care of Lily and me and find us a good home.

I never thought for once that she was lying. In her mind she did just exactly what she said.

But Matthew was different. If Matthew said everything was okay, then everything was okay. If he said no one would hurt me, then no one would hurt me. It didn't mean I wasn't terrified as we hopped off one blue-and-white bus and onto another — and then yet another — thinking of as many memories of Momma as I could possibly dredge up (Mrs. Dahl and her cattle, Momma's taste for banana and mayonnaise sandwiches or the way she would eat all the way around the crust first, saving the insides — the *guts* she called them — for last) because thinking of Momma helped quash that notion of being scared half to death.

I love you like bananas love mayonnaise, she'd say, and I'd just shake my head and laugh, watching her prance around our home in her black shift dresses and beehive hairdos.

That bus took us past buildings that looked like the apartment buildings I remembered from Ogallala, short buildings splayed over the tawny lawn, made of pressed clay bricks, brick red. There were parking lots as wide as the buildings themselves. Electrical wires running alongside the street, making the air through the open bus window buzz. We drove through slummy neighborhoods, past run-down, boarded-up houses, past ratty cars and rough-looking people who loitered along the cracked sidewalks. Just loitered. We passed American flags, flying in the stubborn wind, patches of dirt showing through the deadening grass on the side of the street, past bushes with puny leaves, brown and tumbling to the ground, and trees, naked trees, hundreds of thousands of them.

There was an enormous parking lot that we passed, with pieces of cars. When I asked about those cars, Matthew told me it was called a junkyard, and I asked him what's a person possibly to do with cars without wheels or doors.

"They use 'em for parts," he said, leaving me to wonder what good wheels or doors do without a car. But I found myself searching for Momma and Daddy's Bluebird nonetheless, for the upside-down car, the smashed-in hood, the broken headlights, the mirrors that hung from the door by a string, bumpers and fenders squished down to half their size. This is the image I'd carried in my mind for all those years, a snapshot on the front page of the paper: *I-80 Crash Leaves Two Dead.* Momma and Daddy's names were never mentioned. They were called *casualties,* a word I didn't even know at the time.

"Where are we going?" I asked for a third and final time.

A smile flickered on Matthew lips as he said, "You'll see."

"Where did Matthew take you that day?" Louise Flores asks. I think of Matthew living in that house with me all those years, all those years that Joseph kept me locked inside. I wondered what Matthew thought about that, or maybe he didn't think about it at all because he had been a kid and Joseph was his father, and he didn't find it the least bit strange. Living in that home with Joseph and Miriam had become commonplace to me after all that time. I had to look real far inside my heart to realize that being cooped up like that, it was wrong. I thought maybe it was the same way with Matthew. That was the way it had always been since he was a kid. He never saw Miriam come and go. He never saw me leave.

And besides, Joseph said that no one would believe me. Not a soul. It was his word against mine. And I was a child. A child that no one — *no one* — besides him and Miriam wanted.

"Where did he take you?" Ms. Flores asks again, and I say, "To the zoo."

"The zoo?" she asks, like there's a million places in the world she'd rather go.

And I say, "Yes, ma'am," with a smile on my face as big as the sun because there wasn't any place in the world I would've rather been except for maybe with Momma and Daddy.

The zoo. I had been to a tiny zoo before, in Lincoln, but we'd never been to Omaha before. We saw antelopes and cheetahs that day, gorillas and rhinos. We went for a train ride, and into a giant dome that looked just like the desert inside, a real live desert. Matthew spent just about every penny he owned on me there at that zoo, buying me popcorn, too!

I loved every minute of it, though the truth of the matter was that I was a little scared of the people. Lots of people. I didn't know a whole lot about people back then. What I did know was summed up into the scattering of people in my life, and all of them packed into three categories: good, bad and otherwise. It wasn't just that I hadn't been outside of that Omaha home for years. It was that I hadn't seen a whole lot of folks, other than Joseph and Miriam, Isaac, Matthew and, from time to time, every six months or so, Ms. Amber Adler. I stared at all the people we passed and wondered, over and over again, if they were good or bad.

Or if maybe, they were otherwise.

But Matthew held my hand tight the entire time; he didn't ever let go. I felt safe when I was with Matthew, like he was going to protect me, though I knew that sooner or later I'd have to go home, back to Joseph and Miriam's home. As it was, it was sooner rather than later because Matthew said we couldn't risk Joseph getting home before us. We couldn't take a chance of him knowing I'd been gone.

Because then, Matthew said, Joseph would be mad. Real mad.

And then I wondered what he might do.

That night I dreamed of antelope. Antelope in a herd, running throughout the African savannah. Free and uninhibited as I only wished I could be.

HEIDI

We're getting ready for bed when Willow steps into my bedroom and says good-night, her voice apprehensive in that way that it almost always is. Zoe is on my bed staring blindly at some sitcom on the TV, and I grimace internally every time someone on screen says the word *damn* or *hell* or a couple shares a romantic kiss, not quite certain when we graduated from the Disney Channel to *this*. Is my twelve-year-old daughter old enough to watch *this*, to grasp the sexual innuendos and adult humor that suffuse the TV screen?

But she stares blindly, not laughing along with the audience as some man slips on an icy patch in a parking lot, falling onto his rear end, a carton of eggs soaring from his hands and into midair.

Her gaze turns to Willow as she enters, a coldhearted stare in her warm brown eyes.

She scrabbles for the remote control and

turns the volume louder, trying to drown out the sound of Willow's spineless good-night.

Zoe is upset at me, upset that I forgot to pick her up from soccer practice, that I got sidetracked at the clinic with Willow and the baby. That she had to wait an extra hour, maybe more, with Coach Sam while he called — and then called again — my cell phone to remind me of my daughter waiting at Eckhart Park as the Chicago sun sank lower and lower below the horizon. By the time we arrived, her teammates were long gone and Coach Sam had grown cold and antsy, though he faked a smile and told me it was all right when I apologized for the umpteenth time for my delay.

Zoe didn't speak to me when we arrived home; she didn't speak to Willow. She showered and climbed inside the bed, saying that she wanted to be alone. This, of course, didn't surprise me in the least, and I could see in her vacant eyes, in the sulky expression that expropriated her face, that she hated me, as she hated most everything. I'd made it to that never-ending list that included math homework and beans and that nagging substitute teacher. That list of things she hated. Me.

But the baby. The baby on the other hand

was full of smiles. Toothless smiles and mellifluous baby sounds that filled the room like bubbly lullabies. I clung to her greedily, not wanting to share. I prepared a bottle when she began to forage around in the pleats of my shirt for my breast, sneaking off into the kitchen without asking or telling Willow where it was that I was going, or asking whether or not it was okay to feed the baby because if I did, she might suggest she do it herself, and then I would have to relinquish the baby, relinquish the baby to her care, and that was something I found I simply could not do. And so I stood in the shadows of the kitchen, feeding Ruby, and tickling her sweet little toes, pressing a terry-cloth dish towel to her mouth to catch the drops of formula that escaped, sliding this way and that down her chin like a pair of pinking shears.

And then: "It's time for her medicine, ma'am," Willow declared, appearing suddenly in the kitchen, a bolt of lightning on an otherwise quiet night. I'd been caught, red-handed, with my hand in the cookie jar, or so they say.

Her words, themselves, were benign, and yet her eyes bore holes into me, there, in the kitchen; she didn't have to say anything to make certain I knew I was in the wrong.

I was fearful of Willow, all of a sudden, fearful that she would hurt me, fearful that she would hurt the child.

Her image, again, did an about-face before my very eyes: helpless young girl with an affinity for hot chocolate, teenage delinquent who'd managed to sneak her way into my home.

She stood there, in the kitchen, arms wide-open for the baby's return. She was cloaked in yet another outdated article of Zoe's clothing: jeans with a hole in the knee, a long-sleeve shirt that, on Willow, mutated into 3/4 length, peppering the lower half of her arms in goose bumps, the hairs of her forearm standing on end. There were socks on her feet, a gaping hole in one of the big toes, and as I stared at that big toe, I found myself considering how naive I'd been, to bring Willow into my home.

What if Chris was right after all, right about Willow?

I hadn't paused to consider the effect it would have on my own family's well-being, for I was far too worried about Willow's well-being to consider Zoe, to consider Chris.

What if Willow couldn't be trusted?

My eyes flashed to the drawer where we keep the Swiss Army knife, hidden among a collection of junk — birthday candles, matches, flashlights that don't work — and I found myself suddenly scared, suddenly wondering who this girl is, who she really truly is, and why she is in my home.

As she stood there, staring at me, she didn't ask the obvious: what was I doing?

But she took the baby from my hands. Just like that. She just took her, leaving me helpless and short of breath. I stood in the kitchen, helping Willow dispense liquid antibiotics into the baby's mouth, and then stood, horrified, as Willow turned away with the baby in her arms. The baby I had just been holding, feeding, and without her, without Ruby, I felt as if something was suddenly lacking from my life. I watched as Willow settled cross-legged onto my sofa and laid that baby in her lap, wrapping her up in the pink fleece blanket like a caterpillar in a cocoon.

I wanted to cry, staring at the all but empty bottle in my hand, the vacancy left in my arms. I found myself wanting, consumed by an impassioned need to hold that baby, my thoughts gripped by the image of Juliet, of Juliet being scraped from my uterus by a curette. It was hard to breathe, nearly impossible, as my thoughts dithered between a longing for that baby — for Ruby — and a longing for my Juliet, my Juliet who'd been discarded as medical waste.

How long this went on, I don't know. I stood there, on the threshold between kitchen and living room, hyperventilating, the carbon dioxide escaping my blood at an alarming rate so that my lips, my fingers, the toes on my feet begin to tingle, and I clung hard — knuckles turning white — to the granite countertop so I wouldn't faint or fall to the ground, imagining my body convulsing on the hardwood floors, envisioning Willow and Zoe standing by and doing nothing, simply watching *Sesame Street* or some sitcom on the TV, until I began to loathe them — the both of them — for this disregard, no matter how hypothetical it might be.

And now I stand in my master bath, Zoe tucked in bed with the ridiculous show on TV, as Willow utters her good-night. She's made it all the way into the bedroom and stands, just shy of the bathroom door, watching as I hang my precious golden chain, my father's wedding band, from a shabby chic hook on the wall, a filigree bird painted a distressed red.

I don't turn to Willow as I mumble, "Good night," and wait until she's left the room to breathe. I slip into a satin nightgown and, locking the bedroom door, join Zoe in bed, sliding the Swiss Army knife under the pillow.

I spend the sleepless night tossing and turning, trying hard not to wake Zoe from sleep, Zoe who turns so that her back is in my direction, hugging the far edge of the bed so our bodies don't connect. Zoe, who used to long to climb in bed with Chris and me, who begged to fill that empty space between Mommy and Daddy's protective bodies, now pushed far enough away that she might fall off the bed.

When I finally do sleep, my dreams are filled with babies. Babies and blood. They are not happy dreams, of cherubs and cherubic babies as I've had in the past, but rather bloody babies, dead babies, empty bassinets. I find myself running from room to room in my satin nightgown, searching for baby Juliet, finding her nowhere. In my dreams, I retrace my steps as if maybe, just maybe, I overlooked her lying in the middle of a room, wrapped up in her fleece blankie. I look in those places where the cats like to hide: in the closet, behind a closed pantry door, under the bed. She's nowhere.

And then I peer down to find my satin nightgown slathered with blood. Like ketchup on a hamburger bun. It's on the nightgown, on my hands, and as I peer at my reflection in a mirror — aging, ten years or more older than I was when I went to bed — I see blood staining my once-auburn hair red.

I wake, in a sweat, from the nightmare, certain — absolutely certain — that somewhere, off in the distance, I hear a baby crying.

I rise from bed and tiptoe across the room. The digital numbers on the alarm clock read 2:17 a.m. I find the hallway dark, save for the feeble light from the kitchen stove that wanders its way into the hall. It's quiet as I press my ear to the office door; there is no sound. No baby cries.

And yet I was so sure.

I lay my hand on the satin nickel knob and turn.

Locked.

I try again, just to be sure, my heart beginning to accelerate in my chest. I'm worried something is wrong on the other side of the door, as a million unwanted thoughts sneak into my mind, everything from Willow rolling over and smothering the baby, to some madman climbing up the fire escape and fleeing with Ruby in his arms.

I need to get inside that room. I need to make certain she's okay.

I could knock on the door and wake Willow from sleep, making her open the door so I can investigate how secure the windows are and whether or not the baby is all right. I could tell her I was worried that something might have happened to the baby.

And if I am right, then my panic would be justified. But if I'm wrong . . .

If I'm wrong, the girls — Willow and Zoe, the both of them — will think I'm insane.

I scamper down the hall to the kitchen junk drawer where we keep a collection of keys — for it's the kind of lock that simply needs to be unlatched with some sharp object; a paper clip would do. I return to the office door again, where I insert the makeshift key, turn clockwise and voilà!

The door opens in a cinch.

I turn the handle ever so gently, not wanting to wake Willow. The door creaks open and there I find her, as I did the night before, her back toward the baby, a pillow placed over her head. The baby is sound asleep, breathing blissfully. She's kicked the green chenille throw from her own tiny body and lies exposed so that I can see the rise and fall of her chest to know that she's alive, not smothered in blood as my dreams persuaded me to believe.

She's sound asleep, eyes and appendages

completely dormant, inert.

I want to take her in my arms and carry her down the hall to the rocking chair in the living room. I want to hold her as she sleeps, well into the morning light, watching out the window as the first buses and cabs of the day appear on the city street. I want to watch the sun rise with Ruby in my grasp, to see the golden pink hues discolor the dark April sky.

And then there are other thoughts that fill my mind, thoughts of taking the baby where Willow cannot find me.

I stare at Ruby, my body pressed into the shadows of the room, becoming a mere silhouette on the wall, a featureless shape backlit by the lightness of the walls, by the pale moonlight that sidles in from behind the pewter-gray drapes, pintuck drapes that always looked a mess to me, wrinkled, puckered. I imagine myself as one of those famous, iconic silhouettes: Jane Austen or Beethoven, or the trashy mudflap girls that grace big rigs and rednecks' trucks, those girls with their hourglass shapes and enormous breasts.

I place my hands on the wall to steady myself; I will myself not to breathe, so that I won't wake Willow, trying hard to extend the time between breaths until I become lightheaded and dizzy.

There is a clock in this room, as well, red digital numbers that drift from 2:21 to 4:18 a.m., all in the blink of an eye as I hover, there, at the foot of the sofa bed, wanting to cover the baby with the chenille throw, to move her, a foot or more from Willow's body so that I don't have to worry about her being smothered or squished flat.

Wanting to lift her up and carry her from this room.

But I can't.

Because then Willow will know.

And she may leave.

WILLOW

In here we wear orange jumpsuits, the word *juvenile* stitched across the back. We sleep in brick rooms, two to a cell, on metal bunk beds, with heavy bars separating us from the concrete corridor where guards — tyrannical women with bodies built like men — stride all night long. We eat at long tables in a cafeteria, from chipped pastel trays loaded with foods from each of the food groups: meat, bread, fruits and vegetables, a glass of milk.

It's not all that bad, not when compared to picking food from the Dumpster and sleeping on the street.

My cell mate is a girl who tells me her name is Diva. The guards call her Shelby. She has plum-colored hair though her eyebrows are a plain old brown. She sings. All the time. All night long. The guards, other inmates tell her to shut up, to put a sock in it, to shut her pie hole, calling the words out from places we can't see. I ask her why she's in here, behind the metal bars like me, sitting on the concrete floor because she swears her bed has been booby-trapped, but all she says is, "You don't want to know," and I'm left wondering.

She's fifteen, maybe sixteen, like me. I see the holes where she was made to remove various piercings: the lip, the septum, the cartilage of her ear. She sticks out her tongue and shows me where it's been pierced, and tells me how her tongue swelled to twice its size when she had it done, how she couldn't talk for days. How some girl she knew split her tongue right in two when she did it. She claims her nipple's been pierced, her belly button. She starts to tell me about something that's been pierced beneath the pants of that orange jumpsuit, about how the guard watched as she was forced to remove the j-bar from her clit before locking her up in the slammer, and then she mutters under her breath, "Fucking dyke."

I turn away, embarrassed, and she starts to sing. Someone tells her to shut her trap. She sings louder, high pitched and off-key, like the grating brakes of a freight train coming to a sudden stop.

The guard fetches me from my cell. She

binds my hands in cuffs, then leads me by the arm to where Louise Flores waits in the cold room with the steel table. She's standing in the corner today, peering out the one window, her back to me when I walk in. She's got on a scratchy-looking cardigan, the color of smoke, a pair of black pants. There's a cup of tea on the table, a cup of juice for me.

"Good morning, Claire," she says as we both take our spots at the table. She doesn't smile. The clock on the wall reads just after ten o'clock.

Ms. Flores motions to the guard to remove my cuffs.

The male guard from the day before is gone. Out of sight. In his place is a middle-aged woman, her gray hair wrapped in a bun. She perches herself where two walls meet, and crosses her arms against herself, the handle of a gun peeking out of a holster.

"I brought you some juice," says Ms. Flores, "and a doughnut," she adds as she sets a paper bag on the table.

Bribery.

Like when Joseph, from time to time, came home with a chocolate chip cookie from the community college's cafeteria, wrapped in cellophane. So that later that night I wouldn't think twice about pulling that big, old T-shirt I wore to bed up over my hips and letting Joseph draw the undies down my thighs.

She sets her glasses on the bridge of her nose and looks back into the notes from the day before. Leaving the Omaha home with Matthew. Riding the buses all the way out to the zoo.

"What happened when you got home that afternoon? From the zoo?" she asks.

"Nothing, ma'am," I say as I reach into the bag and remove a doughnut, double chocolate with sprinkles, and stuff it into my mouth. "I was back home well before Joseph," I mumble. "Well before Isaac. Miriam was in her room, with no sense of time or nothing. I made her lunch and started the laundry, so that later, when I told Joseph I'd done laundry all day, there'd be proof of it — laundry on the line. He'd never know it was a lie."

She hands me a napkin, motioning to my cheek. I wipe at the chocolate residue, then lick my fingers clean. I guzzle the juice.

I tell her how riding the buses with Matthew became more or less a regular thing. We didn't go to the zoo more than the one time because the zoo cost money and money was one thing Matthew didn't have.

We went places we could go without money. We went to parks, and Matthew showed me how to pump the swings, something I'd forgotten since my days back in Ogallala. Sometimes we just walked up and down the streets of Omaha, past the big buildings and all of those people.

And then one day Matthew took me to the library. I remembered how I loved going to the library with Momma. I loved the smell, and the sight of all those books. Thousands of books. Millions of books! Matthew asked me what I wanted to learn about — anything in the whole wide world — and I thought about it long and hard, and then I told Matthew that I wanted to know more about the planets. He nodded his head and said, "Okay. Astronomy it is," and I followed Matthew as he waltzed through the library like he owned the place, and took me to a bunch of books on astronomy, as he called it, the sun, the moon, the stars. The library was quiet, and in that aisle with the astronomy books, Matthew and I were all alone, tucked between the tall bookcases like we were the only people in the whole entire world. We sat on the floor and leaned against the big bookshelves, and one by one I started pulling the books from the shelf and admiring their covers: the black nighttime sky all cluttered up with stars.

Growing up without a mother there were things I wanted to know but had no one to ask. Like why, every now and again, my body started bleeding, and I was made to stuff my underwear with wads of toilet tissue to keep it from ruining my pants. Like why I was growing hair where no hair used to be, and why parts of my body were getting bigger for no apparent reason at all. There wasn't one lady in my life I could ask. The caseworker was the only one, but of course, I couldn't talk to her about those things because she'd want to know why I wasn't just talking to Miriam, 'cause every time Ms. Amber Adler came around, Miriam was taking the little white pills and acting almost normal. Almost. But Miriam was far from normal.

All those questions were about the outside, but I had questions about the inside, too. Especially about Matthew, and this whole strange slew of emotions I felt whenever he was around. I felt an urge to be close to him, and lonely when he wasn't there. I waited each and every day of my life for him to appear at the door once Joseph and Isaac had gone, feeling sad on the days he didn't come.

I was seeing things I'd never seen before when Matthew came and got me out of that house: beautiful women with rippling hair, the color of straw or cinnamon or macaroni and cheese, their faces fancy, dressed in wonderfully complicated clothes: tall leather boots with heels, skintight jeans, pants made of leather, teal pumps, dozens of bangle bracelets flanking an arm, shirts with scoop necks, sweaters with holes where bras showed through the burgundy or jade or navy fabric. Women and men holding hands, and kissing. Smoking cigarettes, talking on phones.

I owned one bra, slipped to me by Joseph with the last parcel of clothing: one that contained brown jumpers and cardigans that bored me to tears, when what I wanted were heels and bangle bracelets. I wanted to slip some see-through shirt over my one bra and let Matthew see.

When Matthew and I lay down, side by side on my bed to read from the pages of whatever book he'd brought me, we lay close, our bodies fused together, our heads sharing the same lumpy pillow. Matthew would slant himself into the bed's headboard, his legs and torso curving their way around my own, his head angled toward mine so we could both see the same microscopic words in the books. One of my favorites was *Anne of Green Gables,* a book I must've asked Matthew a million times to check out, and though I knew he must be getting sick of it, he didn't ever complain. He even said he liked it, too.

But no matter how much I liked that book, still, I'd find it hard to do anything but think about Matthew's hand grazing mine while turning the pages, his jeans brushing against my bare leg beneath the blanket, an elbow accidentally swiping my breast as he redistributed himself on the bed. While Matthew was reading aloud about Anne Shirley and the Cuthberts, I lost myself on the tone of his voice, the smell of him — a hodgepodge of moss and cigarette smoke — the shape of his fingernails, what it would feel like if he slipped those toasty hands up under my sweatshirt and touched my breast.

It would be different from Joseph, that I knew for sure, different from Joseph whose teeth marks were singed into my sallow skin like the branding of cattle.

Matthew and I would lie that way for a real long time, together on the bed, and then sometimes Matthew would sit up quickly, rearrange himself on the other end of the bed.

As if we were doing something wrong.

Ms. Amber Adler continued to come every six months or so. In the days leading up to her arrival, Joseph, with my help, would give Miriam those pills. Like clockwork, Miriam would start to feel better and get out of bed, and we'd air the Miriam stench right out of the house. I'd get to cleaning, and Joseph would appear with a brand-new dress, and he'd sit me down at the kitchen table and give my hair a trim, and by the time the caseworker appeared in her junker car with her too-big Nike bag, the house would smell lemon fresh, Miriam would be acting more or less normal and hanging on the refrigerator door would be some fabricated book report Joseph typed up, my name printed at the top.

"Did you write this?" Ms. Amber Adler asked, clutching the paper in her pretty little hand, and I lied, "Yes, ma'am."

Of course I never wrote any book report. I never went to school. But Joseph looked at her as if it were the God's honest truth and said how my reading and writing were coming along okay, but there was still the issue of my *disorderly behavior,* and Amber Adler would pull me aside and remind me how I was oh so fortunate to have a family like Joseph and Miriam, and that I needed to put more effort into my conduct and *show a little respect.*

The caseworker continued to bring letters from Paul and Lily Zeeger, and from my Little Lily. Big Lily told me how Rose (Lily) was growing up so big. How she wanted to grow her dark hair longer and longer, how she'd recently cut bangs. How she had so many friends: Peyton and Morgan and Faith. How she loved school, and what a brilliant child she was, and how her favorite subject was music. She asked: did I play any musical instruments? Did I like to sing? She'd tell me that Rose (Lily) was a natural musician. She wondered: is it a family trait? As Lily got to reading and writing herself, she would send me notes, too, scribbled on stationery with a simple tree branch and a red bird on front. The stationery had her very own name printed across the front: Rose Zeeger, and every fall, tucked inside, was a brand-new school photo. My Lily was always happy, always smiling, and in those photos I saw how she was growing older, looking more and more like our Momma every day. When I looked in the mirror myself, I didn't see any traces of Momma, but I saw them on Little Lily, in those photos that Joseph forced me to tear to shreds once the caseworker had driven away.

"I started to feel relieved for Lily," I tell Ms. Flores.

"Why is that?" she asks.

"Because Lily was happy with the Zeegers. She was happy in a way that she never would've been if she'd have stayed with me."

I thought of Joseph doing with Lily what he did with me, and just the idea of it made me want to bash his head in with the frying pan, the kind of thoughts that more or less started filling my mind as I grew from an eight-year-old child to a fifteen-year-old girl, one who knew with absolute certainty that Joseph had no business coming into my room.

"Why didn't you tell the caseworker about Joseph?" asks Ms. Flores, adding, "If what you say is true," implying that it was not.

I look away, refuse to answer. I've answered this question before.

"Claire," Ms. Flores snaps, her tone dry. And then, when I don't answer, she goes on, looking at her notes instead of me, "As far as I can tell, Claire, you didn't do a thing to remedy your situation. You could have told Ms. Adler what you claim Joseph was doing to you. You could have informed —" she peeks back at her notes to make sure she's got it right "— Matthew. But you didn't. You chose to take matters into your own hands."

I refuse to answer. I lay my head on the table and close my eyes.

She slaps a blunt hand against the table and I jump; the guard jumps. "Claire," she barks. I will not raise my head. Will not open my eyes. I imagine Momma holding my hand. *Hold still and it won't hurt so much.* "Young lady," she says, "you had better cooperate. Ignoring me will not help a thing. You're in a lot of trouble here. More trouble than you can possibly imagine. You're facing *two* murder charges, in addition to —"

It's then that I lift my head up from that table and stare at her, into Ms. Louise Flores's gray eyes and at her long silver hair, the scratchy cardigan, the wrinkles of her skin, the big teeth like a horse's. The gray brick walls of the small room come closing in around me, the sunlight through the one window suddenly in my eyes. A headache arrives, without warning. I imagine a body, blood, bowels unintentionally let loose on the floor. The front door, open. My legs wobbly, like Jell-O. A voice telling me to go. *Go!*

And I think: *two?*

CHRIS

That baby is whimpering in the background when I finally get a chance to talk to Heidi. I ask Heidi what's wrong, but all she says is, "Waiting for the Tylenol to kick in," and there's a vibration in her voice, a jostling effect as if she's bouncing that baby up and down, up and down, to try to amend the situation. To get that baby to shut up.

"Fever?" I ask, typing away on my laptop. *The securities offered hereby are highly speculative . . .* I'm barely listening as Heidi tells me that the fever isn't so bad — she rattles off some number I couldn't recount if my life depended on it — and then goes on to tell me about their doctor appointment at the clinic in Lakeview.

"DCFS," I remind her.

One quick, easy phone call that could make this all go away.

But all she says is, "Not now, Chris," and then she's quiet. She doesn't want to hear my nagging about the girl and how I think it's utterly insane that she's still cohabitating with us, in a space too small for three, much less five. Or that this whole fiasco might land us both in jail.

The shares are being offered without . . .

She tells me about bringing the baby to the family practitioner at the clinic in Lakeview. How they said the baby belonged to Heidi, in an effort to avoid any suspicious inquiry, and I thought of that, imagining Heidi, at her age, with an infant child. It wasn't so much that Heidi was *too old* to have a baby, but that we'd moved so far past that, past diapers and baby bottles and all that crap.

Apparently it didn't matter so much who the baby belonged to anyway because all the doctor was concerned with was the baby's angry fever as they stood in the office, desperate for some elixir, for some potion to remedy the baby.

I can hear in her voice that she's tired. An image fills my mind: Heidi's hair is a mess; she probably hasn't showered all day. It's likely stringy, like spaghetti noodles, as happens to Heidi when she hasn't given it a good shampoo. There are bags under her haggard brown eyes, big, fat ones to boot, swollen and sore. She's clumsy, I can tell, as in the midst of our conversation a can of pop misses the edge of the countertop and drops to the ground.

There's a crash as I envision sticky brown liquid seeping into the hardwood floors.

"Shit," she snaps, Heidi who never swears. I picture her dropping to all fours to wipe up the mess with a paper towel. Her hair falls in her face and she blows it away. She's a damn mess, desperately in need of a shower and a good night's sleep. Her eyes are erratic, a million thoughts running amok in her mind.

The situation has taken its toll on my wife.

Heidi says that she had lathered enough cream onto the baby's bottom over the past few days that the doctor hardly mentioned the healing red rash. After ruling out all other causes of fever, the doctor used a catheter to get a urine sample and diagnosed the baby with a urinary tract infection.

"How'd she get that?" I ask Heidi, grimacing at the thought of that burning sensation every time the baby peed, of the catheter shooting up the urethra and into her tiny bladder.

"Poor hygiene," she says simply, and I'm reminded of the baby sitting in that shitty diaper for God knows how long. The bacteria in the feces climbing back up into the bladder and kidneys. Festering.

The baby's on antibiotics now, her mother under doctor's orders to wipe from front to back. The very thing Heidi badgered me about when Zoe was still in diapers. I imagine Willow sitting on the sofa now, staring at the TV in a daze, as she's prone to do. She's not eighteen, I remind myself, picturing some kid that still needs to be reminded to wash her hands. To eat her vegetables. To make her bed. To wipe her baby's rump from front to back.

I'm still waiting to hear back from Martin Miller, PI. I'm thinking long and hard of ways to hurry this along, some kind of information I can give him, though my own internet searches have hit a dead end. I considered a picture, but highly doubt Willow Greer would let me snap a photo of her, or that Heidi would give me the A-okay. I consider that old suitcase, brown and worn, the one she tucks beneath the sofa bed when she isn't in the room, as if we might forget it's there. I thought about snooping inside to see if I could find something, some kind of clue, a driver's license or state ID, a cell phone with a contact number.

And then Martin suggested fingerprints, suggested snagging some glass or the remote control, something she touched that would validate an identity she couldn't fake. He walked me through it, how to preserve Willow Greer's fingerprints so he could send them to his lab.

But all that will have to wait until after my trip.

I have yet to receive a tweet from W. Greer, which leads me to believe she's dead. That she did it, like she said she would, that she ended her life.

Or maybe she's lying low in some Chicago condo, wanting the world to *believe* she's dead. How the hell would I know? But still, I check every day, just in case.

"She was interested in her birthmark," Heidi tells me then, interrupting my thoughts.

"Who was?"

"The doctor."

"The baby's birthmark?" I ask, remembering the one that stared at me from the back of the baby's leg when Heidi removed our blue towel from her buttocks and wiped her clean.

"Yeah," she says. "Says it's called a port-wine stain," and I imagine a glass of merlot spilled across the back of that leg. Heidi says something about vascular birthmarks and capillaries expanding and the dilated blood vessels beneath the baby's skin. And that's when she says to me that, according to the doctor, we might want to have them removed. With laser treatment. She says it as if this is something we really might want to consider having done. We. She and me. As if it's our baby we're discussing.

I imagine my wife, talking into the phone with her spaghetti hair and haggard eyes, stating with this blank expression on her face, "The doctor said they can be embarrassing for kids as they get older. That they're easier to treat in infancy because the blood vessels are smaller."

I'm speechless. I can't respond. I open my mouth and close it again. And then, for lack of anything better to say, I ask, "How's Zoe?" and Heidi says, "Fine."

I never say a thing about the birthmark.

As the conversation drifts from birthmarks to the weather, I realize how exhausted Heidi sounds, pulled to the limit, like a stretchy toy that's been yanked too far and won't go back to its original shape. I almost feel sorry. Almost.

But then my mind drifts back to Heidi and me in our prebaby days — before Zoe, before the abortion that rattled Heidi's world much more than she cared to admit — when we would take the steps, two at a time, to the rooftop deck of the apartment where we lived at the time, to watch the fireworks erupt from Navy Pier every Saturday night. I think of the way we sat together, on the same lounge chair, drinking from the same bottle of beer, staring at the city's skyline: the John Hancock Building, the Sears Tower long before it'd been renamed. We had so many aspirations back then: to travel the world and see things — the Great Wall of China, the Blue Caves of Greece — to compete in a triathlon together. Plans that fell by the wayside as soon as we had a kid. I never wanted to be one of those couples, one of those couples so consumed with their individual ambitions and their kids, that the marriage got kicked to the curb, ignored and neglected by seemingly more important aspects of life.

What I wanted in our marriage was for us to be a team. Heidi and me. But these days it feels as if we're nothing but opponents, opponents playing for rival teams. I start to feel bad for her, in this mess with that girl and the baby, all alone.

And yet, I think, considering the haggard eyes and the spaghetti hair, this *is* her doing.

But still, I can't get that note out of my mind, the one in the briefcase with the

single word: *Yes.* I pulled it out at the airport, on the plane. I pulled it out once we'd
checked into our hotel, a luxury hotel in the
heart of New York City. I pulled it out again
after Cassidy, Tom, Henry and I had parted
ways at the check-in desk, and Cassidy had
said, "Toodle-oo," with a one finger wave. I
sat on the crisp, white bed in my stately
room — staring at the view out the window: a bird's-eye view of the building next
door, not ten feet away, nothing but brick
and windows — and pulled that note out
and held it in my hand. I found myself ap-
praising everything about that note: where
she got the purple sticky note, the jagged-
ness of the letters. Was she nervous when
she wrote it, short on time, jarred by the
baby? Or did her handwriting just suck
more than mine?

I wonder when she wrote the note: ten
o'clock, right after we'd gone to bed and
she heard, through the cracks of the door,
Zoe's breathing morph into a snore, or
sometime in the middle of the night, forced
to my briefcase by sleeplessness, by plagu-
ing memories of being hurt by someone that
kept her tossing and turning all night long.
Or maybe it was early in the morning, awak-
ened by the sound of my alarm clock, when
she tiptoed to the briefcase by the front

door as I turned on the shower and stepped inside.

Who knew?

And now, a day later, my meetings done for the day, a rendezvous with Tom, Henry and Cassidy planned in the hotel's bar in some twenty minutes, I debate telling Heidi about the note. But what good would it do? It would throw Heidi into a nosedive, that's what it would do. Having proof that the girl was abused — or at least a claim of abuse — would be enough for Heidi to suggest we keep her. Forever. Like the damn kittens. *They're staying.*

There's a knock at the door. I barely register the sound before Heidi, over the phone, snaps, "Who's that?" and I lie, claiming, "Room service," because I refuse to admit that Cassidy offered to stop by and proofread the offering memorandum — the company profile and financials for some asset we're trying to sell — before we all head down to the hotel bar for a nightcap.

I move from the bed and to the door, telling Heidi how I ordered room service. How I was staying in for the night to finish up the offering memorandum which I was supposed to finish last weekend. How I ordered a turkey club sandwich and cheesecake and how I might tune in for the end of the Cubs game, if I finish the offering memorandum in time.

I slide the door open and find, as expected, Cassidy on the other side, bright red lipstick delineating her lips so that I can think of nothing but those lips.

I raise a finger to my mouth and silently whisper *Shh.*

And then, louder, so Heidi can hear, "Did you bring any ketchup?" and watch as Cassidy stifles a laugh.

I'm going straight to hell, I think as I thank the bogus room service attendant and slam the door closed, grateful when Heidi says she'll let me go so my food doesn't grow cold.

"Love you," I say, and she says, "Me, too."

I toss my phone onto the bed.

I watch Cassidy move across the room with gall. As if this is her room. There's no hesitation about it, no hovering in the doorway waiting to be invited in. Not with Cassidy.

She's changed her clothes. Only Cassidy would change from a dress into a dress for a nightcap, replacing the formal black suit with a Grecian style dress, fitted and sleeveless, the color of rust. She sits on a low yellow armchair slinging one long leg across the other, asking first about the offering memorandum, and then about Heidi.

"She's good," I say, pulling up the offering memorandum on my laptop and handing it to Cassidy, careful not to touch as the computer passes between hands. "Yup, she's good."

And then I excuse myself before I say it a third time, forcing my eyes to stay on *her* eyes and not her legs or her lips, or her breasts in the rust-colored dress. Not big. But not small, either. The kind that work well on Cassidy's lissome frame. Too much extra baggage would throw the whole thing off. She'd be disproportionate, I think as I stand, staring at the display of hotel freebies on the bathroom's black sink — shampoo, conditioner, lotion, soap — as I rip open the soap and wash my face, splashing cold water on the skin so that I'll stop thinking about Cassidy's knockers.

Or her long legs.

Or the lips. Red lips. The color of a cayenne pepper.

She calls to me from the adjoining room, and I step from the bathroom, patting my face dry with a towel. I slide into my own low yellow armchair beside hers, and pull it up to the round table.

We go over the offering memorandum. I focus on words like *shares* and *stocks* and *per unit,* and not the manicured hands that work their way across the computer screen, or the skirt of the rust-colored dress hovering mere millimeters from my leg.

We head downstairs when we finish, standing side by side on the elevator. Cassidy leans close to me to mock a man riding downstairs with us, a man with a bad toupee, as she elongates her neck and laughs out loud, her fingernails grazing the skin on my forearm.

I wonder what others think of us: me with a wedding band, her without.

Do they see us as colleagues in New York on a business trip, or something more than that: me the adulterer and her the mistress?

In the hotel's bar, I snag the steel side chair so that Cassidy is forced onto a low sofa with Tom and Henry. We drink. Too much. We talk. Gossip. Make fun of coworkers and clients, which is far too easy to do. Satirize spouses, and then claim to be kidding when someone's wife becomes the butt of a joke.

Heidi.

Cassidy sips from a Manhattan, leaving ruby red lip marks along the edges of the cocktail glass, and says, "See this, gentlemen, is the reason I'll never get married," and I wonder which it is: that she refuses to be the butt of some joke, or refuses to mock the one she vowed to love in good times and in bad. Sickness and health. So long as they both shall live.

Or maybe it's the whole monogamy thing that dissuades her.

And then, later, in the john, a completely sauced Henry accosts me with a condom. "In case you need this later," he says, and he laughs a haughty laugh with that lewd sense of humor that is Henry Tomlin.

"I hardly think Heidi and I need birth control," I say, but I take it anyway and slide it into my pants pocket, not wanting to be crass and leave it on the bathroom sink.

Henry leans in close, reeking of good old Jack Daniel's Tennessee Whiskey, a throwback to his redneck days, and whispers, "I wasn't talking about Heidi," and gives me a wink.

We lose track of time. Tom orders another round on him, some type of pilsner for Tom and me, more Jack Daniel's for Henry, an Alabama Slammer for Cassidy. She pulls the fruit out — an orange and a maraschino cherry — and eats that first. The bartender announces, "Last call."

I forget about my phone completely, the

one tossed onto the bed, hidden beneath the folds of the white bedspread.

HEIDI

Zoe goes to bed early, riddled with a headache and stuffy nose, the return of spring
allergy season, or maybe just a cold. It's impossible to tell, as is nearly always the case
this time of year, when tree pollens are at
their height, but cold and flu season has yet
to recede from view. So I dole out both pain
relievers and antihistamines, and Zoe falls
into bed, drifting immediately into a drug-
induced sleep, as I kiss her forehead gingerly, leaving the TV on in Chris's and my
bedroom, as the sound of some reality TV
show permeates the walls.

Willow and I sit, perched in the living
room — she, reading silently from *Anne of
Green Gables,* and me on my laptop, feign-
ing work though it's the furthest thing from
my mind. It's been three days since I've
been into the office, three days since anything work related has crossed my mind.

My absence has been felt at work, a happy

bouquet of roses and lilies now taking up residence on my kitchen table with a *Get Well Soon* card. Each morning I prepare my most macabre voice and put in a call to Dana, receptionist extraordinaire, and say that I'm unwell, the flu, I believe, and blame my own foolishness for not getting the vaccine. My temperature hovers somewhere around 102, depending on the day, and my body aches through and through, everything from the hairs on my head to the tips of my toes. I've wrapped myself in blankets and layer upon layer of clothes, and yet I'm overwhelmed by chills, never warm, praying that Zoe doesn't get sick though, being the good mother I am, Zoe, of course, had her vaccine.

But still, I say, before breaking into a coughing fit that sounds really quite sincere, silently giving myself kudos for thespian abilities of which I was unaware I possessed — the compression of air in my lungs, the muculent secretions that erupt from my chest like hot lava from Mauna Loa — *you never know.*

None of it, of course, is true.

I'm finding myself to be quite skilled in the art of lying.

I gaze eagerly at the baby, sound asleep on the floor, waiting impatiently for the first

hint of movement — the fluttering of eyelids, the flicker of a hand — which will eject
me from my chair and to her side a split
second before Willow, like children in a
competitive game of slapjack, both driven
to be the first to spot the jack and whack it
with their hand.

I type meaningless words into the computer screen, evidence that I am working.

My eyes move from Ruby, to Willow, to
the laptop, and back again, a never-ending
circuit that makes me giddy, afflicted with
the sudden sensation of vertigo.

I listen as, from the adjoining wall, the
laughter of Graham and his latest ladylove
drift through the drywall to greet me, the
tone of her voice — flirty and insincere —
indicative of a brief dalliance and nothing
more. Graham's specialty. I watch as Willow's eyes rise up from the book to listen,
to listen to the kittenish laughter and the
shrill tone of voice, and as they intersect
mine, as those icy blue eyes cut through my
own jittery orbs, I find myself looking away
quickly, considering the ochre bruise and
wondering what it would take for someone
like Willow to snap. How much maltreat-
ment and exploitation someone could
handle before losing self-control.

I cannot look at her, into those eyes that

threaten me. I stare at the white walls, instead, a framed photo collage of Chris and Zoe and me, black-and-white photographs in wooden frames, the cats in theirs, the word *family* carved from fiberboard, hand-painted and hung in the middle of the display.

I pat at the pocket of my purple robe and feel for the Swiss Army knife inside.

A precaution. I heed Chris's warning: *How much can you really know about another person?*

And then the baby does start to stir, her eyelids flutter and there's a flicker of the hand, but it's Willow — not me — with her lightning-fast reflexes who reaches the baby first and lifts her from the floor in that rickety way that she does, her arms shaky, her grasp insecure so that for a fraction of a second, or more, I'm certain Ruby will fall. I feel myself rise and step forward to catch the plummeting child, but then Willow's eyes stop me in my tracks, staring at me, smug, taking great delight in my distress. *Ha!* those eyes mock me, and *I beat you,* as if she knew all along that I was waiting. Waiting ever so patiently to hold the baby. To hold that beautiful baby in my arms when she awoke from sleep.

I lift a hand to my mouth to stifle a scream

that threatens to emerge from somewhere deep within.

"Are you okay?" she asks me, as she returns to the chair, bundling Ruby in the pink blanket. And then, when I don't respond fast enough, she asks again, "ma'am?"

My hand drops from my gaping mouth to my splintered heart and I lie, "yes, just fine," finding that lying is so easy to do as an air of serenity disguises my turbulent state, the tempestuous clouds that roll in before a storm.

I'm aware suddenly of the TV in the bedroom, blaringly loud. The reality show has broken for commercial, and suddenly we are being screamed at, chided and admonished, to buy some sort of fabric softener which smells of eucalyptus leaves. It enrages me; the sound of it, loud and emphatic, might wake Zoe from sleep. I curse it out loud, that damned commercial, I curse the TV and the network and the eucalyptus fabric softener which I will never buy. I march down the hall to turn the TV off, pressing *power* so vehemently that the TV slides two inches or more on the console, scratching the wall. Behind me, in the queen-size bed, beneath the matelassé comforter, Zoe rolls over onto a side, her hands still clutching the remote control though she sleeps.

She lets out a sleepy sigh.

My heart drums loudly in my chest, overwhelmed by that sense of being completely out of control. Powerless. On the verge of going mad. As I stand there, in the bedroom, staring at the blank TV screen, I feel overcome by a sudden wave of nausea, my legs turn to jelly and, for one split second, I'm certain I've gone into cardiac arrest.

I inch into the bathroom as blackness sweeps across my eyes like window cleaner splashed on a dirty pane. I drop onto the edge of the bathtub and set my head beneath my legs, forcing the blood back up to my brain.

And then I reach for the faucet and turn the water on so that Zoe, if she awakes from her anesthetized doze, will not hear me cry.

And that's when I see it: the filigree bird painted a distressed red, the shabby chic hook on the wall. An extra hole, poorly plastered and painted, a reminder that when Chris hung the hook, he hung it askew.

I purchased the hook from a flea market in Kane County, on a road trip Jennifer and I made some six, maybe, seven years ago. The forty-some miles out of the city and to St. Charles was the closest either of us had been to a vacation in years. As Jennifer and

I scoured through antiques and collectibles for things we didn't need, the girls, Zoe and Taylor, rode behind in a red wagon, stuffing themselves with hot dogs and popcorn to stay quiet and satisfied.

The hook, completely bare.

I grope at my neck but come up empty, as I knew with certainty I would do, for I recall hanging the chain — the golden chain with my father's wedding band, the words *The beginning of forever* engraved along its inside — from the filigree bird before I kissed Zoe on the forehead good-night. Before I left the bedroom — dimming the lights — and returned to the kitchen to clean pots and pans that awaited me on the cooling stove. Before I gathered the foul-smelling plastic bag from the garbage can and marched it down the hall to the chute. Before I settled down with my laptop to type meaningless words onto the screen, waiting fruitlessly for Ruby to stir.

She has taken my father's wedding ring.

All at once, it's as if he's died again, my father. I'm teleported to the morning my mother phoned from their Cleveland home. He'd been sick for months and so it should have come as no surprise to me, the fact that he was dead. And yet the news of it, the very words slipping from my mother's tongue, her tone newsy rather than sorrowful — *he's dead* — completely bowled me over, left me stupefied. For weeks I went on believing it was a mistake, a misunderstanding, certainly this couldn't be true. There was the funeral and the burial, of course, and I watched as some man resembling my father — but cold and rubbery, his features pliable and strange — was lowered into the ground, and then, like the dutiful daughter I was, I tossed my roses on top of the casket because it was what my mother carried when they were wed. Lavender roses.

Though I believed in my heart of hearts it wasn't my father inside that box.

I tried phoning him each and every day, my father, worried when he didn't answer his cell phone. From time to time my mother would answer, and in her kindest, gentlest voice she'd say, "Heidi, dear, you can't keep calling like this," and when I continued to call, she suggested to me, to Chris, that I see someone, someone who could help me sort through my grief. But I refused.

As I refused to see someone — a counselor, a shrink — as the ob-gyn suggested I do after he killed Juliet, after he appropriated my womb.

It's nearing ten o'clock in New York City.

371

I call Chris from a cell phone stashed in my pocket, to tell him that Willow has stolen from me, and yet his cell phone rings and rings without an answer.

I wait ten minutes and then try again, knowing that Chris is a night owl, and so he is certainly awake, certainly slaving away on some offering memorandum that he swore he'd be writing.

Or so he said.

When again there is no response, I text a message: Call me. ASAP. And proceed to wait futilely for twenty minutes or more.

And then I begin to seethe.

I search online for a phone number for the Manhattan hotel and put in a call, asking reception to transfer me to Chris Wood's room. I whisper for Zoe's sake, and she asks me more than once to repeat myself. There's a pause as the woman tries to make the connection, but then she comes back on the line and says apologetically, "There's no answer in that room, ma'am. Would you like to leave a message?"

I hang up the phone.

I consider calling again and asking to be transferred to Cassidy Knudsen's room.

I consider a red-eye flight out to New York, a surprise appearance in the lobby of his hotel, desperate to catch him and

372

Cassidy flitting about, laughing at some joke the rest of the world is not privy to. I see Cassidy in her hotel-issued robe, Chris in his, champagne delivered via room service, and strawberries. Yes, of course, strawberries.

The Do Not Disturb door hanger placed on the handle.

I can feel the blood creeping up my neck, making my ears ring. My pulse loud enough that Zoe, sound asleep, can certainly hear. My heartbeat is so erratic it makes me dizzy, and I drop my head again beneath my legs to catch my breath, thinking evil thoughts toward my husband and *that* woman, thoughts of planes bound for Denver bursting into flames and crashing to the ground.

"It's time for Ruby's medicine," I hear then, the timid voice of *that girl,* that kleptomaniac who has stolen my father's wedding band from me.

I want to scream, and yet, instead, with astounding control, I say, "You took my father's wedding ring. You took the ring," and I want to grab her by the neck and shake the living daylights out of her because she took the one thing in the world that meant the most to me.

But I remain on the edge of the bathtub, running my hand along the fleece robe, along the straight edge of the Swiss Army knife tucked safely inside, considering its many tools, or weapons if you may: a corkscrew, scissors, a gimlet, and of course, a blade.

"What?" she asks feebly, hurt, as if she's the one who's been laid to waste. Pillaged. Plundered. Her voice is light, barely audible, as she shakes her head desperately, frantically, and whispers, "No."

But her eyes don't look at mine, and she's begun to fidget with her hands. She blinks rapidly, her fair skin turning red. Telltale signs of deceit. I rise to my feet and, as I do, she retreats backward, quickly, and out of the room, prattling in an undertone something or other about Jesus and forgiveness and mercy.

A confession.

"Where is it?" I ask, following her into the living room, my footsteps delicate but fast, a half step faster than her own, so that I quickly narrow the gap. I drift across the room in my sheepskin slippers and turn her by the arm so that she's forced to look at me, forced to maintain eye contact as only the best perjurer can. She steps away quickly; I've intruded upon her space. She sets her arms behind herself so I cannot touch them again.

"Where is my father's wedding band?" I demand this time, aware of the way the baby watches us from the floor, gnawing on a polka dot sock she's pulled from a foot, her pale pink piggies hovering midair, completely insouciant to the tension surrounding her, filling the room, making it hard to breathe.

"I don't have it," Willow lies, her voice as spineless as an earthworm or a leech. "I promise, ma'am, I don't have the ring," she says, but her eyes remain shifty, scheming, and in place of an impressionable, naive young woman, as I had once perceived her to be, I see someone, instead, who's wily and astute. Artful and sly.

She evades my stare, twitches uncomfortably in her own skin as if it's suddenly the skin of a porcupine, riddled with quills.

An act.

Her words come out staccato-like, abrupt and clipped, an outpouring of denials: *I didn't do it,* and *I swear,* her hands overgesticulating, her face turning red.

A charade.

She mocks me with her lies and her tomfoolery, with the naive eyes that are anything but naive. She knew exactly what she was doing, from that very first day I spotted

375

her at the Fullerton Station, waiting in the rain.

Waiting for someone like me to take the bait.

"What did you do with it?" I ask frantically. "What did you do with the ring?"

"I don't have it," she says again, "I don't have the ring," shaking her head briskly from side to side, the bob of a pendulum.

But I insist, "You do. You took it. From the bathroom hook. You took my father's ring."

"Ma'am," she pleads, and it's pathetic almost, the tone of her voice, heartbreaking, really, if it wasn't such a sham. She retreats a step and I follow, quickly, the abruptness of the movement, of my movement, a single step but no more, making her flinch, a wince escaping from somewhere deep within.

My hand gropes for the Swiss Army knife in the pocket of the purple robe, clutching tightly as I utter the simple word, "Go."

I feel it tremble in my hand, that knife. And I think to myself, *Don't make me . . .*

She's shaking her head, swiftly from side to side, the sepia hair falling into her bulging eyes, her lips parting to mouth a single word: *No.* And then she's begging me to let her stay, begging me not to make her go.

Outside it's begun to rain, again, raindrops tap, tap, tapping at the bay window, though it's a drizzle and not quite a storm, not yet at least.

Though there's no telling what the night will bring.

"Go," I say again. "Go now. Before I call the police," and I take a step for the phone sitting on the kitchen countertop.

"Please, don't," she begs, and then, "Please don't make me go," and she's staring out the window, at the rain.

"You took the ring," I insist. "Give me the ring."

"Please, ma'am," she says, and then, "Heidi," as if trying to reach me on a more personal level, and yet it strikes me as inappropriate, presumptuous even. The audacity of it reminds me of her impudence, her overconfidence; the rest is just a pretense, a work of fiction. A pathetic display used to slink into my home and steal from me. I wonder what else she took: the Polish pottery, my grandmother's pearls, Chris's class ring.

"Mrs. Wood," I state.

"I don't have the ring, Mrs. Wood. I swear to you. I don't have the ring."

"Then you sold it," I maintain. "Where did you sell it, Willow? The pawnshop?"

377

There's one in Lincoln Park, I picture it clear as day, a storefront on Clark with the sign: *We Buy Gold.* I think of myself, that afternoon, lying down for a brief nap. Did she pawn the ring while I was asleep? But no, I hung the chain on the hook tonight, before I kissed Zoe good-night and dimmed the lights, cleaned the kitchen and settled down with my laptop to work. Or not work. To pretend to work.

Or maybe that was last night, I think, feeling suddenly lost and confused, not knowing which day it is, or which way is up.

But knowing with certainty that she took the ring.

"How much did you get for it?" I ask then, all of a sudden, and when she doesn't respond, I ask it again, "How much did you get for my father's wedding ring?" wondering — *five hundred, a thousand?* — all the while stroking the smooth edge of the Swiss Army knife with my hand, running my thumb along the blade until it most certainly bleeds. I don't feel it, the blood, but I visualize it, a drop, maybe two, that seeps onto the purple robe.

And then she's gathering her things from around the home — baby bottles and formula; she's collecting the torn jeans and leather lace-up boots, the army-green coat, the vintage suitcase from the office down the hall — and dragging them to the front door, where she drops them in a heap, turning to me sullenly, the phony despair replaced with a stoic expression in her eyes.

But when she moves to lift the baby from the floor, I intercede.

Over my dead body, is what I'm thinking, but what I say is, "You can't take care of her. You know that as well as I do. She would have died from that infection if it wasn't for me."

An untreated urinary tract infection could lead to sepsis.

Without treatment, a person could die.

But those weren't my words; those came from the doctor at the clinic, didn't they? It was the doctor who told us that, wanting to know how long this had been going on, the baby's persistent irritability and that untamed fever.

"A week, maybe two," Willow had said regretfully, but I'd mocked her candor and said, "Just a few days, dear, not a week," knowing what the doctor would think of us if we had let the infection go on for weeks, had allowed the fever to carry on that long. I'd rolled my eyes at the doctor then, there in the tawdry office and said of Willow, "She has such a poor sense of time. Teenagers, you know? One day, one week, it makes no difference to them," and the doctor, perhaps the mother of a teen or a preteen herself, had nodded her head and agreed.

The lying, these days, it's just so easy a thing to do. It comes naturally, automatically, until I can no longer tell what's fact, what's fiction.

"You take that baby," I say, "and I'll be forced to call the police. Child endangerment, in addition to theft. She's safer here, with me."

She needs to understand that the baby is better off with me. "When I met you," I remind her, "she had a fever. Blisters on her rear end, patches of eczema across her skin. She hadn't been bathed in weeks, and you were all but out of food. It's a wonder she wasn't hypothermic, emaciated or dead.

"Besides," I tack on, inching closer to the baby, knowing good and well I will fight for her if I need to, that I will draw the knife from the robe and argue self-defense.

But I can see already, by the resignation in her eyes, that I will not need to fight. The baby, for her, is a burden, a weight. The visceral feelings — that undeniable need to hold the baby, the sense of floating purposelessly adrift when she's not in my embrace — those are mine. All mine. That longing that stems from the tips of my toes, all the way to my entrails. Mine.

"You hardly need a baby slowing you down," knowing as well as she does that she likely has someone in hot pursuit. Whom, I hardly know, but I register she does, the man or woman who delivered that ochre bruise, I assume.

"You'll take care of her," she states. Not so much as a question, but a need. I need you to take care of her.

I say that I will. My face softens, for the baby's sake, and the words cascade from my mouth like a waterfall. "Oh, I will," I promise, "I will take such good care of her," like a child who's been blessed with a new kitten.

"But I can't have you in my home," I say then, my voice tightening, as I walk a fine line between caring for that baby and needing Willow out of my house, "not when you've been stealing from me," and she protests, "I didn't —" and I interrupt with, "Just go."

I don't want to hear it, the lies and denials, any excuses about needing money for this or that, when it's clear I'm not buying her opening story. She took my father's wedding ring, plain and simple, and sold it at the pawnshop.

And now she must go.

She doesn't say goodbye to me. She asks again, "You will take care of her. Of Ruby?" but the words come out half hearted and not genuine, for it's proper etiquette, she must assume, to make sure the baby is in good hands before she goes. But there's a hesitation, nonetheless, a brief hesitation as she eyes the baby and quite possibly her blue eyes fill with tears. Fake tears, I tell myself, nothing more.

And then she steps toward the baby and runs a hand across her head; she whispers a goodbye before she goes, wiping those artificial tears on the back of a sleeve.

"I'll treat her as if she were my very own," I avow, closing and locking the door as she leaves. I watch from the bay window to make sure she's gone, moping down the city street in the cold April rain. And then I turn to the baby girl, completely enraptured by her doughy cheeks, her snow-white hair, her toothless mouth that unfolds into a radiant smile, and think: *Mine. All mine.*

WILLOW

At some point when I wasn't paying attention, I turned sixteen.

And that was when it happened, all of it in about three weeks.

It was the end of winter, and I was feeling antsy for spring, but for whatever reason, the snow kept falling from the ominous, gray sky. I was freezing cold each time Matthew and I took the buses around town, and the sweatshirt and gym shoes never seemed to do. The cold winter air blew into each and every bus stop, and since most of my clothes were dresses and jumpers from Joseph, my legs were completely bare.

At night, as I slept on that bed with the thin patchwork quilt, with only an oversize T-shirt to keep me warm, I trembled, my body covered in goose pimples, which quadrupled each time Joseph pulled that T-shirt up over my head.

I thought of all the ways I'd kill him if I

could. Thinking of Momma and "I love you likes" got replaced with thinking of Joseph and all the ways I'd do him in if I could. Pushing him down the stairs. Hitting him over the head with a frying pan. Setting the whole Omaha home on fire while he was asleep.

But then what would I do?

I hate you like arachnophobes hate spiders. I hate you like cats hate dogs.

One lifeless winter day, Matthew and I caught the bus and headed to the library. I remember that I was excited 'cause that day, Matthew was going to show me how to use the computers. I'd never used a computer before.

We hadn't gone more than a block down the street when Matthew asked if I was cold and when I told him I was, he sneaked an arm around my back and pulled me close to him. In an instant, it was as if there wasn't another soul on that bus but Matthew and me. Like the whole rest of the world had disappeared. Matthew's arm felt warm, strong, secure.

I turned my head and peeked up at him, wondering if those chocolate eyes might explain it to me what just happened. How my insides got all gooey, how my hands turned to slime. Matthew didn't say anything, nor did his eyes. He was looking out the window like he didn't even notice what happened, but inside I wondered if he felt that change like me after all.

We went to the library, and pulling up two chairs to one computer, Matthew showed me a world I'd never known before. He showed me something called the internet, where I could look up anything I'd ever wanted to know about the planets or jungle animals or spiders; he showed me how I could play games.

There was music on there, too, on the computer. We slipped on the library's headphones, and Matthew put some music on, kind of loud, but I liked it. I liked the sound of the bass right there in my ear. I thought of Momma. Of spinning around the room to Patsy Cline.

Going to the library became Matthew's and my regular thing. It was my favorite thing to do. The library was quiet and warm, even though right outside the big glass doors, the world was cold and loud. The building was big, four-stories or more, tucked right there in between all those huge buildings. Sometimes I just liked to ride the elevators, up, down, up, down, even if we didn't go anywhere at all. We talked a lot there, Matthew and me, and if he told me once he told me a thousand times that he was gonna get me out of that house and away from Joseph. He just had to figure out how, is all. By then I'd started thinking a lot about the world outside of Omaha, and it made life there with Joseph and Miriam even worse. I wanted more than anything to leave, to run as far away as I could, but Matthew said to wait. He was going to figure it out for me; he said not to worry, and so I didn't.

But what I really looked forward to there at the library was tucking ourselves into some vacant aisle — just us. We'd sit on the floor and sprawl our legs out before us, and lean up against the towering shelves. We'd skim through the books for random facts and take turns saying them aloud, like *Did you know fresh eggs will sink but a rotten egg will float?* Or *Did you know 89 percent of the human brain is made up of water?* just like we did when we were kids and Matthew would pass by my room at night. I read books about Audrey Hepburn and Patsy Cline. I looked up that place where Lily now lived, Colorado, and learned more about the flat plains of the thirty-eighth state and about the Continental Divide. I learned more about that Magnificent Mile Momma used to talk about, and I learned about Chicago, the Windy City, City of Broad Shoulders.

"Did you know Arthur Rubloff came up with the name *Magnificent Mile* in 1947?" I asked, but Matthew just said to me, "What's the Magnificent Mile?"

And then one day we're sitting there, in one of those vacant aisles, when all of a sudden Matthew found my hand tucked in the kangaroo pouch of that orange sweatshirt and pressed it between his. Matthew had held my hand before, on those buses, or when I was scared, but this time it was something different because this time I could tell Matthew was scared, too. His hand was all sweaty-like, and when he grabbed for it, I felt my heart grow three times inside of me, as if it was going to burst right there from my chest. I didn't know what it was that I was feeling and I wanted so badly to ask someone, anyone.

But most of all I wanted to ask Momma.

We pretended for a long time that it wasn't happening, that we weren't holding hands. We just went on searching for random facts in the books with each of our free hands, while the hands that were joined, they were like their own independent beings or something. They were something different.

But it didn't stop my heart from beating out of control, my brain unable to grasp any of the words inside the heavy library books.

And then all of a sudden Matthew was sitting closer and I didn't remember it happening. I didn't remember it happening at all, but suddenly, his leg was pressed up against mine, and his hip was touching mine, and suddenly we were reading from the same book while the other had been set aside. A book on engineering, whatever in the world that is. I couldn't have made heads or tails of it even if I tried, but I didn't try because I couldn't think of anything other than my hand pressed in between Matthew's hands, or what it sounded like when he turned his head toward mine and softly said my name.

Claire.

Matthew said it like a whisper, my name. I could feel the breath emerge from his lips more than I could actually hear my name.

I turned to look at him and he was so close. He was right there. Breathing on me. Noses all but touching.

I didn't know what I was supposed to do: lean in or pull back, the other way. But I knew, in my heart, what I wanted to do, and so I leaned in to Matthew and settled my lips upon his lips, lips that were coarse and dry, but also tender and delicious, I thought, as a tongue slipped through those lips and into my mouth and I felt everything inside me turn to goo.

I knew then what was happening to me: I was in love with Matthew.

His tongue disappeared almost as quickly as it appeared, his lips withdrew from mine. He pulled away, though he didn't let go of my hand, his eyes darting across the pages of that engineering book until he uttered some stupid facts, nervously, about kilometers and watts, though I had no idea what it meant. I had no idea what any of it meant. I could hardly hear his words. I could hardly stop thinking about his lips and his tongue and his hand.

The way he tasted.

The way he smelled.

After that, when Matthew and I went to the library, we weren't so consumed with those books and finding meaningless facts in the pages to share with one another. We'd sneak down whatever vacant aisle we could find, and there, hidden from the world by those tall, tall bookcases, Matthew would press his lips to my lips, would slide his tongue into my mouth. His hands would hold my hands, sometimes, but sometimes they would stray, they would wander away from my hands and to my face, my arms, my chest, between my legs, slipping cold and unsure up under that bright orange sweatshirt and into the sole bra Joseph had given to me.

CHRIS

I pass through Chicago on the way to Denver for a meeting with a potential client. Face-to-face meetings are big in the world of investment banking; we have a quota for our firm, how many meetings we're to attend each month. Twenty. That's what our CEO says. Twenty face-to-face meetings with clients. Skype won't do. FaceTime doesn't work. Even though I'm eight hundred miles away, giving presentations to try to entice potential investors to purchase shares of an IPO for another client, I'm to pop into the office for the client meeting, then catch up in Denver with Tom, Henry, Cassidy and the rest of the crew later in the day.

I take the first flight out of LaGuardia at 6:00 a.m., landing me in Chicago at 7:28 a.m., local time. The meeting is at nine, barely enough time to gather my luggage from baggage claim and catch a cab to the Loop.

The client meeting goes exceptionally well. They usually do. Apparently I have some charm I don't know about, a tender face that makes people want to put their trust in me. It's the reason I'm usually at the forefront of meetings with potential clients. It has nothing to do with an impressive MBA or the years of experience I have tucked beneath my belt. It's all about my smile, and the boyish good looks my mother swore would get me in trouble someday.

I have an afternoon flight out of O'Hare, to the Mile High City; not enough time to go home, shower, shave, change out of the rancid suit jacket I've worn for days — though I've managed to short myself on clean socks and underwear, and my lucky tie, for this never-ending trip to hell and back. I put in a call to Heidi, never thinking in a million years that she'd do me this favor, and yet she does, she packs a spare bag of clothes and offers to meet me at an Asian grill for a quick bite.

It's only been forty-some hours since I've seen Heidi, and yet there's something different about her, something casual, something that conflicts with the Heidi I left the other morning, asleep in bed, the overthinking, premeditative Heidi she evolved into somewhere along the path of our marriage. I see it in her step, as she walks briskly down Michigan Avenue, right there where the Mag Mile crosses the Chicago River, at the Michigan Avenue Bridge, completely un-ruffled by the hubbub of the city. There's a bounce in her step, and she's dressed in a dress, a stone-colored dress that just skims the ankle, surprisingly fitted and chic, not quite what I'm used to seeing on Heidi. She looks amazing. And yet, she's got the damn baby strapped to her in one of those baby slings, and when I ask, "What the heck is that?" she tells me it's called a Moby Wrap, as if this is the most normal thing in the whole entire world, her, wearing someone else's baby like luggage.

"Where's her mother?" I ask, searching left and right, up and down for the girl. "You didn't leave her at home?" I ask. "Alone?" I'm prepared to go into some big diatribe about that girl stealing my big-screen TV, and how she was never, *ever* to be left unattended in our home.

But Heidi smiles kindly and says that she dropped her off at the library, on the way to meet me for lunch. That the girl wanted to check out a few books. *Black Beauty,* she says, and *A Wrinkle in Time,* tacking on, "The classics," knowing good and well the only thing I read as a kid was the *Wall Street Journal.* She says that she thought I'd prefer it if Willow didn't join us for lunch, a statement I can't altogether argue with; I just happen to wish she'd left the baby at the library, too.

And then Heidi steps forward and kisses me, an impromptu kiss, that's not too short and is entirely sweet, the kind of thing my Heidi would hardly ever do, not in public at least. Heidi is a strict opponent of PDA. She's been like this for years, forever maybe, scowling when she sees some couple kissing on a corner or at the bus stop, even a quick peck, the *have a good day* kind of kiss normal couples share all the time. She presses close to me, the napping baby sandwiched in between, running her hands up and down my arms. Her hands are warm to the touch, vulnerable in a way that Heidi rarely is. Her lips press firmly to mine, decisively, and she whispers, "I missed you," and as I draw slowly away, I know those words, those simple, golden words, and the desiring tone of her voice will stay with me all day.

We eat lunch. I order crab rangoon, Heidi the chicken pad thai. I tell her about my week; she tells me about hers. I apologize for the gazillionth time for missing her call last night, but unlike the seething voice mail she left me a mere twelve hours ago, this time she shrugs mercifully and says it's okay. What I tell her is that I fell fast asleep, completely bushed from the week. I say that I had a beer or two — maybe three — with dinner, and I didn't hear my phone ring.

I don't tell her about drinks in the hotel bar; I don't tell her about Cassidy proofreading the offering memorandum in my hotel room, alone. That wouldn't be very sensible; in fact, it'd be downright dumb. I don't mention Cassidy's lissome frame or the profile of her breasts in the rust-colored dress, though still they're on my mind, like some greedy little kid wishing for candy.

"What did you need to tell me?" I ask, and she laughs wholeheartedly and says, "I can't even remember anymore," as the waiter refills our glasses of water.

Heidi's smile is sympathetic, the epitome of the submissive wife. Her hair is clean — no more spaghetti hair — and there's some sort of musky-perfumy scent coming from her, something I hardly recognize anymore in my wife. I didn't even know Heidi still owned perfume. Or maybe it's the shampoo.

Her words come out solicitous, as she says, "You must be so tired, Chris. You're always on the go."

And I admit I am — tired. And then she tells me about the baby, how the antibiotic has been helping her get better. She's feeling better and sleeping better, which, in turn, means Heidi's sleeping. I can see that her eyes look rested, she's found the time to take a shower and put makeup on, not much — a dab of blush, maybe some lip gloss — but enough that there's color to her skin; she's not a frightening white.

Maybe that was all that she needed, I think. A good night's sleep.

"When I get home," I say, "we're going to need to talk about all this. The whole Willow situation," and though I'm expecting some sort of backlash — casual Heidi to disappear and be replaced with uptight Heidi once again — it doesn't come.

She simply says, "Of course. Yes, let's talk. When you get back from Denver. But," she adds, massaging my free hand — the one that isn't stuffing deep fried dumplings into my mouth like I haven't eaten for a week — and then lacing her fingers through mine and offering a squeeze, "I have a feeling everything is going to be just fine. You'll see. It'll all work out."

And I find myself, somehow, convinced that it will be fine.

We say our goodbyes and exchange bags:

me taking the clean socks and undies, my lucky tie, Heidi carrying away my dirty laundry like some dutiful 1950s housewife.

I watch as she heads off, down the street, veering in and out of pedestrian traffic, heading in the opposite direction of the library.

I take a peek inside the bag, to make sure she brought it, that she brought my financial calculator, because I said the ones from the office sucked, citing their microscopic digits and keys that don't work as the cause though Heidi never asked. But in reality, it was the only small thing I could remember that the elusive Willow Greer had touched inside my home — that first day, in my office, when she leaned over to retrieve it from the floor, a shaky hand tracing each and every key, leaving behind an unmistakable identity neither she nor I could see — the only thing that would be within reason for Heidi to bring to me when we met for lunch.

I could hardly suggest she bring the remote control, baby bottles, the old suitcase.

And then I hurry to meet Martin Miller before I board the next plane.

WILLOW

On one of her prearranged visits, Ms. Adler arrived with a letter from the Zeegers, as usual, though this one was completely different. She appeared on the front stoop, stomping the snow off her big fleecy boots before coming into the home. Joseph took her coat from her and laid it over the arm of a chair, and we all went into the kitchen where, as usual, we sat around the wooden table and a doped-up Miriam served us cookies and tea.

This letter though, wasn't about my Lily and how well she was doing in school and how big she was growing up to be. No this letter was completely different. This letter made the blood in my veins run cold, the air in the room too thin to breathe. I grasped that letter in my shaking hands and read aloud — as Joseph made me do so he wouldn't be left in the dark — about how ten months before, Big Lily found herself suddenly, curiously pregnant, and how Rose (Lily) had become a big sister in December. The letter gushed with the minutia of the baby's pale eyes and delicate hair, her gentle demeanor, the musical sound of her coo. This, Big Lily explained, was what she and Paul had always dreamed of: to have a baby of their own. Her name was Calla, as in the Calla Lily, half of a whole, and my Lily — no longer a Lily but now a Rose — was excluded. Left out. Not the baby she and Paul had always dreamed of.

"But how?" I whined. "She wasn't . . . I thought . . ." I set the letter on the table and swallowed hard against a bulge in my throat. I would not let Joseph see me cry, or Isaac who stood, back to the wall, a smirk on his ugly face.

The caseworker was all smiles. "How wonderful," she said, and, "What a wonderful surprise. Imagine Rose — a sister," as if *Rose* hadn't been a sister all along. My sister. Mine. "Sometimes," she explained to me, her voice dumbed down like I was some idiot, "this happens. I suppose they were never truly infertile. Just —" her voice wavered off for a split second before she added "— unlucky."

Unlucky to have Little Lily in their life

rather than the baby they'd always dreamed of.

There was no mention of my Lily in that letter, other than the simple blurb that she was a big sister. The rest of the note oozed with details of Calla's life: how she slept peacefully throughout the night, how for Lily, giving birth to her own flesh and blood had been sublime. There was a photo attached: Big Lily and Calla, my Lily hovering in the background like an afterthought. Her hair was a mess, red sauce dribbled down the front of a plain white shirt.

But Calla was pristine, in the softest-looking mauve one piece, a denim headband with bow on her head.

There was no letter from my Lily included. No third-grade school picture, no stationery with the red bird and tree, no distorted name printed across the front: *Rose Zeeger.*

My Lily had been replaced.

It plagued me for days. I stayed awake night after night wondering what would happen to my Lily. Would the Zeegers overlook her for the rest of her life, not good enough now that they had their own flesh and blood? Would they decide that two children were one too many, and would Lily be sent back to that group home to await a lousy foster home like the one I was living in? Would she stay in that group home forever, or until she turned eighteen, and was sent out into the world to fend for herself, to live like a waif on some Colorado or Nebraska street? I could only imagine. I conjured up visions of the Zeegers ignoring her, forcing her to wear that stained white shirt for the rest of her life. The very name haunted me in the middle of the night: *Calla. Calla.*

I hated it. I hated her.

Calla had ruined my Lily's life.

The days went on. I spent every waking hour reading and rereading that letter from Big Lily, staring at that photo of Big Lily and the baby, my Lily pushed so far into the background she almost fell out of the picture.

This photo, unlike all the others, Joseph let me keep. In fact, he taped it up to that flowery wallpaper lest I forget that this baby, that *Calla,* was plundering my Lily's happy childhood.

But what could I do?

HEIDI

I spend the night in the rocking chair, hardly able to take my eyes off the sweet baby. When Zoe awakes and asks where Willow is, her cross eyes scanning the closed office door as she slides down the hall with a half-asleep gait, I say, in a hushed tone, "Still sleeping," though I know good and well that isn't true.

I don't think about her at all. I don't think about Willow.

Zoe departs for school, and the day comes and goes. I hardly take notice. Other than a quick lunch with Chris, the baby and I don't leave home. We spend much of the day in the rocking chair, my strides calculated, rhythmic as Ruby sleeps on my lap, soundly, like a newborn babe. I can think of little but the shape of her eyes, can do little but count the milia on her nose. I watch as, out the window, the sun rises and then moments later, it begins to set, slipping beneath the massive skyscrapers that dot the city sky, staining the gauzy clouds a deep pink, a navy blue, a tea rose. Out the window, people awaken, commencing their workday; they return home, a second later, the day through. Breakfast, lunch and dinner come and go; my phone rings, there's the bleep of the intercom system — someone or something beckoning me from the first floor — and yet I can't be bothered, won't be bothered, can't take my eyes off the baby as she sleeps, and then awakens; sleeps, and then awakens, foraging in the folds of a fitted dress when she wants to eat and it's then, and only then, that I rise from the rocking chair and prepare a bottle for her to consume. As afternoon gives way to evening, I watch Ruby sleep while crepuscular rays fill the sky, straight lines that spill downward from the descending sun. Shafts of light, the Fingers of God.

I don't mind the clock, completely oblivious to the aluminum hand that spins around the circular face, pointing at this Roman numeral, and then that. This Roman number, and then that. I hear neighbors in the hallway, coming home from work; I smell their dinners wafting under the door and through the walls: enchiladas and baked chicken, pork chops. My phone rings, and then rings again, but I can't be bothered to rise from the chair and answer it, convincing myself it's merely some telemarketer, or an automated message from Zoe's superintendent about some upcoming meeting at the school which doesn't concern me, pertaining only to graduating seniors or to the parents of students with special needs.

And then the front door bursts open, suddenly, violently, and there Zoe stands in her pink jersey and pink shorts, her feet cloaked in a pair of muddy cleats. Her shin guards are on, the hot-pink socks that stretch all the way to her knees caked with mud. Her hair is woven into a double French braid, a unifying hairdo one of the team mothers has taken to giving the Lucky Charms each and every game day, complete with some kind of homemade scrunchie that matches their uniforms.

And she demands, "Where were you?" while tossing her backpack to the hardwood floor with a thud. She's glaring at me from the open doorway and I watch as, behind her, a neighbor passes by with a pizza box in hand, trying hard to ignore the angry tone of Zoe's voice. The smell of it drifts into the room to greet me, and it's then that I realize I'm hungry. "You missed my game," she says, not giving me a chance to come up with some counterfeit response to the initial question. *I forgot* or *I got caught up at work and couldn't leave.*

Instead, all I can manage is, "I'm sorry," knowing the words sound fraudulent because, in fact, they are. I'm not sorry, not sorry that I missed Zoe's game because then I wouldn't have had this time with Ruby, rocking here in this chair with Ruby in my arms.

"I tried calling you," she says. Her hands are placed on her hips, and there's a pout on her face. She looks to the kitchen and back again, aware that I've started nothing for dinner, aware that in the near twilight, I'm all but sitting in the dark. She flips a light switch on over the kitchen table, and I find myself blinded by the light, waiting for my eyes to adjust.

The baby lets out a moan, and I coo, "There now," wondering if it's the bright light or the surly tone of Zoe's voice that upsets her.

"Why didn't you answer your phone?" Zoe barks out then. "I tried calling you. You missed the game. You missed the game completely," she cries and for a second, I picture it: Zoe, at her game, with the rest of the Lucky Charms, refusing to acknowledge her mother's presence, as is the case each and every game. It's quite the quandary, it is: she doesn't want me there, and yet, she doesn't want to be the only one without a mother in tow.

But I don't answer this. I don't answer Zoe's question: *Why didn't you answer your phone?* Instead, I ask, "How did you get home?"

"Do you hear me, Mom?" she asks, and I realize that I don't like that tone of her voice one bit. That sour tone of voice she's taken with me as if she's in charge and I'm the pliant one.

"Yes, Zoe, I heard you, but I asked you a question, as well. How did you get home?"

There's a huff. A retreat into the kitchen to ransack cabinets for something to eat, slamming this one and that. And then, "Coach paid for a cab. He couldn't stay there all night, waiting, you know? Like the other night. He has a life." A pause, followed by, "You owe him fourteen dollars." She yanks a bottle of water from the refrigerator door and states, "Ms. Marcue says she's been trying to call you. She says you haven't returned her calls." Then, with a box of Saltine crackers and the water, Zoe heads out of the room. She's gone about five feet when she pauses, stops dead in her tracks beside the closed office door and asks, "Why haven't you returned her calls?"

"I've been busy, Zoe. You know that," I respond, knowing that in Zoe's preteen mind she can't make sense of it, how caring for an infant could classify as *busy*. Busy is doodling on a forearm and texting friends, eluding homework and salivating over the handsome Coach Sam. *Busy* is not the inexhaustible hours it takes to raise a child.

"Well, are you going to call her back?" she asks. Her French braids hang long, their tail ends wrapping around the sides of her neck. She looks older to me than twelve, when she isn't smiling and I can't see the braces that remind me she's still a child. I'm aware, for the first time in forever, of the sudden arrival of breasts. Were they there all along, and I simply failed to notice? Or has she turned into a young woman overnight?

"Yes," I say, "of course."

"When?" she interrogates.

"Soon. I will call her soon."

"That baby's not yours, you know," she says out of nowhere, noticing the tender way I cradle Ruby in my arms, the way I massage her head.

"Why would you say such a thing?" I ask, my voice quiet, hurt.

"It's like you think she's yours or something. It's weird," and then, "Where's Willow?" she asks drily, as if her words didn't just blindside me, didn't just punch me in the gut, and I say, sullenly, winded by the abuse, "She wasn't feeling well. She went to bed early," stating it in a hushed tone so that Zoe will believe.

"The flu," I say, "it's going around."

But Zoe, thinking perhaps about my fraudulent phone calls to Dana, receptionist extraordinaire, rolls her eyes and says cynically, "Yeah, right," and then she leaves, down the hall and into her bedroom, banging the door closed.

And I return to Ruby, on my lap, rocking until blackness takes over the sky, until there is nothing left to see out that window but a smattering of stars and the electrified buildings here, there and everywhere.

WILLOW

I started seeing more and more of Matthew. Most often we went to the library where we sneaked down one aisle or another to read books, sometimes, and to kiss. We went as early as we could, after Joseph and Isaac had left that Omaha home, because if we waited too long there would be kids from schools filling the study tables at the ends of the aisles, loud and obnoxious, even up by the engineering books where no one else cared to go. But when we got there earlier in the day, around noon, the library was almost silent, kids at school, adults working, and we could move about that aisle as if we were the only souls in the whole entire world. Even the librarians stayed away — since no one ever checked out the engineering books, there were never any books to shelve. Only once did some librarian stop us and ask, with a tone more curious than disapproving, "No school today?" And though I stopped dead in my tracks, my heart forgetting to beat — absolutely certain she was gonna send me back to Joseph — it was Matthew who said, like he'd had this answer all ready to go for a long, long time, "We're homeschooled," and that librarian nodded her head and said, "How nice," and walked away. I didn't even know what that meant anyway: *homeschool.* But Matthew did.

And that was the end of it. No one ever asked what we were doing there again: two kids out of school in the middle of the day.

Matthew touched me in a way that was far different than Joseph ever did. Matthew's hands were considerate, whereas Joseph's were not. Matthew's hands moved slow and gentle, but Joseph's did not. I thought of Matthew's hands as an eraser of sorts, as if them touching me could erase that image of Joseph's hands right on out of my mind.

Matthew talked more and more about getting me out of that home. But he said he knew his father wouldn't let me leave. And Matthew didn't have the money to take care of himself, much less me. Matthew never told me where he stayed once he left that homeless shelter. Not the truth anyway. He talked about sleeping on a buddy's couch,

410

or a friend letting him sleep on a cot in some storefront he owned, but when he said these things, he looked away, like when he talked about riding barges on the Missouri River, and I knew that he was lying. Matthew always looked tired. He started looking old. His skin was weathered, like maybe he was living on the streets somewhere, I didn't know.

But still, he talked about getting me out of that home. He talked about places outside of Omaha he wanted to see. The mountains, the beach. He talked about saving money. He talked about other ways he could get money: stealing women's purses or robbing a bank. I didn't think Matthew had it in him, but if it got me out of that home with Joseph and Miriam then, I thought, *okay.* Just so long as no one got hurt.

Maybe, he said, and *one day.*

There were times when Matthew wanted to kiss me there, in that Omaha home, in my bedroom. There were times he wanted to lie beside me on the bed for reasons other than to read.

I didn't know what Matthew did and didn't know about Joseph, about what he did when he came into my room. I was too afraid to tell Matthew for fear he wouldn't believe me. *It's my word against yours,* Joseph said. *No one will believe you.*

And besides, Joseph reminded me. I was a child that no one wanted. No one but him and Miriam.

Matthew and my library trips continued throughout the fall and into winter. There were weeks, maybe more, when Joseph stayed home and didn't go to work. *Winter break,* he said, and there he was in that house with me all day long and I didn't see Matthew at all. But I thought about him. I thought about his hands on me, his lips on mine, the way he said my name. *Claire.* The snow fell from the sky, thick and heavy, coating the lawn with a layer of white. I stared out the window at that never-ending snow and thought of snowmen and sledding and snowball fights with Momma and Daddy back in Ogallala. But here, the snow was just another reason to stay inside. The temperatures were cold, in and out of that Omaha home, the windows drafty, the heat set to no more than sixty-eight degrees. I was cold all the time.

Joseph went back to work, and Matthew returned. Winter continued on and on for nearly forever, and though the calendar had turned to March, the weather outside resembled anything but spring. Cold and gray, icicles clinging to the rooftops of the homes

412

on our block.

And then, one early March day, Matthew came to fetch me to the library, excited to show me some new program he'd discovered on the computer. He was excited that day when he arrived, more animated than I'd seen him in a long, long time. The sky was the color of charcoal, the breath from our mouth that kind that flowed into the air like smoke.

But what Matthew and I didn't know was that Joseph wasn't feeling well that day. We didn't know as we hopped on that blue bus and headed past the Woodman building, that Joseph was lecturing over at the community college, and starting to feel a headache coming on, and that, as we pulled our chairs up to the computer, he was thinking about cancelling his afternoon classes so he could go home and rest. There was no way we could've known as we put change into the vending machine for a bag of chips, that he was packing up his stuff in his black backpack to go, or that, as we later settled down in the engineering aisle to peer through the books and to kiss, Joseph was in his car, driving home.

The house was quiet when we came in, the cold wind all but pushing us through the front door. Matthew was talking about

413

his mother, about Miriam, about how, if he was ever a vegetable like her, he'd just want someone to shoot him, to take him out of his misery.

I was stunned, staring at him with my mouth gaping wide, so that I didn't see Joseph parked on the edge of the corduroy recliner, gazing at us with his hawkish, hostile eyes. He was unmoving, still like a statue. Matthew froze in the doorway, and that's what made me freeze, too, made me turn to see Joseph, with a lamp base in his hands, the flocked lamp shade tossed to the ground beside his big, heavy boots.

What happened next, I could hardly explain. Joseph's words were eerily calm as he asked us where we'd been.

"A walk," Matthew said, and Joseph said nothing, twirling that lamp cord around and around in his hand, giving it a slight tug to check the tension.

And then Joseph wanted to know where I'd gotten the clothes, the clothes Matthew hung onto between visits so that Joseph wouldn't see.

It had been a long time since Joseph and Matthew had laid eyes on one another. Joseph had no way of knowing that while he worked, Matthew was in and out of that very home.

Joseph wanted me to say it, to tell him that we'd gone for a walk because lying lips, just like the thoughts of the wicked, were an abomination to God. He wanted me to say it aloud. He wanted the words to come from my mouth.

And they did.

And then he looked toward his son and said, "What did I always teach you, Matthew? Bad company ruins good morals. Isn't that what I always said?"

And then it happened, just like that. Joseph was moving across the room, striking Matthew with that lamp base again and again on the side of the head. There were words my Momma only ever muttered under her breath hurled at the top of their lungs.

I tried to stop Joseph, to get him to stop beating Matthew, but he knocked me down to the cold, hard floor. It took a minute to get my bearings, to get back up on my feet, but before I knew it, Joseph had me on the floor again, and this time, there was blood oozing from my nose, thick and red and sticky.

It happened so fast.

The sound of the lamp base against solid bone.

A streak of crimson blood soared through

the air, splattering on the oatmeal-colored wall.

Epithets muttered between gasping breaths: *son of a bitch* and *bastard* and *prick.*

Random objects used as weapons: the telephone, a vase. The TV's remote control. Breaking glass. A cry. More blood.

Me, on the floor, in the tornado position, feeling the ground shake as though an earthquake was passing through.

And then Isaac was there, too, home from school or work I assumed, and Isaac and Joseph were beating Matthew so badly I don't know how he managed to stay on his own two feet. I was crying out loud, *Stop!* And *Leave him alone!* But no one was listening to me. Matthew groped for a candlestick and managed to connect with the side of Isaac's head, immobilizing him for a split second.

Isaac lost his balance and staggered, thrust a hand to his own head.

And when Matthew raised that candlestick, Joseph managed to knock it right on out of his hand.

I don't know how long it went on. Thirty seconds? Thirty minutes? It seemed like forever, that I knew for sure.

And there was nothing I could do.

"So this was in self-defense, then?" asks

Louise Flores. "Is that what you're implying?" She thrusts up the sleeves of the scratchy cardigan and fans a spare sheet of paper against her head. She's sweating. The day outside must be warm, spring morphing into summer. Beads of perspiration form on the bridge of her nose, in the wrinkles of her raisin-like skin. I see the sun through the lone window, pouring across the dismal room and filling the darkness with light.

"Yes, Ms. Flores," I say, "of course."

I still see Matthew when I close my eyes: the sight of him with blood streaked throughout his dark brown hair, running crossways down his face. He looked like he was ten years old that day, there in the living room, with Joseph and Isaac ganging up on him. I hated that I couldn't do anything to stop it, but even worse, I hated what I knew Matthew was feeling: powerless and weak. His eyes gazed past mine and I knew that more than anything, he felt ashamed.

"After some time," I admit to Ms. Flores, "Matthew left. He didn't want to, you know. He didn't want to leave me there in that home with them. But there was nothing he could do."

I tell her how Matthew managed to drag himself out the front door and leave that ugly March afternoon.

I see it, still, Matthew all but crawling out the front door. I hear Joseph and Isaac laughing.

I hear them heckle Matthew as he crawled away.

"To where?" she asks. "Where did Matthew go?"

"I don't know," I say. "I don't know."

I picture it: his sorry eyes settling on mine before he turned and moved out that door. Joseph and Isaac laughing mockingly, taunting Matthew out the door.

They figured they'd won.

But I knew this was far from through.

"And then what happened? Once Matthew had left?"

I pull back my hair and show her the crater Joseph left behind when he pummeled me with that lamp. He waited until Matthew was out of sight — Isaac still snickering, still calling Matthew a pussy out the front window — and he turned to me with the meanest eyes I'd ever seen in my whole entire life. He picked the lamp base up from the floor — dented at both ends — and smacked me point blank on the side of my head. I don't remember it hurting so much, but I do remember its crippling effects: the way my body lost all feeling, lost its ability to stand on my own two feet, the way I crumpled to the floor and Isaac stood, watching and pointing. Laughing. I remember the blackness that crept in from the edges of my eyes until I could no longer see, the ugly words and voices in the background that ebbed until all was silent.

When I awoke I was in that bedroom of mine, on the bed, on top of the patchwork quilt, the door locked from the outside.

CHRIS

I'm in my Denver hotel room, washing up for bed, dead tired.

I've got the smallest room in the hotel, but even that goes for over two hundred bucks a night. The view out the window could be any other city, any other night. To me, it all looks the same anymore, big buildings, thousands of lights.

I've got on some pajama pants, blue seersucker, a little snug, an undershirt. On the bed sits my open laptop.

The day's newspaper, the *Denver Post,* which I picked up on the way out of the airport, lies ignored. The furthest I got was a front page blurb on the weather — cold — and the day's lottery numbers.

I didn't win.

I'm tired, the exhaustion marking my face. I stare at myself in the mirror and think that I am looking older. That I am *getting* older. That I can't keep up this pace much longer.

I'm ruminating on other jobs: college professor, maybe management consulting, as I brush my teeth. I'm imaging myself at the front of a crowded auditorium, standing before the podium, lecturing on global capitalism before a bunch of cocky kids who used to be me. Back when I was consumed with money. Money, money, money. I'd take a huge pay cut teaching, that's for sure, but Heidi and I would make due, I think, spitting toothpaste into the bathroom sink.

We'd put the condo on the market, maybe rent for a while. Maybe Zoe could go to public school, even though I know that won't fly. But maybe. Hell, maybe we'd move to suburbia, buy a single family home with a fenced-in yard, get a dog. We'd take the train in to work. Live the real American dream.

It could work.

I'm thinking what it would be like to be home for dinner, what it would be like to lie in bed beside my wife, every night. I'm picturing Heidi that afternoon at that Asian grill, the way she leaned in close to me, pressed her lips to mine. The way she laid her hand on mine, the way she uttered those words *You must be so tired, Chris,* concerned for once about *me,* her husband, and not just foreign refugees from around the world.

Mindful of *my* needs and not just those of homeless girls and stray cats.

Maybe something was changing.

I pine for the olden days: Heidi at that benefit dinner in her vintage red dress, dancing with me after everyone else had left the building, after the dimmed lights had been flipped back on and the catering staff was cleaning up the room. She was a college student at the time, and so she had nothing more than a dorm room to her name. I was right out of school, paying more in student loans than the national debt. I was dirt poor, living in a studio apartment in Roscoe Village, which we took a cab to, running wildly up the steps of the walkup apartment, me, forward, and Heidi, gracefully, in reverse, undressing each other along the way.

We never made it to the bed, but fell to the floor right behind the door.

By morning, I expected that she'd be gone. Because certainly someone that amazing, with her beautiful brown eyes, wouldn't want a thing to do with me in the light of day.

But I was wrong.

We stayed in bed half the day, watching the pedestrians who moved up and down Belmont through the windows. That and

The Price Is Right. Then later, when we finally did get up and get dressed, Heidi sporting my Bears sweatshirt, thrown over her own red dress, we went shopping for antiques, buying an old beer tap handle because it was the only thing we could afford.

Heidi stayed with me for three days. Living in my undershirts and boxer shorts, surviving on takeout and delivery. I went to work in the morning and when I came home, she was there.

She was easygoing in a way I thought she'd always be, but that was long before Zoe and cancer and the heavy weight of reality. I think about that weight, how it must deplete her. I think of Heidi, caring more about the rest of the world and everyone else's insatiable needs than she does her own.

I stand in the bathroom in that Denver hotel, thinking to myself, *I miss Heidi,* when there's a knock on the door, a light rat-a-tat-tat, and I know who it is before I ever glance through the peephole.

I open the door and there she is. Not Heidi, of course. Though there's a split second of *what-if?* What if it is Heidi, flown all the way to Denver to see me, abandoning that girl and her baby who have consumed our home, swallowing my wife whole. What if she made arrangements for Zoe to stay with Jennifer, hopped a flight out to Denver and now here she is, to spend the night with me?

But the scene that greets me instead is something else entirely, Cassidy Knudsen letting herself into my room. She's wearing leggings, black and tight, with some sort of baggy tunic whose V-neck exposes the basin between her breasts, a valley, a ravine set between neighboring hills, the skin soft and pale, up for grabs. She wears some sort of pendant necklace, with a long copper chain that forces the eyes to the V of that tunic, forces the eyes down to where the charm sits tucked beneath the shirt, at the end of the copper chain. The makeup on her face is barely there, save for the bright red lipstick that seems to have become a matter of course, the norm. There are heels on her feet, four-inch heels, red, like the lipstick.

She lets herself in, as always, without waiting to be invited.

And there I stand, in my pajama pants and undershirt, still clutching a toothbrush in my hand.

"I didn't know you were stopping by," I say, "or I would've . . ." my voice drifts off and I'm not sure what to say. I glance around the room to see the day's clothing in a pile on the floor, the seersucker pants that cling to my legs like plastic wrap.

She doesn't have to tell me why she's there; I know what she's come to do. She moves quickly, her hands on me, her lips on mine, stating in an undertone, "I can't tell you how long I've wanted to do this," and I say, "Cassidy," though I'm not sure if the word comes out argumentative or inviting. I make a feeble attempt to slide away, out of reach, though deep inside my mind screams at me to let her. To push those forgotten memories of another Heidi out of my mind, and let Cassidy do as she pleases, whatever she came here to do.

And then she's touching me, but her hands are cold, different from Heidi's in so many ways. They are bold and presumptuous, not waiting to get acquainted before they dive right in, full steam ahead. She's doing everything wrong, not the way Heidi would do it, Heidi who is indulgent in the way she touches me, tender, and I find myself thinking about Heidi, suddenly, desperately, longing for Heidi, wishing it were Heidi here in this hotel room, with me.

I'm thinking what Heidi would say if she knew what was happening right now, how it would make her feel. Heidi who is wholesome, generous beyond belief; Heidi who refuses to smash a spider with a shoe.

"Stop," I say, pushing her away, gently at first, and then harder. "Stop, Cassidy," I say, "I can't do this. I can't do this to Heidi."

I want Heidi. I miss Heidi.

I miss my wife.

But Cassidy is staring at me with this morose look on her face, and she says, "You've *got* to be kidding, Chris," and it's not that she's had her feelings hurt or that she's feeling embarrassed that she's been refused. *"Heidi?"* she asks. She stares at me with puppy-dog eyes, big and blue, pouting, saying my wife's name as if it is low-grade.

It isn't that Cassidy can't believe she's been turned down.

It's that she can't believe she's been turned down for *Heidi.*

I miss Heidi and her goodness, her virtue. I miss that she cares for homeless cats, and illiterate men, and children in countries whose names I can't say. Azerbaijan and Kyrgyzstan and Bahrain.

I can't stand to stay there, in that room, with Cassidy. My pulse beats loudly in my ear. My hands are clammy, my balance off, as I thrust my feet into a pair of loafers waiting by the door, Cassidy's voice in the background calling me by name, laughing, saying *Don't go,* leaving me dizzy. Vertigo. I lay

a hand on the wall to steady myself as
Cassidy continues to incant my name, to
reveal herself to me as if it might just change
my mind.

WILLOW

What I tell Ms. Flores is that Joseph brought me meals twice a day, and twice a day he removed them from my room. I tell her that he wouldn't let me out, even to pee. From time to time he'd come to empty a jar he had given me (though the smell of my own pee never went with it), and that every night he came to call, unlocking and thrusting open that bedroom door and telling me to undress.

I tell her that every night, after he'd gone to bed, I checked that door to make sure it was locked.

I tell her that I sat there, day in and day out, praying that one day he might forget to lock the door.

I tell her that Matthew never came around, that I didn't see him again after that day he limped out the front door.

I tell her that I didn't see Isaac, though I heard his voice, echoing throughout the home, and knew that he was there, moving in and out of a world I could no longer see.

I tell her that I watched out the bedroom window as the snow melted away, leaving gaping puddles along the sidewalks and in the potholed street.

I tell her that once a day I was allowed to leave the room, only to defecate. I tell her how Joseph stood in the doorway and watched me go. I tell her how once I didn't make it to the toilet in time, and how Joseph made me sit in it for days, until my rear end was covered in a rash meant only for babies. I tell her how he laughed, how I heard Joseph and Isaac talking later about how I shit my pants.

I tell her how one night, by the grace of God, after Joseph paid me a visit, he slipped out the bedroom door and forgot to lock it as he left. I sat on the bed, waiting for the awful sound of the metallic key jingling in the lock, but there was none. Just the whine of floorboards as he moved through the home, the heavy sound of him climbing into his bed, the fuss of the mattress springs when he laid his immense body upon it. I waited for an hour at least, just to make sure, before I stood from the bed and wandered across the cold room, before I inched a shaking hand onto that bronze lever and opened the door.

I tell Ms. Flores how I found the knife in a kitchen drawer, the biggest one from a twelve-piece cutlery set, a chef's knife, at least eight inches long or more. I tell her how I stood there in that darkened kitchen, watching the faint glow of the moon in the distance and thinking, though there was no need to think because I'd already decided. The house was quiet, but for the hiss of the furnace and the movement of water through pipes.

But of course, I don't know one way or another because that night, before Matthew arrived, I didn't step one foot out of my room.

I tell her how I tiptoed into the bedroom and how I watched Joseph sleep. How I watched his fiendish body upon the big bed, how I heard him snore. Ms. Flores is scribbling maniacally across her paper now, making sure she gets the details just right. The way Joseph's eyes flew open as I approached the bed, the squeaky floorboards awakening him from sleep. How he sat upright in bed, the look in his eyes not scared but confused. How he mumbled, "How did you . . ." before I jammed that chef's knife into his chest. *How did you get out of your room?* was what he was gonna say. But I didn't give him a chance. That's what I tell her. His eyes, his mouth, gaped open and his hands felt blindly for the knife before I tore it out and thrust it in again. And again. Six times they said. That's what they told me when they found me.

But of course, how would I know because that night, I didn't step foot in Joseph and Miriam's room.

What I knew, but what I didn't tell Ms. Flores, was that someone older than eighteen would be tried as an adult. But not someone who was sixteen, someone like me who'd never been in trouble with the law. I wouldn't get in as much trouble as Matthew would if they knew, if they knew the truth. I knew that 'cause Daddy had told me, back when I was just a kid and we were watching some story on the news. Some story about a sixteen-year-old who murdered her folks. Daddy said kids sometimes got away with it, while adults went to jail, plain and simple. If they didn't get executed. I remember that I'd asked Daddy: *What's executed?* But he never did say though I figured it out nonetheless.

"And Miriam?" asks Ms. Flores.

"What about Miriam?"

"Tell me what happened to Miriam."

"She didn't wake up," I say. Not that I know one way or the other since I wasn't

431

there, in that room. I claim that she lay there, sound asleep, while I thrust that chef's knife in and out of Joseph's chest.

But Ms. Flores is bound and determined. She sets her pen on the table and double-checks the tape recorder to make sure it's still working. She's got to get this on tape. My confession. "Then why did you kill her, too?" she asks and my spit catches in my throat and I choke.

Miriam? I almost ask aloud.

But then I hear Matthew's voice in my mind and slowly, even slower than molasses in January, it sinks in.

If I was ever a vegetable like my mom, I'd want someone to just shoot me. To take me out of my misery.

And that's just what he did.

HEIDI

In the early afternoon when Ruby is asleep, I walk through the condo collecting items of clothing thrown at random here and there: Ruby's jumpsuits stuffed helter-skelter in the cushions of the sofa, discarded socks of Zoe's left beside the front door. I drop them into a heaping laundry basket, make my way into Chris's and my bedroom and retrieve an overused bra slung over the door handle. I lift his suitcase from the floor, the one we exchanged at the Asian grill on Michigan Avenue, and begin to sort through its contents: button-down oxfords, work pants stuffed into a ball in the corner of the bag. I lift the pants from the bag, checking the pockets for pens and pen caps, handfuls of coins, the type of random things that typically materialize from Chris's pockets while in the wash. Bottle caps and binder clips, an entire package of travel tissues that disintegrate into a million pieces, and —

My hand lands on something I recognize almost instantly, even before pulling the shiny blue package from the pocket, the words *her pleasure* socking me in the gut. I double over before the bed, dropping the laundry basket to the floor. Some kind of gravelly sound emerges from me, a gritty, desperate gasp for air. I press a hand — two hands — to my mouth to silence the squall that wells up inside me, a sudden, violent storm brewing deep inside my bowels.

I stare at that condom wrapper, confirming everything I believed to be true.

My husband is having an affair with Cassidy Knudsen.

I envision the two of them in ostentatious hotels in San Francisco, New York City and now Denver, their bodies coalescing between Egyptian cotton sheets. I see them in Chris's uninhabited office during nonbusiness hours, and me, stupidly falling for another cover story: working on an offering memorandum or writing a prospectus, doing due diligence on one company or another.

These burdens — the long hours, the endless business trips — were his alibi, his attempt to camouflage a secret liaison with another woman.

My head spins, imagining Chris, in the

kitchen, humbly admitting that Cassidy Knudsen would be joining him on his last trip. I picture the two of them together, later on in their hotel room, laughing about it, laughing about how piqued I'd been to discover that she'd be there. I picture the two of them taking pleasure in my unease and insecurity, in my jealousy.

It's a business trip, Chris had said. *Strictly business.*

And yet . . .

I put it all together in my head: the unanswered phone call, the contraceptive in the pocket of Chris's work pants. The proof, finally, that I've longed for for so long.

I cross the bedroom to the dresser and remove from the top drawer various items that I lay across the bed: a set of matching underwear — lace bra and panties — in a pale shade of pink.

I stare at those items, long and hard, knowing what needs to be done to settle the score.

WILLOW

Of course everything I told Louise Flores was not the truth.

She had me write it all down, in my own words, on a fresh sheet of notebook paper. She paced the room, her heels clicking on the concrete floors, while I wrote it all down, about the chef's knife, and Joseph with his gaping eyes. I even made up a thing or two about Miriam, how she was asleep when I went into the room, but I did her in nonetheless, just because I could.

She gazes at me, shaking her head and says, "You're just lucky you're a juvenile, Claire. Do you have any idea what would happen to you if you were tried as an adult?"

I shrug my shoulders and say, "There's no death penalty in Illinois."

She stops her pacing all of a sudden and peers over a shoulder at me.

"But you didn't commit the crime in Illinois, Claire," she says. "You were in *Ne-*

braska," where I know good and well murderers can be put to death by lethal injection.

Especially those over eighteen, those who commit murders that are willful and premeditated.

Like waiting until someone is asleep before creeping into their room with a knife.

I didn't want Matthew to get in any trouble. 'Cause I knew that what he did, he did for me. Never did I stop thinking of Matthew, not one day since I left. I thought about him every single day, and at night, when I lay down on the bed, I thought of him and cried, quiet-like so Mrs. Wood and Mr. Wood wouldn't hear. I wondered where he was. Wondered if he was okay.

When she's got it all, the whole grand confession in writing and on tape, she tells the guard to bring me back to my room where Diva sits on the floor and sings, tapping her long vermillion fingernails against the bars of our cage for a percussion effect though someone screams at her to shut up. I ignore her interrogation — *Where have you been all day?* — and climb onto my bunk, pulling a thin white sheet over me, all the way up over my head.

I close my eyes and remember that night, the things I didn't tell Ms. Flores.

Heidi

Beside me, on the bed, lay a set of matching underwear, lace bra and panties, in a pale shade of pink. I slip into them and drift to the open closet doors, reaching deep inside. In the back I find what I'm looking for, hung from a department store hanger, still covered in plastic sheeting, a knot tied at its base. Never worn. I loosen the knot and gently lift the plastic from the dress. Dropping it to the floor, I remember the day I made the purchase, some seven months ago, the day I called Chris's favorite steakhouse in the old, refurbished brownstone on Ontario Street, and made reservations for a quieter table away from the bar, the very one where Chris proposed to me. I'd planned for Zoe to stay with Jennifer and Taylor, had left work early to get my hair done, a side-swept chignon to partner with the new dress, a pair of black pumps with a kitten heel.

I release the dress from its hanger, remembering how Chris had called before I ever had a chance to wear it, griping about some last-minute task, and in the background, there was *her* voice — Cassidy's — beckoning *my husband,* stealing him away from our anniversary date.

"I'll make it up to you," he'd promised, his disappointment diluted over the phone, as if maybe, just maybe, he didn't care at all, "Soon."

I run my fingers over the dress, a crepe shift dress with buttons up the back, black. I drape it over my head, letting it slide down, over the pink bra and panties, and then stare at my reflection in the full-length mirror. I remember that October night, the night of our anniversary, I remember that it was Graham who had come over instead, beckoned by the sound of the TV on a night he knew I shouldn't be home. He stood in the doorway, sympathy carpeting his face, knowing, without my needing to tell him, what had happened: me, in a robe and slippers in place of the little black dress, my hair dazzling in its side-swept chignon, *The Price Is Right* on the TV. A frozen TV dinner baking in the oven.

"He doesn't deserve you," was all he said, and then, in a throwback to long lost college days, we played a round of century club with Chris's adored pale ales, until we were drunk and bloated and my memories of being stood up by my work-obsessed husband had become hazy and opaque. I passed out on the sofa, waking the next morning to empty bottles of beer — over a dozen of them strewn upon the coffee table and floor — a vase of flowers set at their center, Chris's weak attempt at a pardon.

He was out the door before I awoke.

I trace my eyes in a dark liner, sweeping a smoky shadow across the lids. I smear Bordeaux lipstick onto my lips and smack them together, wiping away the excess with a tissue. I tie my hair into a messy knot on the top of my head, sad in comparison to that beautiful sixty-dollar chignon, I think, reaching into the depths of the closet for the box containing the black pumps with their kitten heels. I roll a pair of nylons up my legs and slip into the heels, standing before the mirror.

I pass by the baby, sound asleep on the pink fleece blanket, on the floor. I watch her for a short time, refusing to stay too long and divert my course. I watch to make sure she is asleep, that she will not notice my absence, and then I walk into the hallway and gently close the door.

I don't take the time to catch my breath; I refuse to slow down and think.

Graham opens the door before my knuckles rap for a second time. There he stands, impeccable and smiling, in a pair of jeans and an undershirt. He takes in the dress and hair, the overblown makeup, eyeing me from top to bottom. "Ooh la la," he says as I reach back and begin to unfasten the buttons from my dress. His laptop sits on the tufted sofa cushions, abandoned; Nina Simone warbles throughout the room.

"What are you . . . ?" Graham starts, leading me inside and closing the door. I lift that dress up over my head, exposing the pale pink beneath. His eyes fall to the pink, to the lace, getting lost long enough to affirm that Chris's perception of Graham is far from true.

"You don't want to do this," he says to me, but I say that I do.

I step toward him, taking in the paragon, the ideal that is Graham, letting his warm hands wander across my midriff, wrapping around to the small of my back.

And Graham, being the good friend that he is, is happy to oblige. He's more than happy to do me this favor. An act of goodwill. A common courtesy, I think as he leads

me past the tufted sofa and onto an unmade
bed.

WILLOW

It was late. The house was silent. Joseph had come and gone.

I was awoken by a scream, a thick, throaty scream that forced me straight up in bed.

I remember the moon through the window, incandescent on an otherwise black night. I remember that there was silence following that scream, so much silence that I wondered whether or not it had only been a dream. I lay in bed, staring at that moon, willing my heart to slow down, my breath to return to me from wherever it went when I heard that scream. The clouds floated by the moon slowly, lazily, the knobby arms of the big, old trees now shadows in the night. They stirred in the air, their branches reaching out to touch one another, to clasp hands.

And then I heard it: the clink of a metallic key in the lock, the frantic turning of the door's handle. What I expected to see was Joseph, his silhouette against the faint glow of some light from down the hall. But instead it was Matthew who tore into my room with a deranged look in his eye, his convulsive hand bearing a sharp knife that dripped blood across my bed as he said, "Come on, Claire. Get up." And I reached for his outstretched hand and let him pull me from bed.

"You need to go, Claire," he said to me, sweeping me close, tight, in a bear hug. "You need to run." He tossed clothes into my hands: the sweatshirt and gym shoes, a pair of enormous pants, and told me to get dressed. "Hurry," he said, his voice rattling.

"Why?" I asked, and then, "Where?"

"There's a bag," he said, "by the front door. A suitcase. It has everything you'll need." And he pulled on my hand and led me down the hall, through a house that was nearly silent, the door to Joseph and Miriam's bedroom pulled closed. I cringed as I passed that bedroom door, fearful of what was or wasn't on the other side.

I couldn't decide what was worse: what was there or what I imagined to be there, though there was no way to know for sure.

"But what about Joseph?" I asked, though I knew, between the blood and the closed door, by the fact that Matthew and I were moving freely down the wooden steps —

making no effort to mute the sounds of the squeaky floors — that Joseph was dead.

That the scream had belonged to Joseph.

That the blood on the knife was his.

He clutched me by the hand on the bottom step and forced me into him. He whispered into my ear, "I know what he did to you," and I felt my legs give, knowing he knew my secret. Knowing he knew Joseph's secret. Somehow it was a weight off, the fact that I no longer had to carry that baggage alone. I imagined, all those years, Joseph welcoming himself onto the bed beside me, and Matthew, on the other side of the wall, listening. I clung to Matthew there, at the bottom of the steps, not wanting to go, though he said again, "You have to go, Claire. You have to go *now,*" and unclasped my hands from the small of his back.

"Where?" I asked, my voice anxious and scared. I'd never been on my own before in my whole entire life.

"There's a cab," he said, "outside. Waiting. He'll take you to the bus station," and it was only then that I noticed the headlights of a car parked at the curb.

"But I don't want to go," I cried, my eyes darting to Matthew, ambiguous in the blackness of the night. "I want to stay with you." And I clung to him like Velcro, wrapping my arms around his back and for a second he let me, just a split second, before he unclamped my fingers and pried me away. I was crying, this heaving cry that came from somewhere deep within. "Come with me," I begged, weeping so hard that I had to force the words out between breaths. *Come. With. Me.* Matthew was the only person I had in the whole wide world. Momma had left me. Lily had left me. And now Matthew was leaving me, too.

"Claire."

"Come with me," I pleaded like the child I was. I stamped my foot and threw my arms across myself with a pout on my face. "Come with me, come with me," and I tried pulling on his arm and dragging him to the door, toward that front door that stood open, the window to the side of the door smashed in, shards of jagged glass strewn upon the floor.

I froze solid for a second and stared.

This is how Matthew had found his way in.

"You have to go, Claire." Matthew jammed money into my hand, a stack of cash, and hurried to grab the leather suitcase from the floor, towing me behind him by the hand. "Go now," he said, "before . . ." but he didn't finish. "Just go," he said, but as he did, he pulled me close, absorbing me in his arms. He was shaking; he'd broken out in a cold sweat. He didn't want me to go any more than I wanted to go. I knew that. And yet he thrust that suitcase into my fickle hand and pushed — actually *pushed* — me through the door, as I carefully stepped over the broken glass on my way out.

I looked back once, only once, to see him standing in the doorway, the knife hidden behind his back, his face bound in wistfulness and melancholy. He, too, was sad.

I remember that the night was crisp, something only my brain perceived, not the rest of me. There was the knowledge that it was cold — like someone told me or something — but I never felt that it was cold. Like I was sleepwalking or something, in a dream. I could hear myself sobbing like I was watching it on TV. An observer, not a participant. I don't remember telling the driver — a short, shadowy man, nothing more than a muddled voice to me, a pair of eyes in the rearview mirror — where to take me. It was as if he knew. I got in the car and he sped off, down the choppy street, driving fast and jerky, and I remember thinking that he must have heard Matthew say to hurry or something because he was going so fast.

Matthew must have told him. I clung to the door handle and braced myself for every turn, wondering if this is what it felt like when Momma died, when that Datsun Bluebird started spinning somersaults down the road.

The building that the driver pulled up to was short and gray, the word *Greyhound* written across the brick in big blue letters. It was on the corner of some street, a city street that was all but abandoned at this time of night. Outside, an older woman stood, with her sparse gray hair, puffing on a cigarette, her free hand thrust deep in the pocket of a flimsy coat.

"Seventeen dollars," the cabdriver said with a grating voice, and sitting like a birdbrain in the backseat of that cab, I asked, "Huh?"

He pointed to the stack of money in my trembling hand and said again, "Seventeen dollars," and I counted out the fare from the cash Matthew had handed me, and carried that leather suitcase inside, watching the woman as I passed by.

"Spare some change," she said to me, but I folded up that money and squeezed it in my hand, real tight so she wouldn't see.

Inside I found a vending machine, and the first thing I did was slip in a dollar and press the red button. A soda dropped down, faster than expected, and I took it and sank sideways into the rows of empty chairs. Out the window, it was still dark, the first whiff of daylight creeping up from the bottom of the sky. A grumpy old man sat behind the ticket booth, counting dollar bills into a register, grunting all the while he did so. I could hear a TV, though I didn't see it, the sound of early morning news, traffic and the day's weather.

I didn't know what I was doing here. I didn't know what I was supposed to do, where I was supposed to go. It hadn't sunk in yet: the fact that Joseph was dead. Tears clung to my cheeks, my eyes feeling fat and puffy from crying. My heart hadn't slowed its pace, a relentless gallop that made my head start to spin. Tucked beneath the sweatshirt, on a white undershirt, were splotches of blood that had spattered me when Matthew came tearing into my room.

Joseph's blood.

I was sure of it. I tried hard to piece the bits and pieces together: the broken glass, the knife, the guttural scream that awoke me from sleep. Matthew appearing in the door, his words: *Go now. Before* . . . Before what? I sat there and wondered. Before the police arrived. Before Isaac appeared. It had

449

yet to really hit me: the fact that I was on my own. That I no longer belonged to Joseph. That he would no longer be coming into my room.

I sat there for I don't know how long. Taking slow sips of my soda, listening to the TV. It was warm in the bus station, and bright. I stared for some time at a fluorescent light flickering on the ceiling and watched as a man came into the station in jeans and a tattered T-shirt, a *Huskers* cap on his head. I thought that he should've been cold with just the T-shirt on, but he didn't look cold. He looked at me, out of the corner of his eye, trying to make it seem as if he wasn't staring. But I could tell he was. He carried an overstuffed duffel bag in one hand, too much stuff inside to zip it clear shut.

He nodded, kind of a half nod, as if saying *I see you,* and then walked, smack dab to a chart on the wall, and when he got there he just stood and stared. I saw the words on the wall above that chart.

Departures.

Arrivals.

The bus schedule.

I waited until he purchased a ticket to Chicago from the grumpy man behind the booth and then sulked into a hard chair on the other side of the station, and pulled that cap over his eyes and appeared to sleep. I slid from my chair — wiping my eyes with the back of a sleeve — and wandered to that chart on the wall, staring at so many words and numbers it made me dizzy. Kearney. Columbus. Chicago. Cincinnati.

And then I saw it, two words so unexpected, I knew they were meant to be: *Fort Collins.*

Fort Collins. The same words that I'd seen time and again on the return address labels of those letters Big Lily sent me from her home in Colorado. My Lily, little Lily, lived in Fort Collins, Colorado.

It was time to go to her. To see my sister again.

Heidi

Graham stands three feet away in the darkened room, watching with gluttonous eyes as I lower my undergarments to the ground, the pale pink bra falling upon the kitten heels and pink panties, beside sheer nylons now wadded into a ball and cast aside.

His eyes look me up and down deliberately, unhurriedly, coming to a standstill on the diagonal scar, red and ever-present, running from my belly button down, its tail end lost amid pubic hairs. A constant reminder.

I dismiss that scar, telling myself it simply isn't true, reminding myself of the baby, sound asleep on the pink fleece blanket next door.

Graham says nothing as his warm hands come to rest on my waistline and he leads me to the bed, setting me down on a gray duvet that slips halfway to the bedroom floor, beside pillows that have yet to be replaced since morning. I stare past him, at a

452

ceiling fan — brushed nickel with cherry blades — blowing papers one by one from a dresser and onto the floor, Graham's latest work in progress, though he's so caught up in the moment he fails to notice, fails to notice how the breeze of the ceiling fan spawns gooseflesh upon my bare arms, my legs, my chest.

He stands at the end of the bed, slipping an undershirt up over his head and as he does so, as I lean in to run my hands down the oblique and abdominal muscles that line his torso, the faint, fair hair, the alcove of a belly button, the antique brass button that affixes his jeans, I hear it.

I hear the baby cry.

Louder than the blare of a car horn, an unexpected peal of thunder, the roar of a steam engine.

I stand up quickly, gathering my clothing from the bedroom, the living room floor; Graham, deaf to the baby's cry, begs me not to leave. "Heidi," he says, his voice placating in a way that I bet makes it impossible for women to say no. "What's wrong?" His eyes stare at me, at my eyes, as I step into the dress, clinging to the nylons, the panties in my hand. I secure the buttons up my back — mismatched and irregular.

"It's just —" I say, feeling flushed, unable

to let go of the sensation of Graham's hands, his eyes, on my body, staring at me in a way Chris no longer stares. "I forgot there was something. Something I needed to do."

I hear the crying when I am still in Graham's doorway, loud, wretched crying, and I begin to run, the frantic clamor of kitten heels pounding on a wooden floor, as Graham calls to me by name.

"Heidi."

But he doesn't follow.

When I come into my home, there she is, the baby, sprawled across a pink blanket, on the floor.

Sound asleep.

It is not what I imagined.

What I expected to find was the blanket folded over her like the edges of an omelet, a handful of fleece stuffed in her angry hand. Her skin cardinal red, her cry thorny, like goose grass, rasping, scratchy, as if she's been crying for days, weeks, more.

Instead, she is silent, save for the delicate inhalation and exhalation of air. She lies inert on the pink blanket, her features calm and composed while I stand there in the doorway, gasping for breath.

She is asleep, I tell myself, finding it utterly impossible, for I was certain — as certain as I live and breathe — that I heard a baby cry.

I run to the child and sweep her tiny figure from the floor, up into my arms, waking her from her daze.

"There now," I croon quietly into her ear. "Mommy is here. Mommy won't ever leave you again."

WILLOW

Matthew had given me near everything I
could possibly need inside that suitcase:
money, and lots of it, some food: candy bars
and granola bars and cookies. I didn't know
for sure how he happened upon the money.
I settled into the bus, clutching it close to
me, the only possession in the world that
was mine. As the bus crisscrossed rural Nebraska, the sun making its ascent into the
late-winter sky, I laid it upon my rickety lap
and opened the clasp to reveal a book like
all those he'd slipped into my bedroom
when I was a kid: *The Fifty States.* I
skimmed through it, seeing that he'd left
messages for me in messy black ink,
smudged between the slippery pages of the
thick book. Beside Alaska: *Too cold.* Nebraska: *No way.* Illinois: *Maybe.* A guide-
book to my future: that was Matthew's intent.

Montana: *A good place to hide.*

I wondered if that was what I needed to do: find a place to hide. Would someone be looking for me? Joseph, maybe, or maybe the police. No, I reminded myself. Not Joseph. Joseph was dead.

I closed my eyes and tried to sleep, but sleep didn't come easily. All I could see were Matthew's deranged eyes as he tore into my room, the watery blood — colorless in the darkness of the room — on the knife. I heard Joseph's scream over and over again, a ringing in my ears, and tried hard not to imagine what had happened when I left, to wonder where Matthew was right then and there, and whether or not he was okay.

I had this suspicion that everyone was looking at me, that everyone *knew.* I sunk low into the seat and tried to hide, refusing to make eye contact with anyone, refusing to force out a stale hello, even to the man who sat on the other side of the aisle, in his own teal chair, in a black suit and clerical collar, leafing through a worn copy of the Bible.

Especially not the man on the other side of the aisle.

I closed my eyes and tried hard to pretend that he wasn't there, that he couldn't detect my sins, sniff them out like a bloodhound on a scent trail.

Sometime after noon I started to recognize the scenery out that tinted window: gigantic green signs with town names I knew, their names written in bold white letters: North Platte and Sutherland and Roscoe. A plaque lining the road: *Entering Keith County.* Familiar whitewashed barns and cattle fencing, an abandoned wooden farmhouse sloping so far in one direction I was certain, even eight years ago, the last time I laid eyes on it, it would slide right over onto the yellowing grass and collapse. I found myself sitting upright, my nose pressed to the frigid glass, hearing Momma's voice against the drone of the bus's engine: *I love you like pigs love slop.*

And then that bus veered off the road toward Highway 61, signs leading the way to Lake McConaughy where I built many a sandcastle as a kid, Momma waking up with the urge to go on the brightest of summer days and loading Lily and me into the Bluebird for the short drive to the lake. She never remembered the sunscreen, and we always burned to a crisp, all of us, comparing freckles and pink noses later in the day, pressing on the tips of our noses until they turned white. I stared out the window while that bus pulled right on into the Conoco parking lot, right there beside the Super 8 and the Comfort Inn, just across from the Wendy's where Momma and I ate so long ago it was like another life. The Pamida was there and the truck stop; just like I remembered. I remembered it all. The bus was passing through Ogallala on the way to Fort Collins. This was Ogallala.

I was home.

When the bus came to a stop and passengers unloaded and headed into the Conoco to use the restroom and grab a snack, I had the strongest urge to snatch that suitcase and run. My heart was thumping loud and heavy in my chest, arms and hands quivering. I went so far as to push past the handful of new riders who were boarding the bus for the next leg of the trip. "Excuse me," and "Pardon me," I muttered as I pushed the suitcase ahead of me, lumbering down the narrow aisle in a clumsy manner. I got more than one dirty look. A girl with longish hair the color of pralines parroted, "Excuse *you*," as I passed by too close, stepping on her fancy shoe. But I didn't care.

I convinced myself that I had the tiniest inkling how to get home, to the prefab house, though chances were good I didn't know how to do it when I was eight years old. But it didn't matter. I could've laid down in a roadside ditch somewhere in

Ogallala and it still would've felt like home. I could feel it in my blood and in my pores. Ogallala. Home. And wrapped up in all that: Momma and Daddy. There was this silly thought filling my mind: maybe Momma was still here. Maybe it was just a whole big misunderstanding. I'd walk back to the pre-fab home, and there Momma would be with Daddy and baby Lily, who was *not* Rose, who did *not* have a sister who was *not* me. And all of a sudden, walking through the rasping screen door, I'd be eight years old again and it would be as if time hadn't happened. Time had stood still. Momma was alive, her energy and enthusiasm filling the flavorless rooms of that tiny home as it used to do. The house would be exactly the same as we'd left it. There would be no other family living there, no little girl sleeping in my bed. And I'd never have heard of a man named Joseph. *Just a mistake,* I told myself as I climbed down those enormous bus steps and onto the Conoco parking lot. The cold air startled me — begged me to change my mind — but I ignored it. I started off, across the parking lot, toward the street, a look of defiance streaked across my face. A refusal to believe what I knew inside me to be true. *Just a whole big misunderstanding.*

Momma is alive. Daddy is alive. My feet

pounded on the pavement, fast and determined. The suitcase was awkward, smacking my right leg with each and every step I took.

What I found out was that I did remember how to get to that prefab house. Maybe my mind didn't know, but my feet certainly did 'cause they carried me right on out of that parking lot, down Prospector Drive. The suitcase didn't bother me, nor did the blustery air. I was on autopilot, or cruise control as Daddy used to say about driving the truck when I asked how come he didn't get tired with all that driving. My mind was stuck on Momma and this expectation that she was still alive as I trudged past the old brick buildings I remembered from when I was a kid, under leafless trees that spotted First, Second, Third and Fourth Streets, beside the carbon copy white homes and low-lying telephone wires. In time the trees and the homes began to multiply, the small, nearly deserted town drifting away. And then onto Spruce Street with its mobile homes and open land and billboards, nearly a mile's walk with cars soaring by at speeds that made the hair whirl around my head.

My legs burned by the time I arrived at Canyon Drive. My fingers were numb, my nose oozing snot from its nares. My arm was nearly asleep from the weight of the suitcase, my leg likely lacerated from where it rubbed back and forth, back and forth, all along the way.

The house was smaller than I remembered, the white siding more like oatmeal than snow. What once felt like an entire stairwell to the front door were instead only four small crooked steps, the aluminum handrail missing half its winding, taupe spindles. There was a basketball net, which there never used to be, a Honda hatchback in the drive. Red. Not the Bluebird I was used to seeing.

I stood, on the opposite side of Canyon Drive, staring at that house that used to be mine. Gathering the courage to turn the knob on the front door, hoping and praying I'd find Momma on the other side, though of course, deep down, somewhere far inside, I knew she was dead, but I tried hard to ignore that notion, to imagine the *what-if* instead. There was a split-second thought: if I didn't try, I'd never know, and that was a good thing, 'cause not knowing was better than proof that Momma and Daddy were dead. I'd been eight years old, a stupid kid after all. Maybe all those things they told me had been a lie, just one of all the other lies Joseph told me. I made believe Momma had been searching for me all this time, that my face had been like one of those other missing kids they plaster on the back of milk cartons, the black-and-white images with an age progressed photo beside it, what some smarty-pants thought I might look like when I was sixteen. *If you think you have seen Claire, please call 1-800-I-am-lost.* I imagined the wording: *Claire was last seen at her home on Canyon Drive, in Ogallala, Nebraska. Her hair is the color of snot, her eyes a bizarre blue. She has a small scar under her chin, a space between her two front teeth. She was last seen wearing . . .*

What *was* I wearing, that night Amber Adler came to tell me my parents were dead? That periwinkle T-shirt I used to own, the one with the bright red tube of lipstick and the frisky inscription: *SWAK,* kiss marks flecking its edges. Or maybe a party dress or a polka dot tank top or maybe . . .

This is what I'm thinking about when the door to that prefab home jolts open, the sound of kids arguing annihilating the silence. The sound of a mother's voice — not *my* mother, but *a* mother: stern and tired — telling them to Shut. Their. Mouths. Please.

There they were, three of them — no four, I saw then, the mother carrying an infant in a seat in her arms — pouncing down those four crooked steps like a litter of playful kittens. The two freestanding children elbowed one another all the way down the stairs, calling each other names: fart-face and booger-brain. It was two boys, each in jeans and tennis shoes, thick winter coats and fur bomber hats. The mother had a blanket — pink — draped over that baby. A girl. Maybe the girl she always wanted, I thought, as the mother propelled the boys forward with a gentle shove and told them to hurry. Get in the car. They were going to be late. One of the boys spun then suddenly crying huge crocodile tears. "You hit me," he screamed at his mother.

"Daniel," she said, her tone flat. "Get in the car." But he continued his outburst right there, at the bottom of the steps, as the older boy climbed into the hatchback as he was told, and the mother secured the baby carrier into the car. The boy, Daniel, maybe five or six years old, crossed his arms across himself and pouted, that bottom lip of his almost covering the top one. I stared in awe, thinking how I never, ever would've talked to Momma that way, never would've called Lily a fart-face or booger-brain. I decided then and there that I didn't like this little boy, not one bit at all. I didn't like the way his wayward brown hair crept from the edges of his bomber hat, or the way his too-big coat hung farther down on the left side than the right, the sleeve on the left completely covering a gloved hand. I didn't like his navy blue boots or the nasty frown on his long face.

But what really bothered me was that he thought whatever errand they were about to run was the worst thing in the world that could happen. Clearly he'd never met a man like Joseph.

What I wouldn't give for a trip to the Safeway right then and there. I thought about helping Momma push the shopping cart around, and tickling Lily's little piggies so she wouldn't fuss. I remembered the heavenly scent of fresh baked doughnuts in the bakery's display case, the way Momma would tell me to pick one for each of us for the next day's breakfast.

There I was, picturing cake doughnuts oozing with rainbow-covered sprinkles, long johns coated with chocolate icing, when that lady started toward me, and instinctively my feet began a retreat. "Can I help you?" she asked, coming down the driveway to where I stood on the opposite side of the street, staring at her family. Her eyes, brown and runny, lined with bags, were tired, her hair slick, as though she hadn't found the time for a shower that day. "Are you lost, honey?"

And things came at me quickly, things I hadn't seen before: the green shamrocks taped to the windows of the home, shamrocks we never used to own. The black lettering on the mailbox: *Brigman.* A dog barking from the front window, big, like a German shepherd, its head poking through lacy curtains that were never there. A wooden rocking chair on the tiny front porch, a gnome holding a welcome sign. That boy with the ugly pout on his face or the older one, who now reemerged from the car to see who the heck his mother was talking to, who walked down the drive to meet his mother, who asked again, "Is there something I can help you with?" as I turned around and began to run.

This was not my home.

The realization stole the breath right from my lungs and I found myself gasping for air as I tore down Canyon Drive, past parked cars and fenced-in yards, mailboxes and splotchy lawns, kicking the gravel up from the street as I ran. The world spun in hurried circles. I cut through a lawn, in case that woman in her red hatchback, Mrs. *Brigman,* tried to follow. I tripped over a boulder and landed splat on the ground in the back of some stranger's yard. The knees of my pants were soaking wet, muddy from the melting snow. The suitcase fell open and emptied itself onto the soggy lawn, the books and dollar bills peppering the snow. I grabbed quickly, stuffing my belongings back into place before slamming the suitcase closed.

I didn't see it right away. In fact, I almost didn't see it at all. I was standing up, hoping and praying someone wasn't at the back window of that home watching me, when something — bright in the otherwise white snow — caught my eye, and I reached down and picked it up, and there, in my hand, was a photo of Momma, the very same one Joseph had years ago forced me to tear to shreds. That photo Joseph made me march down the steps of the Omaha home and throw into the trash. I remember that day, Matthew and Isaac sitting at the table watching me, watching as I dropped the hundreds of pieces of Momma into the garbage can before I walked upstairs, like Joseph had told me to do, to pray. Pray for God's forgiveness.

Matthew had pulled those pieces from the garbage can and, like a jigsaw puzzle, taped them back together. A million pieces of

Scotch tape lined the back of that picture, making it thick and sturdy, white, ragged creases lining Momma's beautiful face, her long black hair, her sapphire eyes. I held Momma in my hands, there, in her peridot-colored dress — a *frock* as Momma used to call it, the bateau neckline and cap sleeves seamed by Joseph's poisonous hand.

Where had Matthew kept it all those years since he pulled it from the trash?

Why had he kept it from me for so long?

But of course, I knew why. He was worried Joseph would see.

But he didn't have to worry anymore.

It had been years since I'd seen Momma. In my mind, the black hair had dissolved, the blue eyes had become diluted, like a watered-down can of pop. Her smile had shrunk to half its size, and only sometimes did I remember she wore bright red lipstick on the days when Daddy was home. But there she was: the pitch-black hair and sapphire eyes, berry bliss lipstick smoothed on her lips. And she was laughing. I could hear it, the laughter, from that photograph, and I could see Momma, just seconds after I'd snapped that crooked photo, snatch the camera from my hand and take a shot of me, and after we'd developed the roll at the Safeway, we each held on to the photo of the other, so we'd always be together even when we weren't together. *I love you like x's love o's,* she'd said, planting a big red kiss on my cheek, and I'd stared at that kiss in the rearview mirror of the old Datsun Bluebird, refusing to wipe my cheek clean.

I pressed that photo of Momma to my heart and knew then, bawling my eyes out in the backyard of some stranger's home, on my knees in the vanishing March snow, that Momma was there even if she wasn't there.

Momma would never, ever, ever in a million years leave me.

HEIDI

I press my baby into me and sink into the rocking chair, vowing never, ever, *ever* to leave her again. She's begun to cry now, her cry angry and infuriated as she seizes strands of my hair in the palm of her hand and pulls, hard, howling without cease, the kind of cry that forces the breath from her lungs, and she finds herself gasping, suddenly, for air. I rise from the chair and begin to tread throughout the room, aware of the murmur of Nina Simone that seeps through the wall from Graham's home: *I Put a Spell on You,* playing louder now than ever before.

Or is that simply my imagination?

Is he trying to drown out the sound of my baby's indignant cry? Or send me a message? I envision Graham, at that moment, still unclad, wondering why it was I had to leave when I'd only just arrived.

And then, I think, what would he do, there

in his home, with his undershirt discarded, his jeans unzipped; would he phone a lady friend to fill the space where I'd just been? I try not to think about it, to think about some beautiful blonde woman taking my place on the edge of the unmade bed, and Graham, blind to the change, aware only of some woman's hands on him. I will the image out of my mind: me on Graham's bed, his body hovering above mine. I think what I would have done, how far I would have gone had it not been for the baby.

But no, I remind myself. The baby was asleep. Or was she? I wonder, finding myself suddenly oh-so confused, mindful of the cry — desperate and helpless, completely forlorn — that I heard from Graham's room. That cry plays over and over again in my mind, a soundtrack to accompany the scene: Graham slipping an undershirt up over his head, the oblique and abdominal muscles, the faint, fair hair, the brass button of his jeans.

And then: that cry.

The baby did cry, I tell myself. She was not asleep.

I move the baby back and forth, up and down in a gentle seesaw motion, anything to calm her down. She's angry with me for leaving. I say it over and over again, "I'm so sorry. Mommy will never, ever leave you again," and I smother her with kisses in a weak attempt at an apology.

I am not a good mother, I tell myself. A good mother wouldn't have left her alone and walked out of the room. A moment of weakness, I think, remembering all too well the condom abandoned in the pocket of Chris's trousers, and the thought of it, the thought of that shiny blue wrapper, sends me into a rapid descent: heartbeat unsettled, hands that feel like sludge.

In the kitchen, I prepare a bottle, knowing, as I always do, as the baby nuzzles her nose into the black crepe dress, that she is hungry. I set the formula into the bottle, add water and shake: a counterfeit reproduction of the sustenance her mother is meant to provide. I try to remember why it was that I decided to bottle feed my baby, why I did not breast feed. Or did I breast feed? And I find that, standing there, in the kitchen, I cannot remember. *Cancer,* I tell myself, but then: *cancer?*

Or was that — the cancer — simply a figment of my imagination, and I wonder about that line on my abdomen, the very one Graham traced with a fingertip — the one he almost asked about until I pressed my fingers to my lips and whispered *shhh*

— and wonder where it came from, that scar, whether or not it's a scar at all.

And then a word settles in my mind, ugly and vile and I shake my head posthaste to get it out.

Abortion.

But no. I press the baby into me, knowing that can't be true.

That doctor with the balding head said that she, my Juliet, had been discarded as medical waste. He said that medical waste is incinerated after leaving the hospital, and I was left with a vision that kept me awake for years on end, that filled my dreams with dread: baby Juliet in a two-thousand-degree kiln, being tossed around like cement in a cement mixer so that all sides of her were exposed to the heat, her tiny soul escaping as gas into the earth's atmosphere.

I shake my head again, vehemently, and say out loud, "No."

I peer down at the baby in my arms and think: Juliet is here. She is safe.

Perhaps it's a birthmark, I think then, that scar on my abdomen, like the one on my baby's leg. Do such things — birthmarks — pass from generation to generation? I think back to the day before, chatting with patrons on the "L" train en route to lunch with Chris in the Chicago Loop as they complimented my adorable baby, and said how much alike we looked, my baby and me, those words every mother in the world longs to hear. *She has your eyes,* one said, and another, *She has your smile,* and as they did, I traced a finger over the curve of the baby's upper lip, that prominent V in the middle that is somehow said to resemble the bow of Cupid.

Just like Zoe's. Just like mine.

"It runs in the family," I'd said, of that resplendent smile my baby revealed at the appropriate time, as if she'd known all along that she was the topic of conversation, the one who everyone was staring at, ogling.

But she's mine, I thought, pressing her close to me, refusing to think about Willow, pushing the name Ruby far from my mind. *All mine.*

And then there's the buzz of the intercom, pulling me from my thoughts; it's loud and incredibly rude as I set that fraudulent breast milk into my baby's mouth, and whether it's the milk itself or the blare of the intercom, I honestly can't say, but the baby thrusts the bottle out with a tongue and again begins to scream.

I walk to the window and peer out, onto the street below, to see Jennifer, my best friend, Jennifer, standing by the plate-glass door with a cup of Starbucks coffee in each hand. Dressed in hospital scrubs and a jean jacket, her hair blowing in the incessant Chicago wind. I duck frantically down before she can see me, before she can see me standing by the bay window eyeing her, and hoping that she will leave. I cannot see Jennifer *now.* She will stare at my dress, the buttons mismatched, the dark makeup, laden with a decided desperation, now running its course down my cheek. The pink panties and nylons in a ball, the black heels once again pulled from their cardboard box in vain.

And she will want to know what happened. She will ask about Graham. She will ask about my baby.

And what will I say? How will I explain?

The intercom buzzes again and I rise to my knees, clutching a screaming baby in my arms, peering out of the bay window to see Jennifer, blocking the sun from her eyes with the back of a hand, peer upward to the window that she knows is mine, and I plunge again to the ground, uncertain as to whether or not she saw me there in the window, eyeing her from up above. I all but drop the baby on the ground, as the two of us hover, together, in the mere twenty-four inches of space beneath the windowsill.

"Shh," I beg the baby with a despair in my voice that mimics her own. "Hush. *Please,*" I say, as my knees begin to ache.

My phone is ringing, and I know without having to look at the display screen, that it is Jennifer, wondering where I am. She's been told I'm sick, for sure, if and when she called the office to see if I was there. Dana, receptionist extraordinaire, told her of my unrelenting flu, and my best friend has come to deliver coffee — or perhaps an Earl Grey tea — to make me feel well. And here I am hiding from her, on my knees on the hardwood floor, begging the child to be still, to be quiet.

And then the phone settles and the intercom settles and, with the exception of the baby, all is quiet. I rise cautiously from my knees to see that Jennifer is gone, out of sight, here one minute, gone the next. I search down the block for the faded denim of a jean jacket, but spy only my neighbor, an older lady from down the hall toting an empty granny cart en route to the grocery store.

I exhale deeply — certain I'm off the hook — and plead with my baby to drink the bottle, as I set it warily on her tongue and will her to drink. "Please, honey," I say, or attempt to say, before a knock at the door makes me jump right on out of my skin. The knock is light, and yet knowing and determined. Jennifer, I'm certain, who slipped through the plate-glass door with her Starbucks cups when old Mrs. Green left for the grocery store. *Sneaky, sneaky,* I think as I hear her calling me through the door.

"Heidi," she says and then there's that knock again — that damn *tap, tap, tap* — which speaks louder than any words possibly can. She knows I am here.

"Heidi," she says again, as I begin to run through the home, with the baby in my arms, as far away from the door as I can possibly go. I imagine we're being trailed by carbon monoxide and must find a place where we can breathe. Jennifer's voice is diluted by the distance as I hover in the corner of Chris's and my bedroom, tilting the blinds upward so those who come and go on the city street down below will not see — and yet I'm certain I hear her utter *I saw you* and *I know you're there* from where she stands in the hall, tap, tap, tapping on the wooden pane of the door for my attention.

They will take my baby. They will take my baby from me. I beg, "Please, Juliet, *please* be quiet," panic-stricken that she won't take the bottle, that she won't stop crying. That word — *Juliet* — it slips from my tongue, utterly wrong and yet so undeniably right. But the crying . . . the crying won't stop. I'm with baby Zoe all over again, in the midst of an episode of colic, and she's screaming, writhing in pain, but with Zoe, I don't remember the need to hide, to crouch on my bedroom floor and hide.

How long we wait, I cannot say. One minute, one hour, I don't know, but I jostle my baby silently and beg her to stop. The frequency of Jennifer's tap, tap, tapping gets less and less until it altogether ceases; my phone rings and then stops, rings and then stops, the house phone, the cell phone.

I watch out the bedroom window with its upward slanting blinds as Jennifer appears, turning circles on the street below as if utterly confused. She peers up, at the bay window in our living room and stares, and it's only as she departs down the street, tossing one of the Starbucks cups in a nearby garbage bin, that I emerge from the bedroom and seek out my phone, the one which, from the hallway, Jennifer most certainly heard ring. Three times, or so the phone tells me, three missed calls, an awaiting voice mail. A text message.

Where r u?

WILLOW

Louise Flores beckons me again. A guard arrives at the cell I share with Diva, demanding I put my hands through the portal so she can cuff them before she opens the door. I climb down from the top tier of the bunk bed and place my hands behind my back.

We walk through the prison together.

Today Ms. Flores wants to talk about the baby, Calla. I sit down across from her, on a spent seat with its inflexible back. "Why did you take the baby?" she asks, and I picture that night, standing in the darkened woods, staring through the treasure-trove of windows of the A-frame home.

After visiting the old prefab home in Ogallala, I found my way back to the Conoco where I begged and pleaded with the ticket lady to trade my obsolete ticket in for a new one. I'd missed the bus to Fort Collins, of course. For twenty bucks she said she would. Grudgingly. It was dark by then. The next bus wouldn't arrive until the middle of the night: 3:05 a.m.

But I hadn't gone to the Conoco right away. After I'd stopped sniveling in that stranger's yard, I made my way over to the cemetery off Fifth Street and laid down on the lawn, right between Momma and Daddy.

And then I got myself together and did what needed to be done.

Every single light in the A-frame must've been turned on. I saw everything as if I was in that house with them all, a fly on the wall. I saw Paul Zeeger in an upstairs room, slipping off a tie. Big Lily, cradling that gosh darn baby in her arms, rocking her back and forth in a subliminal sway, her hand sweeping across the baby's stupid head. The dog, at her feet, began a happy dance, and when Big Lily meandered to the back door to let it outside, I hid behind an enormous tree. "Go, Tyson," she said with a slight kick to his behind, "Hurry up," and then she closed the door, and that dog, with its amazing snout, sought me out in the trees and licked me. I pushed it away, whispered *Go!* in whatever firm voice I could muster, letting my eyes run their course through the home. The fireplace was on, a TV in the

480

Zeeger bedroom (where Paul now lay, spread out across the bed) tuned in to the news.

And then there was Lily, Little Lily, *my* Lily, in a bedroom, all alone, braiding the hair of a baby doll. She sat on the edge of a purple bed with that doll pressed between her legs, winding the strands around her fingers. My Lily wasn't a baby anymore. In fact, she was older than I'd been when Momma and Daddy died.

And she was beautiful. Absolutely beautiful. Just like Momma had been.

"Why didn't you just take Rose?" Ms. Flores asks as she breaks off a bite of muffin and sets it in her mouth, letting it slowly dissolve. "Rose was your sister after all."

"Lily," I snap. "Her name is Lily," I say, imagining the way she tired of braiding the doll's hair — maybe she didn't know how to do it, or maybe she was just tired of playing with the doll, I don't know — but I saw the way she spun that doll around and stared into her acrylic eyes for a split second before she flung it across the room. The doll's head smashed into the purple wall and fell like a brick from the sky. At the same time, Paul and Big Lily jumped, but it was Big Lily — beckoned by the sound of my Lily's cry — who placed the baby in a cradle and climbed the steps to my Lily's room.

Lily hated Baby Calla. That's what I told myself. And she was taking it out on that doll. I watched as she rose from the bed in a horse-print nightgown and plaid slippers and walked to where that toy lay facedown on the ground and kicked it with a vengeance.

Ms. Flores stares at me and then gives in. Sort of. "Fine," she says. "Lily. Rose. Whatever. Answer the question, Claire. Why didn't you take your sister instead of the baby?"

The truth was that my Lily had a grand life. Before. Before Paul and Big Lily decided to replace her with the *baby they always dreamed of.* There wasn't a thing I could give my Lily. My only possessions in the entire world were stuffed inside a suitcase Matthew had given me: dollar bills that were quickly dwindling away, a couple of books, the photograph of Momma.

"I couldn't take care of Lily," I tell Ms. Flores, "if I took her from that home."

"But you could take care of the baby? You could take care of Calla?"

I shrug and say weakly, "That's not what I meant."

"Then what did you *mean,* Claire?" she

condemns, her lips thin, her eyebrows puckered. She removes her glasses and sets them on the table. My Lily could have that life again. The one with beach vacations and pink–and–mint-green bikes and Montessori schools. I just needed to fix things. And so, when Big Lily climbed up those steps and Paul rolled over onto his side and pretended he couldn't hear the outburst my Lily was having, I let myself into the A-frame home, through a back door that had been left unlocked when the cocker spaniel was let outside to pee. I slipped my hands under that sleeping baby's pink blanket and lifted her from the cradle, careful of her head like Momma always told me when Lily was a baby, and with that baby in tow, I walked out the wooden patio door and into the starless March night.

CHRIS

I oversleep.

When I finally do wake up, the hangover is immense: a splitting headache, the despotic sunlight blinding my eyes. I wake up to the impatient sound of my cell phone ringing, the tone, in my alcohol-induced state, out of place, jarring. Henry. His voice on the other end of the line, like a drill sergeant's, calling out orders. "Where the hell are you?" he asks. It's after nine.

I don't have time to shower. I reek of tequila as I wait for the elevator at the end of the hall, my hair still smelling of rancid cigarette smoke from some bar I wandered to last night. My eyes are bloodshot, my hands still clammy. I forget my notes, the ones that tell me what I'm supposed to say to the group of potential investors awaiting me in the eighth-floor conference room, the ones we're hoping to impress. As I slink into the conference room, all eyes are on me. I taste alcohol on my breath, stomach-churning in the morning light. Gastric acid propels upward and into my mouth before I choke on it, forcing it back down.

"Better late than never," Henry slurs beneath his breath as I wipe my mouth on the back of a sleeve. I catch sight of Cassidy, leaned in close to some venture capitalist named Ted. She's got her lips pressed so close to his ear, I imagine the way he feels her breath, the tingle of it on his skin. He turns to look at her all at once, and together they laugh in unison, laughter that I'm sure is at my expense.

I run my fingers through my hair.

At some point, Tom pulls me aside, tells me to get it together. He hands me a mug of coffee, as if the caffeine might change things, make my speech less slurred, my thoughts crystal clear. I dig into the depths of my briefcase for financial documents which are nowhere. I yank crumbled notes, memos out instead, the purple sticky note with the sole word: *Yes.*

The coffee settles me some. We take a midmorning break, and I return to my room to change my clothes, comb my hair. I find the missing financial documents strewn upon a table and place them in my briefcase. I brush my teeth; between the caffeine and the toothpaste, the taste of alcohol begins to slowly ebb away. I all but overdose on pain medication for the splitting headache.

When I return, Cassidy and Ted are sharing a bagel with cream cheese from a single plate. They're leaned in close together. She licks her fingers with an overzealous tongue and leans in close to whisper something to him. Their eyes turn to mine and again they laugh. I imagine Cassidy, in my hotel room, unbuttoning the buttons of a starch-white tunic so that I will stay. And I imagine me, forcing on a pair of loafers and running through the door. I imagine that she left that hotel room and sought out Ted. Ted, a fortysomething venture capitalist with a tungsten wedding band on his left hand. Based on the looks of things, he, unlike me, didn't turn her away. He let her unbutton that blouse, let her reveal what was hidden beneath.

I hear Heidi in my head, hear her chant *femme fatale* over and over again in my head: a rallying cry. *Women unite!* I wonder about Ted's wife. I wonder if she's pretty. I wonder if they have kids.

I'm not in the least bit let down. More than anything, I'm relieved, seeing now that Cassidy would've chosen any member of the male species to keep her company for the night. I'm grateful it wasn't me.

Because then I'd be the one sitting like an ass at the conference table, drooling all over a bagel with cream cheese, watching the way her tongue wraps its way around a finger as she licks it clean.

When my phone rings, I find it in my pocket and see on the display screen: *Martin Miller,* the PI I hired to track our Willow down. I hurry, quickly, from the conference room and into the hallway, an eighth-floor balcony that looks down into the hotel's atrium below, filled with banquet tables and plush sofas, tropical flowers and fish, dozens of big, fat koi that swim in ponds throughout the atrium.

Martin's voice is reticent. He's found something. I lay my hand on the balcony rail to steady myself, staring down on eight floors of nothingness that, when combined with the aftereffects of too much alcohol, make me woozy.

"What is it?" I ask, my voice discomposed. The koi, eight floors below, are little more than white-and-orange smudges in the water.

Martin says that he's emailing me a newspaper article he found, dated the middle of March. There's no mention of a Willow. Or a Ruby. But he says it might just be our girl.

I wait for the email to come through on my phone, my limbs numb by the time my phone vibrates the email's arrival.

I open the article and there, staring me in the eye, is Willow Greer. Except that she's not Willow Greer. The caption reads, Claire Dalloway, wanted for questioning in the death of an Omaha man and his wife, and for the kidnapping of an infant girl abducted March 16 from her home in Fort Collins, Colorado.

I skim the article and see that this Claire Dalloway may be armed, dangerous, that this man and his wife, Joseph and Miriam Abrahanson, were stabbed to death in their Omaha home while they slept. I read about the baby, Calla Zeeger, born to a lady named Lily and a man named Paul. In Fort Collins. Colorado. There are identifying features: the color of her eyes, the shade of her sparse hair, a close-up of a birthmark on the back of a leg. A port-wine stain, the article states, shaped like the state of Alaska.

There is a reward. For her return.

I read about Joseph and Miriam Abrahamson, Ms. Dalloway's foster family, who graciously welcomed Claire into their home upon the death of her own parents when she was eight years old.

I read how they were murdered in their beds while they slept.

"The Abrahamsons have boys, as well," Martin is telling me. "Two sons, two biological sons," he adds. "Isaac and Matthew, both in their twenties. The oldest son, Isaac, has an alibi for the night in question. He works the third shift, stacking shelves at Walmart. He came home early in the morning of March 19 to find his parents dead, in bed.

"The other son, Matthew Abrahamson, is on the run. Like Claire Dalloway, wanted for questioning in the murder."

"You didn't tell anyone, did you, Martin?" I ask desperately.

"No, Chris, of course not. But we'll need to," he says. "We'll need to turn your girl in. If she's the one," he says, and I think, of course, of course we do.

"Twenty-four hours," I beg. "Just give me twenty-four hours," and he says okay. I need to get to Heidi myself, I need to be the one to tell her.

I wonder if he means it, if Martin really will give me twenty-four hours before he phones the police.

There is a reward, I reread. *For her return.*

Good God, I think, telling Martin that I have to go. I must call Heidi. I must warn

489

her. I dial the numbers, press send.

The phone rings and rings but there is no answer.

My eyes reread the words: *Armed. Dangerous.*

Stabbed.

Death.

WILLOW

The bus ride to Chicago was long. Over twenty-three hours to be exact, with some sixteen stops. Twice we had to gather all our belongings and move to a different bus, one that was going the same way as us. I saw more of the world than I'd ever seen: the mountains of Colorado that shrunk as we crossed the state, and became near nothingness, only cattle farm after cattle farm with so many cows jam-packed inside, it made me claustrophobic just looking at them all, fighting for food from the trough. We retraced our steps through Nebraska, crossed over the Missouri River, and were welcomed to Iowa by the people of the state, or so the sign on the side of the road said.

I chose Chicago because of Momma. There I was, staring at another big chart on the bus station wall. *Arrivals* and *Departures* it said. And I saw that word *Chicago,* and thought of Momma and her list of *one days,* and how she didn't get to cross too much off that list before the Bluebird went tumbling down the road. I didn't see Switzerland on that list, nor did I see Paris, but I did see Chicago, and I thought of that Magnificent Mile Momma longed to see — the one with the Gucci and Prada stores where she wanted to shop.

I thought that if Momma couldn't see it for herself, then I'd see it for her.

The baby slept peacefully, wrapped up in the soft pink blanket on my lap. I didn't dare set her or the suitcase down and so the three of us, we shared one seat. She slept much of the time but when her eyes were open I held her so she could see through the window, first the sunset and, later, the sunrise over the Gateway to the West, a city that used to be my home. At some gas station stop at a town called Brush, I lugged the baby and suitcase inside and purchased formula, like Momma used to feed Lily, and a plastic bottle. When the baby finally did fuss at some point in the night, I thrust that bottle in her mouth and watched her suck herself back to sleep.

I didn't think much about the baby being cute, or the way she wrapped her tiny hand around my finger and squeezed. I wasn't thinking about how her eyes watched me,

492

or the words *Little Sister* scrawled across her shirt.

What I was thinking about were those sea anemones, the ones in a book Matthew had brought for me when I was a kid: would-be murderers in delicate, angelic bodies. I thought of their wispy tentacles when the baby twined her hand around my finger, I considered their brilliant colors when the baby looked and me and beamed. They looked like flowers but they were not. Instead, they were predators of the sea. Immortal. Injecting paralyzing venom into their prey so they could eat them alive.

This baby was a sea anemone.

I thought that I hated her, I did. But as the bus drifted across the country, and the baby held tight to my little finger, and from time to time just stared at me or smiled, I had to remind myself that she was evil, as if that thought just kept slipping from my mind. I told myself I wasn't going to like her. Not one bit.

But in the end, I did.

As we boarded a new bus in Denver, some girl slid into the seat beside me, dropped down into the chair like a plane crashing from the sky, and asked, "What's your baby's name?" I opened my mouth but no sound came out. "What's the matter?" she asked. "Cat got your tongue?"

The girl was all skin and bones, her cheeks hollowed in. She wore clothes that were too big on her, an unshapely coat that just drooped. Her hair was dark, her eyes dark. Around her neck she wore a dog collar with spikes.

"No, it's . . ." I stuttered, unable to come up with a name.

"She's gotta have a name, don't she?" not even flinching when I couldn't tell her my baby's name. Course I couldn't say the baby's name was Calla. Then she might have known. "How about *Ruby*?" she asked then, as she gazed out the window, watching as the bus bypassed a Ruby Tuesday restaurant on the side of the road. There it sat, right before the expressway entrance. Karma, I believed.

I stared at those words, the big bold red letters. I'd never known anyone named Ruby before. I thought of that brilliant red gemstone, red, the color of blood.

"Ruby," I repeated, as if tasting the word in my mouth. Savoring it. And then, "I like it. Yeah. Ruby," I said again.

And she said, "Ruby," ingraining the word in my mind.

The girl had a bruise the size of Mount

Everest on her head, slashes across a wrist that she tried to cover by yanking down the sleeve of a green coat. She caught the bus in Denver, and by Omaha she was gone. I tried not to look at the bruise, but my eyes found it near impossible not to stray to the purple goose egg on her head. "What?" she asked nonchalantly. "This?" She swept her hair down, to cover the bruise. "Let's just say my boyfriend's an ass," she said, and then asked me, "What brings a girl like you out on the road in the middle of the night? With," she adds, pinching the baby's tiny nose, "a babe."

We got to talking, that girl and me. She had a low-key approach that I liked, a way of holding my eyes when she talked. "Let's just say we needed a change of scenery," I said and with that, we stopped asking about where we were going and where we'd been because we both knew the other had come from someplace ugly.

We had a stopover in Kearney, Nebraska, during which time the girl poured a bottle of reddish hair dye over my head and I did the same to her. It didn't sit long enough, and so, instead of ginger hair, as depicted on the box, I remained snot colored, tinged with red. The girl shimmied out of a pair of torn jeans and a sweater. "Here," she said, thrusting the clothing into my already jam-packed hands. "Switch."

I slipped the baby into her tattooed hands, a half butterfly on each palm that, when pressed together, made it complete. "A tiger swallowtail," she said when I asked. In the stall of the bathroom — the walls covered with ink: *Benny loves Jane* and *Rita is a gay* — I took off the pants Matthew had given me and pulled the sweatshirt up over my head. I left on the undershirt, the one dotted with Joseph's blood. This, I couldn't dare let her see. I slipped on that girl's clothing: the jeans and sweater, a hooded coat the color of green olives and leather boots with frayed brown shoelaces. When I emerged from the stall, she was holding the baby in a single arm, a safety pin in her right hand.

"What's that for?" I asked, watching as she removed a course of earrings from her ear: an angel's wings, a cross, red lips.

"It'll only hurt for a second," she replied and with that I held the baby while she thrust that pin through my ear and set the earring inside the swollen lobes. I screamed, squeezing the baby unintentionally, and Ruby, she screamed, too.

We tossed the empty bottles of hair dye into the trash and then the girl pulled me close, streaking eyeliner across my eyes. I'd never worn makeup before, nothing other than a hint of pale pink rouge Momma swept across my cheeks every now and then. I looked at myself in the filmy mirror: the hair, the earring, the dark mysterious eyes.

The reflection that stared back was anything but mine.

"What's your name?" she asked, slipping the eyeliner into my pocket, the pocket of that green coat that used to be hers. And then she took a pair of scissors to my hair. I didn't object. I held very still, watching in the mirror as she snipped erratic strands from my head. "You know," she confessed, tossing the wet clumps of hair to the bathroom tile, "I used to want to be a beautician."

I stared at my reflection and thought it best that she was not. My mop was misshapen: longer on one side than the other, lanky bangs that hid my eyes.

"My mother was a beautician," I said, then wondered what Momma would think of me now. Would she be disappointed in me, or would she see that I was doing what needed to be done? I was taking good care of Lily, just like I told her I would. "My name is Claire."

"Claire?" she asked and I nodded my

head. "Claire what?"

Her own reddish hair she'd dyed dirty blond. She took the scissors to her hair, too, and on the dingy floor the strands coalesced.

"Claire Dalloway."

She tossed it all in the trash: the scissors, the safety pin, what she could collect of the hair from that floor. She opened her own bag and dumped its guts into the bin: a torn magazine, an ID, a half-eaten bag of Skittles, a phone. And then she reached inside the black garbage bag and snatched the Skittles, having changed her mind. The rest she left behind.

The girl was standing in the bathroom, hand on the door. Someone on the other side knocked, a heavy, thumping blow. "Hang on," she snapped, and then, to me, "I'm Willow," she said, "Willow Greer," and I knew after she left that bathroom, I'd never lay eyes on her again.

"I'll meet you at the bus," she fudged, and with that, I hoisted the slipping baby onto a hip and watched my former self walk out the yellowing veneer door and into the gas station, past a line of waiting women who'd lost their patience.

She wasn't on the bus when I returned.

HEIDI

She'll have nothing to do with the bottle.

I try again and again to set the formula-filled bottle into Juliet's mouth, but she'll have nothing to do with it. I press my lips to her forehead; it's cool. No fever. I change her diaper and attempt a pacifier, I spread diaper rash cream onto a healed rash, but nothing will do, nothing will soothe my child.

And it's in the way that she nuzzles her nose into the black crepe dress that the answer comes to me, the answer, utterly simple: that one thing only a mother can provide.

I sit down in the rocking chair and, reaching behind me with a single arm, begin to unfasten the mismatched buttons up my back, sliding my arms out of the dress so that before Juliet, I am exposed. *Nothing she hasn't seen before,* I think, recalling those nights in my mind that I sat down with Juliet, in the sleigh glider in the nursery with its pale pink walls and damask sheets, and pressed her to my breast so she could drink her fill, until her hunger eased and she drank herself asleep, her eyes slowly becoming too heavy to hold open, and there, in the nursery, with only the glow of the moon to keep us company, my Juliet would suckle until she drifted to sleep. I recall the way she would slurp insatiably at times, staring at me with her huge brown anime eyes as if I was the best thing in the world, her eyes filled to the brim with love and awe. Love and awe for me.

But Juliet, I'm noticing, eyeing the child before me, Juliet's eyes are blue.

It's no matter, I tell myself, knowing how babies' eyes can change on a dime. Brown one minute, blue the next, and yet there's something different about it, about those eyes, about the way they stare at me.

I place my breast beside Juliet's mouth, and watch in admiration as she locates the nipple, and as she latches on, I find it all so familiar, the tingling sensation in my breast, the release of oxytocin that fills me with a sense of calm. I run a hand across my Juliet's head and whisper, "There now, pretty baby," as I watch for the rhythmic sucking and swallowing action, for the big brown eyes to stare at me with awe. Love. Wanting me and only me.

But instead there is exasperation in those eyes, those blue eyes that look at me untrustingly, as if I've pulled a fast one on her, before she begins to cry. I slide a finger between her mouth and my breast, and attempt to reposition her, certain that she hasn't latched on correctly. I try cradling her in either arm, and offer milk from either breast; and then, when this doesn't work, I move Juliet and myself to the couch, where I lie on my back, with her sprawled across my chest: biological nurturing, or so it's called, the way nature prescribed. Just as my lactation consultant, Angela, suggested I do when Zoe had trouble nursing.

I think of my lactation consultant, of Angela, of how I will phone her for advice if this doesn't work. And Angela will come as she always used to do, and she will help position Juliet so that she will eat; she will once again explain to me breast compression to increase milk flow, and before I know it Juliet will suckle as she used to do.

And then there's a sound in the hallway, footsteps that are loud and impatient, and I curse Jennifer, sneaking into my building again when someone was coming or going, not even bothering, this time, to buzz the intercom or call my cell. Trespassing, I think, wondering where I've left my Swiss Army knife.

I lie on the couch, with my black crepe dress pulled down to my waist, and Juliet, floundering like a fish out of water, on my chest, about to scream.

There's no time to escape into the recesses of my bedroom for a place to hide before Juliet lets out a bloodcurdling scream and the front door flings open, and I see him, standing on the other side of the wooden door, staring at my attire, the black dress, the streaks of makeup dried to my skin.

His mouth formed in the perfect loop, his eyebrows raised in question.

His hair stands on end, in a jumble, as my heart beats fast, the room spinning laps around me. Juliet is screaming into my ear, her fitful body becoming hard to hold.

Not Jennifer at all.

But Chris.

WILLOW

That bus dropped us off in Chicago, the baby and me. *Ruby,* I reminded myself as I stepped out of the station and onto a bustling city street. It was cold outside, and windy. *The Windy City,* I called to mind, thinking of those days in the Omaha library with Matthew, looking up Chicago in the pages of the books.

I'd never seen anything like Chicago in my whole entire life. There were people everywhere. Cars and buses, buildings that soared into the clouds. Skyscrapers, I told myself, knowing now where they got that name. I turned and over my shoulder I saw it: a building with antennas that scraped the sky. It had to be a hundred floors or more, that building, twice as high — three times as high! — as any of those buildings in Omaha had been.

It didn't take long to figure out I had nowhere to go. People stared at me, and it wasn't a stare that was kind or concerned, but mean, judgmental, uncaring. I hid at first, the baby and me, in whatever dark alley we could find, leaned up against mildewed brick buildings, beside doors that were locked and barred. There were smelly garbage bins and Dumpsters down those alleys, and sometimes there were rats. I spent my days sitting on concrete — wet from the rain — staring up at the steel grating of the fire escapes. And hiding. I was certain they were coming for us, that Paul and Lily Zeeger were coming, that Joseph was coming. But it occurred to me then, after a day or two, that with all those people there in Chicago, there was no way they were ever gonna find me, no way at all.

And Joseph, well, Joseph was still dead.

And then, when I wasn't worrying about the Zeegers coming for me, or Joseph, I was worrying about other stuff: what to eat and where to sleep, for the money Matthew had given me was all but gone. It was cold out there, cold during the day, cold during the night, the wind making it hard sometimes to walk in a straight line. It took me only a night, maybe two, to figure out how I'd have to forage in the garbage for food, after restaurants tossed their leftovers in the trash at closing time. I'd hover in the alley where they couldn't see — just waiting, begging the baby to keep quiet — and then I'd pick through the Dumpster for something to eat. I saved whatever money I had left for the baby, for Ruby, for her bottles of formula.

I was scared, for about a million and one reasons, but the thing that scared me the most was that something might happen to that baby, something bad. I didn't want to hurt her. I was only doing what needed to be done, I reminded myself time and again when the baby spent the night in a fuss, screaming till she cried herself to sleep.

I liked Chicago, I did. I liked the buildings and the anonymity of it, the fact that no one in the world was going to find me there, in the Windy City. But it was the train that delighted me the most, that train that soared over the city streets, and then down, down, down underground. I spent nearly all my money on one of those train passes, so that Ruby and I could ride the train as much as we pleased. The "L" I heard someone or other call it, and I had to remind myself "L" when my brain started mixing it up with every other letter of the alphabet: R, P, Q. When the day was cold or rainy, or we were otherwise bored, we'd climb on the train, the baby and me, and ride.

I realized quickly that there was a library

there along the brown line of that train. It said so right on the map: *Library.* I was pretty sure it was an omen, a sign.

I climbed up the steps to the train platform one cold, rainy April day after we'd been in the city a week, maybe two. I had that baby tucked up inside my coat to keep her dry and warm. And we waited there, on that platform, beside men and women with too-big umbrellas and their briefcases and bags. They stared, they pointed fingers, they whispered. About the baby. About me. I looked away, pretended not to notice, letting my hair fall into my eyes so I couldn't see the way they stared, the way they pointed.

The first train that came, it was too crowded. I didn't like the crowds, being so close to strangers that I could smell their perfume, their shampoo; being so close that they could smell my stench, days upon days of body odor and sweat, of the sour smell of spoiled milk and seafood that drifted from the garbage by which we slept, enfolding the baby and me in a noxious stench.

And so I told the baby we'd wait, we'd wait for another one. And I stood there, watching as everyone else climbed on board, not a single one of them paying me the time of day.

But then I saw it: a woman hesitated a split second before boarding that train, the only person in the whole entire city of Chicago who'd ever hesitated for me. But then she, too, climbed on board that train and out the window she stared, at the baby and me, though I looked away, my eyes like stone, pretending that I couldn't see.

That next brown line train that came by, I got on, being hurled through Chicago and toward the library, a great big redbrick building in the heart of the city, its green roof spotted with winged creatures that kept watch over me. But I wasn't scared.

I didn't think I'd ever see that woman again.

But then I did.

CHRIS

I'm utterly speechless, my mouth hanging open, my tongue unable to produce words. Heidi lays on her back on the living room sofa, completely topless, some black dress I've never seen before pushed down beneath her chest. Her hair is in shambles, some kind of updo that has since come undone. Makeup dribbles down her face: dark eyeliner I've never seen my wife wear, dark lipstick that's smeared everywhere. The baby is screaming, out of control, and I have to remind myself that Heidi would never hurt that baby.

Heidi loves babies.

And yet I'm not so sure.

I glance around our home, taking in the emptiness, entirely aware that the door to my office — to Willow's aka *Claire's* — room is sealed shut. "Heidi," I say then as I cautiously let myself into my own home and close the door, "where is Willow?"

I whisper in case Claire is there, hiding behind the closed door with a knife. I tell myself that Claire has done this, that Claire has rendered my wife topless, the baby frantic. And yet there are no restraints, no belts or cuffs binding Heidi to the couch.

My words come out unsteady, without rhythm. I don't even know how they manage to emerge. My throat is dry, like sand; my tongue feels like it's grown to two times its size. An image of Cassidy Knudsen half-naked haunts me, alternating places with an image of a man and a woman stabbed to death in their bed.

"Heidi," I say again, and I see then, the way that she presses that baby to her chest. Heidi would never hurt that baby, I remind myself again, paralyzed by the scene before me, trying to figure out what the hell is going on. And then it comes to me, all of a sudden, what it is that Heidi's trying to do. *My God!*

My heart stops beating altogether; I lose the ability to breathe.

Suddenly I'm bounding across the room, fully prepared to snatch that baby from Heidi's hands.

Heidi rises to her feet all of a sudden, before I can catch her, clutching the baby like it's hers. I think of that birthmark on the baby's leg. *The doctor said we really might want to have it removed,* she's said. She and me. Like it was our baby they were talking about. Our baby.

This was never about Willow, I realize then and there, that sudden, obsessive desire Heidi had to help some homeless girl she'd seen on the train.

This was about the baby.

And suddenly I'm not worried about Willow — *Claire* — hiding out on the other side of the office door; I'm worried Heidi has done something to hurt the girl.

"Where's Willow?" I ask again, standing a foot, maybe two, shy of Heidi and the baby. And then again, when she doesn't answer, *"Where's Willow, Heidi?"*

Heidi's voice is flat, nearly impossible to hear thanks to the baby. But I read her lips anyway, the simple proclamation: "She's gone."

Wake up, wake up, wake up! my mind screams, certain this is only the aftereffects of last night's drinking binge. Certainly this can't be *real.*

"She's gone," I repeat more to myself than Heidi, and then, "Where?" And a dozen possibilities float through my head, a dozen possibilities that scare the shit out of me, each one worse than the next.

But Heidi doesn't answer the question.

The baby struggles in her arms. I grab a blanket from the arm of a chair and try to hand it to Heidi, to get her to cover up. "Give me the baby," I say to my wife, and then, when she shakes her head and backs farther and farther away — toward the bay window, stepping on a cat's tail in the middle of retreat — a compromise: "Just let me hold Ruby so you can fix your dress," I suggest, unprepared for the impetuousness that takes over Heidi's obliging brown eyes. Her eyes look demented, her skin flaming red.

And then she begins to scream.

Her words come out deranged, like some head case you'd see on TV. Illogical terms that oddly make sense to me. There are words: *baby* and *Juliet. Juliet.* She must say that word a dozen times or more: *Juliet.*

She's pissed that I called that baby Ruby. The baby is not Ruby, Heidi reminds me: she's Juliet. But no, I think recalling the article Martin Miller sent to me; this baby is not Ruby nor Juliet.

This baby is Calla.

"Heidi," I say. "This baby is . . ."

"Juliet," she snaps again and again and again. "Juliet!" she screams, frightening the baby all the more.

I can hardly place the name, it's so far flung from memory. And yet it's there, in bits and pieces. Heidi — years ago — lying on a hospital bed, cloaked in a hospital gown and tears; Heidi flushing her contraceptives, pill by pill down the john, pretending not to cry.

But now she's calling me names: liar and murderer and thief. She doesn't mean to, I know she doesn't, and yet she's squeezing that baby unintentionally, and the baby is crying — howling like a wolf at the goddamn moon — and Heidi is crying, too, tears that flow down her cheeks like water down a drain.

"You're mistaken," I say, as gently as I can. Heidi has convinced herself that the baby, that *this* baby, is the one she lost eleven years ago to cancer. And I could explain the idiocy of this — the fact that *that* baby is dead, the fact that *if* that baby were still alive, he or she would be eleven years old — but I realize all too clearly that the woman standing before me is not my wife.

I step forward and reach my hands out to the baby, but Heidi snatches her away. "This baby, Heidi. This baby is not . . ." and I could go on, but I don't. I'm terrified by the unstable look in her eyes, of what she might do to that baby. Not intentionally.

Heidi would never hurt a baby, not intentionally anyway.

And yet I don't know.

"Just let me hold the baby," I say, and then to appease her, "just let me hold Juliet." And I'm thinking of all the things I should have done when we lost that baby. I should have consoled her more, I think; that's what I should have done. I should have taken her to a shrink as her ob-gyn said to do. Among other things.

But Heidi said she was okay. She said she was fine, after we'd made the decision to abort that child so the doctor could treat Heidi's cancer. And yet I ignored the sadness I saw in her, the craving, the need. I figured if we ignored it, it would go away, like a stray cat, a pesky sibling.

She's quiet for a moment, watching me. I'm certain she'll give in, if only I can convince her that it's for the baby's good. "Let me make her a bottle," I say, my voice as soft as silk. "She's hungry, Heidi. Just let me make her a bottle."

The words come out pleading, desperate. But Heidi doesn't give in. She can read right through me, Heidi who knows me so well.

She brushes past me and into the kitchen, where she rummages through drawers. I grab her by an elbow as she passes by, but she shoves me in a way I never thought my wife capable of, enough that I lose my balance and almost fall. By the time I get my bearings, I find her in the middle of the kitchen, holding a Swiss Army knife in the palm of a hand, the sharp blade aimed at me.

I should have seen this coming; I should have known. I go through the past few days in my head, trying to figure out what I overlooked, some desperate cry of Heidi's for help.

A breakdown, that's what was happening. A mental breakdown. A psychotic break.

But how did I not see it coming? Did I ignore the warning signs?

"Go away, Chris," she says.

She doesn't have it in her to use that knife — or so I tell myself — but even I'm not sure.

"Heidi," I whisper, but she thrusts that knife into the air, stabbing the oxygen in the room. I glance at a clock on the wall and know that Zoe will be home soon.

For once in my life I don't think about me. I think about Heidi, Zoe, the baby.

And I lunge. It's not enough to gain control, but enough to knock the knife out of her hand. It lands on the hardwood floor with a thunk, leaving a chip in the oak floor that we'll forever remember: a reminder of this day. We scramble for the knife, the both of us, the baby thrashing in Heidi's unstable hands, her cry slowly caving in to exhaustion and fear. I charge for the Swiss Army knife on the kitchen floor, sliding headfirst, like a baserunner into second base, coming up with it in my hands.

And it's then that Heidi turns — before I have a chance to get to my feet — and sprints, down the narrow hall, slamming the door and locking herself and the baby in the bedroom.

She's crying; Heidi is crying. I can hear her through the door, sputtering some kind of mystifying diatribe about babies and Juliet, Cassidy and Graham, our neighbor Graham, the man from next door. Graham. I could call Graham for help. But there is no time. I try to reason with her — *Heidi, please, open the door. Let's talk. Let's just talk this out.* — but she won't be reasoned with.

I think of all the pseudo-weapons that are in that room and the adjoining bathroom: nail clippers, a nail file. Electrical sockets.

And then there are the windows, five floors up from the concrete below.

I don't think twice. I reach for the phone

and dial 911.

"It's my wife," I say desperately to the dispatcher on the other end of the line when she asks the nature of my emergency. "I'm afraid she's . . . I don't know . . . She needs help," I say then, shaking my head quickly from side to side; I don't know what Heidi may do. Take her own life; take the baby's life? Thirty minutes ago I would have said no, never, not Heidi.

But now I didn't know.

"Just come," I command instead, and I rattle off the address.

And then I hurry toward the bedroom door, fully prepared to knock it to the ground.

HEIDI

I don't know what happens first.

They take my blood. They hold me down on the starch-white gurney, two men do, two men in face masks and bouffant caps, their hands clad in latex gloves. They hold me down while a third injects a needle into me and takes my blood; he steals my blood from me. Chris stands idly by behind a utility cart as I kick and scream, thrusting my body from the bed, until the men with the masks and the caps and the gloves press their weight into me until I can no longer move. Their alien faces stare at me: their massive, hairless heads, their frightening opaque eyes. They have no mouths, no noses as they probe me with this and that and I scream as Chris watches from afar, saying nothing.

And then they sit me down at a table, a folding table of sorts with three padded black chairs, a clock on the wall, the requisite one-way mirror you see on TV.

Not the aliens. No not the aliens. Some-one else. Someone else entirely.

I don't know what happens first.

"My daughter. I need to see my daugh-ter," I continue to chant, but they say to me that if I cooperate I'll be able to see my daughter soon. *If I cooperate.* But whether it happens before or after the blood, I don't know. I can't say. There's a woman there, an older woman with long silver hair and I'm watching as my Juliet gets passed from one person's arms to the next, to the next, before she disappears.

"Do something!" I beg of Chris, but he ig-nores this, standing there in a room with dozens of desks and chairs. He ignores *me,* staring past me and through me, but never at me as they lead me into a room and close the door where Chris can no longer see. I wonder if I am invisible, if that's that reason Chris cannot see me. Like air, oxygen, ghosts. Perhaps I am a ghost, an apparition; perhaps I am dead. Perhaps they did not take my blood but rather injected me with potassium chloride so that I would die, there on the gurney with the men in face masks. But my hands are bound in cuffs, and the woman with the long silver hair, she can see me. She asks questions about a

518

Claire Dalloway, setting photographs on the table between us, gruesome images taking up residence in my mind, gory, bloody images of a man, spilled across a bed, a woman beside him, her torso strewn upon his, each slathered with blood. Carmine blood, thick and gooey, absorbing into the tawny sheets.

I remember the blood on Willow's undershirt and I begin to scream.

"Where have they taken the baby?" I cry out, trying in vain to free my hands from their cuffs, so that the handcuffs scrape the inner lining of my wrist. My hands are bound behind my back so that I can hardly move, a guard forcing me into my chair each time I attempt to stand, to rise from my perch and find my baby. "Where have they taken my Juliet?" I plead again when she fails to respond. And then I hear it, clear as day: I hear my baby cry. My eyes dash around the soundproofed room, searching every nook and cranny for my Juliet. She's here. She's here somewhere.

"She's in good hands," the woman says, but she doesn't tell me where. I drop my head beneath the table to see: is she there? Hidden beneath the table?

"Mrs. Wood?" the woman asks, tapping on the table to get my attention. She's impatient and short-tempered, this woman with her tape recorder and her felt-tip pens. "Mrs. Wood, what are you doing, Mrs. Wood?"

But no. Only a washed-out tile floor, varnished with coffee stains, and smut, grime, filth.

"I need to see my baby," I say, raising up to look her in the eye. "I *have* to see my baby."

There's a moment of silence. The woman, Louise Flores, the assistant state's attorney or so she says she is, stares at me with dull gray eyes. And then: "You must be mistaken, Mrs. Wood. The baby you brought in," she tells me, "that baby is Calla Zeeger. She is not your baby."

And I'm gripped with a sudden onset of wrath and fury, and I find myself rising with great difficulty to my feet and screaming at her, that she's wrong, that the baby is mine. *Mine!* I ignore the pain I feel in my arms, my back as I stretch them in ways I didn't know I could move, like women whose children are pinned beneath cars, finding they can suddenly lift four thousand pounds in a single motion, in one single hoist.

A guard is coming at me quickly, ordering me to sit down. "Sit down now," he barks, and I see him then, I see him clearly: a Perro de Presa Canario with a coarse brindle coat bounding across the room, barring razor-sharp teeth, growling — a rasping, gravelly growl: a warning. Slobber dribbles from his wide-open mouth, his teeth like spears, his eyes intent on his next meal. His hands are firm on me, on my shoulders, pressing me into the chair so that it hurts along the ridges of my shoulders where his hands meet my flesh. And he bites, that Presa Canario does, he bites quickly, unexpectedly, tearing the skin, so that blood runs its course down my arm, and I stare at that blood, blood which the others — the woman, the man — do not see. Blood which is invisible, like me.

I sit. But I don't stay seated. I stand again from my chair and push past the guard, losing balance and crashing headfirst into the wall. "I need to see my daughter!" I scream. "My daughter. My daughter," over and over again, maybe a thousand times or more, before I fall to the ground in tears.

And then that woman decides that she'll leave, then and there, with an autonomy that no longer belongs to me, rising from her chair. "I think we're through here," she says, her gray eyes not making contact with mine.

I hear her say something about the need for a psych consult, the words *delusional*

521

and *disorder* suffusing the room long after she leaves.

And then the blood. And the gurney. And the men with the face masks and gloves. Aliens. My ears ring as they inject me with needles and probes. But what comes first, I can't say. I don't know what happens first, how Chris comes to loiter at the far end of the room behind the utility cart, watching as aliens inject me and take my blood, as they administer a lethal dose of potassium chloride so that I will die. "Stop them!" I demand of Chris, but he ignores this, again, as he ignores me, and once again I am invisible, a phantom, a spook.

My Chris, who never cries, is wet with tears. He stands, still as a statue, behind that utility cart, refusing to move. I'll never forgive him for this.

And then I am tired, oh so very tired all of a sudden, the fatigue weighing on me like a thousand bricks there on the gurney while the men with the face masks and gloves watch, they watch as I stare at the tubular flourescent lights that line the ceiling tiles, my eyes suddenly becoming too heavy to hold open and I wonder, in that final moment before I go to sleep, what else they will take from me.

I want to beg Chris to stop them, to plead

with him to do something, but I find that I can no longer speak.

I awake in a room on a bed with a window that overlooks a green grassy park. A woman stands before that window in a pair of wide-leg pants and a button-down shirt, her back to me, staring out at the scenery. There is wallpaper on the walls: herringbone stripes in ecru and sage, and hardwood on the floor.

When I try to move I find myself bound to the bed; the chime of metal on metal makes the woman turn to me, to stare at me with gracious green eyes and a smile.

"Heidi," she says most pleasantly, as if we know one another, as if we're friends. But I don't know this woman; I don't know her at all. But I find that I like that smile, a smile that makes me half-certain the men with the face masks, the woman with the questions, the potassium chloride, and the dog — the Presa Canario with its coarse brindle hair — were all a dream. I peer down to my arms and find no blood, no cavernous teeth marks left in the skin, no bandages to stop the bleeding. My eyes bound around the sterile room, searching for Juliet, behind the sheer curtains, in the folds of the bedspread.

"Where have they taken my baby?" I ask

weakly, the words tired and paltry, my mouth like cotton. I can no longer scream. I pull dispiritedly on the handcuffs, trying to free myself from the bed.

"They're for your own safety," the woman says as she moves closer and sits in a chair beside the bed, an armchair she pulls close, skidding it across the tile floor as she says to me, "You're in good hands, Heidi. You are safe. The baby is safe," and I don't know if it's the compassion in her voice, or my overwhelming fatigue and despair, but I begin to weep. She snatches two, and then three, tissues from a dispenser on the bedside table and presses them to my face, for I cannot reach with my own hands. I pull away at first, away from this stranger's touch, but find myself leaning into it then, into the warmth of her hands, the softness of the tissue.

She tells me her name, a name I instantly forget, save for the title that precedes it. *Doctor.* And yet she doesn't look like a doctor at all, for there is no lab coat, no stethoscope. No balding head.

"We just want to make you feel better, that's all," she says, her voice pleasant and accommodating, as she runs that tissue across my cheek and wipes the tears from my eyes. Her hands, they smell of honey and coriander, reminding me of my mother's cooking. My mind drifts back to my childhood home, the chunky farm table around which the four of us sat: my mother, my father, my brother and me. But my thoughts get stuck on my father, my father who is dead. I see the casket being lowered into the ground, lavender roses in the palm of my hand, my mother beside me, ever stoic, waiting for me to disintegrate into a million pieces in that graveyard, the one saturated by rain. Or wait — I wonder — was it the other way around? Was I the one who watched my mother, waiting for her to disintegrate?

I long to reach out and hold his wedding band, my father's wedding band, in the palm of my hand, to wrap my fingers around the golden chain, but I'm affixed to the bed and cannot budge.

"Where is my baby?" I ask again, but she only says that she is safe.

She tells me without my asking that she has kids, too. Three of them. Two boys and a daughter named Maggie, only three months old, and it's only then that I notice the baby weight on the woman's otherwise slender frame, baby weight that has yet to fade. It's this, the mention of her own children, that makes it easier to talk, easier to reveal the secrets I've held inside for so long.

Ruby, Juliet, Ruby, Juliet, and I remember then, that famous Rubin's vase.

And so we talk about the sleepless nights and the fatigue. I tell her that Juliet has yet to sleep through the night, though my thoughts are heavy and opaque, words trapped in the sky on a cloudy day. I explain how she's been ill — a urinary tract infection, I say — making it all the more difficult, to console a child who's in pain. And the kind woman nods her head and agrees, and she tells me of her Maggie, born with a congenital heart disease, forced to undergo surgery just days after she left her mother's womb. And I know then that this doctor, she understands. She understands what I'm saying.

And then she asks about Willow, not in the way the other woman did, but kinder, more gentle. She asks when she left, and why. "Why did she leave?" she asks, and so I tell her. I tell her about my father's wedding band and the golden chain. About discovering the filigree bird hook with its distressed red finish completely bare, though I knew that I'd hung the chain there.

But no, I think, yanking again on hands that are bound to the bed in handcuffs, trying hard to peer down and prove to myself that the chain is there, around my neck as it should be. I ask the woman for it, for my father's wedding band on the golden chain, but she peers beneath the neckline of a hospital gown and tells me there is no chain, no wedding band there.

And it's then that my mind replays a scene, obscured somehow, by fog. Like a movie I'd seen in the past, the character's names and title of the film long gone, but snippets of the movie left here and there in the recesses of my memory. Quotations, love scenes, a passionate kiss.

But in this scene, I offer medication to Zoe on the palm of my hand, two oblong white pills, and then I watch from the edge of a bed as she thrusts the pills into her mouth without a glance. I watch as she swallows, then, with a long swig of water. And then I return to the bathroom to replace a prescription pill bottle into an open medicine cabinet, the word *Ambien* staring me straight in the eye, beside pain relievers, beside antihistamines. And then I quietly close the door.

"Why didn't you report her to the police?" the woman asks when I tell her about the wedding ring. I shrug my shoulders, on the verge of tears, and say that I don't know. I don't know why I didn't call the police.

527

But I do know, don't I?

And then there I am again, closing the door to the medicine cabinet and watching Zoe, anesthetized by my Ambien and not an antihistamine at all, drift off to sleep so that she won't be awoken in the night. And I recall the words, my words running that night through my mind: *there's no telling what the night will bring.*

I see myself remove the golden chain from around my neck and begin to hang it on the filigree bird, but then I don't. I stop just short and conceal it, instead, in the palm of my hand, kissing Zoe on the forehead in the adjoining master bedroom before I leave the room.

And I step into the living room to find Willow in a chair, my Juliet sound asleep on the floor. I set to cleaning the remains of dinner, and in my visions, in this foggy memory — or maybe not a memory at all, but a daydream, a fantasy — as I discard leftover spaghetti into a plastic garbage bag, I watch from a distance as the golden wedding chain and band tumbles from my hand and into the garbage bag, comingling with hardening noodles and bloodred spaghetti sauce, and then I hoist the plastic bag out into the hall and down the garbage chute.

But no, I think, shaking my head. That

528

can't be. This is not true.

Willow took my father's ring. She killed that man and then she took my father's wedding ring. She is a murderer, a thief.

"Is there more?" the woman asks of me as she watches me shake my head from side to side like the bob of a grandfather clock. "Do you have any idea where Willow might be?"

It can't be. Willow took that ring, I remember then and there, the way I sat on the edge of the bathtub, water running so that Zoe — sick with a cold, or maybe allergies — would not hear me cry. The way I looked up and discovered the hook completely bare, the way I tried in vain to call Chris for advice, but he was too busy with Cassidy Knudsen to answer my call.

I no longer know what's fact and what's fiction. Fantasy or reality. I tell her that no, I don't know where Willow is. I bark the words, suddenly furious and longing for my father, for my father to stroke my head and tell me that everything will be okay.

It's all coming at me quickly now, images of Willow, of Ruby, of Zoe, of Juliet. Images of blood and bodies and babies, unborn fetuses being removed from my womb.

But that kind woman who's name I don't know, who's name I can't remember, it's then that she *does* stroke a hand over my head as my father would do; she says that everything will be all right, and I want to ask, "Daddy?"

But I know what she would say, how she would look at me if I called her by my father's name.

"We'll figure it all out," she promises, and I find myself leaning into the mollifying words, finding the words themselves, the conciliatory tone of voice to be exhausting, as I close my eyes and let them lull me back to sleep.

By the time Chris arrives, it's dark outside, the world on the other side of the single window now black.

"You called them," I say, my quivering voice holding Chris responsible for this entire mess. For the fact that they've taken Juliet, my Juliet. "You called the police," I scream at him and I begin to curse, attempting in vain to rise from the bed and lunge at him, but finding instead that I'm tethered to it, my hands still bound to the bed in cuffs.

"Is that necessary?" Chris asks of a nurse who passes through the room attending to the various tubing and needles that are injected into the veins of my arms. Injected by aliens in face masks and bouffant caps.

"Is that *really* necessary," but the nurse says drily, "It's for her own protection," and I know what she says to him then, what she whispers to Chris then, about how she heard I ran headlong across a room and into the brick wall, as evidenced by a purple bruise now forming on the top of my head.

"She's agitated," the nurse says to Chris then, as if I can't hear, as if I'm not in the very same room. "She's due for more medication soon."

And I wonder what kind of medication, and whether or not they will hold me down, on the bed, and administer the medication with a syringe, once again. Or whether I'll be allowed to take pills, oblong pills in the palm of a hand, and I think again of the Ambien.

No, I tell myself. Antihistamines. Pain relievers. Not Ambien.

I would never give Zoe sleeping pills.

But I find that I don't know.

"You did this to me," I cry quietly, but Chris holds his hands up in the air, a look of innocence glued to his weary face. He's disheveled, the tidy appearance that usually describes his trim brown hair, his bright brown eyes and winsome smile now clouded over with fatigue, concern and something more, something I can't put my finger on.

He could incriminate me, my Chris, who likes to point fingers and dodge blame. He could say that I was the one to lock myself in the bedroom with Juliet, but he does not.

He could say he was worried I would hurt the baby, our baby, and I would laugh, wouldn't I? I would laugh. A cynical, mocking laugh, though he knows as well as I that I was standing there, on the edge of a fire escape, about to lose my balance when Chris forced himself into the bedroom.

But he didn't tell the police about this when they arrived; no he did not.

He sits on the edge of my bed and reaches for my hand. And there I am, drowning, sinking farther and farther beneath the ocean's current, the waves washing over me while I scream silently, involuntarily drawing breaths, my throat in spasms, choking on mouthfuls of salt water that fill my lungs.

"We're going to figure this out, Heidi," he says to me, then as he runs his fingers along my hand and up an arm, unaware of the way I gag and retch there on the bed, suffocating. I become submerged beneath the water while Chris and Zoe, the both of them, stand on the shore and watch.

The nurse steps from the room, saying to Chris, "Just five minutes, and then she needs to rest," before allowing the door to drift closed until it is just Chris and me. I hear her words, muffled, from afar, and then the water again, a large breaking wave that pulls me under the sea.

And I see Chris, then, I see that he has spotted me from a distance and he dives into the water making his way ever so slowly to me.

"Zoe needs you," he says, and then, after a pause, "I need you," offering a life belt, something for me to hold on to as I flounder in rapid waters, trying desperately to swim.

WILLOW

It wasn't long before the police found me, over on Michigan Avenue, staring through the windows of the Prada store. I was mesmerized; I couldn't move. Staring through the big ol' window of that shop, I couldn't think of anything else but seeing Momma in those fancy-schmancy dresses, the ones that hung in the sparkly store window, from headless mannequins. How Momma would have loved those dresses!

The police hung on to me for a little while, but they didn't keep me for long. Turned out that, once again, I was a kid no one wanted.

I celebrated my seventeenth birthday in a group home settled right in between Omaha and Lincoln, so that sometimes we'd drive on over to the Platte River and hike, through the woodlands that overlooked that broad river that was usually filled up with mud. There were twelve of us girls in that group home, living with a husband and wife we called Nan and Joe. We all had chores that varied from week to week, like cleaning the kitchen or doing the wash. Nan cooked dinner for us each night, and each night we sat down around the table to eat, all of us at one big table like some kind of mismatching family.

It was a lot like that home I found myself living in after Momma and Daddy died except that this time, I wanted to be there.

There were other folks who came and went, like Ms. Adler, and some nice lady named Kathy who wanted to talk again and again about the things that Joseph did to me. She made me say over and over again that *this was not my fault,* until one day, she said, I'd actually start believing those very words, believing that what Joseph did to me, it was wrong. Believing that what happened to my Lily, her getting adopted by the Zeeger family and all, that was not my fault. Momma was not mad at me.

In fact, she told me once, looking at me with a pair of emerald-green eyes, "Your Momma would be proud."

But still, there were nights when I lay down in bed, and I heard him — heard Joseph — sneaking into my room. I heard the squeal of the door, the grumble of floorboards beneath his feet, the sound of his huffing and puffing right on into my ear; I felt his damp, calloused hands yank the clothing from my body, heard his words crippling me, paralyzing me so that I couldn't scream. *An eye that mocks a father and scorns to obey a mother will be picked out by the ravens of the valley and eaten by the vultures,* he said, hissing the words right on into my ear until I'd wake up, in a sweat, searching everywhere in that room for Joseph, in the closet and under the beds, sure that he was somewhere.

Every single squeak and creak, every time someone or other got up to use the restroom, I was sure it was Joseph, coming for me, coming to slide his hot beastly body in bed beside me, and it would take nearly forever for me to remember: Joseph was dead.

I must've made myself say it a hundred times a day — *Joseph is dead* — until one day maybe I'd start believing those words, too.

There were cupcakes for my birthday, chocolate ones with chocolate icing, just like Momma used to make. In the days leading up to my birthday, Paul and Lily Zeeger drove from their home in Fort Collins with Rose and Calla in tow. I wasn't allowed to see Calla anymore, wasn't allowed to touch her, and so she and Paul, they stood outside, on the front lawn of that group home, waiting for Big Lily and Little Lily, waiting for *Rose*. But I could see her through the window, how Calla had grown so big. How she was walking. From time to time Paul tried to scoop her up into his arms, but she pushed him away because by then, Calla was over a year old and didn't want to be held. I watched as she wobbled around the lawn and once or twice or three times, fell to her hands and knees on the dirt and then popped right on up again like an old game of Whac-A-Mole. But there Paul was every time, ready to wipe the dirt off her knees and see if she was okay. I could see it now, though I couldn't see it before: Paul was a good daddy.

Big Lily gazed at me from across the living room and said, "If only I'd have known . . ." and just like that, her voice drifted off and tears settled in her pretty eyes. "Your letters . . ." she said, and then, "I thought you were happy."

Mrs. Wood longed for babies. She deserved her more than me. And she'd care for her, for Calla, for Ruby, better than I ever could. I knew that for sure. I knew that my being there, in that home with them, was problematic for Mr. and Mrs. Wood. I heard them talking about it all the time, Mr. Wood talking about police and jail and getting arrested. And I didn't want to cause any trouble, not for them, for Mrs. Wood, who had been so kind.

But I never stole any ring.

Those detectives, they found fingerprints on the knife, on the bedroom doorknob there in that Omaha home, fingerprints that were not mine. Didn't matter what I said or didn't say; they knew the truth.

I wondered if Matthew knew about fingerprints. I wondered if he left them there on purpose so I couldn't take the blame.

And the Zeegers, well, they refused to press charges about the kidnapping, though I wanted them to. I wanted someone to take the blame for what had happened. But they didn't. They decided, what with Momma dying, and me getting stuck with Joseph for all those years, I'd been through enough. But they said I wasn't allowed to see Calla, not then, not ever again, only through that living room window when they brought Lily to see me. I got to see Lily twice a year, just two out of every 365 days, and only ever *supervised visits,* which was why Big Lily was always there, in the room with Lily and me, and sometimes Ms. Adler and sometimes Nan and Joe — in case I tried to grab

Lily and run. Seeing that lady, Kathy, that was supposed to be my penance, too, but as it was, I liked talking to Kathy a lot. It wasn't punishment at all.

One day, out of the clear blue, Ms. Flores had shown up in that jail and told me I was free to go. But not free to go anywhere I chose. No, she said, I was still a *minor*. And being a minor meant I was still a ward of the state. And she smiled with those big horse-like teeth of hers, a smug look like the very fact that I was still a prisoner made her as happy as pie.

It was then that Ms. Amber Adler picked me up in her junker car with the too-big Nike bag and drove me to the group home, and there, helped me settle into a big blue bedroom that I would share with three girls. She said, "If only you would have told me, Claire," and just like Big Lily, her voice drifted off and her eyes got sad. But then she told me she was sorry for what happened, like it was her fault or something, what Joseph was doing to me. She said she should've made unannounced visits, or talked to my school teachers herself. Then she would've known, she told me, she would've known I wasn't going to school. "But Joseph . . ." she said, letting her sad voice wander off for a minute or two. "I thought . . ." and she didn't have to finish that sentence 'cause I knew what she was gonna say anyway. Joseph, she thought, was kind.

"A perfect fit," she'd said that day I went to live with Joseph and Miriam. Blessed and fortuitous.

Cursed and damned.

But they never found Matthew. They had the fingerprints from the knife, the door handle, but nothing to compare them with. They asked me questions, lots of questions. About Matthew. About Matthew and me.

But I didn't know where he had gone. Not that I would have told them anyway if I did.

I saw that Paul and Lily loved my Lily very much. And Lily, she loved Calla, too. They were a real family. My Lily, she barely knew me anymore. The times they came to call, there in that home between Omaha and Lincoln, she hugged me because Mrs. Zeeger told her to hug me, but otherwise she held back, eyeing me like the stranger I was. I could tell by her eyes that she had some vague recollection of me, a hazy memory from a dream, all but obliterated in the morning light. The last time she saw me I was eight years old. The last time she saw me, I was happy, carefree, smiling.

It was Louise Flores who told me what

happened to the Wood family. About how things weren't quite right in Mrs. Wood's head. "The funny thing about delusions," she said more to herself than to me, as she packed up her files and paperwork, considering her job done, just like Ms. Adler and her list of things to do, "is that a person can act relatively normal while they're having them. Their delusions aren't entirely out of the realm of possibility." She tried to explain it to me, a post-traumatic something or other kind of thing, about how Mrs. Wood was probably never okay after her father died, she said, and then, as if that wasn't bad enough, she got sick with cancer and had to abort her baby.

She couldn't have any more kids. And Mrs. Wood, well, she wanted kids. And that thought made me feel sad 'cause Mrs. Wood was the nicest anyone had been to me in a long time, and never for a minute did I think she was a bad person. I thought she was just a little bit confused.

From time to time I received a note in the mail there in that group home with no name, no return address. Just random facts scribbled on scraps of paper.

Did you know you can't sneeze with your eyes open?

Did you know camels have three eyelids?
Did you know a snail has 25,000 teeth?
Did you know sea otters hold hands when
sleeping so they never, ever drift apart?

ACKNOWLEDGMENTS

Writing can be a solitary task. We sit behind a computer screen or lock ourselves in a room with a notebook and pen, and obsess over fictional characters. Some days, we find ourselves talking to imaginary people more than any real human beings in our lives. While the rest of the world is asleep, our characters are tormenting us in the middle of the night, demanding that we make them say *this* or do *that*.

Writing is a solitary task, and yet book publication is anything but. I feel so fortunate to have so many amazing people on my book publication team: my extraordinary literary agent, Rachael Dillon Fried, my brilliant editor, Erika Imranyi, my publicist, Emer Flounders, and all the other dedicated, hardworking and all-around wonderful people at Harlequin and Sanford Greenburger Associates — the editorial, publicity, sales and marketing teams, and various other literary agents and assistants I've had the privilege to meet (and those working hard behind the scenes who I have yet to meet)! I'm so proud to be part of the Harlequin and Sanford Greenburger families.

And then, of course, there are the incredible authors I've met throughout the journey, those who have reached out to me, offered mentoring and guidance, an ear to listen and all the emotional support an author needs and, on top of it all, have helped generously promote each other's work as if it is their own. Thank you, thank you, thank you! I'm so honored to be a part of this amazing writing community.

Although I wrote my first novel in private, it was wonderful being able to share *Pretty Baby* with family and friends throughout the process. While writing this novel, I was also busy promoting my first, and so a huge thank-you to family and friends who helped hold my life together for me this past year or so: my parents, Lee and Ellen Kubica, and my sisters, Michelle Shemanek and Sara Kahlenberg, and their families; the entire Kubica and Kyrychenko families; my dear friends, who I won't name individually for fear of leaving someone out, but I hope you know who you are (special shout-out to

Beth Schillen — you are awesome)! I've been humbled by the way each and every one of you has shared in all the excitement of book publication, whether helping promote my books, spreading the word to family and friends, inviting me to speak at your book clubs, watching my children so I could attend out-of-state conferences and book tours, or just reading my books and asking the best questions about the writing process. I wrote *The Good Girl* in secret, but with *Pretty Baby* I had a cheering squad! I can never thank you enough.

And lastly, for my husband, Pete, and my children — thank you for the patience, the support, the encouragement. I couldn't have done it without you!

I love you all like x's love o's.

ABOUT THE AUTHOR

Mary Kubica holds a Bachelor of Arts degree from Miami University in Oxford, Ohio, in History and American Literature. She lives outside of Chicago with her husband and two children and enjoys photography, gardening and caring for the animals at a local shelter.